*Chronicle Worlds:
Feyland*

WINDRIFT BOOKS

Subscribe to our newsletter for news of upcoming titles in this series, and to be eligible for draws for paperbacks, e-books and more – *http://smarturl.it/chronicles-news*

CHRONICLE WORLDS: FEYLAND

No part of this work may be reproduced or transmitted in any form or by any means, electronic or mechanical, including photocopying and recording, or by any information storage or retrieval system without the proper written permission of the appropriate copyright holder listed below, unless such copying is expressly permitted by federal and international copyright law. Permission must be obtained from the individual copyright owners as identified herein.

The stories in this book are fiction. Any resemblance to any person, place, or event—whether computer-generated, faery-enchanted, or portal-introduced—is purely coincidental.

ALL RIGHTS RESERVED.

Chronicle Worlds: Feyland copyright © 2016 Samuel Peralta and Windrift Books.

"Chronicle Worlds" by Samuel Peralta, copyright © 2016 Samuel Peralta. Used by permission of the author.

"Entering Feyland" by Anthea Sharp, copyright © 2016 Anthea Sharp. Used by permission of the author.

"MeadowRue" by Joseph Robert Lewis, copyright © 2016 Joseph Robert Lewis. Used by permission of the author.

"The Skeptic" by Lindsay Edmunds, copyright © 2016 Lindsay Edmunds. Used by permission of the author.

"The Sword of Atui" by Eric Kent Edstrom, copyright © 2016 Eric Kent Edstrom. Used by permission of the author.

"The Huntsman and the Old Fox" by Brigid Collins, copyright © 2016 Brigid Collins. Used by permission of the author.

"Unicorn Magic" by Roz Marshall, copyright © 2016 Roz Marshall. Used by permission of the author.

"City of Iron and Light" by Jon Frater, copyright © 2016 Jon Frater. Used by permission of the author.

"The Gossamer Shard" by David Adams, copyright © 2016 David Adams. Used by permission of the author.

"The Glitchy Goblin" by K. J. Colt, copyright © 2016 K. J. Colt. Used by permission of the author.

"On Guard" by Deb Logan, copyright © 2016 Deb Logan. Used by permission of the author.

"An Artist's Instinct" by Andrea Luhman, copyright © 2016 Andrea Luhman. Used by permission of the author.

"Tech Support" by James T. Wood, copyright © 2016 James T. Wood. Used by permission of the author.

"Brea's Tale: Passage" by Anthea Sharp, copyright © 2016 Anthea Sharp. Used by permission of the author.

All other text copyright © 2016 by Samuel Peralta.

Edited by Ellen Campbell (http://ellencampbell.thirdscribe.com/ellen-campbell-editor/)

Cover art and design by Adam Hall (www.aroundthepages.com)

Print formatting by Therin Knite (www.knitedaydesign.com)

Chronicle Worlds: Feyland is set in the world of Feyland, created by *USA Today* bestselling author Anthea Sharp. Find out more at https://antheasharp.com/the-feyland-series

Chronicle Worlds: Feyland is part of *The Future Chronicles* series produced by Samuel Peralta. Get *The Future Chronicles – Special Edition* anthology free via www.smarturl.it/free-anthology

978-1-988268-01-9

Chronicle Worlds: Feyland

STORY SYNOPSES

MeadowRue (*Joseph Robert Lewis*)
After years of servitude in both the Bright and Dark Courts, MeadowRue escaped to the Dusk Vale to live a happy life knitting scarves, brewing tea, and chatting with the river hags. But when a mortal girl stumbles into the Vale, it isn't long before the deadly Black Knight and the cruel Bright Lance come hunting for her soul, and only MeadowRue can save her.

The Skeptic (*Lindsay Edmunds*)
Sam Sammish is a professional debunker. He earns his living mocking "airy-fairy" ideas, meaning anything he doesn't believe. When the parents of a teenage girl obsessed with playing Feyland ask him to debunk the game, he readily agrees. But on entering Feyland, he finds a magical world that he cannot control.

The Sword of Atui (*Eric Kent Edstrom*)
A country boy going by the gamer handle "Fasster" codes a highly illegal mod for Feyland. The mod is a sword that will make him invincible in the game. But when a mischievous fairy sends him on a tricky side quest he must test his weapon—and wits—against a foe who cannot be killed.

The Huntsman and the Old Fox (*Brigid Collins*)
Decades ago, Marylan used to play games professionally. Now,

her granddaughter's excited to show off her favorite game, Feyland. But the wonder of full immersion in a virtual faerie world fades under Marylan's frustration with the unfamiliar mechanics, and one particular faerie starts to feel a little too real, and far too dangerous.

Unicorn Magic (*Roz Marshall*)
Feyland: a new computer game that allows Scottish teenager Corinne MacArthur to escape the sadness that haunts her everyday life after the loss of a loved one. It's a game where legends come to life, the lines between reality and fantasy become blurred, and the impossible becomes—probable?

City of Iron and Light (*Jon Frater*)
A lonely teen finds solace in the game Feyland, where she'd rather spend time gaming than her real life. But she isn't prepared for the trouble she encounters when she collides with the Dark Queen's Royal Guard. There's only one escape open to her…and it's not back to reality.

The Gossamer Shard (*David Adams*)
They say that every time someone says: "I don't believe in fairies", a fairy dies. If only it were that simple. Sometimes when a powerful fey dies, the strength of its desire to live forestalls death. They can break the rules, slipping out of one game and into another entirely…

The Glitchy Goblin (*K. J. Colt*)
Any substance that delights, excites, and satisfies has the power to control, to spur addiction, to enslave. The Realm of Faerie

is about to be introduced to such a substance—sweet-tasting, mind-altering, the nectar of the gods. Chocolate.

On Guard (*Deb Logan*)
Wallace, a fierce Norwegian Forest cat, has guarded the boy since he was an infant. Despite advancing age, Wallace isn't about to shirk his duty now that the boy is old enough to play a dangerous game. Wallace doesn't understand his boy's fascination with Feyland, but he knows a threat when he sees one.

An Artist's Instinct (*Andrea Luhman*)
Agatha keeps failing at life, both her real one and her simulated one. As the daughter of a world-class opera star, she's humiliated at losing another choir audition. With no date to the winter formal, Agatha can't even get an in-game invitation to the Master Bard level in Feyland. Her new friends Jane and Zack offer to help, but what they each encounter in Feyland makes Agatha suspect the boundaries between game and reality have changed.

Tech Support (*James T. Wood*)
Ranjeet Nagar of Kochi, India, works in a call center to support his aging parents. When a demon from the game he supports attacks a woman in real life he must risk his job, beg his ex-fiancé for help, and brave the game world to face a very real threat.

Brea's Tale: Passage (*Anthea Sharp*)
Part human girl, part water creature, Brea Cairgead only wants

to find out where she fits in the Realm of Faerie. But when she unwittingly aids two mortal gamers who stumble into the Realm, her future takes a frightening twist. She is given an impossible choice: carry out a dangerous mission, or face the eternal fury of the Dark Queen…

CONTENTS

Foreword (*Samuel Peralta*)..1

Introduction (Anthea Sharp)..5

MeadowRue (*Joseph Robert Lewis*)....................................9

The Skeptic (*Lindsay Edmunds*)..39

The Sword of Atui (*Eric Kent Edstrom*)............................65

The Huntsman and the Old Fox (*Brigid Collins*)............95

Unicorn Magic (*Roz Marshall*)..125

City of Iron and Light (*Jon Frater*).................................151

The Gossamer Shard (*David Adams*)..............................185

The Glitchy Goblin (*K. J. Colt*)......................................217

On Guard (*Deb Logan*)...251

An Artist's Instinct (*Andrea Luhman*)............................261

Tech Support (*James T. Wood*)..305

Brea's Tale: Passage (*Anthea Sharp*)................................347

A Note to Readers..369

FOREWORD
Chronicle Worlds
by Samuel Peralta

I've always been about taking risks, starting with poetry, my first love affair with writing. Although I'd won awards and found online success, when I risked the next step of trying to place my work with a major literary publisher, my *magnum opus* spent a year languishing on an editor's desk, only to be rejected.

I decided to risk it all and start over again, in speculative fiction. The goal was to build on my literary craft, but in a more mainstream genre, a direction suggested by the works of Margaret Atwood and Kazuo Ishiguro. My first story, "Trauma Room", was a flash-fiction sample piece, to convince folks who'd never heard of me to take a chance. It worked.

Three other stories I'd written were quickly placed in three separate science fiction anthologies: "Hereafter" in David Gatewood's *Synchronic*, "Liberty: Seeking a Writ of Habeas Corpus for a Non-Human Being" in Hugo award winner John Joseph Adams's *Help Fund My Robot Army*, and "Humanity" in *The Robot Chronicles*, which I organized (just in case my other two stories hadn't placed) and brought to fruition with David Gatewood.

Released in turn, all three anthologies marched up the Amazon bestseller charts. In just over two months from the publication of "Hereafter"—which was eventually named a *Best American Science Fiction and Fantasy* notable short story—I hit the Top 10 Science Fiction Authors on Amazon, peaking at #8.

When I approached authors and editor with the concept for what would become *The Robot Chronicles*, I had no inkling of how powerful the idea of a continuing anthology series would become. We followed it up with *The Telepath Chronicles, The Alien Chronicles*, and then in quick succession *A.I., Dragon, Z*, and on, and still readers wanted more.

Two years and fourteen titles later, *The Future Chronicles* series is now arguably one of the most well-known anthology series born of the digital publishing revolution, yet adhering to the principle that we are, as Gatewood has put it, "a place where a reader can reliably expect quality storytelling from start to finish."

Over 150 contributing authors, illustrators, editors, and an expanse of loyal *Chronicles* readers have powered each *Chronicles* title to become, by turns, the #1 Anthology title on Amazon, in its speculative fiction genre, whether science fiction, fantasy, or horror.

I've been told that this success and commitment to literary quality has also helped inspire other publishers to take risks with independent anthologies and anthology series—and the results are amazing. We've seen the charts rocked by the *Beyond the Stars* series, the *UnCommon Anthologies* series, the *Mosaics* series, the *Canyons of the Damned* series, *Clones: The Anthology*, *Interspecies*, and many more in the works.

The Future Chronicles itself has taken new risks with its continuing *Alt.History* line of titles, and the *Illustrated Chronicles* project. To our amazement here at the *Chronicles*, despite the risks, readers continue to embrace these new titles.

And so we come to *Chronicle Worlds*. In this line of anthologies, authors chart stories not around a single theme—A.I., immortality, doomsday—but set in shared universes, or in already-imagined worlds, exploring the potential of these rich worlds with more characters, more history, more imagined futures.

Worlds such as these…

…A universe of far-flung planets and colonial starships with a singular mission, as envisioned in *New York Times* bestselling author Hugh Howey's *Half Way Home*…

…A steampunk world of aristocrats and artists, scholars and

scientists, detectives and criminal masterminds—and a mysterious island floating among the clouds, as imagined in *Drifting Isle*…

…A universe of conflict, of alien invasion, and of human resistance in the face of overwhelming odds, as dramatized by *USA Today* bestselling author Nick Webb's *Legacy Fleet*…

…A universe where humankind, fleeing a dying system, has found a second chance, but in a system already populated by a sentient culture, the worlds of *Paradisi*…

…Or a world where an immersive, virtual reality game is the gateway to an all-too-real, fantasy realm, as mapped out in USA Today bestselling author Anthea Sharp's *Feyland*.

It's my pleasure to introduce you to the *Chronicle Worlds* series, and this landmark collection, *Chronicle Worlds: Feyland*. Welcome.

———

Samuel Peralta is a physicist and storyteller. An award-winning author, he is the creator and driving force behind the bestselling speculative fiction anthology series The Future Chronicles.

www.amazon.com/author/samuelperalta

INTRODUCTION
Entering Feyland
by Anthea Sharp

Who hasn't dreamed of stepping into a fantastical world and escaping the tedium of everyday life?

Virtual worlds have always fascinated me – whether it's opening a book and plunging into the story between the pages, or getting lost wandering around *Zork* (and later *World of Warcraft*). I grew up reading a lot, including volumes of old-school fairy tales, and also playing computer games. A few years ago, after playing massively multiplayer online games (MMOs) fairly intensively, and also performing in a Celtic band and singing old ballads, I started to think about the parallels between the new world of gaming and fairy tales of old.

Gaming	*Faerie*
Lose sense of time	*Time moves strangely*
Filled with enticing worlds	*Famously enchanting otherworld*
Immersive and magical experiences	*Immersive and magical experiences*
Gamers get sucked in and lost in the worlds	*Mortals get sucked in and lost in the Realm*

My mind wouldn't let go of the similarities. Wouldn't it be cool to actually go to a magical land via a game? And why not the most magical of all – the Realm of Faerie? Thus the *Feyland* series was born.

Portal fantasy has been around for a long time, and the idea of falling into a game isn't new (*Jumanji*, Tad Williams' *Otherworld* series, and several anime shows, like *Sword Art Online*, explore this concept) – but in addition to the virtual world, I was struck by the fact that for centuries, right here in the regular world, there is a long tradition of lore and tales about another land that exists beside our own reality.

Fairyland.

Glimpsed at the edges of twilight and dawn, the Realm of Faerie has always been a liminal place—there and not there, real and not real. Much like virtual reality and game worlds. I imagined that as gaming developed, it, too, would reach that state of between-ness – and maybe even forge a connection with the ancient world of Faerie, given the right conditions. Who's to say what might happen when we can step so easily between the borders of one world and into another?

The *Feyland* books draw deeply on faerie lore, including the Seelie and Unseelie (Bright and Dark) Courts of the Fae. Many of the story lines in the series are based on ancient ballads and tales: *Tamlin, Childe Roland, The White Hart* – plus poetry by W.B. Yeats, and a wealth of Celtic music and mysticism.

In addition to folklore, the books are also influenced by many (perhaps too many) hours playing *World of Warcraft* in a fabulous guild (shoutout to Fates Legion on Alexstrasza!) and immersing myself in the engrossing virtual worlds of *Azeroth* and beyond. But imagining that a player could really enter a world and subsequently transition into the Realm of Faerie, I knew I had to set my books in a near-distant future where virtual reality gaming was fully immersive. The *Feyland* series takes place in an indeterminate time ahead of our own, where gravcars hover over broken pavement, the rich elite have embedded wrist chips, and sim-gaming can transport you to places you've never imagined.

In 2010, when I wrote the first *Feyland* book, Virtual Reality gaming setups were entering a new era (Oculus Rift's prototype was invented that year). While we aren't yet at full sensory immersion, that day is coming ever closer. In the meantime, we have the power of story to plunge into and let our imaginations take us deep into new worlds.

This collection is a landmark collaboration between one of the finest anthologists in science fiction and fantasy today, Samuel Peralta, and the group of authors who make up *The Future Chronicles*. When the idea of playing in other authors' worlds came up, I lightheartedly mentioned that people might want to write in my world of Feyland. I was pleasantly shocked when a bunch of authors took my suggestion and ran with it – and I'm delighted that *Feyland* is the first *Chronicle Worlds* to see publication.

The intersection of virtual reality gaming and ancient faerie lore has made for a rich and fantastical playground for story ideas to grow. I'm delighted to share these twelve tales of wild and wonderful takes on Feyland, VR gaming, and tricky faerie magic. Keep your wits about you, carry a bit of iron on your person, and game on!

Anthea Sharp is the author of the USA Today *bestselling Feyland, with over 200,000 copies sold worldwide, and counting. The first book in the series is free at all digital retailers.*

http://antheasharp.com/the-feyland-series

MeadowRue
by Joseph Robert Lewis

"AND THEN THE GOBLIN SAYS, well, at least I'm not mortal!"

We all laugh. Jenny probably tells this joke more than once a week, but Peg and I still laugh anyway, mostly because out of the three of us, Jenny is the only one who has never actually met a human in person. Lucky her.

"I still can't believe I let that girl get away," Peg mutters, clawing at her scraggly hair, which is dripping with mud. A toad tumbles out between her knobby fingers and swims away. "I almost had her when that boy…"

"…that boy Tamlin stole her away from you," I finish for her with a smile.

"The miserable, bloody Feyguard!" Peg snarls.

"Indeed, the Feyguard." I nod understandingly. I don't have any particular fascination with humans myself, but I can sympathize with theirs. Everyone needs a hobby. Mine is knitting.

I sit by the edge of the bog and chat with Jenny and Peg a bit longer, but there's no news and Peg seems eager to check her many snares throughout the distant rivers for hapless humans. Not that we've heard of many lately, but still, it helps to pass the time. Personally, I hope she never catches one.

So we say our farewells and I wander back up the narrow path to my home, looking forward to a few hours of just sitting by the window, sipping my red bramble tea, and reading the *Lays of Belaradoc* for the hundredth time. And maybe then I'll take a break to step out into the garden to spend some time with the dormice who live in the hazel to help them weave the switches into shady domes and pet their soft, furry tummies.

The stars are lovely this evening, but there are only a few because it's always early evening here in the Dusk Vale. I know that might sound a bit dull to some people, but it's never too hot or too bright at noon and never too cold or too dark at night. It's always dim and cool. Always perfect for candles and sweaters, and that suits me just fine. I have a lovely collection of spider-silk sweaters. I knitted them myself.

I put my hand on the wicker door of my wicker house with thoughts of tea on my mind when I smell something strange. Something foul.

Glancing about, I see nothing, hear nothing. Just the grove and the soft evening breeze playing through the tall grasses. But then I see it. The mushroom. An ugly white stalk with an angry red cap where there wasn't one before.

And then there's a second, and a third, all rising from the earth in a ring just a few dozen paces up the trail from my front door. Frozen and disbelieving, I watch them pop up from the loam, one by one, all sickly white and poisonous red, a dozen of them, more! My heart leaps up into my throat as my stomach drops into my shoes.

They're coming! They've found me!

The Huntsman, it must be the Huntsman! He'll come charging through the ring with his cackling riders and his howling hounds, horns blowing and beasts snarling, an entire company of blades and fangs and flames all rushing down upon me!

A light appears in the ring of mushrooms, just a brief flash, and then… her. Just her.

A human.

I can't move. Of all the things fair and foul that I had imagined coming through that ring, this was the least expected, and I don't know what to do. She's looking at me. Looking right at me. Maybe if I don't move she can't see me. No, wait, I think that's trolls, not humans.

She's a little taller than me, very dark brown-skinned and very bright pink-haired, round-faced and pear-shaped. The small spots on her face don't look like freckles, and the spectacles resting on her spotted nose are so thick that her eyes are enlarged and distorted.

And she's wearing silver armor, with a silver sword on her hip.

A knight! Why did it have to be a knight? All covered in iron and steel. I can feel myself growing weaker already, my strength and magic waning in the presence of the hideous metal.

This is going to end badly. Horribly. I should run, I should fly, dash away into a hole with my dormice or soar up to the owl's roost in the tallest ash, quickly, before she speaks, before she can cast some vile enchantment—

"Hi there!" The girl waves her hand like a puppy wagging its tail. "Oh, I mean, greetings, fair stranger!"

I blink and my hand instinctively waves back, though with less enthusiasm than hers. My mouth is dry, but I manage to whisper, "Good even."

She starts toward me, casting excited looks up at the steep mossy walls of the vale to the east and west, the slender ash trees and the sleepy willows, the softly waving hazel and hawthorn, and my own small home nestled in the brambles.

"So pretty," she whispers to herself. And then she strides down the trail to stand in front of me and I draw back a step as she says, "Hi, hello, good evening! What news, my lady? Everything okay here? Anything I can do for you, Miss Fairy Elf Person?"

I blink, feeling a bit frozen. "Is this a trick?" I peer at her. "CloverMist? Is that you?"

"Oh, sorry, manners." She bows dramatically. "I'm Kandess the Daring, at your service." She straightens up and extends her open hand to me.

Slowly, cautiously, I touch her hand gingerly, pinching a single one of her fingers between two of mine and shaking it once. "MeadowRue. A pleasure, I'm sure."

"MeadowRue? That's so pretty." The knight called Kandess appears to be under some devious curse that forces her to smile all the time and to talk too loudly. Puck's doing, no doubt. She looks up at the fireflies glowing in the eternal shadows. "Wow, this area is so much more detailed than the early levels, huh?

I'll have to remember to message Jabari about this place." Then she focuses on me again. "So, Lady MeadowRue, how can I be of assistance to you?"

"I… You…" I frown, struggling to make sense of her. She's nothing like the last mortal girl. The last one was clever and cruel, and cold. This one is practically made of sunshine. "I don't need anything, thank you. You can go." I wave her gently back toward the ring of mushrooms. "Please."

"Really? Are you sure?" Kandess's smile falters a bit, but it still clings to her dimpled cheeks. "You don't need me to fetch ten willow wands, or hunt down the dastardly bear that's been eating your prized pumpkins, or find your little brother who's lost in the woods?"

"I… what? No." I shake my head and massage my eyes. This one must be mad, her mind broken by some vile spirit, perhaps by the cruel Queen herself. Poor thing! Still, she is a mortal, and trouble follows wherever they go, and I can't risk bringing any trouble here. "No, there's nothing I need. Please leave, good lady. Go on, back where you came from." Again, I shoo her toward the mushrooms.

"Well, I'm not going to leave. I only just got here." Her smile is definitely drooping now on one side. "I mean, come on, there must be some quest line in this area. What, am I not high enough level to get it? Do I need to grind a bit more? Is that the problem?"

"There is no problem, brave Kandess," I assure her, trying to match her smile and failing, I'm sure. "Everything is absolutely fine here." And it will stay that way if you would just go!

"Oh wait." She looks around the glen, peering through

the leaves. "Is someone making you say that? Are we being watched? Is there some sort of Big Bad controlling you with an evil curse?"

"No. If you would just listen to me!" I glare at her. Why does this always happen to me? I'm too soft-spoken, I suppose. Maybe I should work on that, for next time. If there is a next time. I hope there isn't a next time!

"Fear not, fair maiden!" Kandess draws her sword, assumes a war-like stance, and begins creeping into the shadows of the woods off the trail. "I will find the villain and free you from his power."

"No!"

But she's already slinking away. If she wasn't listening to me face-to-face, I doubt shouting at her backside will do much good. This is bad. Very bad. The stink of mortality is all over her. How long before the Queen's hounds catch the scent? How long before the Huntsman comes looking for her, looking to steal her mortal soul so Her Majesty can break through the world-skein and return to the land of the humans?

But more importantly, how long before they find me?

Not long, surely.

I shrink to the size of a butterfly and whisk through the air on wings of sorrowful laughter and sparkling hope. The forest looms enormous above me, but I plunge through it as easily as falling rain and the bright white trees and their dark green leaves melt into a soft blur around me. A quick circle of the groves and slopes around my home reveals no sign that anyone from the Courts has come (yet!), so I flit past the human intruder to land in front of her, and return to my natural size.

Kandess the Daring stumbles back at my sudden appearance, but before she can spout off any more of her courageous nonsense, I hold up my hands to silence her and say, "Brave Kandess, there is indeed a task that only the truest of warriors can complete for me."

"That's more like it!" She beams and bobs her head, causing her huge nimbus of pink hair to bob with her. "What's the problem?"

"I…" My mind goes blank. Of course it does. I can't lie, and I haven't had to think quickly on my feet in ages. "I… lost my knitting needle." This is true, I did lose a needle once, and while it only took me a moment to make a replacement, the original is still missing. My prime suspect remains a certain gray dormouse I have named Norbert the Needle Nibbler. "I ask that you find it and return it to me for a most handsome reward." Returning to wherever she came from without being killed by the Queen is a fairly handsome reward, in my mind.

"Was it stolen by a wizard? Is it a magic needle?" The girl's eyes are practically sparkling with curiosity and eagerness.

"A magic needle? Oh, well, indeed, yes." I nod. "From a certain point of view." It turns spider-silk into comfy sweaters, and I think that's pretty magical. Sort of.

"Where did you last see your needle?" she asks.

"I don't quite remember, but you might begin your search near a ring of red-capped mushrooms."

The knightly girl's smile vanishes. "Seriously? Is this some kind of trick? Your needle is back where I came in on this level?"

I sigh and look away to the faint stars in the east. I hate

playing at words like this, dancing around the truth. It tires me so much. It's one of the many reasons why my only two friends in the world are river hags. "You know, once upon a time mortals came to this realm through proper portals in sacred groves, and they were filled with fear and awe at the sight of true, living magic. But now you come here through your sim games and all you care about is grinding, and leveling, and aggro. And what is aggro, anyway?"

"Wait, what?" Kandess stares at me. "Back up a sec. Things here just got super meta. What kind of game is this?"

"One that I am not enjoying." I point back toward the mushroom ring. "You have to leave now. It isn't safe for you, or me, even here in the borderlands."

"Wait, you're no NPC. Are you another player? Or an admin?"

"Go, please!" I want to steer her back toward the trail, but I don't dare touch her steel-clad arm. Being this close to so much iron is giving me a headache. I need a cup of tea!

"No." She grins and folds her arms over her chest. "What if I stay right here? What's the worst that can happen?"

Thunder booms across the twilight sky and a dark figure appears in the shadows just a stone's throw away from us. The warrior is armored in midnight plate, no hint of flesh exposed, no glimpse of face offered. All we can see is the obsidian armor and the obsidian blade of the Dark Queen's champion.

A burning lump forms in my throat as my flesh runs cold, and I whisper, "That can."

"Wicked! Who the hell is this guy?" Kandess asks. "Some kind of Black Knight?"

I don't answer. I run.

There isn't time to feel guilty about leaving the human girl to her fate. There isn't even time to think of leaving her behind as bait to cover my escape. I just run.

BOOM!

I stumble to a halt only a few dashed paces from where I began, frozen at the sight before me. Where there were shadows a moment ago, now there is a tall warrior armored not in heavy plate but in light shimmering chainmail crafted of golden, gossamer threads woven through the cast-off scales of the Dawnspire dragons. In his fist the warrior grasps a spear so terrifyingly bright that it has no form beyond the blinding white shape of the shaft and blade.

And the girl called Kandess calls out, "Sweet! Who the hell is that?"

"The…" I swallow as I straighten up and curl my hands into fists to steady them. "The Bright Lance, champion of the Bright King." I exhale slowly. "And also… my former fiancé."

"You say that like it's a bad thing," Kandess observes. "Is it a bad thing?"

"It is," I agree. "It is a very bad thing."

"Well, maybe you should try to… Hey, Shell-head, back off! Yeah, you! Hya! Have at thee!" Kandess shouts at the Black Knight, waving her sword in wild circles over her head. The Knight growls something back at her, but I can't hear it, I can't even watch the duel erupting behind me at all because my eyes are fixed on the golden warrior standing before me. I can barely breathe. I'd forgotten what he was like to look upon.

"MeadowRue?" The Lance smiles his perfect smile, displaying his perfect white teeth, dazzling against the light golden hairs of his close-cropped beard and his long flowing golden hair. "Ah, MeadowRue. Together again, at long last. You know, the King tripled the price on your head after you went over to the Dark Court, but now that I see you with my own eyes again, I don't know if I can bear to surrender you to him. Perhaps I will keep you for myself, as was intended from the very start."

"No, I will not go with you." I can barely say the words. I know I have no power to defeat him. Escape is my only hope, and a threadbare hope at that.

"So what's the deal here?" Kandess yells over the clangor of her battle with the Black Knight. "Are these guys working together?"

"No." I shake my head, unable to tear my eyes away from the golden face of the Lance. "They each want us for their masters. And should either one capture us, I fear they will take your soul… and my head."

"Wow, wicked plot line. Sounds like we've got a decent boss fight on our hands. You're some sort of spellcaster, right?" Kandess sounds more than calm, she almost sounds excited, barely focused on her duel at all. "Think we can beat these guys together?"

I shake my head, still staring at the Lance, who begins walking slowly toward me, still flashing that dazzling smile, still grasping his blinding spear. "No. We have no chance of victory, not in a hundred worlds, not in a thousand lifetimes."

Kandess sighs. "All right, Debbie Downer. I guess I'll handle them both on my own. Watch how a first-class tank operates solo!"

She lunges at the Black Knight and I hear the sharp clangor of blade on blade grow louder and faster behind me, but still I keep my eyes on the Lance.

"You know," he says casually. "You never really told me why you wouldn't marry me. Have you thought of a reason yet? Or are you really just a traitor at heart?"

"I told you my reason the day I left," I say, trying to keep my voice as calm as his and not betray my quaking nerves. "I am a living soul, and I refuse to be treated as a pawn in your Court games."

"You were created by the King himself to be my wife," he points out.

"I was also created with free will, and as long as my will is my own, I will not marry you or any other tyrant who orders when he should ask, and who cannot comprehend the meaning of the word No." The words sound bolder than I feel. I want to run. I should be running.

Behind me the duel between the two knights carries on, and I can hear Kandess huffing and gasping for breath now as she dashes and lunges through the brambles.

"We all have our roles to play," the Lance says. He extends his empty hand to me. "And if you return to your proper place now, and beg our forgiveness, you may yet live the grand life intended for you. I still love you, MeadowRue."

I laugh. Really laugh, right in his face. I can barely believe I'm doing it, but I can't help but laugh at him now, and more than a little of my fear shakes out with the laughter. "You love me? You don't even know me. We barely spoke a dozen words in the Bright Court. Back then, I barely knew myself. How can you possibly love me?"

"Because you are lovely beyond compare." He smiles, still holding out his hand.

"What sort of idiotic answer is that?" I pass my hand over my face and take on the features of the wretched goblin woman that I wore when I served the Dark Queen and deceived the last mortal girl. "Am I lovely now? I am still myself, but few would call me lovely."

The Lance's handsome smile twists into a mask of seething rage. "You will wear your true face, and you will return to the Bright Court with me to answer for your crimes!"

Just then a terrific crash of steel on stone turns my head and I see Kandess lying dazed on the ground with the Black Knight standing over her. But instead of delivering the killing blow, the Knight marches toward us, saying, "Stand down, Lance. The Queen commands that MeadowRue be returned to the Dark Court to suffer for her broken oaths."

And for the first time, the Lance takes his burning gaze off me to glare at the Knight. "Oh, I think not, you vile dog."

"Villain fight!" Kandess scrambles up to her knees to grab my arm and yanks me away from the two warriors just as they raise their weapons and the flaring brilliance of the Lance's spear claws at the smoking darkness of the Knight's sword.

"This is awesome," Kandess whispers in my ear. "We let one kill the other, and then we only have to beat the winner, and he'll probably be really weak from the fight!"

But the two warriors remain unmoved, glaring in silence.

"I will not be the first to deal a treacherous blow against the Dark Court," the Lance announces. "So strike, you foul creature, and learn what true valor is!"

"Still the maniac? Still the mindless lapdog?" The Black Knight laughs with the all the mirth of a thousand knives clawing across a wall of ice. "Attack me if you wish to die, but I will not cross this Rubicon for you."

"Damn it. It looks like they need a little encouragement," Kandess whispers to me. Then she shouts, "Don't worry, Goldilocks, it's okay to be scared. I fought him a minute ago and he was pretty tough. Perfectly okay to back down. No one will call you a pathetic, cringing little coward!"

"Silence, girl!" the Lance roars. "I will not be goaded like some simple child!"

"Whoa, settle down," Kandess says. "Look, if you're not up to it, then maybe I'll just roll out with Tall, Dark, and Armored over there. That's fine, too."

"Silence, mortal! Your soul belongs to the Bright King!" The Lance slams the butt of his spear into the earth and it flares twice as brightly as before, forcing us to turn away and shade our eyes with our hands.

"She is for the Dark Queen!" The Black Knight raises his sword and his entire body is suddenly enveloped in a dark mist that hides all but his upraised sword.

"Yes!" Kandess whispers. "Time to rock and roll!"

"No!" I shove the mortal girl away from me and stride back out between the two warriors. "There will be no duel here."

"Rue! What are you doing?" Kandess wails.

"If they fight each other in open combat, it could ignite

a war between the Courts and thousands of innocents would die, and I won't have a single person suffer so needlessly." I look from the flaming Lance to the smoking Knight. "Moreover, I am not some trinket to be claimed by the meager virtue of a thug's skill in brutality, or murder. I go where I choose, and I choose neither of you, nor your cruel masters." My heart is racing. I have no idea what I'm saying or what I'll do when they come after me a few seconds from now, but these words have been simmering in my heart for so long that I can't contain them any longer. I only wish I had thought to practice a better speech than whatever I'm babbling now.

"The Queen saved your life when you came to her," the Knight reminds me.

"The King gave you your life in the first place," the Lance argues.

"You owe her much," the Knight growls.

"You owe him more," the Lance booms.

"How much?" Kandess calls out.

We all turn to look at her.

"How much is owed?" The girl steps out from the shadows and approaches the would-be killing ground. "I mean, what does she need to pay to clear all these debts? Gold? Jewels? Some sort of dangerous errand?"

"No, no! Stop!" I wave her back. "There will be no duel, and no ransom either. I owe the Queen nothing. I served her loyally in return for her protection, and I left as freely as I came. And I owe the King even less, for he created me to be less than a person, to be a gift, to be owned by some stranger. My life is my own, and I will not pretend to buy it from anyone else."

"Such lovely sentiments," the Lance remarks. "So noble. So lofty. A pity that nothing that spills from your treacherous lips is of any consequence." His spear roars as it burns brighter still.

"Your life is forfeit," the Knight snarls at me. "My Lady commands your return at once!"

My heart is racing, my hands are shaking, and I can barely breathe. These people… they're not people at all. They're monsters, animals, beasts! They're slaves to their own pride and rage and fear of their masters.

I cannot reason with them.

I cannot change them.

I wish I could just knit their lips closed, and their eyes closed, and their fingers closed forever, and leave them silent and harmless on a distant mountain peak where I would never have to see them again…

…wait. A place where I never have to see them again?

I turn to Kandess, my hand outstretched. "Take my hand if you want to see tomorrow."

Her eyes meet mine, and I feel her hot, sweaty palm slam against mine. I close my eyes and spin my arcane magicks inward, calling on every shred of strength that I have to overcome the mass of iron encasing the girl's body.

The Lance bellows and the Knight screams.

Lightning flashes, thunder roars…

…and then all is silence and darkness.

I feel weak and sick, my head spinning and my limbs shaking hot and cold at the same time as a thin veil of perspiration trickles down my cheeks and the small of my back. I open my weary eyes and see Kandess still staring at me, her eyes impossibly wide, her face awash with sweat, her breath coming thin and quick between her parted lips.

"What just happened?" she whispers.

Still clutching her hot, clammy hand, I look around at the low silvery trees draped in Old Man's Beard and the thick clumps of pale moss adrift in the sluggish waters of the Gray Bog on every side of us. We're standing on an island of sorts, an island so small that perhaps I should only call it a small mound of soft, damp earth surrounded by the dark, glittering pools of the swamp. It's so small that we can't take more than a step apart before slipping into the water, though I suppose if we stand here too long, we'll sink the poor lump straight down to the bottom all the same.

"I moved us," I say softly, still teetering on the verge of collapse. "Both of us, all at once. Not very far, but far enough, I think."

She looks around at the quiet swamp. A fish swishes through the water. A night heron cries out. And the girl asks in a voice as soft as silk, "Are we safe here?"

"For the moment." I nod and we let go of each other's hands. Instantly I feel stronger and clearer, and I step away from her steely armor to stand at the water's edge. I'm not sure if this will work, but it's the only idea I have, so I have to try. I kneel by the water and plunge my face just below the freezing surface and I yell into the bubbling murk, "Jenny! Peg!"

I sit up, shivering as the frigid water pours off my face and hair.

"What was that? Are you okay?" Kandess asks, but I don't answer. I'm still wiping the cold bog water from my eyes, and she says, "Is this where we come up with a new strategy? Fetch some sort of magical swamp mud that will help us… somehow?"

"No." I shake my head and pull my sweater tighter around my shoulders. "No, none of that. Nothing like that. What would be the point? The Lance, the Knight, they've lived their whole lives like this. Serving the Courts. Making everyone else serve them. That's all they know, circles of power, circles of slavery. It's who they are. And I'm not going to waste my time and sanity trying to change them."

"But… but that's what we do!" Kandess kneels beside me. "We're heroes! This is what we do, we fight evil and injustice, and we don't give up until we've made the world a better place."

I stare into the murk, watching threads of silvery silt-water swirling like clouds. "If you wish to be a hero, then by all means, be a hero. But that is not the life for me."

"Why not?" She touches my hand gently. "You're smart, you're passionate, you're powerful. You could rally the people to rise up against these Court punks, and, I don't know, start your own Court!"

I smile. "Crown myself the Dusk Queen? No, thank you."

"But…" There's a deep sense of confusion in her eyes. She's genuinely lost for words. "But we have to. We can't let them win! Those psychos? We can't let them go on treating people like this."

I sigh and squeeze her hand. "You've a noble heart, Kandess the Daring, and if you choose to spend your days fighting evil in the hopes of creating a better world for future generations, then I wish you well. But I have no heart for that life. Nor the stomach, neither."

"Oh, Rue." She squeezes my hand back.

I nod at her. "The world needs heroes, I know it all too well, but the world needs someone to make sweaters and candles that smell like old books, too. They want me to be a trophy, and you want me to be a hero. And yes, someone needs to slay the dragons, surely, but someone also needs to protect the dormice and the vales, and even wayward girls with silver swords." A crooked smile curls my lip. "That's what I want to do, and what I've been doing, and what I will go on doing if I survive this day."

"Oh." Her eyes drift away from me, gazing out over the bog, her thoughts wandering somewhere I cannot follow.

"But Kandess, there's more to life than just what we do," I say, drawing her eyes back to me. "There's also what we feel, too. And I don't want to feel angry, or frightened, or tired from fighting or worrying. I want to feel happy. I want to enjoy living, every day."

"Well, I…" She frowns. "I want that too. But we owe it to—"

"No." I hold up my hand and look her sternly in the eyes. "We don't owe anyone anything. My first breath was taken in slavery. The first thing I saw was a golden King, and the first thing I heard was that I was the property of the Lance, to serve and obey him for all time. I hadn't even spoken my own name yet, and already my life was set and sold for all eternity."

Can she even comprehend that? She, a mortal? Has anyone ever lived a life like mine in her world? Maybe not, and I certainly hope not, but I want her to understand. I want someone, somewhere, to understand, so I continue, "My first three days of life were passed in a golden cage, dressed like a doll, ordered about like a pet, ignored like a dumb object. I was so confused by it all. But then…" I exhale slowly. "Then he struck me. The Lance. Because I questioned him. Questioned the notion of our marriage. He hit me… and I left. I ran. I just… ran. I didn't know anyone in the world, and I had no idea where to go. I just ran away into the wild."

Kandess stares at me, her eyes shimmering with tears, her lip pushing out into a sad pout.

"For days I ran, and for days they hunted me with phoenixes and sundogs." I pause. "I barely slept. It was hour after hour of fear, shaking at every sound, running until I was too exhausted to move. Just fear and fatigue, day after day. But then Puck found me and brought me to the Dark Court, and I lived there in safety for a time." I look down into the bog at my wavering, rippling reflection. "It was… passable. I was still ordered about, but only as much as anyone else. But then I saw the Queen steal the soul of that girl, that mean, selfish human girl, and I… I just didn't want to have anything to do with that world anymore."

I'm crying a little, but I don't care. I've told this story to myself so many times. It feels good to tell it to someone else. A silence falls over us. The bog is still. I close my eyes and feel… calm. Quiet. Free.

"You're a survivor," Kandess says. "That's what they call it, when something like that happens to you and you get away. You're a survivor."

"No." I shake my head, frowning. That word, survivor, it sounds all wrong in my head. "No, I'm MeadowRue. And yes, something horrible happened to me once, but that isn't what I am, or who am I. I am… quiet, and I like being alone, which doesn't feel lonely at all, and I love knitting, and poems, and dormice, even ones that nibble on my knitting needles." I smile at the thought of little Norbert.

Another long silence falls, and we hear only the croaking of a toad in the distance.

"My friend died," Kandess whispers. "She killed herself. Four months ago."

I blink and wipe at my tears and look at her, silently bidding her to go on.

"They bullied her. Kids at school. For… being fat, and… I don't know, being different." The girl looks away, shaking her head. "Every day. Until she couldn't take it anymore, and they found her… with a bunch of pills, in the bathroom." Kandess takes a long breath and exhales slowly. "So I, uh… I started this vlog where I talk about bullying, and abuse, and shelters…" She trails off.

I only understand about a half of what she says, but I'm sure it's the important half. "I'm truly sorry about your friend."

She nods and shivers. "So what will you do now? I mean, if you won't fight these jerks, will you go on the run again?"

"Yes," I nod. "But only a short distance, this time." I look back down at the water, and I smile. They're coming.

"What's that?" Kandess points at the swamp and stands up sharply, backing away from the murk. "What are they? There's two of them!"

"They're my friends," I say as the two heads break the surface. "Kandess, allow me to introduce Jenny Greenteeth and Peg Powler."

I know my friends are far from lovely and won't be receiving any Court invitations anytime soon, but they have their charms, their kindnesses. Jenny and Peg protect their toads and their eels, keep their rivers clean and healthy, and only rarely trouble those on the shores. But no one seems to care about that. They only care about what the hags look like, and how they smell, and where they live. Typical.

"Ladies, this is Kandess the Daring," I introduce the human girl to my friends. "And before you ask, no, you can't eat her."

"Oh poo," Peg pouts. "You're such a tease, Rue!"

"But I do have some good news," I continue smoothly, smiling at them. "I've decided to join you two in the river realm."

"Lovely!" Jenny cackles. "Rue 'O the River!"

"Oh, very nice!" Peg claps. "And three is such a lucky number! A magic number!"

"I certainly hope it is." I slip off my shoes and step down into the soft mud, feeling the biting chill of the water. "Oh dear frog, that's cold! It may take me a few moments to sort out my change. I've never done this before."

"Wait!" Kandess catches my wrist. "You're going to live in the rivers? You're just going to let the Lance scare you off? You won't even fight for your home here?"

I look at her and shrug. "Home is where you make it, and I want my home to be somewhere I feel safe and happy. I don't want to go back to being scared and tired again, not even for a single day. I'm sorry, but I hope you can understand that."

She nods a little and lets go of my arm. "I—"

The brush on the far side of the bog rustles and crackles with the sound of heavy boots crushing the undergrowth, and the Lance and the Knight stumble through the veil of hanging moss at nearly the same moment, still a fair distance from us across the water, but only a dozen paces apart from each other.

"They found us!" Kandess cries, drawing her sword.

"I'm not ready!" I wade out into the freezing water and try to focus on my changes. I've never lived in the water before. I'll need scales, and fins…

"Oh, what shiny things," Peg hisses at the Lance. "I like shiny things."

"Oh dear me, I want a taste of the shadowy one!" Jenny giggles.

The two river hags plunge back down into the murk and emerge again only a moment later on the far side of the bog, throwing their arms up around the necks of the two armored warriors, and try to drag them back down into the cold water.

Kandess barks out a relieved laugh at the sight of the two dripping hags caressing and sweet-talking the outraged men, and I wade out a bit farther as I clad my legs in tiny verdant scales that remind me of the leaves of the brambles and the hazel outside my cottage window. The chill of the water quickly fades as I transform myself, spreading the scales up my chest and down my arms and across my face. Slender fins of deepest indigo and darkest gold extend from my calves and forearms, and thin gills spread across ribs under my dress. As I walk farther out into the bog, I feel the water rise to lift me, letting me float. Swimming here is effortless, like flying in a dream, my hair spreading out around me in delicate black fans. It's wonderful.

I turn to look back at Kandess. "It's done. Everything is all right now. The Courts don't care much for the river realm, or the river folk. I'll be safe. I suppose I'll have to learn to knit my sweaters and scarves from reeds and moss now. And maybe I'll raise otters, or turtles. I do like turtles. But try not to worry, and don't look so sorrowfully at me!"

"I'll try." She smiles sadly and waves. "I guess this is goodbye. Good luck, MeadowRue. I mean, fare thee well."

"Farewell to you, dear Kandess. I hope you find your own happiness one day, young hero."

A pair of high shrieks and huge splashes turn my head and I see Jenny and Peg crashing down into the bog as the Lance and Knight stagger back up onto the banks, dripping and cursing. The sight makes me smile. I swim out a bit farther and feel my gills breathing easily through the soft, slow water, and I slip beneath the surface.

"MeadowRue!"

Kandess's voice sounds strange and muted, but I hear it clearly enough and I swim back up to see her still standing on the lonely little mound in the center of the swamp with the Knight and Lance circling quickly along opposite banks toward her.

"MeadowRue!" she cries. "How do I get home?"

I blink and a shiver runs down my legs as I realize that I don't know, so all I can call back to her is, "I don't know!"

The two warriors reach the places on the banks closest to

the little island, and each one takes his terrible weapon to begin felling the ancient willows to bridge the bog.

"MeadowRue?" Kandess points her sword at the Lance, and then at the Knight. "Uhm, I can't log out of the game. Something's wrong with the system. Help!"

Damn! She needs to get back to the mushroom ring, but she can't get back there, not on her own, and I can't help her now… Can anyone help her? I blink. Of course!

"The Feyguard… Kandess, call the Feyguard!" I call out. "You must scream for them to come so they know you are in terrible peril. Do it now!"

"Call the what? Who are you talking about?"

I roll my eyes. Of course she doesn't know who the Feyguard are, not if she still thinks she's just playing her sim game. I suppose I was hoping for too much, thinking that she might understand where she really is by now. So I plunge into the water and race forward, shooting like an emerald arrow and feeling the cool river flowing over my skin like a living caress. Then I put my feet beneath me and kick upwards, flying up from the bog toward the mound where I grab Kandess's wrist and yank her down toward the swamp.

"I beg your pardon, sweet Kandess, but you must scream!" And I sink my teeth into the warm brown skin of her hand.

The sound of her scream is ear-piercing and sets my skin to crawling, just as I hear the wooden groans of two willow trees breaking at their spines and crashing down across the bog. Two sets of armored boots clang across the makeshift bridges, but still I bite and still she screams.

BOOM!

The young man appears from nowhere, perhaps from a flash of light, perhaps from the twilight sky itself. I only catch a glimpse of him through my thick wet locks, a youth in silver armor with fine brown hair falling across his bright green eyes. As he grabs Kandess's arm, he whispers softly into her ear, "…and let's get you out of here before…" I see the steel in his eyes, and I see a calm come over Kandess, just for an instant, and then the warm hand is wrenched from my mouth, a flash of light dazzles my eyes, and the Lance and the Knight dash onto the little mound, face to face, all alone.

Kandess, and her rescuer, are gone.

I push back from the little island with only the top of my head and my eyes above the surface. The water tastes cool and sweet and rich, and I smile to myself. I should have done this ages ago.

The Bright Lance turns his terrible, beautiful visage on me one last time, shakes his blinding spear, and vanishes. The Black Knight sheathes his sword, and the dark mist takes him away. And finally, finally, the Gray Bog looks like itself once more. No more smoke, no more sun, no more shouting, no more crashing about. It's dim and quiet, and still, and after a few moments I hear a toad croak and a heron cry.

Smiling, I slip below the surface and float, weightless, hovering in my new world humming with strange new life and strange new friends. I wonder if I really can knit a sweater from moss, and whether I can brew a cup of tea from orchids and lilies. I can't wait to find out…

* * *

Kandess awoke in the dark, in her sim chair. With her mind still wrapped in sleepy cobwebs, she pushed off the gloves and the headset of her gaming rig and sat up with a yawn. Squinting at the clock, she wondered where she had left off in the game. She couldn't remember logging out from Feyland.

No matter. She'd figure it out when she logged back in tomorrow.

As she paced over to her desk, she felt her hand throbbing and she rubbed it absently. Must have slept on it funny, she mused.

Outside her door, she could hear her parents talking over the TV. Something about planning a party for someone at work. Whatever.

Kandess plunked down in her chair and picked up her screen. Without thinking, she pulled the box of tissues closer and opened the drawer beside her right knee. The individually wrapped candies crinkled and rolled inside it.

She woke up her screen and opened her vlog channel. The new video that she uploaded yesterday was pretty good, she thought. Lots of good advice about how to document and report harassment. Who to tell. What to do if they didn't listen. Websites. Phone numbers. Then she looked down below the video and swallowed.

Three hundred new comments.

"…shut up, you fat piece of…

"…back in the kitchen and make me a…"

"…die in a fire."

She exhaled slowly and bit her lip. Just like the last six videos.

"…face like a tumor, a fat tumor…"

"…harass this, you blubbery bitch…"

"…another morbidly obese feminist idiot who can't get a date."

She tried to just breathe as she tried to think of something powerful and intelligent to say to the first commenter. Something that would show them that she wasn't scared of them, that she wasn't going away, that they couldn't break her, or silence her, and that she was going to keep on fighting until she beat them.

"…stupid cow…"

"…couldn't even bang you if I put a bag on your head…"

"…just kill yourself already."

Kandess wiped her eyes and started to type, but the throbbing in her hand made her stop. She paused for a long moment, massaging her hand as she stared at the vicious words, and then her finger slowly traveled up the screen to the Admin Settings. She scrolled down.

Delete account?

She paused, trying to breathe with her eyes full of hot tears and her skin pricking with gooseflesh.

No.

Not delete. Not run away. Never that. The videos were good. They helped people. That was important. Making things was important. Protecting things was important. Big or small. It all mattered. This mattered.

She scrolled back up a little.

Disable comments?

Tap.

Comments disabled.

She looked back at her video and now the three hundred little knives in her chest were gone. There was only her video, her face, her message. Just her. She didn't have to see them or hear them, and neither did anyone else. She blinked and wondered, why didn't I do that ages ago?

Kandess exhaled again, and this time some of the heat and shivering seemed to flow out with it. She pushed the tissues back into the corner and nudged the drawer shut with her knee. Drumming her fingers on her desk, she stared at the wall, wondering what to do with the rest of her evening. More gaming?

No. Not tonight.

She picked up her messenger and sent a text to Jabari: You free?

Jabari: Yeah.

Kandess: Nachos and Trek marathon?

Jabari: Hell yeah!

Kandess: Cool. I'll get the nachos. Be over in twenty!

And then she got up and strode out of her room with a smile.

A WORD FROM JOSEPH ROBERT LEWIS

I've been reading stories about people getting sucked into fantasy worlds through computers and video games for years, and I've always wanted to write one myself. Especially after seeing more recent anime series like *Sword Art Online* and *.hack//Sign*. So I was very excited to be invited to write for this *Chronicle Worlds* anthology, more so after I started reading Anthea Sharp's *Feyland* stories and learned more about the world she had created.

Portal fantasies have a long and glorious tradition, including such classic works as the *Chronicles of Narnia* and *John Carter of Mars*. An ordinary person magically steps into a fantastical world! The very idea tugs at that desire in all of us to escape from our mundane lives into some Other place, to be some Other person. The computer-as-portal is simply the modern version of the Wardrobe, and I really enjoyed playing in this genre.

When I read the first *Feyland* book, I discovered so many prominent characters in both the human world and the Fey world, scientists and warriors, teenagers and royalty. And yet my attention kept wandering to the supporting cast, all the strange people and creatures hovering at the edges of the Dark Court. Who were they? Where did they come from? And when I learned the name of the fairy who helped to deceive Jennet, I knew I had found my own heroine: MeadowRue.

The story of MeadowRue is full of the things I like best: a strange new world, lots of fun dialogue, complicated characters who still manage to be really heroic or really villainous (no brooding anti-heroes for me!), a few heart-felt moments that I hope will resonate with my daughters, and plenty of jokes about fantasy tropes. Because if it's not fun, then why would anyone read it?

You can find all of my own fantasy series like *Elf Saga* and *Aetherium* on my website at www.josephrobertlewis.com, where you can also join my mailing list to hear about upcoming books and free offers, as well as follow my blog, my Facebook page, my Twitter, my Tumblr, and my 1998 Geocities homepage covered in blinking "Under Construction" graphics (just kidding… probably).

The Skeptic
by Lindsay Edmunds

ONE TRUE THING ABOUT SAM SAMMISH: he knew what he didn't like. He made an excellent living from a niche vid show and a well-monetized website, both called *Things That Are Wrong*. These attracted armies of followers who enjoyed the way he slaughtered, eviscerated, and roasted his targets. These targets included airy-fairy ideas, meaning anything Sam Sammish didn't believe, and useless people, meaning anyone who failed to live up to Sam Sammish's standards for worthiness.

He debunked folk tales, tall tales, urban myths, rural myths, and ancient myths. He debunked magic and the charlatans who claimed to practice it, and magical thinking in general. He debunked extra-sensory perception, psychic communication, ghosts, witches, devils, angels, spirit guides, alien abductions, and little green men. He turned the long knives of his sharp mind on literature, art, and music. ("Ninety-nine percent of it is fantasy," he said with a superior smile he encouraged his fans to emulate.) He loathed spirituality in all its manifestations, although he was careful not to attack the mainstream religions. He went after only smaller sects such as Wicca and paganism, whose anger did not matter to him or to his advertisers.

He disliked poor people unless they were willing to work hard all the time. Then they were all right.

He disliked young women who failed to meet his standards for beauty and old people because he could not see the point of them existing at all. Overweight people of either sex and any age were objects of particular scorn because Sam Sammish himself was lean and buff, and ate a carefully controlled diet, which he never tired of telling his audience about in detail.

Things That Are Wrong interspersed its debunking segments with video of things such as an elderly couple dancing in public where people had to look at them, or a teenage girl singing a heartfelt ballad she had written herself. A howler was video of a pudgy young woman giving art lessons to flabby, badly dressed old people with spotted skin and wrinkles. None of them could draw or paint at all. That was a trifecta for *Things That Are Wrong*: extra pounds, old age, and art.

The segments on wrong people were more popular than the segments on wrong ideas. This made sense. A finite number of airhead ideas were useful for *Things That Are Wrong*, but there were an infinite number of stupid people. What a gold mine they were!

Of course, Sam Sammish had enemies, people who hated his guts, but as long as his advertisers did not care, neither did he. Every morning he looked in the mirror and saw a handsome, dark-haired devil with fire in his eyes. He walked out his door with a spring in his step: another day, another dump truck full of people failing to do things right, and another boxcar full of money for him. Life was good.

In his palatial and extremely well-guarded office high above the city, he pondered requests from viewers. His fans were so good at coming up with topics for *Things That Are Wrong* that he had fired his entire research department. Why pay people to do something that others would do for free?

The request from Bradley and Chakonine Wright got his attention right away. Their video showed a handsome couple, neither of them carrying an extra pound. Bradley had blonde hair in a brush cut and wore an expensive dark blue suit with a red tie. Chakonine was lithe and beautiful with short black hair. She wore a cropped black top over white jeans. They both looked great.

"Our daughter Lenna is addicted to a Full-D game called Feyland," Bradley Wright said. "It's the one that puts gamers into a fairyland."

"Lenna claims it's not a game," Chakonine Wright said. "She says she's been to the Faerie Realm, it's realer than the life she has with us, and she wants to go there and never come back."

Sam Sammish snorted with disgust. He'd heard of Feyland. The whole world had heard of Feyland. The developer, VirtuMax, was cleaning up with that one. Its stock had gone through the roof because some people always fell for airy-fairy ideas. What suckers.

Chakonine held up a photo of Lenna. She looked to be thirteen or fourteen. Her hair was neither blonde nor black, but a weird muddy shade as if the two colors had been mixed together. Sam noted that unlike her parents, she was overweight.

He requested and got a video conference with the Wrights that same morning.

"We want you to debunk Feyland," Bradley said. "Really go after it. Tear it to pieces."

"Feyland is stupid, of course," Sam said to the Wrights. "But why would what I say on my show have any influence on your daughter? Unless she's a fan of mine," he added.

The Wrights paused for an uncomfortable second. Bradley spoke with a little hesitation in his voice. "When you debunk Feyland, we want you to feature Lenna, too. We have video of her playing the game. We have recordings of what she said. She does not know this."

Sam was a bit surprised. He had no compunction about humiliating children, but he had never had parents request him to do so.

"We're afraid for her!" Chakonine cried. "We've taken away her sim equipment, but she just sneaks out to a sim cafe or goes to her friend Bree's house and plays there. When we got a doctor to prescribe an antidepressant, she flushed all the pills down the toilet."

"We can't keep her locked up," Bradley said. "It's illegal."

"My opinion of Feyland and the delusionals who play it is even lower than yours," Sam said. "If you are willing to sign a contract saying that you agree to my featuring Lenna on my show and on my website, I agree, too."

The Wrights spoke together: "Yes." Five seconds after they received the contract, they returned it, signed.

Sam decided that the most effective way to debunk Feyland was to enter it himself. He would show the video of Lenna while talking over it about his experience with the game. They would edit the audio so that every time Lenna spoke, he would cut her off and cut her down.

The first step was to get Feyland thoroughly researched. He needed to have a detailed map of the terrain and to know in advance the answer to every riddle. He was about to bark out a command to his researchers when he remembered that he had fired all of them. This was a problem, but not an insurmountable one. His secretary, a pretty young woman named Robin, made the requisite contacts. By the end of the day, people working for freelancers' pay and no benefits, which was pretty funny to Sam, had compiled extensive background material on the game levels, the characters and their possible quests, and how to win every challenge.

He ordered a Full-D sim system, charging it to Things That Are Wrong, Inc., and had it set up in his home office. Robin provided login instructions, character notes, and answers. A hack by Enrico, his staff geek, enabled Sam to switch views between the background material and the simming system, so he did not have to go to the trouble of memorizing anything.

This was going to be easy.

At seven o'clock on a Friday evening, Sam Sammish got suited up in the Full-D paraphernalia. How could anyone believe that Feyland was real? "Reality" was obviously being simulated by expensive technology.

Moody music began to play in his helmet. "Yeah, yeah," he said to the game. "Bring on the golden glowing words of welcome."

WELCOME TO FEYLAND
A VirtuMax Production
Version 1.1
A wondrous place where adventure awaits.

Sam laughed into his helmet. *Take only screen shots, leave only money,* he thought. Although he knew that a player's thoughts could influence game activity, nothing happened at all. This made him laugh again.

A list of character classes appeared, but Sam paid no attention to it. He had already made his choice: the Knight. Noble, courageous, and true, wearing armor and wielding a sword, the Knight could kill anything.

Sam made his avatar the image of himself and took the onscreen name of Sam the Man.

More golden light, a blat of pretentious music, a blip of nausea, and he was in. He stood in a clearing in the middle of a circle of mushrooms with white-spotted red caps. Amanita mushrooms, which were poisonous. Sam considered that they were probably the only honest element in Feyland: this game was poison for the mind, and the mushrooms symbolized that.

"Oooh, into the mystic," Sam said. He swiped his sword around the circle, decapitating every mushroom. Squinting in the bright sun, he spied a narrow path and stomped out of the clearing. The air was sweet with the scent of flowers, and rolling green meadows lay under a pure blue sky. However, Sam was not impressed. He switched views to review the first challenge. Got it, he thought. I find an ugly little Non-Player-Character and bring him milk.

On the doorstep of the airiest-fairiest cottage Sam had ever seen or wanted to sat a hideous creature that seemed to be male. He was covered with brown hair, his large ears were misshapen, and his nose was a triangular deformity hanging off the center of his face. Sam had to bring free milk to a loser. Just the way to start a game.

"I want milk," the thing said, holding out a wooden bowl.

"Right," Sam said, grabbing the bowl and running as fast as a suit of silver armor would permit over the rise behind the cottage. He knew he had to sing to a damn cow. Spotting her, he bawled out a little ditty he sang on his show now and then. Not coincidentally, he wrote it himself:

Here come the idiots
One by one,
Pop 'em in the truth oven,
Until they're done.

The cow came over anyway. Wrinkling his nose in distaste, because the cow smelled like a cow, Sam milked her in quick jerks. She raised a hind leg, kicked the bowl away, and fled to another part of the field. With a string of curses, he retrieved the bowl, sang the "Here come the idiots" song, watched the fool cow return, and again began to milk her. Perspiration began to trickle down his neck.

"Nice touch, making the players sweat in the sun," he said.

He half-filled the bowl and set it aside because the smell of warm milk nauseated him. The cow looked at him with her gentle brown eyes. He picked up his sword, slaughtered her where she stood, and carried the wooden bowl back to the creature who waited in front of the cottage.

"Ah, thank you!" the thing cried when it saw the bowl.

"Here," Sam said. He dumped the bowl of milk onto the creature's head. The creature looked up at Sam with a stunned expression. Tears began to roll down his face, mingling with the rivulets of spilled milk. He tried to lap the milk with his thick black tongue.

"The programmers must have expected some players to dump the milk on your head," Sam said. "I'm not surprised. With that bowl on your head, you look better."

The creature continued to cry. "Milksop," Sam said, pleased at his own joke.

* * *

In the Realm of Faerie, members of the Dark and Bright Courts observed the headless mushrooms, the dead cow lying in a spreading circle of blood, and the tears on the face of the creature who had asked for milk. They observed Sam Sammish, who seemed to be distracted by something. He was not at that moment entirely in Feyland.

Without consultation, because they could read each other's minds on this particular subject, the Bright King and the Dark Queen met high on a green hill between their two courts. Clouds moved quickly across the face of the sun, casting them in and out of shadow.

"Sister," the Bright King said to the Dark Queen, "I would like to make some mischief with this one. Shall we let him in?"

"Brother," said the Dark Queen to the Bright King, "I could use this one's bitter mortal essence. I say yes."

They spoke to the creature on the cottage doorstep, who brightened a bit and gave Sam a crooked smile. Sam watched as the creature raised a hand to trace an elaborate path in the air, as if painting something Sam could not see. A ghostly pathway appeared, leading into a gray forest. Sam headed out to victory over Feyland.

* * *

Sam hoped to find another circle of mushrooms. Killing that first group had been fun. A plant can't run away from you, or cry aloud when it loses its head. However, the forest he entered had no Amanitas or any other kind of be-headable fungi. It was entirely bleached of color. Trees, brush, flowers, sky, and grass all were shades of gray. The air smelled like dead leaves and mud. He severed some gray blossoms from their stems and some twisted gray tree limbs from their trunks, but that was not too entertaining.

Sam did not see any obvious path forward, nor did anything appear to challenge him. "Get on with it," he said to Feyland. "I knew this game was stupid, but I didn't expect it to be boring, too."

As if responding to his command, glowing lights appeared

and beckoned him forward. Getting closer, Sam observed that at the center of each light was a delicate fairy. Of course, he thought, fairy lights. "Turn on your brights and step on the gas," he said to them. "I want to finish this game sometime tonight."

The fairies raced ahead and he galumphed behind under the weight of the silver full-body armor. His back hurt. His legs ached. Sweat trickled down inside his armor and drove him crazy.

Breathing hard, he caught up to a pair of laggard fairies. Because he was angry, he knocked them to the ground with his sword. They lay on their backs staring up at him with their great eyes. He was about to finish them off when they vanished. In their place appeared a female creature even more hideous than the male one on whom Sam had dumped the milk.

She was, first of all, grotesquely fat. In one hand she held a joint of meat, on which she gnawed with enthusiasm. In the other hand she held a tankard brimming with a pale amber liquid, from which she drank when she was not making a pig of herself with the joint. Three black hairs protruded from a large mole on her face, which was creased and wrinkled like an old boot. She wore a skirt and blouse so dirty that Sam could not tell what color they were meant to be. In a few places, the seams had given way, exposing rolls of fat.

Typical fat woman, Sam thought. She gets her clothes too small thinking that will make her look thinner. He called up the background information to find out what challenge she would present and how to answer it.

But there was nothing on her at all.

"Damn freelancers," Sam muttered. He would dock their pay for that. He would dock their pay for not telling him about the gray forest, too. At this rate, they would get nothing at all. This, at least, was a pleasing notion.

"Tell me what to do next," he said to the woman, "or feel my blade on your neck." He waved his sword in her face. She smiled, showing her bad teeth.

"Here's a riddle for you," she said. "What's got a hide like steel, a heart like a cinder, and no brains at all?"

"You mean me," Sam said. He had been attacked like this before. Still, it was odd that a character in a computer game knew how to recite the standard criticisms leveled against him by wimps and losers. It was as if she had researched *him*.

"Do you think I care about your opinion?" he said. "You are the ugliest woman I have ever seen."

The woman then did a strange thing. Setting down the joint and tankard of ale, she walked over to the nearest tree and began to climb it, not as an ordinary person would but as one who could defy gravity. She trod straight up the tall trunk, perpendicular to the forest floor. With a heave of revulsion, Sam saw that the soles of her feet had suckers on them. The woman walked up and down the trunk several times, apparently thinking about something.

Abruptly, she pulled her suckered feet free of the tree trunk and jumped down. She walked straight up to Sam, coming so close he could see the bad capillaries on her nose and smell her sour breath.

"Go away," she said. She flicked her fingers and a golden path appeared in the gray forest.

"Where does it go?" Sam asked. "I assume gold is good."

"A smart man like you shouldn't worry about that. It's just a game, isn't it?"

The woman levitated a few inches off the ground and took off at high speed. As if she piloted a floating grav-car, she zoomed and zipped among the trees and was soon out of sight.

Sam thought, then regretted thinking, that the gray forest reminded him of death. Shaking off a feeling of uneasiness, he lit out for the golden path.

Quickly, the world turned green and gentle, and the air sang with music. Sam admitted that the tunes were pleasant. They helped him relax and forget that playing this game was a waste of his precious time. He began to look about him, and saw playhouse-sized houses that were detailed, intricate, and individual in their artistry.

A house did not have a single porch, but two or three porches, one for every floor. The porches did not just have railings, but carved railings painted in every color of the rainbow. Sam noted particularly one porch with six curved archways that had cutouts and spiraling decorations. From the tops of each archway hung six potted fern plants, and each differed from the other. In the front yard was a garden in full bloom. Sam stopped to examine the plants and found that they, too, were individual. Even the flowers on a single plant did not look entirely alike.

He kept walking, past a house as elaborate as a castle with its towers and turrets, and a whitewashed house with a brick chimney from which came wisps of smoke. The forest stretched before him in all directions. Although he sensed that he was being watched, no characters came out to challenge him.

This forest must have cost a fortune in programmers' salaries and overtime. Sam wondered what the point was. He checked the Feyland background material: no information about this level of the game. He decided then and there to reduce the freelance researchers' pay to zero. Let them whine their heads off; they would not get a penny from him. The only person who had done work worth paying for was the geek who hacked the Full-D sim system to enable him to access the background view in the first place. What was that geek's name? Encito? He could stay on staff.

The golden path led on and on and on, past more houses as fantastic as the first ones and gardens riotous with color and form, each one unlike all the others. The strange, hypnotic music continued.

Something was wrong. This was not how Feyland was supposed to work.

It was with honest relief that Sam finally saw fairy lights like the ones he had seen before. This time he decided it would be imprudent to hurt them. He followed the lights until he found himself in a circle of gold, copper, and silver trees. In the center of the circle was a gold throne on which was seated a gold man wearing a crimson robe. Around him a great many creatures were making merry.

Sam remembered enough about the background material to know that he was in the Bright Court before the Bright King.

"Sam Sammish," the Bright King said, "Do you believe in me?"

"Is that a riddle?" Sam asked, wondering how the Bright King knew his full name.

"No," the Bright King said.

"You are lines of code," Sam said. "Impressive, I admit, like your forest."

The Bright King said something Sam could not hear. Around Sam's armored feet appeared a dozen spotted puppies with long ears and enormous paws. One bit his right foot and took the armor off as cleanly as a can-opener takes off a lid. Sam stared down at his naked white foot and at the teeth of the puppy, which were sharp as razors and, obviously, much stronger.

"Have at him," the Bright King said.

All twelve puppies leapt upon Sam, gnawing his armor with glee. When he fell trying to escape, it was short work for them to remove the shining silver metal in jagged pieces. The puppies played with the scraps as other puppies play with chew toys. Tugs-of-war broke out all around Sam, who sat on the ground wearing long red underwear with an unbuttoned drop seat.

"Very funny," Sam said, regarding his red-clad self. "Har-de-har-har."

"Puppies!" commanded the Bright King, "Let our honored guest rise."

The puppies scattered. Sam got to his feet and fastened the drop seat of his underwear. "I suppose there are game scenarios where the Knight loses his armor," he said. "The programmers had to put something under it, or the game wouldn't be rated for all ages."

"Sam Sammich," said a colorfully dressed little man with an annoying grin on his face. "We are not done with you." He shoved Sam toward the throne of the Bright King.

Sam stumbled into a cunning loop of rope and found himself hoisted skyward. "Oh [expletive deleted]," he yelled as he dangled by one leg upside down. Back in the mortal world in Full-D sim, he was dizzy and disoriented. He could do nothing as various creatures gathered around to bat at him as if he were a piñata.

"Just a game!" they cried as they swatted him. He spun around, not slowly, and added nausea to his list of discomforts.

"Just a game! Just a game!"

"What do you think of Feyland now?"

Sam tried to abort the game, but he was not adroit while spinning around upside down in space wearing long red underwear, so he could not. He heard a slashing noise, as of a sword cutting rope, and fell to the ground. For a moment, all went dark. When he regained his senses, he saw a wondrous sight:

The most beautiful girl in the world stood before him. She had long blonde hair with wispy bangs and wore a crown of flowers that matched her ankle-length dress, which was fringed in white feathers. Her feet were bare. She looked at Sam calmly, as if she could see straight through him. She seemed to be a pure, clear band of consciousness, meeting a pure, clear band of consciousness within him. Sam had not believed until that instant that he had a soul, but she changed his mind. "Oh," he said.

In one arm, she cradled a fold of her dress. Looking at her

belly, Sam realized that she was pregnant. He felt both hot and cold.

"What is your name?" he asked.

The girl considered the question for a few moments. "Fay," she said.

"You are expecting a baby," Sam said. Speaking those words aloud felt like broken glass in his throat.

"Aye, soon."

But you belong to me, he wanted to cry. In desperation he fell back on the observation that she carried a few extra pounds not attributable to her pregnancy. However, this did no good; he loved her, he wanted her.

As he gazed up at her, she shape-shifted into the ugly hag he had met in the forest. Fat, warty, and wrinkled, she looked upon him with the same calm, soul-piercing gaze as before.

"You did not see me as I am," she said. "Now, you will see me no more in this world."

She again became the beautiful girl of Sam's dreams, then vanished. Alone and stunned, Sam knelt in his red underwear in the court of the Bright King.

"It is time you met my sister," the king said.

The world swam in darkness. Sam woke, still in red underwear and on his knees, in a midnight-colored world. On a throne made of gnarled vines sat a woman whose beauty inspired terror rather than attraction. She looked down at Sam with black eyes as deep and fathomless as the ocean. Bonfires blazed purple in the shadows. Creatures danced about, but not in a way that implied invitation to join them.

Sam heard a laugh that caused his heart to flutter like a

trapped bird. All the cruelty of the world was in it. He knew that the horrible sound came from nearby on his right, but Sam would not turn to see who or what could laugh like that. He did not have to turn around. The Black Knight, faceless behind his black armor, stepped directly in front of Sam and laughed again.

With the last of his strength, Sam tried again to quit the game. He was right side up now, he should be able to do it with ease. *But he couldn't.* It was as if he were being prevented from leaving Feyland. He remembered the mocking words so recently thrown at him, "Just a game?"

"Fool," said the Dark Queen. "If a great wave were approaching, you would stand on the shore proclaiming you did not believe in great waves while all the animals ran for the hills."

She moved her hand as if in sign language. Before Sam stood every Feyland creature whom he had wronged: the cow he had slaughtered, the creature on whom he had dumped the bowl of milk, the fairies he had injured, and even the red and white-spotted Amanita mushrooms he had beheaded.

Sam looked for Fay. Not there.

"I won't waste a riddle on you," the Dark Queen said, raising a crystal sphere high above her head. Sam watched her make more sign language gestures, every movement causing silver tracings to appear in the darkness. Her pale fingernails looked like claws.

She pointed at him, and he reeled in agony. The pain in his chest felt like death. "Oh God," he cried as he fell to the floor.

"You don't believe in God," remarked the Dark Queen

Sam rolled this way and that, clutching his chest. A crescent moon cast faint light on his contorted face. Candles flickered. Goblins and wraiths gathered round to watch and wait.

"Now," the Dark Queen said with a wicked smile. "Look up and behold a tiny sliver of your mortal essence that I have trapped for my own use."

Sam saw a small flame twisting helplessly within the crystal sphere the queen held aloft. It seemed to be made of many colors, although they were dark and subdued. Even in his pain, he wondered about that. He had colors inside him?

"Bitter," the queen said. "I am pleased."

This cannot be happening to me, Sam thought. *I have a vid show. I have a website. I have fans who hang on my every word.*

The Dark Queen's laughter chilled his blood.

"Sam Sammish," she said, "With this I curse you: The woman named Fay will come to you in dreams, day and night. You will long to return to her. But if you try, you will find the way to the Realm of Faerie blocked by flaming swords."

The gold light that swirled around Sam hurt like a burn. He cried out one word, "Water," before he fell unconscious in the sim chair.

When he woke up, his chest felt empty and cold. He ached from head to toe. He no longer felt like a man.

The helmet. The gloves. He had to take them off. Pain shot through his arms as he struggled to lift the helmet from his head. Wincing, he peeled the gloves from his hands. There was a large bruise on the back of his left hand. His right little finger did not work right.

On his hands and knees he found his bedroom. He slept

for eighteen hours and woke up thinking he was a little better. However, the room went round and round when he tried to get out of bed. His stomach heaved with nausea. He crawled to the bathroom and crawled back again.

When his secretary Robin called to ask what was going on, he said he was sick with flu. No, there was nothing she could do for him. No, he didn't need to see a doctor. That afternoon Fay came to him in a lucid dream. She looked just as she did before, same long flowered dress, same soulful gaze. "You complete me," Sam said, tears running down his cheeks. "How can you not be mine?"

The dream ended. The wounded place in Sam's chest throbbed with pain. He lay in his sour bed, afraid to fall asleep again.

For several weeks, viewers who tuned into *Things That Are Wrong* saw reruns.

However, people can survive with missing parts, sometimes many of them. Sam's bruises healed, and the nausea went away. The painful emptiness in his chest became a routine feeling. He began to eat real meals again and sleep regular hours. However, he could not return to *Things That Are Wrong*. He tried, but the hurtful words he once said with relish now died on his tongue.

His quitting the show did not much trouble the advertisers. They found someone to take his place within two days. Sam was glad. The show did not matter. The show had never mattered.

Sam stayed inside his penthouse apartment for several months, where he did nothing at all except spend his money and play Feyland over and over. He put on weight and grew pale and flabby. One night Fay came to him and held up a baby boy who had her blonde hair and blue eyes. "My son," she said. When Sam stretched out his arms to hold them both, they moved far away. He woke up in darkness. The wound in his chest twitched.

* * *

In the meantime, the troubles between Lenna and her parents had solved themselves. Or rather, Lenna had figured out a way to make it seem as if they had.

Out of the blue, she announced to her parents that she intended to be a better person. That day she began a diet to lose weight and to use her parents' exercise machines. She colored her hair a pretty shade of red and let her mother instruct her on the use of makeup. Using her mother's charge card, she bought a lot of new clothes. She brought up her grades. Although she didn't want ever to become too popular—popularity was a nuisance when you had better things on your mind—she grew into a role as a well-liked, if somewhat mysterious, girl.

For all these things, she asked only one condition: that she could play Feyland whenever she wanted. "I know it's just a game," she said to her parents, smiling almost invisibly.

* * *

Sam moved into a one-room apartment in a high-rise for single low-income people. With the last of his money, he bribed the owner of a sim cafe to take him on as a helper (read: waiter-janitor-customer service guy). The owner ran his sim cafe according to the motto "The customer is always right." That suited Sam fine. "Yessir, Nossir, Yes'm, No'm," he said all day, never varying his tone. Customers asked rude questions and made absurd demands. These things did not bother him. In fact, it pleased him to delegate responsibility for being right. He had never been right about anything in his entire life.

Employees of the sim café could use the gaming equipment in off-hours. After a double shift of customer insults and tiresome work, Sam sat down to play Feyland in the small hours of the morning. As he worked through the levels of the game, so familiar now, he remembered the beautiful world to which he could no longer return. The Dark Queen had cursed him with exile, and she seemed unlikely to break her promise.

Weariness overcame him, and he fell into troubled sleep without moving from where he sat. In a dream, Fay came to him.

"Sam Sammish," she said. "You do not need to play Feyland to go on a quest. You are on one now. Choose to admit it. Will you meet the challenges and solve the riddles? I cannot undo the Dark Queen's curse, but if you live with honor and humility, you will see me again."

Sam woke up and looked around the dark, empty café. *This is the current level of my quest,* he thought.

He walked home in the dim light of a new day. As he approached his high rise, he saw in the shadows an elderly woman carrying two bulging plastic bags. *What is she doing out at this hour?* he wondered. One of the bags ripped, spilling boxes and cans of food onto the sidewalk. Sam ran to her side and helped gather up the groceries.

"Where do you live?" he asked, hoping she had a home.

The woman pointed at the high rise.

"In that place?" Sam said. "I live there, too."

"I was at the food bank," she said. "If you get there later than four in the morning, all the good things are gone."

In a flash, Sam saw how it was for this old woman: She had to force her tired bones out of bed in the middle of the night so she could eat. Yet she was still in the game, playing with all the strength that remained to her. He could not think of anything to say for a moment.

"What's your name?" he finally asked.

"Marina Fluvanna," she said.

"My name is Sam Sammish."

Marina looked up at him with a glint of amusement in her eyes. "You had that vid show," she said.

"Not anymore," Sam said.

"Good," Marina said.

Sam put all the boxes and cans in the remaining unbroken bag and carried it in both arms. The bag was heavy. He did not know how Marina had walked as far as she had with all those groceries.

At the security door of the high rise, Marina fumbled for the correct code. She pulled at the door with both hands, leaning against its heavy weight as if trying to get a sailboat to come about in a high wind.

"Wait," said Sam. "I'll help you." He set down the bag and opened the door. He and Marina walked through the labyrinthine maze that led to the bank of elevators. They shot up to the thirtieth floor and walked another maze to get to Marina's tiny cell, smaller by half than Sam's. She was the first resident Sam had ever talked to. He often went a week without even *seeing* another resident.

"Do you want some coffee?" Marina asked. There was no mistaking the hopefulness in her voice. Sam did not want coffee, but he said yes. She boiled water on an electric plate and added a spoonful of instant coffee to each of two dingy white cups, one with a chipped rim. Sam noticed she took the chipped cup for herself. She punched holes in a small can of milk and poured the milk into a little flowered pitcher. She served him a slice of white toast with "berry" jam that tasted violently of sweetener and chemicals.

"What I would like before I die," Marina said, looking dreamily into her coffee cup, "is to taste real cream again."

After he had drunk the coffee and eaten the toast, Sam said he had to do some errands. In an hour, he returned from a 24-hour grocery with three pints of cream, two new coffee mugs, a loaf of freshly baked French bread, a pound of butter, a pound of sugar, and strawberry jam labeled "100% fruit." Marina's jaw dropped.

"Not needed," she said, even though she eyed the food hungrily.

"Yes, needed," Sam said. In his own apartment, which seemed suddenly spacious, he thought, *I've completed my first task: I got cream for Marina Fluvanna.*

He considered his situation. His job was terrible, but he could not quit because he needed what little money it provided. Maybe that did not matter. He flashed back to the sight of the sliver of his mortal essence twisting and turning in the Dark Queen's crystal sphere. He had been surprised it had colors. He had been surprised he *had* a mortal essence. But Fay had seen. Fay had known.

She had said that she would return if he performed his tasks with honor. When she came again, he wanted her to smile and say, "Level up, Sam. Level up."

A WORD FROM LINDSAY EDMUNDS

One day several months ago, I saw Samuel Peralta's Facebook post about a new series called *Chronicle Worlds* and knew at once I wanted to be part of it. I loved the premise behind Anthea Sharp's *Feyland* series: What if a computer game was a gateway to the Realm of Faerie?

I was not intimidated by the prospect of playing in another writer's fictional universe. Instead, I was delighted. Feyland was a marvelous gift: a highly detailed, intricate place full of color and magic. Everything I needed was already there.

My story, "The Skeptic," is about a professional debunker named Sam Sammish. He enters Feyland to mock and sneer at it, which turns out to be unwise. The story was fun to write.

In 2011, I self-published my first book, *Cel & Anna*, about a computer that spontaneously develops consciousness and falls in love with its owner. That book was followed by tales of good and evil e-beasts roaming the internet (*Warning: Something Else Is Happening*), a mother and daughter bound by a shared gift of psychic power (*Blood Psychics*), and a young girl who seeks adventure in the world outside her gated utopian community (*New Sun Rising: Ten Stories*).

For a long time, I kept thinking up complicated explanations for what I write. These confused everyone, and eventually I wised up. Here's what I do: I write fairy tales for the internet age. I've done it from the beginning.

Cel the computer is an elf. The good and evil e-beasts are faerie tribes. The young girl's utopian home, where ghosts are commonplace and spirituality saturates the very air, is a type of fairyland. I grew up loving fairy tales and wrote my thesis on Emily Dickinson's use of fantasy in her poetry. It is logical I ended up where I have.

Fiction writing is my part-time job. (My full-time job is as an editor working with medical/scientific researchers for whom English is a second language.) I believe in regular hours, practice, and structure. A wild imagination is not much good, I discovered, until it is tame enough to be ridden.

Take a look at my website. Subscribe to my newsletter while you are there. You will get a free Imagination ebook with great quotes and beautiful images. The first quote is from Albert Einstein. (Who knew he loved fairy tales?) The images come from several sources. Some are photos I took at the Chautauqua Institution, a western New York summer community.

http://www.lindsayedmunds.com

The Sword of Atui
by Eric Kent Edstrom

SYSTEM TEMPERATURE ALARM: 85°C

The pop-up alert covered Fasster's terminal window, interrupting the flow of code streaming from his fingers and into his clunky old keyboard.

He muttered a few choice curses and pushed away from the 32 inch flatscreen wired into his system. The Feyland game mod he was writing would have to wait until the system cooled. That's what you got for over-clocking your rig. But since Dad wouldn't spring for an updated system and a thirteen-year-old couldn't earn enough money mowing lawns to buy one, that's just how it was.

The temperature alarm couldn't have come at a worse time. He was so close to finishing his mod he could taste it.

There was only one solution.

With a grunt he yanked open his bedroom window. The

blade edge of winter sliced into his second story bedroom, stinging his face. A rustle of leaves curled across the back yard like waves piling on a distant shore. Farther off, the neighbor's swaybacked mare whinnied in the darkness, probably to warn off Fasster's errant hound Nodo.

Beneath those sounds was silence. Far in the distance, the sky glowed amber from the lights of Milwaukee.

Fasster called for Nodo to come home, and began pulling on warmer clothes. The only good thing about the chill Wisconsin winter was that it supplied a free source of cooling for his straining gaming rig.

* * *

The box fan in the window rattled and complained, blasting frosty air into Fasster's bedroom from outside. Now bundled in long underwear, wool sweater, winter parka, and wool socks, he had to breathe on his fingers every few minutes to keep them from going numb. But the cold air had greatly improved his system's performance.

The system temperature now hovered at 78°C. Well within operating limits.

Nodo, exhausted and panting from his adventures harassing the neighbor's horse, was curled under Fasster's desk. The dog's body would keep Fasster's feet nice and toasty.

Now he could install his newest mod into his sim system and go into the game. The gloves and helmet would keep him warm enough. He hoped. Once inside, he wouldn't know if his body was getting frostbite or not.

He prepared the code file for his mod.

SwAtui.xlc

The trick now was to get it on a Feyland server without the anti-virus wardens noticing. In his favor was the fact that his mod file was not, in fact, a virus. It was a game object. A sword. His plan to get it installed was so simple, he was amazed nobody else had thought of it.

He entered the commands, fingers flying across his keyboard in a blur. It came down to this: he sent an email to a Feyland customer support rep. But this was not just any CSR, this lady was a high-level developer whose own system was always logged into the Feyland administrative backdoor. That was key.

Fasster's email contained a link to a screenshot of an error message. But when she clicked on it, the link would run a bit of executable code in the background to install the SwAtui.xlc file on the Feyland servers.

If things went as planned, she'd never notice.

Once he invoked the mod, Fasster's character would conquer the entirely of Feyland. If he had been old enough to grow a long mustache, he would have twisted it while he laughed with malicious glee. As it was, he stroked the peach fuzz on his upper lip and chuckled.

The code would fire him a message as soon as it executed, so all he had to do now was wait.

Fasster hit the bathroom, ate a candy bar, and sucked down a can of energy drink. He tiptoed downstairs to make sure Dad wasn't going to interrupt him. Finally some good luck. The old man was conked out on the sofa, a late night talk show blaring on the TV. Pretty much where he'd been ever since Mom had moved out two months ago.

By the time he'd returned to his freezing bedroom and snuggled his feet beneath his snoring hound, the code activation notice had appeared in his inbox.

This was it. This was the day he became king of the world. Maybe Dad wouldn't care, and Mom wouldn't even know about it, and his so-called friends at school would keep picking on him and cutting him out of their conversations during lunch period—but in Feyland, he would reign above all. He wouldn't need any of them then.

He geared up in his gloves and helmet, then wrapped a scarf around his face to protect his nose and cheeks from the icy air.

His system was rickety, but he knew guys online who gamed ten hours a day on flicker rigs his dad would have been ashamed of. He couldn't complain.

"Here goes nothing!"

His stomach lurched and he fell into the game.

* * *

The sun stood on the horizon, seemingly very far off. A sea-like prairie stretched away before Fasster, tall grass flickering from emerald to sage as the breeze ruffled the stalks. As inviting as it looked, he'd stay away from the Horselands for this outing. This time he was headed back to a side quest he'd never been able to beat. It was the perfect test for his mod.

Today he would slay Hig-Tuli, the Rage Bear of Deller's Cave.

He put his fingers in his mouth and whistled for his mount. As usual, he heard the bark before he appeared. He'd used a third party plugin called X-Jen's Familiar-Maker to re-skin Feyland's standard horse. It now looked just like Nodo, except he was the size of a horse.

With a bound, Fasster hopped on Nodo's back and hugged his neck and gave him the command to run: "Fly, you fool!"

Wind blew back Fasster's hair, which he kept super long in game. Dad made him cut it short in real life. The mid-summer heat wasn't too bad beneath the hazy sky, a nice change from last time. For some reason, his leather armor always made him sweat and chafe.

With a quiet command, he told Nodo to take him to Nym, the creature who would give him the quest.

He found the fuzzy little critter in its usual spot, lounging beneath a willow and grooming itself. More feline than humanoid, the creature's furry ears twitched into alertness as Nodo tromped toward him. Or her. Fasster didn't know which Nym was. And perhaps Nym didn't know either.

Without turning to face him, Nym sighed and straightened its waistcoat. "Well met, Fasster. I must confess I'm surprised at your willingness to die and die and die and die and die and die—"

"This time will be different," Fasster said. He didn't bother dismounting. He and Nym had gone through this routine a dozen times.

With a sigh, Nym recited its spiel. "Hig-Tuli guards a

treasure rare, a relic sacred and powerful: the Talisman of the Heart. Slay the Beast and bring me the Talisman. Complete this quest and I shall grant you a boon."

Keep your boon, Fasster thought. With his mod, nothing in this world would be denied him. Still, he knew better than to speak his thoughts to the mercurial creature until he'd tested things out.

"I shall bring you the Talisman or die trying."

"'Tis not a quest to go on alone," Nym warned for the umpteenth time. "To defeat Hig-Tuli, one needs a powerful ally."

Fasster ignored this warning as he had done many times before. "There are three of us. Me, myself, and I."

Nym laughed and finally turned to face Fasster. The cat eyes squinted with mirth, mouth parting to flash needle-pointed teeth. "I said a *powerful* ally, not a stupid one."

Biting back a curse, Fasster turned Nodo away from the creek and left the giggling Nym behind. He knew better than to respond. Nym always had to have the last word.

Fasster told Nodo to take him to Deller's Cave so he wouldn't have to steer yet again through the same winding path. And so leaving his mount on autopilot, he turned his attention to bringing his mod into existence.

"Powerful ally," he mumbled. "I'll show you a powerful ally, little kitten."

Despite the outward bravado, he found himself hesitating. The downside of failure would be pretty bad. If he got caught, some sysadmin would kick him out of the game. Probably ban him forever.

But if he didn't get caught, he would own the game and destroy all opposition.

And that was totally worth the risk. Maybe here, at least, he could be powerful.

He closed his eyes and relaxed. Nodo's easy bounds over the terrain soothed him, gave him confidence. Already they had entered Whileaway Forest, bringing the scent of pine and earth to his nose. Somewhere ahead was the mountain and Dellar's Cave.

With a deep breath, Fasster pictured his mod and spoke the words. "I summon thee, Sword of Absolute, Total, and Utter Invincibility!"

Thrusting out his right hand, he willed the weapon into existence.

There wasn't so much as a flicker of light. No sudden swell of orchestral music. Not even a magical chime.

Instead, the object just appeared in his hand. Like any good magical weapon, the sword was light and perfectly balanced. And it would hold a razor's edge without sharpening no matter how much armor or bone he chopped through.

Fasster admired the weapon, a longsword as common looking and inconspicuous as could be. One would find hundreds of such weapons as loot on the bodies of lesser goblins and rogues or in level-one treasure chests.

But this... this plain, faintly rusted blade, was part of the genius of the mod. Nobody who faced him, or even gave him a cursory glance, would suspect the powers of the Sword of Absolute, Total, and Utter Invincibility.

The Sword of Atui.

He slashed the air. Oh, this was going to be good. Hig-Tuli

wouldn't give the blade a second look as she charged, spittle drooping from her ravenous jaws, bellowing animal curses and reaching with her immense claws to rend him to pieces.

He only hoped her severed head would retain a moment of consciousness to realize just what had happened, to see who had vanquished her. Warmth filled Fasster's chest, and a feeling he'd never felt before made his face split into a grin.

Pride.

The feeling wisped away like candle smoke in a breeze as he beheld what lay around the final bend.

* * *

A raiding party of no less than twelve jerks was congregated at the cave's maw. With that many raiders, there was no way Hig-Tuli would survive. And if they killed her before Fasster did, he would have to wait weeks for her to respawn. Assuming she ever did. The thought that his victory might be stolen made Fasster's blood sizzle in his brain.

A druid wearing a red cloak embroidered with verdant ivy vines turned away from the scrum of raiders and spotted Fasster. Black locks plumed from the hood which masked the druid's face.

It was too late to retreat, so Fasster dismounted and sent Nodo off to sniff around in the bushes. The reskin of his mount had a bug that overlooked a horse's tendency to eat grass. Fasster was vaguely embarrassed when Nodo starting munching away and trying to flick flies away with his cropped tail.

"Hail, sir," said the druid in a feminine alto. "By the looks of you, you're a stealth archer." The druid paused and took in Fasster's loadout of equipment. "And it appears you have secondary skills in one-handed weapons."

By now the rest of the raiding party had convened behind the druid. A tank wearing nothing but a loincloth and three hundred pounds of muscle nudged the red cloaked figure. He braced a club the size of a parking meter on his shoulder. "You no invited. We no share XP with raid crashers."

A chorus of agreement burbled from the others. From the looks of them they were all equipped with magic weapons. They had way more scars and achievement tattoos than players Fasster usually saw on this level.

A wave of defiant irritation arose in Fasster's heart. "I didn't come here to join your pathetic raiding party."

Muscle Tank laughed. "You fight Rage Bear by self?"

Fasster let silence be his answer. He couldn't help but rest his hand on the pommel of his rusty sword.

The others laughed and shook their heads at his stupidity. All save the druid. With feather light steps, the red cloak approached. Long, nimble fingers pulled the hood back to reveal a mane of raven hair framing a face of such delicate beauty that Fasster wanted to take back all of his previous words and pledge his life and honor to her.

When she spoke, her words were soft with concern. "Do you truly mean to fight Hig-Tuli alone? Again?"

Fasster swallowed, conscious of the smirks aimed his way from all of the other raiders. He stiffened and jutted his chin forward. "I do." His voice sounded weak in his own ears. "But how do you know I've tried before?"

She smiled and stepped closer. Fasster thought her heard the tinkle of wind chimes as she moved. Her presence made him slightly dizzy and the air smelled of strange and intoxicating flowers. "It's one of my talents. I can see the past." Her eyes—large and luminous—dropped to Fasster's sword, then snapped up to meet his gaze.

There was no way she could know about the Sword of Atui. Was there?

She pulled her hood up and turned to address the raiding party. "I believe Fasster was led here by Fate to assist us, though he knows it not. I say we include him."

Fasster blinked. He hadn't told her his name. And he certainly didn't want to join the group.

Except he would do it if it would please her.

The smirks all disappeared. The Muscle Tank's face went red with fury, but amazingly he said nothing. A knight—visor lifted to expose a hard face with ebony eyes--even wore a look of interest. Next to him a cliché dwarf fighter with two axes strapped to his back stroked his braided beard and gave Fasster a reappraising look.

"What's your name?" Fasster called to the druid.

The beautiful red-cloaked woman did not respond. Instead, a spellcaster bearing a twisted staff ambled near. He was outwardly elderly, but had the bearing of an excited ten-year-old. "Everyone knows Jaconde."

"Not me."

"How is that possible? She's legendary."

"I play solo and I don't chitchat in towns."

Jaconde calmly addressed the party. "Our stealthy friend

has been in Deller's Cave several times before. He's faced Hig-Tuli, and has met many honorable deaths."

The party laughed, but this time they seemed to give him different looks. Their eyes squinted and the smiles seemed to include him rather than mock him. Three witches—all dressed alike in black robes—conferred in cackling mumbles.

In unison, they spoke. "Lonely! Sullen! Bitter!"

Jaconde smiled sadly. "True."

The witches pointed gnarled fingers at Fasster and repeated their declaration. Or maybe it was a denunciation.

Jaconde's face turned dark and she was clearly losing patience. "Anyone can change."

"He dies alone! Alone he dies! He dies alone!" the witches cried, eyes flaming at Fasster.

Before Jaconde could respond, Fasster stepped forward. "Fine. I'll go in alone. I was going to anyway."

"No." Jaconde turned away from the witches and they bowed their heads. She challenged the rest of the raiders with her eyes, each in turn bowed to her will. Fasster was not surprised. Just being in her presence made him want to please her.

Even so, this was not at all what Fasster had wanted. Killing the bear—Hig-Tuli—was meant to be a test of his new weapon. He'd never intended to do it in front of an audience.

He pursed his lips as a new thought filled his brain.

Audience…

Would it not be better to have an audience for his triumph? A band of witnesses to testify that he had, in fact, single-handedly defeated Hig-Tuli?

Yes, he thought. That would be better. And Jaconde would

see him do it too. That would impress her. He so desperately wanted to impress her.

Jaconde's voice interrupted his musings of glory. "Fasster, please tell us what to expect in the cave."

Conscious of the eyes bathing him with attention, he cleared his throat. "As you all know, Hig-Tuli is a rage bear. She is tough as a dragon, with a health meter a mile long. She is always pacing in the cavern at the end of the entry tunnel. Even with my stealth skills, I can only get within twenty meters before she senses my presence. She'll hear the tank—and you other stumble-footed clods—well before that. An arrow will get a stealth bonus, but that might as well be a pinprick. The best I've ever done was three arrows into her flank and one critical eye shot. That didn't even slow her down. Two swipes of her claws and I was out." Fasster deliberately eyed the Muscle Tank, whose name, it turned out, was Krahp. "You might be able to take three or four swipes."

Krahp grunted something that was clearly against the Feyland Terms of Service and flexed his pecs.

Okay, Fasster grudgingly admitted, maybe Krahp could take five swipes from Hig-Tuli.

Fasster was warming to having an attentive audience and was about to go on, but Jaconde interrupted him. Not by speaking, but simply by taking one step forward. All eyes followed her.

With a voice barely above a whisper, she assigned the raiders their roles in the attack. Each nodded respectfully and took their place in one of two lines. Fasster saw the red-cloaked leader was dividing the force into two waves, each roughly balanced with melee and range specialists or casters.

His eyes lingered on two female archers with blond braids. They were identical twins. They wore forest green genie pants, flowy crop top blouses, and curly-toed boots. Strictly speaking, the outfits were utterly impractical, especially for a raid. But wow!

"That's Eve and Riah," said the elderly spellcaster, nudging Fasster's shoulder. His name was Doodoodalf ("everyone just calls me Dalf"), which confirmed to Fasster he was actually talking to a ten-year-old. "The twins are the two finest archers I've ever seen. They're also pretty handy with their bows."

Fasster allowed himself a chuckle, but couldn't help but appraise the competition. He was no slouch with a bow, but these players were higher level. And the more he studied their equipment, the higher he estimated their experience was. Each of the twins bore Relic Bows, unique and endowed with powerful charms. No way to know what they would do just by looking, but the scrollwork and runes carved in the supple wood spoke of ancient magics.

"And you," Jaconde said to Fasster, "I want you to go in last."

"Last?" Fasster blurted. "But I was going to scout out the situation."

The woman's hood shadowed her face, but Fasster thought he detected amusement in the chime tinkles coming from her. "You've already scouted it. Twelve times."

"But—"

She was suddenly standing toe to toe with him. The rest of

the world went out of focus and the sounds of the raiders' conversations dulled to an unintelligible warble. Chimes sounded again and her floral scent made him woozy.

Jaconde placed her delicate hand on his chest. Heat seemed to sear his skin beneath his leathers. It didn't exactly hurt, but it made his heart race and his vision swim. Only two points of light remained in the world. Glimmers from Jaconde's eyes.

Her whisper floated in his mind, as if she had somehow bypassed his ears and spoken directly into his brain. "Hold back. Watch the others to find the beast's weakness. Then strike."

Like the flip of a switch, vision and sound returned. Jaconde was already—impossibly—disappearing into the mouth of the cave.

"How does it feel?" Dalf asked.

"How does what feel?"

"The armor buff Jaconde just cast on your ass. What else?"

So that's what she'd done, cast a protective spell to improve his armor rating. The buff would probably last for the fight with Hig-Tuli, then wear off.

"I've never heard of her doing that for anyone before," Dalf said as they moved to the end of their assigned line. "You must be very special indeed." He flicked a finger against Fasster's shoulder, making an odd thunk.

Fasster looked down, surprised to discover his leather armor replaced by… vines. He ran his fingers along the ivy armor, lingering on a sprout of leaves on one shoulder—like a living epaulet. He couldn't help but marvel. His armor was quite literally alive. He swung his arms and twisted, surprised at how supple it was.

As the last raiders disappeared into the cave, Fasster took a final glance at the world of daylight. It was the same Feyland he'd been exploring for over a year, but for some reason it felt different.

Shrugging, he followed Dalf into the dark and chill guts of Deller's Cave.

* * *

A caster at the front of the procession had produced a dim ball of red light. It made the moisture trickling down the walls look like blood.

Dalf chanted quietly, preparing some spell or other. Fasster had never liked being a caster in games. Learning spells had always felt vaguely like homework.

A dissonant chime sounded in his head, followed by a woman's stern voice. "System Temperature Warning 83°C."

"Dammit," he breathed.

Dalf gave him a concerned glance.

"It's nothing. My rig is overheating a little."

"You rockin' an overclocked spark wagon?"

"Yeah. But it's more wagon than spark."

Dalf chuckled. "I'm driving a fourth generation FullD. Got it for Christmas. My brother had a fit when he…"

Fasster tuned out the mage's ramblings. He didn't understand why was his rig was overheating. With his bedroom open and the fan going, it should be below freezing in his room by now. Fasster spat with disgust. There was only one answer. Dad had come upstairs and felt the draft coming from Fasster's room.

He'd barged in and shut the window. He'd probably mumbled something about not being made of money and heating bills or some other nonsense.

At least Dad hadn't pulled Fasster from the game. The last time he'd done that, Fasster had suffered the worst migraine of his life.

He tried to calculate how much time this encounter with Hig-Tuli would take. The problem was that the more intense the game got, the more cycles his rig needed to keep up.

If the system got above 93°C, the operating system would override Fasster's already-dangerous overrides and shut down. And if he was in-game when that happened… There was a reason why the User License included a disclaimer about simming on overclocked rigs.

A shut down could put him in a coma for weeks. If he was lucky.

A gut-twisting roar filled the tunnel with waves of rage. Hig-Tuli had discovered the raiding party. Ahead, the twins sprinted forward, nocking arrows as they ran.

"Something went wrong," Dalf said.

"Krahp?"

The old-looking spellcaster nodded, a wry smile twisting his mustaches. "Aye, Krahp happens."

If Jaconde had let Fasster finish briefing them, he would have been able to tell her about the side tunnel. But since he was the only stealth expert in the group, perhaps nobody would have used it anyway.

"Come with me," Fasster said to Dalf. "I know how we can

get behind the bear." He needed to get this encounter over with and surface from the sim, and quick.

Dalf tapped his staff on the floor and soft blue light shone forth. "Lead on, my friend."

Fasster dragged his hand along the cool wet stone of the wall. "The tunnel opening moves, but it's always on this wall somewhere."

Dalf shook his staff and the top glowed with a ball of flickery amber light. The bloody walls turned to honey.

"Thanks, but the opening is invisible."

"Then how did you find it the first time?"

"I fell through it once when I was running awa—uh, regrouping."

His hand suddenly slid up to the wrist into the rock wall. "Aha! Follow me." He plunged through the illusory wall and into the ink-black side passage.

Fasster was thankful for Dalf's stafflight. Usually he lit a torch in here, but the smoke always made him choke and that alerted Hig-Tuli.

The sound of battle dulled as they plunged deeper into the narrow passage. "Careful here," Fasster said as he knelt to squeeze through a particularly narrow point. "Ice spiders."

Dalf made a dismissive spitting noise. "Stand aside. I'll fry 'em."

Fasster did as he was told. Dalf muttered for a moment and thrust his staff into the narrowing. A burst of flame, like someone torching a pool of gasoline, flashed for a split moment. Shrill cries of ice spiders followed immediately after. "Flee! Flee!" they shrieked in pipsqueak voices. "The sneak-who-dies is returned with magical fire!"

"I didn't know they could talk," Dalf said, face drooping with obvious regret. "I've toasted thousands of those little devils in my day."

Fasster scrambled through the narrowing tunnel. Dalf emerged after him, regal robes and beard smudged with soot. The passage widened and turned a corner before coming to an apparent dead end. Fasster skidded to a stop.

"There's a narrow ledge on the other side of the wall. It's at Hig-Tuli's shoulder height, so don't think for one second you're out of range of her claws."

Taking a deep breath, he stepped through the wall and into chaos.

* * *

Having never been on a raid before, Fasster was momentarily stunned by the cacophony of blasts and roars and cries that met him in the cave. The great Hig-Tuli stood on her hind legs in the center of the cavern, taking great swipes at Krahp. Though he'd seen her many times before, her size took his breath away. This was no mere grizzly bear, this was a monster the size of a minivan.

Her black fur stood up at the hackles as she battled the raiders. Upon her hind feet, she towered over her adversaries, a raging giant. Mouth open, lips pulled back, her teeth glistened in the flashes of magic bolts and flames coming from the casters. Drips of slaver dangled from her great maw. And if this wasn't fearful enough, her eyes glowed red, showing that her Rage Might was upon her.

Blood streamed from gaping claw marks on each of Krahp's shoulders and ran in rivulets down his chest. Face contorted with battle madness, he met the rage bear blow for blow. His club swung in huge arcs, and made the bear's furry hide ripple with every impact. Already, the beast's pelt was pincushioned with arrows. A glance told Fasster that the twins would soon be out of arrows.

"Where's Jaconde?" Fasster asked into the air as he searched for their leader.

The bear was encircled by raiders. The knight stumbled and tottered, swinging wildly. His helm had been caved in, misaligning his visor and blinding him. The stocky axe-wielding dwarf hurled more curses at the bear than he did blows. But when he did choose to swing, the blades seemed to bounce off the bear with no effect.

"Egads!" Dalf shouted. His face was drawn and he seemed to stagger back. "She's immune!"

"What?"

"To magic. Look!"

At first Fasster didn't know what he was supposed to see. But then a caster sent a fireball at the bear's face. It should have left her as crispy as a match head. Instead, the eldritch fire glanced off the great beast like a ping pong ball and fizzled into a wisp of smoke.

System Temperature Alarm: 89°C

Fasster drew his sword. He had to end this now.

"Hold!" Dalf yelled, grabbing Fasster's shoulder. "If you jump into the melee you'll be dead in two seconds."

Fasster smirked and leapt from his perch, rusty blade high

overhead. This was it. With all his might, he swung it at the bear's skull as he descended.

The blow sent a numbing shock up his arm, as if he'd struck a granite boulder instead of a bear's skull.

He landed awkwardly and stumbled into Hig-Tuli's rump. The stink of carrion and dank unmentionable excretions filled his nose. Roars and curses continued to whirl like a tornado of clashing metal and screams.

Someone grabbed hold of Fasster and yanked him back. Hig-Tuli's claw swiped through the air, fanning Fasster's hair back with a death whisper.

So close. But he was still alive.

System Temperature Alarm: 90°C

But how could Hig-Tuli still live? He had delivered the killing blow with the Sword of Absolute, Total, and Utter Invincibility.

"It doesn't work," he cried, casting a hateful look at the sword.

Krahp suddenly shrieked like a nine-year-old girl on a roller coaster. A second later his body struck the wall near Dalf and slid to the floor. He did not move again.

Jaconde was shaking Fasster and saying something he couldn't hear.

"What?" Fasster cried.

She put her mouth to his ear. "The sword won't work against her."

"Why?"

"No magic can reach her."

The red-cloaked druid had pulled him out of immediate

danger. But with Krahp down, Hig-Tuli was making short work of the remaining raiders. The knight and the dwarf were already dead and mangled. As he watched, their bodies disappeared into the glowing blue light that meant the characters were being revived at some distant graveyard.

"Perhaps we should retreat," Jaconde said. She didn't sound disappointed or upset. Just matter-of-fact.

He jerked her hand from his shoulder, furious. Once his rig cooled he was going to have it out with that quest-giver Nym. Hadn't the little kitty told him he needed a powerful ally? Well, here he was, raiding with the most powerful players he'd ever seen. What good had it done him?

With disgust and bitter anger in his heart, he flung the sword away from him. It glanced from the stone wall with a spark and clattered to the ground. He started to draw his bow. Maybe if he got two eye shots…

Jaconde's whisper suddenly filled his head. "The beast will be vanquished by no weapon, magical or common." She pressed a hand to his forehead, just like his mom used to do when she checked him for a fever. "Remember what Nym told you was your quest. Perhaps focus on that instead of Hig-Tuli."

In an instant, Jaconde was gone, leaving only the hint of her perfume and the quickly fading ring of windchimes.

Her words continued to swirl in his mind until they began to coalesce into a totally new idea. Like the first tiny pebble that starts an avalanche.

He recalled Nym's exact words. He'd certainly heard them enough times. But now he truly *heard* them. *"Hig-Tuli guards a treasure rare, a relic sacred and powerful: the Talisman of the*

Heart. Slay the beast and bring me the Talisman. Complete this quest and I shall grant you a boon."

Slay the beast…

What if the "beast" wasn't Hig-Tuli?

Certainty hit him like a mace to the head. Fasster's eyes lifted to the monster just in time to see her take out all three witches with one blow. Their bodies plumed into black smoke and seemed to retreat from the cave as if being sucked into a great vacuum cleaner.

"Fasster, to me. I'll pull you up." Dalf still stood atop the ledge by the secret tunnel. He lowered his staff for Fasster to grasp.

The bear lumbered between them, blocking escape.

But Fasster needed no escape.

System Temperature Alarm: 91°C

Slowly he pulled his bow from his shoulder and set it on the floor. He did the same with his quiver of arrows. Swallowing hard, he took a step toward the bear. Arms out, palms forward, he bowed.

"What are you *doing*?" cried Dalf. Desperate, he fired a bolt of lightning. It struck the bear but bounced off with a weak sizzle.

Fasster straightened, and met the bear's gaze. Though his guts felt like they'd turned to water and his heart rammed in his chest, he kept a smile on his face. "Well met, Hig-Tuli. I am in search of a powerful ally."

The red glow of Rage Might faded from the great bear's eyes, replaced by golden warmth. She dropped to all fours and bent a foreleg as she nodded in a bow. "And you have found one."

Dalf swore and jumped down from the ledge. "You cannot be serious!"

Hig-Tuli sat and licked a forepaw. Eyes squinting, she made a spitting noise. "Oh, how I detest the taste of blood."

Now that she was calm, the Rage Bear of Dellar's Cave looked more like a giant stuffed animal than the indomitable end-of-level boss she was.

"I seek the Talisman of the Heart."

"Why did you not just ask?" Hig-Tuli said wearily. The arrows in her hide fell out and clinked on the floor, the wounds healed.

"Nym made it sound like I had to kill you."

Like a weary human, the bear blew out a great sigh. "That explains the recent onslaught of lunatics storming in here. Nym is such a naughty little kitty. I shall have to speak to her."

System Temperature Alarm: 92°C

"The Talisman of the Heart?" Fasster prompted, already preparing his exit from the game.

The bear shrugged, paws up. "Oh, you are it. Everyone is."

* * *

A half hour later, after Fasster's system had cooled to safe levels, he left Nodo grazing along the bank of the creek, enjoying the thick, juicy grass that grew there. His tail wagged in delight. Ahead stood Nym's willow.

Fasster approached, smiling to himself, proud to have finally fulfilled the quest. But he didn't feel any of the smugness he'd expected to feel. In truth, he didn't know *what* he felt. He was still musing over what it meant that *he* was the Talisman of the Heart.

Nym was not lounging against the willow this time. Instead, the little cat-like being was pacing back and forth, angrily tugging at the bottom of its waistcoat and shaking an angry paw at someone behind the willow's trunk. "I knew it was you. I just *knew* it!"

An answering voice brought Fasster up short. It was Jaconde. "You've had your fill of fun at the expense of that poor young lad."

Nym cried out, "But he was so *easy* to manipulate. I could have watched him get pummeled to death for an age and never weary of it." Paws on hips, Nym's mouth twisted with disgust. "And don't give me that 'poor young lad' nonsense. As if you care about a ridiculous human."

"Believe what you want."

"You just couldn't bear to see me enjoying myself. That's why you followed me out of the Realm and into this foolish game."

Jaconde's chimes climbed in pitch, suggesting amusement. "I'll admit, it was pleasurable to foil your fun. But if I helped the lad improve himself along the way, all the better."

"He is dedicated, I'll give him that," Nym said in grudging tones.

"And his heart is true. I assume you never had a boon to give him, so I prepared one myself."

A delicate hand appeared from behind the willow trunk and placed a tiny object into Nym's.

"You've won this time," Nym said. "But somewhere, sometime…" She stomped a little cat paw and crossed her arms. "She never lets me have the last word! Come here, Fasster. She's gone."

Startled, Fasster approached the angry creature. "You knew I was listening?"

"Of course I did. You couldn't sneak worse if you were wearing bells on your elbows." Nym pulled a pocket watch from her waistcoat and flipped the lid. "I must be running."

"Wait. My boon?"

Nym grinned, eyes squinting mischievously. "And the Talisman of the Heart?"

Fasster spread his arms. "Hig-Tuli said I am the Talisman."

Nym did a double face-paw, and shook its head. "Jaconde got to Hig-Tuli too!"

Growling, the little furry creature handed a tiny wooden box to Fasster. It appeared to be a chest, but sized for a pixie. He thumbed open the hinged lid.

With delicate pinch, he pulled out a necklace. The chain was a golden ivy vine, and hanging from it a charm. A very tiny rusty, common-looking longsword. Engraved along the blade were the words: "Surrender to Conquer."

"What does it do?" Fasster asked.

Nym waved a paw over the charm, eyes closed. Wind suddenly picked up and the sun dimmed. Just as quickly the wind died and sun returned to normal.

Nym gave a sideways nod, as if mildly impressed by the charm. "Speak the words to summon Hig-Tuli whenever you need advice or to talk. But be warned, she'll fight for you only once. After that, you'll never see her again. And you'll never see either me or Jaconde." Nym brushed her paws together as if ridding herself of the whole fiasco. With that, the creature stepped behind the willow and disappeared.

Twenty minutes later, Fasster met up with Dalf at the verge of the Horselands.

Dalph raised his staff in greeting. "Krahp and the twins and the others respawned while you were gone. They wanted to go after Hig-Tuli again, but they can't find Nym."

"And they never will. That was a one-time quest," Fasster said. He paused, suddenly self-conscious. "But how about you and me campaign together. Maybe ask some others to join us?"

"Jaconde?"

"I doubt we'll find her." A bit of sadness descended on Fasster at the knowledge he would never see her again. But her last words about him perked him up. *His heart is true.* Fasster didn't know if she was right about that, but he would try to live up to it.

Fasster urged Nodo forward. Dalf rode next to him on an ostrich named Gottum.

"And the boon?" Dalf prompted uncertainly, as if he feared he was asking an overly personal question.

"A priceless trinket." Fasster lifted the necklace from where it rested over the heart of his ivy armor.

"So you speak in riddles now? Maybe that Nym did something to your head."

"You're the one riding an ostrich, my friend."

"Um, and riding a giant beagle is normal?"

Fasster shook his head and laughed in amazement, realizing

it truly was better to adventure with a friend than to rule the world alone.

With a quick smile at Dalf, Fasster shouted to Nodo. "Fly, you fool!"

A WORD FROM ERIC KENT EDSTROM

Writing in Anthea Sharp's fictional world felt a bit like being invited into her house. I didn't want to break anything, and I was hyper-conscious to mind my manners. But that's no way to write a story!

In fact, this story was inspired by that very feeling. I asked the simple question: what if a Feyland player tried to break the game? I followed that thread right into a rather raucous adventure. By the end, I felt quite at home. Whether I ever get invited back is another question.

Eric Kent Edstrom is the author of the YA speculative fiction trilogy The Undermountain Saga *and the YA dystopian series* The Scion Chronicles. *Learn more at www.ericedstrom.com.*

The Huntsman and the Old Fox
by Brigid Collins

THE SLEEK PLAS-METAL SIM CHAIRS Marylan's twelve-year-old granddaughter eagerly led her to certainly didn't look like the old gaming consoles she'd played on as a girl, eons ago. Marylan frowned at the helmet Stelli shoved into her wrinkled hands. Where was the controller? How did this Full-D system hook up to a TV screen?

And how on earth was playing a sim game supposed to help with her physical therapy? Marylan's frown turned into a full scowl. She may have been a hotshot gamer chick in her youth, but she didn't belong in-game these days. She was supposed to be improving her unsteady gait, not lying in a reclined chair in her daughter's basement and playing a video game, no matter what her therapist said.

Though it was a nice basement, to go with the rest of the nice house. Far nicer than anything Marylan had had growing up. Plump leather couches surrounded a huge vidscreen entertainment center. The two Full-D systems sat in the far corner of the room, away from the wall of window wells. Light spilled from canisters set in the vaulted ceiling. A vaulted ceiling in a basement! Only Marylan's good breeding kept her from clucking at the lavish sight.

Instead, her fingers twitched against the plastic helmet. Its colorful, streamlined design looked too cool for someone Marylan's age to wear. She could tell it wouldn't be at all comfortable. It didn't feel right in her hands. Admittedly, many decades had passed since the last time she'd held a controller. She wasn't even certain she could manage the trick of playing a game these days. The fact that she wouldn't be touching a controller now didn't help any. Simming—entering the virtual reality of a sim game—boggled her mind.

Oblivious to her grandmother's discomfort, Stelli plopped into one of the two chairs and jammed her own helmet over her head. "This is so exciting! Mom says you used to play in old screenie game tournaments when you were my age. Were you like Spark Jaxley? She's the most prime gamer ever!"

Marylan pasted on a smile and gingerly placed the helmet over her head before shuffling over to the other chair, keeping her steps tiny and deliberate. The visor blurred her vision. She wished her daughter hadn't fed Stelli so many stories about her days gaming. Now Stelli had all these ideas about her grandmother's skill level. How could Marylan bear it if she disappointed her granddaughter in this gaming session?

"I did play in some tournaments. I'm not sure I'll be as good at simming, though. What button do you push to jump?"

Stelli giggled. "No buttons, grandma. You make small gestures and the gloves pick them up as commands."

All geared up, Marylan sat back in the sim chair, feeling ridiculous. She was too old to be learning new game systems. The helmet pressed awkwardly against her head, and the urge to get up and go have a cup of tea instead made her feel even more out of place. Anything to avoid what was sure to be an embarrassing and frustrating afternoon of gaming.

But as Stelli directed her to select the golden F icon of her favorite game, and the title screen for Feyland filled her vision, Marylan knew it was too late for that.

* * *

The Queen of Midnight's depthless eyes flickered as she spoke the words of the quest for the ninth time.

"Mortal effort shall unlock the door."

Sealgaire bared his teeth and drew his hunting knife. Its sharp rasp against the sheath did not bring the usual sense of comfort and power along with it. He'd killed the Queen of Midnight eight times already. Tonight, he had to defeat her. Every hour he remained here, more of his strength trickled away.

The script of Feyland's final level unfolded around him. Lanterns of faerie flame hung from every branch of the enormous oaks that ringed the wide, stone-paved courtyard. Their light kept the absolute darkness of full night at bay. The gathered members of the court looked on as their queen descended from her throne of tangled roots and branches, two wicked knives of obsidian appearing in her hands as she approached those who had dared enter her court. Behind her throne, surrounded by the last faerie ring of the game, the transparent outline of a closed door shimmered in the lantern light. That closed door hadn't responded to Sealgaire's own attempts to open it. Apparently, the quest would only work for a mortal.

A lightning bolt crackled by Sealgaire's head, zigzagging towards the queen. She slid to the left, the movement not quite natural, even for a faerie. The shot missed.

Sealgaire hissed at the mortal Spellweaver he'd brought with him this time. "I explicitly told you to keep out of the fight!"

The boy shrugged and grinned. "That's boring. I'm not wasting this chance to play the final boss. I'd have to play through like, ten more levels before I get here again. Maybe afterwards you can show me whatever mod you used to make a faerie character?"

Sealgaire gritted his teeth. "I don't need your help, fool. I just need you to stay alive."

He would not let the mortal fail to unlock the door for him. Not this time. This human would survive to the end of the final fight and beyond, unlike the others he'd brought here. He gripped his knife and faced the oncoming queen.

From the un-detailed bark of the trees to the incorrect depictions of faerie court members, Sealgaire picked out more signs of artificiality every time he returned to Feyland's version of the Dark Court. He noticed them more in this mimicry of his own home than throughout the other levels of Feyland. All sound murmured as though it came through a filter, and the most pungent smells lacked the strength to make his nose twitch. Even the colors blurred and faded more than the darkness of night could account for. The wind stirred his hair too stiffly. Everything about this simulation showed weakness, its power a far cry from the terror that lived in the true Dark Court under the Dark Queen.

And yet, each time he challenged and killed the Queen of Midnight, as she was called here, he still moved too slowly and failed to complete the quest. With the game sucking his power away bit by bit, his chance of success and escape dwindled ever lower.

His knife clashed against the queen's two blades, sparks flying without heat. She stepped back and raised one arm. Magic gathered along the black blade, the hum of it vibrating through the air against Sealgaire's skin. Her spell solidified into a long spear of ice aimed at the Spellweaver.

Sealgaire lunged to strike at her abdomen. She dodged out of the way, but the ice spear missed its mark.

"Nice one!" the mortal said.

Sealgaire said nothing and pressed another attack. As always, the Queen of Midnight ignored him except to defend against his attacks. Every time he came to this fight, she focused her wrath on his mortal companions.

The leather grip of his hunting knife squeaked in protest as his fist tightened. His breath squeezed in his lungs, and his lips jerked backwards in the feral snarl of the Wild Hunt. The Queen of Midnight would pay him the respect he was due.

"Hey, watch this!" the mortal said. He waved his staff in a serpentine pattern, preparing to cast a spell.

Sealgaire growled. None of these players took this game seriously, which was why, despite Sealgaire's *real* faerie magic, his mortal traveling companions couldn't stand up to the challenge of the game's final fight.

With a grunt and a quick, economical movement, Sealgaire pushed through the queen's thin defenses and plunged his knife into her back. Her high-pitched shriek pierced his sensitive ears. He braced her while she writhed, until her body vanished in a puff of smoke. He sneered at the unnatural portrayal of death.

"Aww, way to take all the fun out of it," the mortal said. "I was totally gonna fry her."

Sealgaire let a heavy breath out through his nostrils. He'd done it. He'd defeated the Queen of Midnight and gotten a mortal through the experience to unlock the door for him. He had beaten this horrible game.

He was *free*.

Almost free, he corrected himself. *Mortal effort shall unlock the door,* after all. He stomped over to where the mortal stood, ignored the boy's jabbering questions about his "prime character class" and dragged him over to the transparent door behind the throne. Sealgaire could almost smell the deep pine of the forest on the other side, could almost make out the baying of the hunting hounds chasing after their prey. The desire to join them, to charge along a scent trail after prey that quaked and sweated pools of its own fear, surged through him.

"Here," he spat. "Open the door."

The mortal glanced at him, unease tilting his brows together. "There's no option to open it. My display thinks the boss battle is still going on. You tweaked the game somehow, man."

Sealgaire grasped the front of the Spellweaver's robes in both fists. "You didn't even try. Open it! I can't stand this place any longer."

He threw the mortal to the base of the door with a hiss. The mortal scrambled to his feet, glaring.

"Look man, I'm telling you, there's no option to open the door. Whatever hack you did to bring us here early must have broken the game. I thought it was cool at first, but I don't want to play a broken game. I'm logging out."

"*Open* it!" Sealgaire commanded.

If he had to stay in this forsaken game for another day he'd go mad. The longer he lingered within the code, the more his fey essence drained away bit by bit. He didn't know how many more times he could fight against the Queen of Midnight before he simply became a part of this fake world, before he turned into one of these flat NPC characters.

He had to get back to the true Realm, and this ungrateful mortal was going to help him. He reached for the front of the boy's robes once more.

But the Spellweaver had already made the gesture to leave the game, and Sealgaire's fist closed on nothing. He was alone in the courtyard. The fake courtiers, making their familiar shocked faces at the repeated death of their queen, didn't count as company.

Kicking at the sparse grass, Sealgaire let out a howl. He'd been so close! The words of the quest stated that the mortal should have been able to open the door.

"Mortal effort," Sealgaire muttered. "Don't tell me the mortal needs to strike the killing blow." He couldn't count on a human to pull that off.

What he needed was a player who understood the serious nature of this game. Even the ones who were focused on being the best warriors they could be didn't devote all of their effort to a fight that wouldn't have any real consequence if they failed.

Feyland was just a game, after all. Fake battles and fake stakes bred fake warriors.

And those hateful Feyguard were doing everything in their power to keep it that way.

Sealgaire stopped his kicking. The Feyguard!

He'd seen one of them once, when the Wild Hunt had pursued her in her attempt to rescue another mortal from the Dark Court. That girl… he still remembered her scent, the sharpness of her determination and the underlying salt of her fear. The musky scent of her fox form wound through her main scent as a splash of red. He'd caught whiffs of it from time to time since he'd found himself trapped in Feyland, though always far out of reach, as though she had entered the game in a different level. But he knew it was her.

He gave a strained laugh. While he rode at the rear of the Wild Hunt in the Realm, he was the greatest huntsman by far in the world of Feyland. Not even the queen of these simulated faeries could hold her own against him.

He could hunt down the Feyguard girl and bring her here. He could force her to return him to the Realm. Securing her cooperation would expend much of his remaining faerie magic, but it would be worth the cost.

Leaving the faeries of the court to their scripted responses, Sealgaire strode back to the faerie ring that had brought him here. His magic flared as he performed the intricate twist of his fingers that would bring him to the game level of his choosing. Once he locked on the Feyguard's scent, he'd have no trouble following her anywhere she went, so long as she stayed in-game.

His vision blurred as the Midnight Courtyard faded away, but he couldn't stop himself from casting one last glance at the transparent door. It shimmered serenely, as if it weren't blocking his path to the place his very essence yearned to be. His fists shook at his sides, his sharp nails digging into his palms.

He would make sure she stayed in-game. That door would open, even if he had to spill mortal blood to accomplish it.

* * *

"You chose a Kitsune character? You really are like Spark Jaxley!"

Marylan found herself standing in a clearing as realistic as any she could find in real life. Silver-leaved trees surrounded the clearing, and she shivered as the cool breeze carried their scent and rustling to her. She felt the hardness of the dirt under her feet. A circle of mushrooms looped around her and Stelli, who stood beside her in a Spellweaver's outfit, grinning.

She'd struggled to get a hang of the gesture controls while figuring out the character creation system. It had been a long time since she'd played any game, of course, but she'd always loved fantasy games. She'd dithered over her options, torn between choosing the ability to cast magic and knowing she was supposed to be working on her physical movements.

"The description said I could cast magic and fight with this character," Marylan said, looking down at her leather-clad avatar.

"And turn into a fox. That'll be fun for your therapy, huh?"

Marylan joined her granddaughter in laughing. Despite her decision to despise the simming experience, she couldn't help it. She'd never played a game like *this* before. The place felt so real!

"Okay, let's get to my open quest line. We'll meet up with my friends."

Stelli waved her staff, and the world melted away as the faerie ring transported them to a new location. They appeared in another faerie ring outside the wooden walls of a city. A dense forest of oak and curling underbrush grew right up along the wall, and Marylan watched as a crowd of cityfolk and soldiers worked to fortify their defensive line.

Stelli led the way to the gate. While Marylan marveled at the ease of her own movement in the game, Stelli filled her in on the quest.

"The townspeople are plagued every night by a group of fierce faeries known as the Midnight Huntsmen. Our job is to help fight them off once and for all. A whole bunch of people have tried to complete this quest, but it's way harder than the rest of the game has been so far. We're starting to think something's tweaked in the programming."

They stepped up to the city gate, where a guard stopped them. Marylan squinted at him, making out the slight stiffness of his motions that marked him as an NPC. His armor was serviceable, though not of the best quality, and the sword he held could use a good sharpening. He waved them in as Stelli presented a token to him.

"Welcome, my ladies. We need all the help we can get against these foul dark faeries. Be on your guard. Night approaches."

The guard spoke true, and as Marylan followed Stelli into the main square of the town, the sun dipped towards the horizon. The pinks and purples of twilight draped over the city, and the cool breeze developed a chillier snap. More and more lanterns blazed with light as the sky grew darker.

Ten other players stood gathered beside the stone basin of the town's fountain, chattering in rising tones. Stelli greeted her friends with a wave.

"You'll never guess who we were just talking to, Stelli," said a Saboteur.

"Who?"

"Spark Jaxley! You missed it. She logged out five minutes ago."

Stelli moaned and threw her hands up. "Did you ask her to join us? *She* could beat this impossible fight."

"Nah, Spark's not like that. She won't steal the glory from us regular players."

"But wouldn't it be so prime to watch her smash these faeries?" asked a Knight. She pantomimed some fighting move, apparently something Spark Jaxley was known for, and the group laughed.

As Stelli introduced the group, Marylan smiled. These

kids wouldn't have any idea who she was, but in her day, people had said similar things about her gaming. She sighed, remembering the glory of her tournament days. Of course, she also remembered the stress of travel, and of always being in the spotlight. A pang of sympathy for Miss Jaxley softened Marylan's smile.

"My grandma used to play games professionally, just like Spark."

Marylan concealed a wince as the group turned wondering eyes on her.

"And you play a Kitsune, just like her," said the Saboteur. "Maybe some old school gaming skills are just what we need to get through this fight!"

Despite Marylan's protests, the group rallied around this idea. Before she knew it, she had been declared their mascot, their ace-in-the-hole, and the leader of their charge.

At that moment, the sun sank fully below the horizon, and a long, high-pitched wail snaked out of the forest beyond the city.

"On your guard! The Midnight Huntsmen come!" someone shouted from the city wall.

The group of players moved together to the gate, drawing weapons and scrolling through spells in preparation.

A shot of nerves twanged through Marylan as she struggled with the gesture to bring up her own menu screen. She was about to make a total fool of herself. She still didn't have good control over these gestures, and though she was enjoying the ability to walk without the shuffling gait that plagued her real legs, she didn't think she would be able to pull off the sort of dexterity she would need in a fight. These kids were about to be sorely disappointed in their new mascot-leader.

"Don't worry, grandma," Stelli said. "It's just a game, even if it feels totally real."

They arranged themselves to defend the gate, and Marylan peered into the inky blackness of the forest. She couldn't see a thing, and from the way everyone else was squinting, she knew it wasn't just her worn-out vision.

Glancing at her list of abilities, Marylan wondered about her fox form. Changing form in games always granted some sort of shift in abilities. Maybe as a fox she'd be able to hear what she couldn't as a human?

She made the gesture, and suddenly she was on all fours, much closer to the ground. Her vision reduced even further, blurred and gray, but her hearing sharpened. She ignored the group's interjections of "good idea," and focused on the way the foliage rustled in the forest. The sound swelled and faded with the natural flow of the wind straight ahead. But to the left, the hiss came in bursts, punctuated by the soft snap of twigs under light footfalls.

Unable to speak as a fox, Marylan pointed her snout left, towards the oncoming faeries. She found herself slinking forward into the trees, ears pricked and nose primed for the telltale signs of her prey. The other players followed her.

She froze when the harsh odor of dogs hit her nostrils. Her fox body felt an instinctive need to put distance between herself and the hounds, but Marylan fought it and pressed onward, wriggling through the underbrush on her belly. She knew the hounds had caught her scent, too, from the way they set up baying, but by then the others had caught up with her and were prepared for the fight.

The two forces met at a wide, shallow stream. Marylan gaped at the sight of the Midnight Huntsmen. The hounds curled along the ground with glowing green eyes and strings of saliva dripping from their dark muzzles. The horses chomped at their bits and pawed at the ground as if they, too, sought the capture of the prey. Their riders, the Huntsmen themselves, showed terrible faces, pale yet dark with malice. Their leader seemed part animal himself, sporting a pair of ram's horns curling from his forehead. At the sight of the players, he lifted a hunting horn to his cruel lips, and the high-pitched wail rang out again. At such close range, its cry was deafening.

At the sound, a new Huntsman melted out of the trees. Something about this hunter was *wrong*. Marylan's tiny fox heart pounded against her ribs at the sight, the sound, and the smell of him. Of all the impressive simulations in Feyland so far, this hunter truly took her breath away. He didn't even seem to be all that important a member of the Huntsmen, certainly not as visually intimidating as the leader, but his expression was somehow chiseled with more hatred and more drive than the others'. As Marylan watched, he lifted his nose and sniffed. His gaze snapped to the bush she hid in, and a shot of icy fear ran from her skull to the tip of her tail.

With a battle cry, the other players leapt into the stream. Marylan hung back, waiting for a break in the clash of weapons. Could she use her magic in fox form, or did she have to change back?

A hound came bounding towards her hiding place, startling her out of her bush. The hound snarled behind her as she dashed away. Which gesture would turn her back to a human? The swipe? The chop?

She scrambled through the brush. The hound snapped its dripping jaws at her tail. Its warm breath rippled over her fur. Why couldn't she figure out these controls?

The hound's snarls turned to a stabbing yip of pain. Marylan spun to see it collapse and disappear in a puff of black smoke, defeated.

Keeping her belly pressed to the dirt, she slunk into the cover of the undergrowth.

All around her, grunts of pain and frustration rose from both Huntsmen and players. She saw two players fall, their avatars shimmering and disappearing as they lost all HP. But the Huntsmen were losing fighters, too, and the battle remained even.

Marylan's legs quivered and her breath sawed from her lungs. The mess she'd made of this battle proved she had no business playing games at her age. Her human form still eluded her. She desperately needed a rest, and she wouldn't mind if she never set foot in a sim game again. That cup of tea was sounding exceptionally relaxing right now.

She crouched under a bush, panting like a dog, as the two remaining players regrouped in the stream. Marylan allowed a hint of pride to puff through her at Stelli's continued presence. The girl showed promise as a gamer.

The tatters of the Midnight Huntsmen gathered on the opposite bank. Their ram-horned leader scowled and pointed in silent command.

The fearsomely realistic Huntsman still remained. He was hidden from view behind the leader, but Marylan's nose locked on his woodsy smell. She could hardly help it, especially now that their enemy's numbers had been pared down. His scent stood out in sharp contrast against the duller smells of the others.

The other remaining player, the Knight, charged forward to clash with the leader. Stelli leapt forward, too, her staff glowing with arcane light. The Huntsmen raised their weapons. The blades glinted in the faint starlight.

Stelli's spell crashed into her foe in a shower of embers, and the black smoke was curling about her feet before the hunter's back touched the ground.

But the horned leader slashed his long knife at the Knight, and her avatar faded. Stelli gave a shout and swiped her staff at the leader. Her rage-fuelled ice spell sent the leader spinning to the ground.

The action left her wide open to attack from the remaining hunter.

Marylan's sense of wrongness returned full-force as she watched him reach for her granddaughter with his bare hand. The faerie's stance, so feral, so *real*, screamed that they'd made a giant mistake in treating him like one of the other hunters.

Marylan let out a bark. Cold stream water splashed in her snout and eyes as she bounded to Stelli's side. She bared her teeth, and a growl rattled up her chest and throat. Confound these controls! She could hardly save her granddaughter as a fox.

The huntsman turned to sneer at her as he drove his hand

into Stelli's shoulder. Stelli went limp, her eyes rolled back, and her skin turned a sickly pale color.

The huntsman's fist pulsed red as he gripped Stelli's body.

"We wouldn't want anything to happen to this innocent girl's mortal essence," he whispered with a grin that set Marylan's blood roaring in her ears, "would we now, Feyguard?"

* * *

Sealgaire had the Feyguard right where he wanted her.

He'd meddled with the scripted Midnight Huntsmen event, knowing she would come as soon as she heard about the bottleneck in the game level. When he'd smelled her presence in-game an hour ago, he knew he had her.

Oh, she might think she was confusing him by remaining in fox form, but he'd know that scent of determination anywhere.

Yanking his fist from the unconscious girl's shoulder, he wobbled on his legs as a wave of weakness passed through his body. The theft required almost all of his remaining magic, and a spike of panic pricked at his pulse. What if the Feyguard realized how easily she could overcome him right now? What if this last effort failed and the door remained closed?

He shoved aside his fears and rested his fist against a pouch at his hip. "I'll just keep the girl's essence here for the moment. What I do with it later, well, that depends on your cooperation."

The Feyguard fox growled at him, puffed up like a cat and showing all her teeth, still dripping from her sprint across the stream. She was quite adorable, if he was honest. But what he needed from her didn't have a thing to do with her animal form.

"I won't bother being cryptic. You know what I am and where I come from. The Wild Hunt rode here in search of wayward mortals to bring back to the Realm. The others pulled ahead of me, and I found myself entangled in this imitation world. The game finally reacted to my presence and bestowed a quest upon me to open a way out, but I cannot complete it on my own. You will defeat the Queen of Midnight for me and unlock the door back to the Realm as my quest requires, or I will dispose of this girl's essence. I'm under the impression that your position as a member of the Feyguard limits you to the former option."

Without waiting for a response, Sealgaire hefted the girl's body over his shoulder and moved through the trees, heading for the faerie ring. He didn't have to look back to know the Feyguard was following.

The chirps of insects and hoots of owls trickled back into the forest, now that the nightly fight was over. Sealgaire breathed a sigh of relief at the knowledge that tonight's battle was the last he'd ride with the false Wild Hunt. In many ways, his time with them had been more painful than each of his nine visits to the Midnight Courtyard. And in other ways it had been more frightening. Acting as the replica huntsmen did came too easily to him as his faerie essence trickled away.

But he had the Feyguard now, and the door was as good as unlocked. She had the skill to defeat the Queen of Midnight many times over, and the necessary quality of being mortal, per the words of his quest.

Mortal effort shall unlock the door.

The faerie ring materialized out of the underbrush, the mushroom caps glowing under the light of the stars and moon. Sealgaire stepped into the ring and finally glanced back at the fox behind him.

Her eyes were out of focus, the way players got when they were interacting with the game's interface. She must be sorting through her options, trying to decide how to best use her tricks against him. He tightened his grip on the girl.

"Join me, won't you?" he demanded. He let one hand drift to brush against the pouch.

Her eyes widened, then narrowed as she processed his unspoken threat. Her ears pressed flat against her head, and she slunk into the faerie ring.

Once she stood beside him, Sealgaire twisted his fingers. His magic rushed around them, and he directed it to bring them to the game's final level.

He didn't attempt to smother the blast of fierce joy as he felt the faerie ring's tug for the last time. Never again would this sickening jolt pull at him. He had to endure the Midnight Court materializing before his eyes only once more.

As the flawed mirror of his home came into view, Sealgaire slid the girl from his shoulder and placed her on the ground just outside the faerie ring. With her settled, he pulled at his pouch again, letting the fox see that it still pulsed with the mortal's essence. If he had to stay out of this fight, he wouldn't hesitate to give her all the motivation she needed to see it through to the finish for him.

"I don't presume to tell you how to fight your battles, but

I'd think you'd have an easier time of it in your human form," he said. He was surprised to realize how excited he was to watch her at work. Imagine, a mortal who would actually take this fight seriously.

She hesitated a moment more, her fox body twitching. Then she made the shift, her body growing and elongating, pulling upwards.

Into the form of a frail old woman in a Kitsune's armor.

Sealgaire's lungs clenched, sending a jolt of pain through his heart. He'd made a horrible mistake.

"I don't know who—or what—you think you are, but you're going to give me back my granddaughter," she said. "She never did anything to earn your violence. Who taught you how to ask for a favor?"

His chest hurt. His jaw ached where he held it clamped shut. He'd bitten his cheek, and the copper of blood filled his mouth.

Across the courtyard, the Queen of Midnight's eyes flickered as she spoke the words for the tenth time.

* * *

"Where is the Feyguard?" the Huntsman demanded. "She's the only player with the strength to best the queen and send me back to the Realm!"

Standing once more on two legs, Marylan trembled. The energy coursing through her body did not come from fear, but from anger. This faerie creature would regret laying a finger on Stelli, no matter that Marylan was an old woman past her gaming prime.

She'd finally figured out how to shift between her forms, after all.

"I have no idea who this Feyguard you're looking for is. I barely understand how this game works. But believe me, young man, when I say I will make you pay ten times over for every hurt you inflict on my granddaughter."

The hunter shifted his slitted eyes towards the lantern-hung courtyard. Marylan noticed his fists tightening at his sides, an obvious instinctive response to the threat of the oncoming queen.

She watched him watching the queen, read his desire to finish the fight quickly in the tightness of his posture. One hand inched towards the knife in his belt.

With a quick gesture, done correctly this time, Marylan returned to her fox form. She gathered herself and leapt for the hunter's hand, her jaws open and ready to snap down on him.

He dodged aside. His tight restraint as she passed within range of his blade made the fur on her back ripple. She twisted to bite at him as she fell to the leaf-strewn flagstone.

"I didn't bring you here to fight me!" he hissed.

Marylan prepared to make the shift back to her human form. A sizzling light and a flare of heat slammed into her, knocking her off all four paws and dropping her at the roots of a huge oak tree.

Dazed, she blinked embers from her eyes as the hunter screamed a challenge at the queen. He was brandishing his knife at her.

And yet, as the queen came within range of him, he did not attack her, and the queen acted as though she did not see him.

Then she'd passed him, leaving him frothing with fury at her exposed back as she drew closer to Marylan.

Why doesn't he stab the queen right now? Marylan thought.

He turned a scowl on her, his eyes glittering with… desperation. Beyond him, beyond the oncoming queen, beyond Stelli's motionless body, a strange transparent door reflected the eerie light of the lanterns in the courtyard.

Mortal effort shall unlock the door, the queen had said when the fight commenced. Marylan had been too preoccupied with getting Stelli back to pay much attention then, but now she took in the whole level and knew the questline. Somehow, this wild fey creature had gotten himself trapped in the game where he didn't belong. His efforts to force a player to open the door that would take him back home, though dangerous and downright rude, made some sense to Marylan. Despite his poor method of asking, the hunter needed her help.

Two obsidian blades appeared in the queen's pale hands. Marylan's ears flattened against her head as the glow of magic gathered along the edge of the left one.

She couldn't afford to mull over her options. That's not how games were played, and certainly not how they were beaten. She had to trust her instincts and read the game's signals, then base her actions off of that.

The hunter's freedom, and therefore Stelli's life, depended on it.

Marylan leapt up and twisted around, shifting to human form. Could she call up her bow at the same time? She could. Its smooth wood materialized in her hand, and she fired an arrow into the queen's eye as her human feet touched the ground.

The queen shrieked and flitted away, then grimaced with renewed hatred.

A fierce grin spread across Marylan's face. The thrum of energy she'd only ever gotten from the challenge of gaming zinged through her. How had she ever given it up? She was too old? Ha! She could do this for ages.

The flow of the fight pulled at her, and she shifted back into fox form to dart among the faerie courtiers until she found another advantageous spot. This time, when she shifted back to human, she sent a wall of fire burning towards the queen. She shifted again, but the queen's scream of pain and outrage told her she'd hit her mark as she dashed off once more.

She erupted from between two astonished faerie courtiers as a human, and aimed another arrow at the queen's face. But just as she loosed the string, the queen hurled a spear of ice at her. Marylan leapt up, somersaulting in mid-air without thinking, to avoid the projectile. Its chill grazed her back, knocking her off-balance. She tumbled to the flagstone with a crack. Her bow had broken beneath her.

But she had no time to lie there moaning, as much as the fall had reminded her of her true age. The queen was approaching, both obsidian knives drawn.

As the queen bore down on Marylan, she pulled her own knife out to block. The blades met with a grating clash. The queen still had one more knife than Marylan, though. Marylan's blood pounded in her ears, but the hunter's shouts pierced through the roar. Was he cheering for her?

Thinking quickly, Marylan reviewed her options. Her bow was broken, and she'd used her fire spell, but the other three elemental spells remained. With a twitch of her wrist, she shot a blast of wind into the queen's arm, knocking her next attack aside. The queen grunted, and Marylan used the opportunity to dance out of the way.

She glanced back at the hunter, who was leaning forward as though fighting against an invisible force that kept him stuck outside the area of combat. Stelli lay at his feet. Her arm was flung towards Marylan, as if in a plea for rescue.

Marylan narrowed her eyes at the queen. She had to finish this quickly. She had no idea what the hunter's magic might be doing to Stelli's mortal essence, after all.

She waited until the queen stood over a particularly large slab of flagstone, then cast both of her remaining elemental spells at once. The stone melted into a sloppy pool of mud, and the queen fell over, shrieking.

The hunter taunted the queen, but Marylan wasted no time as she rushed towards her fallen foe. Her fingers tightened over the hilt of her knife, getting ready to plunge it into the queen's heart and finish this battle.

A wicked glimmer in the queen's eyes was the only warning Marylan got before a crackling lightning bolt flew at her. She jerked to the side, but the bolt struck her hand, sending her knife spinning through the air and out of the courtyard.

Marylan screamed and clutched her burned hand. She was out of weapons, out of magic, and lying defenseless on the hard flagstones before the Queen of Midnight. Her enemy was climbing out of the muddy mire, her blades glistening in the faerie lantern light.

The pain faded quickly, though, and as her own whimpers

quieted, she became aware of the hunter thundering across the courtyard towards her. His knife was out.

He skidded to a halt, throwing his body between Marylan and her enemy just as the queen brought her first knife down. The blow landed on his back and drove him to his knees beside Marylan. His eyes widened.

"Take it," he grunted, dropping his hunting knife. "Defeat her."

The queen's second knife hit him in the side, and he slumped to the ground.

Behind the queen, the transparent door solidified and creaked open a crack.

Marylan snatched up the offered knife and rolled to her feet. She drove the blade up into the queen's heart up to the hilt. The queen screeched and writhed, then disappeared in a puff of black smoke.

Marylan ignored the victory fanfare ringing through the courtyard, and knelt beside the hunter. He was still alive, his breathing shallower than her own harsh gasps. He looked up at her with unfocused eyes.

"Is the door open?"

Marylan nodded. "It opened when you took that hit for me."

The hunter grimaced. "Should've known. Mortal effort. Faerie quests… are never straightforward." He twitched a finger at the pouch on his hip. "Let her… breathe in her essence… she'll be… good as new."

Marylan reached for the pouch, but stopped when her fingers brushed it. The hunter's breathing grew shallower, his face paler, and an idea came to her.

Marylan made the gesture to bring up her menu. Her fire and air spells had returned, and in another second, so would the water and earth. It was time to see what this elemental system could do.

First she sent fire crawling over the hunter's open wounds. When new skin rippled into place, she once again mixed water and earth, this time sending it into her patient's veins as fresh blood to replace what had spilled on the flagstones. Finally, as he stared up at her with glazed eyes, Marylan blew her air spell into his lungs until his breathing grew even and deep.

The hunter blinked, and Marylan helped him to sit up.

"You cured me," he said, his voice soft with awe. "You didn't have to."

Marylan picked up his hunting knife and offered it to him hilt first. "I think it's time you went home, young man."

The hunter stood and pressed the pouch into her other hand. "Keep the knife. May its power one day repay you for the kindness you've done me today."

Then he turned and strode to the now open door. For a moment, Marylan thought he might look back at her, but he only took a deep breath before pushing the door open and stepping through.

In that split second before the door closed behind him, Marylan got a dazzling glimpse of the Realm beyond the game of Feyland. A courtyard at midnight, full of glittering lights and the dark, terrible forms of fey creatures such as she'd only ever seen in storybook illustrations, lay just across the threshold. The strains of a harp floated in the air. Fair maidens with gossamer wings, and knobby gnomes wearing caps the color of blood cavorted in the open space between the thick trees.

Deep in the murky darkness, a tall faerie crowned with antlers beckoned to the hunter. His piercing red gaze locked with Marylan's as the hunter bowed before him, and Marylan's entire body tingled with a fear the leader of the in-game Midnight Huntsmen could never hope to generate.

Her breath caught in her throat, and she realized how the simulated world of the game, so realistic to her, could drive a true faerie mad. The Courtyard of Midnight seemed so much duller now, like a reflection in a warped and smudged mirror. Feyland, as groundbreaking as its technological and graphical advancements were, was a subpar imitation of the real Realm of Faerie.

Then the door swung closed. The soft snick of a lock engaging sighed through the courtyard, and the door disappeared.

Rocking back on her heels and catching her breath, Marylan put the hunter's knife away in her inventory, then rushed to Stelli's side. She administered the pouch as the huntsman had told her, and soon Stelli's eyes flickered open.

"Did we lose the battle, Grandma?"

Marylan hugged her tight, laughing with relief. Real magic existed, tucked away in a hidden level of a video game, and she had seen it and lived to play the game another day. She considered telling Stelli about what she'd just experienced.

But games and their secrets were always more satisfying when figured out for oneself, and Stelli had proven herself to be an excellent gamer. Perhaps Stelli would find a way to unlock Feyland's secret levels on her own.

"I think we did lose," Marylan finally said, "but I'd like to try it again tomorrow."

* * *

"On your guard! The Midnight Huntsmen come!"

Standing amongst Stelli's friends as they readied themselves to take on the nightly raid once more, Marylan brought up her menu. The gestures weren't giving her trouble anymore, and she wondered why she'd ever let herself get so tangled up over them.

"Are you ready, Grandma?" Stelli asked, rocking back and forth on her toes as she waited.

"Almost," Marylan replied. She swiped through her inventory, searching.

Her bow had returned, intact, upon login, but she moved past it until she came to a hunting knife. The standard Kitsune knife rested beside it, looking rather plain and undetailed in comparison.

Marylan smiled and equipped *Sealgaire's Hunting Knife*. As it appeared in her hand, the familiar thrum of anticipation swept through her. A good simming session lay ahead.

"I'm ready."

A WORD FROM BRIGID COLLINS

I usually write young characters, probably because I am, at the moment, a young-ish person myself (the big Three-Oh draws ever closer). I find myself naturally drawn to writing younger protagonists. So when the image popped into my head of Marylan, an elderly woman who used to be a hotshot gamer chick (and still is, though she doesn't realize it), she certainly surprised the heck out of me. It didn't take long before I knew she was destined to make a run through Feyland, whether she wanted to or not!

I've been a fan of the *Feyland* series from the moment I finished reading the first novella. Getting the chance to write a story of my own in such a rich and wonderful world has been so thrilling, and I'm not ashamed to admit to doing a happy dance when Anthea asked if I wanted to write for the *Chronicle Worlds: Feyland* anthology. I immediately knew I wanted to tell a story involving the Wild Hunt in some way, as I always found them eerie and terrifying in Anthea's original series.

If you enjoyed this story and want to check out more of my work, feel free to visit my website, www.backwrites.wordpress.com. All my pieces and where to find them are listed there, including my fantasy series, *The Songbird River Chronicles*, book 3 of which came out in May of 2016! Be sure to sign up for my newsletter while you're there, which will net you a free short story, as well as periodic news about my releases.

Unicorn Magic
by Roz Marshall

> *"Once you eliminate the impossible, whatever remains, no matter how improbable, must be the truth."*
> — Arthur Conan Doyle, *Sherlock Holmes*

Chapter One
THE SINGER

THE BREATH CAUGHT in Corinne MacArthur's throat. If anyone discovered her here, peering around the trunk of a silvery birch, she would be in all *sorts* of trouble.

She might not know very much, yet, about how to play Feyland, but she was sure she shouldn't be in a place like *this* on her first foray into the game. Surely it was way too advanced a level for a new player like her? But—*that music—that singing…* It was as delicate as rose petals, as pure as a mountain stream and as sweet as marshmallow melt. It captured her senses; filling her mind with its beauty so that for a few precious moments, the awful ache in her heart was replaced by a glowing golden warmth which emanated from the centre of the magical clearing—from him.

The singer.

Standing on a wizened tree stump as if it were a dais on an international stage, the minstrel's voice rang clear and strong across the forest glade. Hair the colour of burnished copper curled around his head like a halo, a smear of freckles gilded his high cheekbones, and over his shoulder hung a drape of heather-coloured plaid.

The crowd around him contained creatures that Corinne had only seen in picture books—elves, pixies, nymphs, and other mythical beings with legs like goats or taller than trees, things that she couldn't even put names to. But they all seemed as wrapped up in his song as she was; hanging on his every word and straining to hear every syllable that spilled from his lips. Even the tiny birds perched on bush and branch had fallen under his thrall, their voices silent and their heads tilted in his direction.

He had a talent for drawing people in; for making his audience feel a part of his song. Looking out over the crowd, he made eye contact with one, then another, and another, each of whom would almost swoon after receiving his attention.

And then, for one heart-stopping second, those green eyes swept over to the edge of the clearing and locked, momentarily, with hers.

It was like a physical blow, driving the air from her lungs

and all coherent thought from her mind. She rocked on her heels, gripping hard on the birch tree lest she fall.

Then panic set in. Had he spotted her? The allure of his song had caused her to forget the precariousness of her situation, and to linger when she should have quietly made her way back to a lower level.

But his gaze moved on around the throng, and she exhaled slowly. *No, he didn't see me.* Her green tunic and brown leather waistcoat gave her excellent camouflage in the forest, and thankfully she'd chosen chestnut brown hair—like her own, in real life—for her archer avatar, rather than the more esoteric options of neon-fuschia or lightning-white that had been on offer. The undergrowth here was heavy, and the tree was sturdy. She was undetected. *For now.* But she'd need to get moving soon.

The last tinkling chords faded like the morning mist, and the troubadour stepped down from his platform, his song at an end.

As if released from a trance woven by his lyrics, there was a collective exhalation of breath from the watchers. Wings unfurled, translucent like the finest stained-glass window, necks cricked, releasing knots under skin as pure as parchment, and legs stretched elegantly like a prima ballerina at the barre before the fey folk began to disperse around the clearing.

Above them, thistle-light tufts of phosphorescence shimmered through the air as bright pixies darted through the trees and skimmed above the heads of the other creatures.

Mouth-watering smells drifted across the dell from an enormous silver table laden with golden plates heaped high with tasty delicacies like honeyed rose-hips and toasted mallow-root. Behind the table, graceful attendants distributed crystal goblets brim-full of translucent nectar or creamy milk.

Before she could stop it, Corinne's stomach rumbled.

She froze, eyes scanning the clearing for any sign she'd been heard, legs tensing in preparation for flight.

But her luck was in. Any noise she'd made had been covered when a tall elf had picked up a pearly harp and begun to strum an ethereal tune. Nearby, a circle of dryads and naiads began to glide and weave in an intricate reel, and she slowly released the breath she'd been holding. *Careful!*

In the corner, a blue-faced creature pulled a winter-white shawl over her head and shuffled over to a grass-covered mound that Corinne hadn't noticed until now. Sitting in regal splendour on a golden throne was a captivating man with eyes the colour of sapphires, an aquiline nose and angular jaw. Above skeins of platinum-blond hair, he wore a circlet of filigreed gold that led Corinne to the inevitable conclusion:

The Bright King.

She'd read about him, of course, in the game's description: *The Bright King presides over the Seelie fey in the Bright Court. He finds mortals amusing—at least until he has no more use for them.*

She shivered at that last thought; and that was her undoing.

* * *

"Look!" called a loud voice from the centre of the crowd. An arm pointed directly at her. "An intruder!"

Dozens of pairs of eyes turned in her direction, and she ducked behind the tree, her heart racing. There were too many of them to fight. She needed to escape, and fast!

Stooping low, she slung her bow over her shoulder and exploded forward in a crouching run. But already she could hear the sound of pursuit—too loud, too close!

Terror turned her legs to rubber, but she pushed the fear away and searched the shrubbery on either side, looking for a hiding place.

She'd barely gone ten paces when a chirruping whistle from a downy willow bush beside the path caught her attention. "Over here!" a voice hissed.

She glanced at the large shrub the mysterious voice had come from, and then over her shoulder towards her pursuers. *The unknown, or the unnerving?* Did she have a choice?

Chapter Two
THE VISION

As the last of her pursuers passed just a few feet in front of her nose, Corinne slowly exhaled.

The woollen cloak her saviour had thrown over both of them had strange properties—it was heavy enough to hide them from her pursuers, yet it was thin like gossamer and she could easily see through it. What class of player could her rescuer be, to have such a magical item? Perhaps a Spellweaver. Or an Illuminer?

She turned to thank him, and stifled a gasp.

Orange eyes glowed in a face that was dark and leathery, deep lines gouged through cheeks that sprouted tufts of long, coarse hair the colour of burnt umber. *What kind of creature is this?*

"Th—thank you for saving me." Surreptitiously, she slid a hand towards the knife tucked into her belt.

"Make no mention of it," he said, in a deep, melodious voice that was much more pleasant to listen to than he was to look at.

She stilled her hand. Perhaps he wasn't to be feared after all. "I'm Corinne. Pleased to meet you."

"Elphin. My pleasure."

"If you don't mind me asking, what class of character are you playing? I should've read the instructions more carefully." And then another thought struck. "Or are you a non-player character?"

"Something of that ilk. Now," orange eyes bored into hers, "let me help you to find your way back. The Bright Court is not a safe place to be."

"So I gathered. But I don't know if I'll be able to leave just yet." She grimaced. "I haven't completed my quest."

His head quirked to the side. "What quest were you set?"

"It was a riddle, I think. I didn't really understand it." She looked up, recalling the strange words the goblin had said in his singsong voice. "*'Only the pure can see the pure, only the pure will find him. Only with love will love be shown, only by love unbind him.'* I thought maybe I had to find a stream, or a pool, so I went hunting through the forest. And ended up here." She jerked her head over her shoulder. "But I probably should be going, right enough. I'm in a sim cafe using rented kit, and I'm sure my time is nearly up."

"Come." He stood up and held out a hand. "Let me take you to a faerie circle."

* * *

Reality bites, so the old expression went. And in Corinne's case, it was almost literally true. Back in the real world—the virtual reality of Feyland left behind in the gaming booth—all her troubles and woes came rushing back. Leaning against the wall outside the sim cafe in the wan Scottish sunshine, the residual glow she'd felt from the mysterious minstrel's song dissipated, leaving her heart-sore and despondent.

"Did you have a good time, dear?" asked her mother as she pulled up at the kerb. "Meet any of your friends?"

"Yes thanks, and no," Corinne answered, stepping into the grav car. If only her mother knew.

"I suppose everyone else must be away lying on a beach in Spain or on a golf course in Florida. If only your father wasn't so busy, we…" She pursed her lips. "But anyway." Mother's face turned serious. "A courier dropped this off—" She nodded her head at a large box in the luggage area.

His ashes. Corinne knew what it was without asking.

"If you want me to go with you when…" Concerned eyes stared at her from under arched eyebrows.

Corinne squared her shoulders. "No, it's okay, mum. I'll take him up Chessaig after dinner."

"Your favourite ride?"

"His favourite. Yes."

* * *

By the time Corinne reached the top of the small hill, carrying her sad burden, it was twilight, the time of day the Scots called 'gloaming'. The sun's last rays gave the silvery trees around her an otherworldly aura and left an amber glow in the sky, which faded to a deep, velvety navy overhead. A sigh of wind rustled the leaves in the trees, and swirled through the lichen-covered granite monoliths that circled the hilltop.

Local legends said that this tumbledown stone circle was an ancient druid temple, but she'd never paid much attention to those folk tales, counting them as fiction, much like the stories she loved to read and the games she liked to play. As far as she was concerned, this was just a place she'd liked to visit, on a route that her horse had enjoyed.

Setting the box on the ground, she raised her face to the sky and turned in a slow circle, until her back was to the wind. Memories crowded her mind.

As if replaying a film, she saw Midnight's ears in front of her and heard the thud of his galloping hooves as they raced up the slopes. Felt the warmth of his shoulder under her hand as she told him what a good boy he'd been. Smelled the sweet smell of his sweat in her nostrils as they headed home from their ride.

She let out a long, shuddering breath, and stooped to pick up the box. This was the right place. His place.

* * *

As the last of Midnight's ashes eddied through the air and were dissipated by the wind, the sun dropped behind the horizon, casting long shadows and leaving uncertain light.

With the back of her hand, Corinne wiped the tears from her cheeks, turned for the path home, then stopped in her tracks with a gasp.

Between two of the standing stones a shadowy figure was silhouetted against the fading light. A cloak mantled his shoulders, and thick curls ruffled in the wind as he gazed across at her, the intensity of his stare drawing her towards him like a magnet.

How could he *be here?*

But the vision slowly faded and burned into nothing and she faltered to a stop, feeling stupid. *I'm seeing things.* How could a character from a computer game appear on a Perthshire hillside? *Impossible.*

Chapter Three
THE QUEST

Her hand on the coffee pot, Mother looked sideways at Corinne. "What would you like to do today? Would you like to start looking for a new horse? Ms. Irving has kept a space for us at the farm, remember, and it's not long till the end of the holidays. There won't be much time once you're back at school. Your father and I thought it could be a birthday present. An early one."

Staring into her bowl of cereal, Corinne shook her head. "It's too soon, Mum, sorry." Midnight was still in her heart, in her mind—and in her dreams.

Last night her sleep had been full of strange fantasy creatures and dark storylines. She'd been chased by unrelenting hounds through a never-ending forest, riding on the back of a proud white steed. A steed who felt just like Midnight.

Ahead of her—always just ahead but never reached—was a shadowy figure with flame-coloured hair and a lyre over his shoulder. The vague sense of terror and exhilaration she'd felt in the dream had stayed with her as she woke and went down to breakfast. It was like Feyland had got a hold of her somehow, drawing her in so that she couldn't stop thinking about it—even while she slept.

Perhaps it was because she hadn't solved the riddle of her first quest. "Could I—could I maybe go back to the sim cafe today? There's a new game I was playing, and I'd like to complete my quest."

"Well, yes, I could drop you off on my way to work. But wouldn't you rather do something outdoors? Or meet some of your friends at the stables?"

"I don't think I'm ready for that, yet." *And nobody will want to see me, anyway.*

* * *

Settling into the sim chair, Corinne pulled the visor over her eyes and pressed the large "F" icon.
'WELCOME TO FEYLAND'

The colour of the text changed from golden-yellow to blood-red, then scattered into tiny fragments, spiralling away as music swelled around her. Briefly, a pair of eyes glowed from the shadows, sending a shiver down her spine, and reminding her of the strange creature who'd helped her yesterday.

Stepping carefully out of the circle of moon-pale mushrooms, she settled her bow over her shoulder and started down the narrow silvery path, brushing against wiry clumps of purple heather as she walked. Closer to the tree line, butterflies flittered through clumps of yellow broom, and framing everything around her were tall, parchment-white birch trees punctuating the darker majesty of fresh-smelling pines.

It was like a perfect summer day, and, for a few seconds, she forgot that this world was not real. Raising her face to the sun, she felt the heat of its rays warm her skin. The programmers really *had* done a good job with this VR. She could actually *smell* and *touch* things here in Feyland. In other games she'd tried, visual and audio experiences were the norm, but not *smell*. She shook her head. Probably taste would work here too, she guessed, but the game instructions had explicitly warned not to let your characters eat or drink anything in-world. Something to do with introducing glitches into the simulation and failing your quest. The exact details had been a bit vague. Worryingly vague.

Opening her eyes, Corinne moved forward again, reciting the riddle under her breath. "Only the pure can see the pure." What on earth did that mean, anyway? Pure water? Pure like snow? But there was hardly likely to be snow here in the middle of summer, even if it *was* a magical land. Pondering this, she entered the cool shade of the forest.

Before she'd walked very far, a flash of light to the side of the path caught her attention. Something large and white was moving through the trees. *Not snow. An animal.* Could this be the answer to her quest?

Quietly, she stepped off the path and made her way through the undergrowth towards her target. Hopping over a small stream, she circled behind some large pine trees, trying to get a better look at the snowy creature. It was white, definitely white, with four legs and a shape quite like... a horse?

That thought must've provoked a tiny noise, because the animal threw its head up in alarm. Her eyes widened as she saw the long, twisted horn protruding from its elegant forehead. Not a horse. *A unicorn!*

Its nostrils flared as it turned its head, searching for the source of the noise that had startled it. She froze in place, not daring to move a muscle or even breathe.

Eventually, the unicorn seemed satisfied that it was safe, and dropped its head again. It was drinking, she saw now, from a small still pool formed where the stream crossed some rockier ground.

She wracked her brains, trying to remember what she knew—anything she knew—about unicorns. Since some of the legends had them similar to horses—obviously the game developers hadn't read the myths about cloven-hoofed, goat-bearded unicorns—and since she liked books, they were a subject she'd read about a couple of times, but mostly in fiction, so she wasn't sure how much of what she'd read was true.

And then she stopped herself, almost laughing. This *was* fiction, wasn't it? It was a game, and the game developers wrote the 'story' of each quest. So what she remembered was probably fine; and what she remembered was that unicorns were tamed by unsullied maidens. *Maybe that's what my riddle means?* She pressed her lips together, narrowing her eyes at the magical creature. *Could taming him be my quest?*

There was only one way to find out. And it *was* only a game, so what could go wrong? She could just try again tomorrow if she messed up.

Taking a deep, quiet breath, she crept silently around the pine trees until she was level with the unicorn's shoulder. Holding a hand out in front of her, she stepped out from behind the tree. "Good boy," she breathed, announcing her presence.

The unicorn's head raised again, but this time he looked more curious than alarmed. Liquid brown eyes surveyed her, and then his head bobbed slightly.

She took another step towards him, and then another, and another until her hand could reach out and touch his muzzle.

A glow of satisfaction suffused her whole body as the animal snuffled her fingers, his whiskers tickling her palm. Another step closer and her other hand was able to reach up and stroke his cheek. His hair was silky-fine and so smooth it was like touching satin, and his muzzle in her other hand felt like expensive velvet. Then he dropped his head so that she cradled it in her arms, and she felt a catch in her chest.

That was what Midnight used to do. He'd stand quietly in his stable, face in her arms, letting her run her fingers through his mane and tickle his chin.

Just like this unicorn was letting her do now.

Could this game somehow tap into her subconscious? For a moment, she became aware of the headset pressing tight on her temples, of the sensors studding the gaming gloves she was wearing. But that couldn't explain the dreams she'd had last night, could it?

She sighed, and, as if taking a cue from her, the unicorn rocked back on its haunches, folded his legs and sank to the ground with a grunt, eyelids drooping.

Sitting on the grass beside him, she cradled his head on her lap, stroking the half-moon of his huge cheekbone. Apart from his horn, he seemed to look and behave very like a horse. And then a thought pulled her up short. Could *he* have been the white creature she was riding in her dream last night, the one that reminded her of Midnight?

Chapter Four
THE WILD HUNT

You're confusing reality and virtuality again, Corinne. Get a grip. She shook her head. This game was confusing. And addictive. She was already wondering what her next quest would be.

But, talking of quests, if she'd completed this one by taming the unicorn, why hadn't the goblin appeared to give her next mission?

Running the riddle over in her mind, she tried to work out what she hadn't done, how she'd failed. *Only the pure can see the pure, only the pure will find him.* She'd found the unicorn now.

Why hadn't she moved on to the next level? Surely a first quest like this shouldn't be so hard?

She was still pondering the rhyme when a chilling noise reached her ears, and the unicorn's head jerked up.

Hounds. Hounds baying like they were on a hunt. *Like in my dream last night.* She jumped up at the same time as the unicorn scrambled to his feet, shimmying his whole body to shake off the dust and then standing to attention, ears pricked in the direction of the hunt.

They were getting closer. Worryingly closer. She looked around. Nowhere to hide here. Then she looked at the unicorn. Could they be hunting him? Her insides turned to ice. *Or her?* Maybe the Bright Court faeries from yesterday somehow knew she was here, and were continuing their chase.

A hoof stamped on the ground, attracting her attention. The unicorn was staring at her; looking her right in the eye. And then he turned his head, deliberately, and looked at his back, before staring meaningfully at her once more.

"You want me to ride?" she asked breathlessly.

He nodded his head and stamped a hoof again.

Ride a unicorn? She felt faint at the thought. Never in her wildest dreams… Well, actually, she *had* dreamed it, hadn't she? Like a premonition. But how had the dream ended? *Did we get away?* She narrowed her eyes, wishing she could remember.

The noise of the hunt followers was obvious now, not just the baying of their hounds. Breaking branches and the thunder of running hooves on peaty ground signalled their approach and quickened her pulse.

Spotting a tall rock to use as a mounting block, she was about to slide onto the unicorn's back when a large creature burst through the bushes, and the unicorn spun to face this new threat.

Swinging the bow from her shoulder, she had an arrow nocked before she recognised the intruder. It was Elphin, her rescuer from yesterday, his breeches snagged and tattered, twigs and leaves stuck in his unruly hair.

He glanced from the unicorn to her, and she was surprised to see fear in his eyes. "Help me," he gasped, his lungs heaving.

"They're after *you*?"

He nodded, hands on his knees as he regained his breath.

Corinne locked eyes with the unicorn, and he bobbed his head again, stepping back to the rock.

"Quickly, over here." She motioned at the rock, and slid onto the unicorn's back. "He'll help us escape."

* * *

The unicorn splashed down the stream, before hopping up the bank. *Masking our scent. Clever.* Behind her, Elphin's breathing became less ragged and she wound her hands into the unicorn's mane as he cantered off through the trees. "Hold on!" she cried, unnecessarily, as Elphin's grip around her waist became vise-like.

Branches whipped around them as they careened through the forest, and more than once she had to duck down over the animal's neck to avoid being swept off its back by a low branch. Behind her, Elphin mirrored her every move as she crouched forward to keep balanced while the unicorn ran, or leaned back when they travelled downhill.

But the hounds were relentless. No matter how fast the unicorn galloped, they couldn't seem to lose the fearsome hunters. Eerie howling and baying echoed through the trees, punctuated at intervals by a creepily atonal hunting horn.

Got to do something about this. Swinging the bow off her shoulders, she twisted round, then recoiled in horror. It was like the hounds of hell were after them; the dark huntsman on his black stallion frenziedly driving the slavering dogs whose savage teeth and glowing red eyes were mere yards behind them.

"Who *are* they? *What* are they?"

"The Wild Hunt," Elphin shouted, his voice higher-pitched than usual.

Nothing about this sounds good. What on earth was going on in this game? She clenched her jaw and aimed into the pack.

Her first arrows went wide of the mark, but after a couple of tries she got the knack of aiming, and managed to hit one of their pursuers. Wounded, it landed at the side of the track with a yelp of surprise. But the rest of the hounds just kept running, their pace not faltering. She ground her teeth. *There aren't enough arrows in my quiver to injure all of them.*

"How can we escape them?"

"I do not know."

Then inspiration struck. She turned towards him. "What about your magical cloak?"

He shook his head. "They hunt by smell, not sight. So it will be of no use."

She put a hand on the unicorn's shoulder, feeling its muscles ripple and bunch as it powered underneath them, making the double burden seem effortless. But he'd eventually tire, she knew that. She glanced behind them again.

The unicorn's long, flowing tail streamed behind them like a lure, and the hounds who followed their every twist and turn were getting close—*too close!*

Corinne swung her bow off her shoulder again, just as a particularly large and vicious grey beast snapped his yellow fangs at the unicorn's hocks, snagging a part of his tail and ripping some of the silvery hairs with a blood-curdling snarl.

The unicorn almost stumbled, and, acting on instinct, Corinne loosed an arrow at the savage hound. It arced through the air and felled the beast, a green-feathered arrow protruding from its chest.

"Well done!" said Elphin, and she gave a grim smile.

But the near-miss reminded Corinne of an old Burns poem they'd studied at school, where Tam O'Shanter's mare had been chased by witches and lost her tail before they escaped. She leaned forward and whispered in the unicorn's ear. "Is there a river somewhere? With a bridge? Maybe they can't cross running water."

An ear flicked to catch her words, and the unicorn changed direction. A minute later they turned onto a dirt road leading through the forest towards distant purple hills. His hooves hammering, the unicorn surged forward, straining to put some extra distance between them and the hunt.

* * *

Elphin exhaled sharply. "Look!"

The trees were thinning now, and in the distance great clouds of white spray plumed overhead, the air shimmering with hundreds of effervescent rainbows. The sound of thundering water drummed in Corinne's ears but her heart quailed as they approached the powerful waterfall. "I—I can't swim," she gasped.

"Trust him," Elphin said, pointing at the unicorn. "He's taken us this far."

Underfoot, the surface had changed and they were now riding along a cobbled road, which became slippery as they neared the water. The unicorn checked his pace, and dropped to a trot as they entered the mist and inclined upwards.

Glancing down, Corinne's stomach leaped into her mouth when she saw the great drop below them to her left. But, somehow, they were arching over it, as if dancing on air.

"Rainbow Bridge," Elphin whispered. "I had heard of it, but never…"

Reaching the other side, the unicorn stopped and spun round.

Across the fearsome chasm, dark shapes howled their frustration and the grim antlered huntsman gnashed his teeth in anger.

It worked! Maybe that poem was based on truth, after all.

Leaning forward, she wrapped her arms around the unicorn's neck, burying her face in his mane. "Good boy. Thank you."

"Yes, you have my eternal gratitude, brave creature." Elphin patted its flank. "You saved my life."

"We should get off now. Give him a rest."

But before they could move, the unicorn stamped a foot and spun round to face away from the river again. He raised his head and stared at a distant hill, before setting off at a brisk trot.

* * *

As they climbed the small hill, Corinne could see trees above them, and when they crested the rise, she realised that they were rowans. Rowans planted in a circle around the summit, like a silvery crown, the air at their centre shimmering slightly in the heat of the afternoon. *A special place.*

The unicorn stopped, and looked round at her.

Throwing her right leg up over its neck, she slid off, then stepped forward as Elphin dismounted behind her.

The unicorn dropped his muzzle into her palm, and she fondled his ears. "Thank you," she murmured. "Thank you *so* much for saving us, and for letting me ride you. It's been—it's been…"

A lump rose in her throat. It had reminded her of riding Midnight: of the special bond they had, of the way he could seem to read her mind. But she couldn't put that into words. A tear trickled down her cheek, and the unicorn pushed his face into her arms. "Thank you," she whispered. "Thank you for the memory."

The unicorn snuffled her fingers one last time, then took a step backwards and looked each of them in the eye. With one final bob of his head, he turned, paced sedately into the circle of trees, and—disappeared.

Chapter Five
THE IMPOSSIBLE

Corinne's jaw dropped open, and she rushed forward. "Wait!" she cried, but Elphin grabbed her arm to still her headlong flight.

"You cannot follow," he said, turning her towards him. "His task here is complete."

Another tear spilled down her face, chasing the first one. Elphin reached out a finger and brushed it gently away.

"M—maybe it's because I completed my quest," she said, trying to convince herself.

"Perhaps," he agreed, but his orange eyes looked troubled.

She stared at his pockmarked face. He was still strange-looking and ugly, but how could she ever have been scared of him? "Will you be okay now? Will the hunt leave you alone?"

He turned and looked back towards the forest. "I hope so." Then he sniffed the air and glanced up at the sky. "But the hour is late. I must go."

She sighed. "So should I. I must be *way* over my time"

He jerked his chin to the left. "Over there is a faerie ring."

Sure enough, a circle of polka-dot mushrooms poked through the grass nearby. "W—will you be in-game tomorrow?"

His eyes clouded. "Yes."

"See you tomorrow, then?"

He nodded solemnly. "I hope so."

* * *

"Thanks for dinner," Corinne said, pushing her chair back from the table. She helped her mother stack dishes in the dishwasher, then glanced at the clock on the wall. "I think I'll go for a little walk before bedtime. Stretch my legs."

"Good idea, after being inside all day," agreed her mother.

If only she knew!

Twenty minutes later, Corinne was striding up Chessaig hill as the evening light faded from the sky and the sun sank into the horizon. *I'll just visit Midnight's place, then I'll head home.* The events of the day whirled around her brain, scrambled memories and hyper-real sensations returning to her as she walked. How could a game seem so lifelike? But Feyland certainly *was* addictive. She'd have to see if she could wangle her way back to the sim cafe tomorrow, and find her next quest.

Pushing through the rowan trees in the almost-dark of the gloaming, her mind on the game, she suddenly stumbled to a halt, unable to believe the sight that met her eyes.

Grazing peacefully on the lush grass on the centre of the hilltop was a grey horse. A beautiful, untethered animal with no sign of headcollar or bridle.

She spun around, eyes scanning the gloom, searching for its owner. But nobody was in sight.

The horse's head raised when he saw her, and he took a step towards her, liquid brown eyes staring intently into her own.

No! It couldn't be. Could it?

The grey took another step forward, and dropped his muzzle into her hand, snuffling at her fingers.

Her heart stopped. This was impossible, wasn't it? *He must be a ghost.*

But a very real, very solid nose nudged her in the ribs, and a very real, very elegant head jerked in the direction of the path.

Not a ghost. Just something impossible and amazing.

She swallowed. "Okay, boy. You want to go with me?"

He bobbed his head.

Taking a deep breath, she put a hand on his neck. "This way," she said, and they set off down the hill towards the stables, together.

EPILOGUE

From the shadow of the trees, Elphin watched them go, his heart heavy.

He could tell the girl carried a burden of sorrow, and that she cared very deeply for horses. *Maybe the unicorn will be good for her, in her real world.* He wanted her to be happy, he truly did.

But, watching them disappear into the gloaming, a niggle of worry ate at his soul. What if she was so happy with the grey that she never returned to Feyland? What if he never saw her again?

What would become of him then?

She didn't know—couldn't know—that their fates were inextricably linked; that Feyland wasn't the simple game she seemed to think it was. But he knew, to his cost, just how treacherous the fey realm could be. And he knew, now, that he needed her help to escape his dark fate.

As the horse and the girl vanished from sight, he squared

his shoulders and turned back towards the forest. He couldn't change what Corinne would choose to do; he could only hope.

Hope.

And dream.

A WORD FROM ROZ MARSHALL

At last year's Edinburgh International Book Festival, I picked up a book on Scottish myths and legends. I was spellbound. Some of those stories kindled my imagination and made me look at my homeland through fresh eyes.

Living in Scotland is awesome. Soaring mountains, inky lochs, thousand-acre skies—just looking at our scenery is an inspiration in itself. And folk tales abound—perhaps a relic of a time when the only thing to do in the long dark winter nights was to sit around the fire and spin a yarn.

It was around this time that I was reading Anthea Sharp's *Feyland*, and thinking about a contribution for Samuel Peralta's *Chronicle Worlds* anthology. Nearly everything I write is set in Scotland, so it seemed natural to combine the two, and to use some of our stories about the 'fairy folk' to inspire my *Feyland* piece.

But as I wrote about Corinne and Elphin, I realised that their full story couldn't be told in five thousand words. They had a bigger tale to tell—a tale that will awaken ambitions, enmity and sleeping kings. In the end, I drafted outlines for a four-part series, *The Celtic Fey*. Part two, *'Kelpie Curse'*, should be available now, and parts three and four will be published soon after. You can check those out on Amazon or on my website: www.rozmarshall.co.uk/books.

As a long-time 'resident' of virtual reality world *Second Life*, I'm no stranger to online gaming. So I loved writing in this universe that combined tech and fable. Oh—and I loved writing about the unicorn. It probably won't be a surprise to readers that, outside of writing, my main spare time activity is horse riding…

Thank-you for reading; thank-you to Samuel for putting together this amazing anthology; and thank-you to Anthea for letting us join her in the fabulous *Feyland*!

City of Iron and Light
by Jon Frater

SABINE COULDN'T RID THE SMELL of singed hobgoblin from her nostrils. It presented her with a stark contrast: the smell of burnt fur combined with the rolling emerald hills of Feyland. Sycamore and larch trees stood in small groves on both sides of the wide earthen path which lay before them, like sentinels who guarded travelers.

Jonny Wonderful's voice was a constant as they walked. The hobgoblins had succumbed quickly, he'd said, due to his fine art of tanking and taunting. Not once did he compliment her use of fire bolts to chase the hobgoblins off. That rankled her worse than the smell. She didn't look forward to hearing her questing partner lecture her all the way to the marketplace.

Jonny talked a lot, usually about himself. He'd managed to tweak the game character setup to give himself crazily elaborate green armor, flowing hair, and pointed ears. She was willing to put up with the grandeur of his company, but only to a certain point.

Finally, she snapped. "Do I have to remind you how we met?" she asked.

"I remember it clearly," he said, as they hiked down a wide road. A stiff breeze rose, dampening the heat of the summer sun. "I had taken a charge to retrieve a lost cow and found myself ambushed by brigands. Struggle though I did, there were too many for me to vanquish alone. I was subdued and treated barbarically."

Sabine chuckled with the memory. "I found you buried up to your chin in mud, and passersby were being invited to saw at your neck with a bamboo sword."

"So it was," Jonny agreed. "For days, nay, weeks, I lingered between life and death. And then, in the distance, I observed a vision of truth and beauty, a Spellweaver with steel in her eyes, a mane of fire, and robes the colors of the rainbow, who bore a fearsome skill with word and staff—"

"Dude," she sighed, "stop the flattery. I saved you because I wanted to. I'm working with you because I want to. You tag and tank the mobs, I nuke them. We have a good system. Don't ruin it."

"My sincerest apologies, my lady," Jonny demurred with a flourish and a bow. He even managed to make his nose touch his knees. Sabine wondered absently if there was a game command to do that. She'd have to look.

She did like Jonny, despite his silly name and obsequious personality. He fought well and told great stories. He helped make the game that much more interesting and no matter where she logged in from, he was always waiting for her nearby. She'd been playing in Feyland a lot more since meeting him.

The quality of gameplay had improved as well. Jonny had introduced her to a new zone which he called the Borderlands. Here, the fights were tougher and mobs dropped better loot, and the feel of the spells, the texture of the environmental effects on her skin and muscles had deepened and broadened. VirtuMax had outdone itself with their newest upgrade. Now anyone on the planet could potentially don their VR gear and create a character and get the same immersive experience. It was almost frightening.

Jonny, true to form, wasn't finished. "I speak as what I am: a rogue, a jack, a saboteur. Merely ask me to be silent and I will obey."

"No," she said. "Just walking is boring. Why don't you tell me about where you come from?"

For a few moments, he remained silent. She sensed a truly ridiculous story in the works. He finally addressed her with a startlingly serious one.

"We were expelled," he said, then paused again. "No, that rings false. We allied ourselves with mortals, broke with the Dark Queen's royal court, and fled."

"Some alliance," Sabine muttered. She almost felt sorry for the big fool.

"Not at all," he said, standing tall again. "It was a fair arrangement. A creature named Bat rules a city of iron and light called Justice. It is unique in all my experience. It's a week's travel from end to end, home to countless refugees from all over the many realms. At its center lies Cloudspire, a building of such height that one sees it rise from the horizon when one is still three days away from the city gates."

Sabine found the idea of an enormous city in Feyland to be an impossible thing. She couldn't even imagine it. "That's amazing."

"Indeed. Justice was quite small in those days. Bat needed help, as the Shadow Warriors who lay siege to Justice gained ground. Aoife and Llyr, our rulers, pledged their aid to his cause in return for the land surrounding the city. He agreed. We named our new home the Cothram Forest, and the rest is as I have told."

"That's insane," Sabine breathed. It had to be part of the new expansion. A zone that was only unlocked at super-high levels, or something. Maybe a beta of some kind. Maybe even an alpha release. The thought of getting a look at such a restricted area made her mouth water.

"You have to take me there," she said.

Jonny laughed deep and long. "My lady," he said as he recovered, "I need do no such thing."

"Why not? It sounds brilliant."

He shook his head gravely. "No fae visits Justice. Few even walk the protected roads that run through the city or the surrounding lands. There are rules of conduct for both sides. There is a treaty we dare not break."

"Well, that sucks," she said, but let it go.

The trees gave way to meadows, dotted with wildflowers. Sabine spent so much time wondering what Jonny's fabled city might look like that she barely noticed when the road turned into a wide valley, with lush green hills on their left and right.

"One thing I don't like about this game," she muttered. "Bags actually get heavy, now."

"We shall be at the marketplace shortly," Jonny said. "Remember the rules. Touch nothing and allow me to do the talking. I know the vendors. I shall get good prices."

She snorted. "You'll get buried in mud again."

"Not today," Jonny insisted. "I may not always properly respect opponents in battle, but my merchant is like a father to me. Or like a humorless older brother."

"Can I at least look around?"

"Surely. Enquire after the wares. Talk to the dealers. Tell the gossips of our exploits. But touch nothing which is not yours."

"Yes, Lord Wonderful." She stopped and offered him a silly, sarcastic curtsy.

Jonny whirled on her, his brow furrowed and his visage dark. She'd never imagined he could be this serious. "Fiery Sabine," he said, "you are my sun, my moon, my friend, my confidant. Our laws matter. Obey them."

She nodded quickly, startled by his demeanor. "All right."

They heard the market before they saw it. Music rose from the far side of the valley and swelled as they approached: flutes, pipes, drums, and strings, interspaced with the tinkling of bells and laughter. Below that, the murmur of a thousand voices all clashed into a veil of white noise. Colorful peaked tents and more permanent structures came into view as they crested a hill.

Over all rose massive ash trees that grew together, trunks entwined and leaves mingling freely far above them. They formed a wide roof over the length of the road, which ran through a gauntlet of stands, stalls, and booths displaying their owners' wares. Tables covered with arcane objects, scrolls, books, and food beckoned. A gnome alchemist and a pair of goblin tinkers worked on opposite sides of the road as Sabine and Jonny passed. Both tried to get their attention.

"Hey, travelers! I got what you need!"

"Howdy ho, dear! Stop for a sweet drink?"

She hesitated, and then continued as she felt Jonny's hand on her shoulder. "Touch nothing."

"Right. I got this." She looked up at him, trying to be as serious as she could. "Really."

"Very well," Jonny said, "I'll make mark with my buyer. Remain vigilant."

She wandered between the stalls, oohing and aahing every so often. She stopped before a poorly kept table cluttered with jewelry that looked like it could have come from a Crestview flea market. Strings of colored glass beads, tarnished silver brooches, and the occasional gold ring, some with set gems and others without. One item grabbed her attention instantly: a purple and gold ovoid lying on its side.

"'Tis a mundane egg," the vendor said. He was a tall, thin fae wearing a black morning coat and a waistcoat. His grin showed too many teeth for her liking, and she had no clue how his spectacles remained perched on the tip of his long nose. "Not a trinket, nor a toy, but an item of great magical power. It can unlock unseen doors and begin the greatest of journeys."

"How much?" she asked.

"If ye need ask, yer pockets are not deep enough."

Sabine shrugged. "I don't know, I have quite a bit."

He narrowed his eyes. "Truly? Show me your bits."

At that moment, a drunken brawl broke out a few stalls down. Tables were shoved, shouts of rage emerged from the combatants, and she heard the unmistakable clang of steel on steel. A cry of "Guards! Guards!" arose from the vendors around her. Her eyes remained fixed on the egg. She could hear something wobbling within, demanding her attention.

The vendor screeched for the duelers to stay away, and then the egg was in Sabine's hand. It pulsed faintly, warm to the touch.

"Thief!" shouted the vendor.

Sabine looked up to see a group of tall soldiers rush up; two broke off to eject the combatants and two more approached her. One bore a fancy seal on his black breastplate. Sabine tried to drop the object, but it was stuck to her fingers. Shaking them didn't help.

"Captain Winhome! Arrest this sticky-fingered one. She's—!"

"I have eyes, Malgrove."

"I was going to buy it," Sabine pleaded. "Really!"

"Your bleating is better spoken from the mouth of a goat, wretched pilferer!"

A sick, falling sensation grabbed her and she found her vision wobbly, reduced to black and white images like a very old movie. Her head felt impossibly heavy. When Sabine opened her mouth to argue all she could say was, "Maaaaah!" She realized that the vendor hadn't been kidding: she now had a goat's voice. She looked down at herself to see hooves where her hands were and the world somehow grown bigger. All at once, she was standing on four short legs, bleating her surprise and anger to a growing crowd of onlookers.

She thought about summoning her staff, but nothing happened except for her feeling ill. Which, she thought in a rising panic, was probably just as well. She was in enough trouble.

"Witnesses!" called the captain. "Come forward!"

One goblin vendor raised a green claw and jumped up and down. "I saw the whole thing! I—" His companion pounded the back of his head, and the goblin calmed down. "No, I didn't."

"Any others?" called Winhome. Silence. "Very well. You'll come with me and stay in a cell until I can inform Her Majesty, the Dark Queen; she will judge you appropriately. Come along."

Winhome reached into a leather belt pouch and pulled out a thin yellow cord. At a spoken command, the rope snaked out and circled Sabine's neck, She struggled at first, but the rope merely tightened its grip on her.

Captain Winhome took the loose end of the rope and strode out of the tent, pulling her away from the merchants and muttering crowds. Small winged pixies jeered at her, changing the color of her hair for a few seconds at a time. Finally, they reached a great wagon pulled by a team of huge warhorses. Upon its bed rested an iron cage with a heavy lock on the door.

Winhome spoke a word; the lock snapped open and the door swung wide. "In, girl."

Without wanting to, Sabine stepped into the prison cart and immediately reverted to her human form. She was thankful enough that her human body had reappeared inside her dress and not on top of it to quietly sit down on the short wooden bench that was built into the floor. An iron cage, she knew, was the perfect way to trap a fae. But she as a player wasn't supposed to end up in one. What was going on here?

The rope now released her, snaking back through the bars to its master. The captain settled himself up front with the driver as she wondered where Jonny Wonderful had gotten to, or what in-game abilities she was going to lose over this.

As the cart pulled away, a giant oak tree and a rainbow-winged butterfly glanced at each other, shrugged, and went about their business.

Like the splash of a pebble in a still pond, the ripples of the morning's events reached Jonny Wonderful before he realized just how badly things had gone. It took some inquiry but he quickly pieced events together and hung his head as he realized that mortals were the same fools all over, and no, he truly could not leave Sabine alone for even a moment. Part of him resented the fact that she needed so much looking after. Part of him feared for her safety. The Dark Queen would not take kindly to a market thief. The girl would, at the very least, stay in a cell while the human world raced past her and eventually forgot about her. To cross the Queen's Guard—much less the Queen herself—meant a very long stay for himself well beyond the Unseelie Court.

"Well then, Sirrah," he muttered to himself, "you dare not delay."

Sabine sat on the bench in her cage, dejected. Her staff

refused to appear when she tried to summon it; she had no better luck with any other item. The lock was heavy, solid, and probably warded. Besides, she had no skill at lock picking. She rocked along with the wagon's motion, wondering what might happen to her.

She perked up as she spied a lone figure chasing the wagon. She squeed as she recognized Jonny on a red and yellow War Raptor. He pulled alongside the wagon, jumped from the flightless bird's back, and landed on the tailgate steps. The War Raptor squawked indignantly and then stopped in the road, dwindling to a speck as the wagon left it behind. "Care to leave this place?"

"Wait, you can pick locks? Iron locks?"

"I would be a poor rogue indeed if there were a cage that could hold me," he replied. She couldn't see what he did, but in a few moments the lock sizzled and popped off. A moment later the door swung open. Sabine noticed that Jonny made an effort not to touch the door itself. "Jump!"

They jumped, dropped, and rolled. The wagon trundled away, the door swinging aimlessly from its hinges. And Jonny's mount had squawked off in the wrong direction.

"One fewer problem to manage," Jonny said. "But now we have a greater need: a place of relative safety for you."

"I could log off the sim. Forever," she suggested.

"No. The Dark Queen would merely arrange things in your world such that you were forced back here. However…"

Sabine noticed that Jonny was staring at her hand. She looked down, surprised to see that she still held the mundane egg in her grasp. That made no sense. "I dropped it when

Winhome put me in the cage," she remembered. "I know I did."

"It's yours," Jonny breathed wonderingly. "It must always have been. The trouble in the market was that mad vendor's doing." He bowed low. "Sabine, you have my apologies twice in one day. I should not have thought poorly of you."

She stared at him. Who was this guy? He was no mere role-player, she knew that now. And she was in way over her head. "What's going on here, Jonny? This isn't just a game, is it?"

"Only if avoiding prison seems like a girl's play to you. The danger you face is quite real." He hesitated a moment as he weighed strategies. "Give your magic item here, and I will grant your wish to see the city of Justice."

"Promises, promises," she teased. But she handed him the mundane egg. "How's this going to work?"

"Within this object is a world waiting to be born. Or, a way to bring an existing world forward." He pulled a vial from his pocket, popped the cap, and emptied the contents into his hands, smearing his palms and the mundane egg. "Dandelion milk makes a wonderful binding agent. Take my hand."

She gripped his hand fiercely. Her heart pounded in her chest and she couldn't slow her breathing. In the distance she heard the clattering of wagon wheels and the stomp of hooves. Winhome had discovered her escape and was coming back for her. "Hurry up!" she said.

"And now, take a step— " he said as he threw the egg down on the packed dirt of the trail. The shattering sound was far too loud for it to have come just from the egg as it broke into pieces. A light flickered and blossomed around them. They stepped into it and were surrounded by thick clouds of gray and white smoke. In a few moments the mist cleared, and Sabine looked around at a completely different world.

"Welcome to the Cothram forest."

She twirled in a circle as she worked to take in the new environment. The plants and trees were entirely different and the air smelled of cherry blossoms and honeysuckle. They stood in a grove of pine and elm trees. She could smell the sap from them. There was no hint of the danger they'd just left. It felt peaceful in a way that Feyland never had.

She lifted her skirts and picked her way through the trees, working to step past shrubs and over clumps of tall grass. She didn't see the strawberry bush nestled against the old pine tree. She did, however, tread too close to it. The bush snapped at her, rearing up and barking loudly. Sabine screamed and ran, flying across the grass and leaping into the low branches of an elm. She gripped its trunk in a death hug as the strawberry bush dashed around the roots, barking and snapping, unable to climb after her.

She heard a sharp whistle and looked down in amazement as Jonny Wonderful caught the bush's attention, and lured it away into the bright daylight. The bush promptly quieted and settled.

Jonny approached the tree and looked up at her. "Strawberries become irritable when they lie in the shade for too long. Luckily, it wasn't a bamboo tree. Those will carry a grudge."

She dropped from the branch, smoothed her skirts, and

glared at him. "Anything else you want to tell me about this place?" she asked.

Jonny indicated the edge of the trees. A clearing lay beyond, and then a wide, bricked road. Well down the road, behind all manner of hills and valleys, stood an immense tower that gleamed like an icicle in the sunlight.

"Cloudspire," Jonny said. "The seat of Mayor Bat's rule. We may walk. The road is safe."

She sighed with relief as she saw the bricks were gray rather than yellow. That would have been too weird. On the other hand, the stone sparkled with mica chips. Their boot heels clicked noisily against the bricks as they walked down the path toward the city.

"How does the protection work? Is it the treaty?"

"It is. While on the roads, we fall under the city's law. The Cothram Fae may not molest any who tread upon it. All else is their territory, over which the city has no claim. Errant wanders have found themselves maimed, duped, or robbed."

"A non-aggression pact," Sabine said, grinning. "Cool. What happens if you meet an unhappy person on the road?"

An unholy scream from above them gave her an answer.

They rained from the sky, not flying as much as falling. Rotted humanoids with gaping holes in their bodies and armor to match. They stank of corruption and landed around Jonny and Sabine, too many for her to count.

"Jonny Wonderful," the leader crowed in a voice that sounded like a mouthful of suet and ants, "Welcome home! We would have a toll, Cothram."

Jonny maneuvered himself between Sabine and the leader

as she took the opportunity to summon her staff. "What toll? This is a free road."

"Bah! Pay us, or—"

A sizzling bolt of fire arced into the group, hitting the speaker square in the chest. He burst into flames instantly and fell silent.

"Or we can fight," Sabine said.

The crowd drew weapons and charged, bellowing wordless battle cries. Sabine gripped her staff and concentrated, blasting a circle of fire in all directions, forcing the corpse horde to retreat. Jonny engaged them with his rapier, driving them back as Sabine kept them at bay, but there were clearly too many of them.

A shout erupted from behind them and suddenly a new combatant entered the field: a tall fae knight with sword and shield, and a suit of black armor with a silver and gold seal on the breastplate. Captain Winhome surged forward with a flurry of blows, raining destruction onto the field.

Jonny and Sabine sensed their opportunity and moved away from the Captain of the Queen's Guard. They maneuvered the mob so that the corpses focused their attention on Winhome. Then, Jonny grabbed Sabine's hand and pulled her toward the edge of the road.

"Jump!" he yelled. A grave yawned open in the ground just beyond the edge of the road and they were gone.

The grave closed over them and the darkness consumed her, penetrated her, broke her into component molecules and then broke each molecule into atoms. She floated in an airless, senseless void. Sabine could barely sense time, couldn't even formulate thoughts. At some point her senses returned and she felt as if she'd slammed into a wall, chest first.

She opened her eyes to see a large room with off-white walls and plush, comfortable looking chairs. A number of disheveled individuals sat in them. Judging by the wings and battered finery, she'd have said they were fey—but in a sorry state. They shivered, they hugged themselves, and one did nothing but stare at the wall. They were clearly out of their element, and as she watched, two more appeared out of nowhere. Jonny wasn't among them.

"Welcome to the airlock," an androgynous voice said.

"Thanks," she muttered. The room wasn't huge, but the uniform color scheme meant she couldn't easily discern where the walls stood. She found herself disliking that. A lot.

"Hello?" she called out. With no answer forthcoming, she sat in a chair, and then a different voice floated from the ceiling.

"Welcome to Justice. May I have a moment of your time?"

Sabine looked up to see a flashing globe the size of a softball hovering above her. "Sure," she answered.

"Thank you." The silver orb glimmered in a flashing pattern of colors which never played out twice in a row. "I have no record of your electromagnetic and astral identity, which is required for all visitors to the city. I have a few questions—"

"Who are you?" asked Sabine.

The ball flashed more brightly. "I am a node of Theopolis, the administrative megabrain," it said. "I process newcomers to the city."

"How do I get out of here?"

The globe dimmed. "Do you wish to depart already?"

"No. I mean—I was with someone else. A friend. His name is Jonny Wonderful."

"Just a moment." The ball flashed more quickly and brightly. "Jonny Wonderful is currently in the Justice Terminal plaza."

Sabine looked around her, beginning to understand. She was here. Jonny's iron city. "This is just the vestibule for the real city, right?"

"Correct. May I ask some questions to properly record your arrival?"

Sabine nodded. "Sure, let's do the interview."

"Of course," Theopolis said. "What is your name?"

"Sabine Jade."

"Thank you, Sabine Jade. Please come this way." The globe floated to the opposite side of the room. It led her to a section of wall that became a darkened area roughly as tall and wide as she was. "Please stand still for a moment, Sabine. Be careful not to move, or you may disrupt the scanning process."

Sabine followed the instructions, keeping her feet on the floor and her back straight. She felt a tickling inside her feet, which spread to her calves, knees, up her body until it reached the top of her head. Her entire form was alive with the weird sensation for almost a minute. It stopped all at once.

"Scan complete," said Theopolis. "I have assigned you a unique identification pattern for verification whenever you enter or leave the city."

She frowned and stepped away from the wall. "How do I use it?"

"It is an automatic response. If you are not cleared for city access, you will not be allowed admittance. If you attempt to force entry, the megabrain will alert the police and you will be detained."

"Sounds like the Dark Queen's system," she grumbled.

"I do not understand that reference," said Theopolis. "The rule ensures maximum safety for all Justice visitors and residents." The voice paused a moment. "Do you wish entry to the city?"

"Can I leave whenever I want?"

"Of course. When you are ready to depart, simply alert the megabrain to your wish to leave."

"Then, sure, I want to enter. For a while."

"Enter at will, Sabine."

The wall glowed briefly, then cleaved, splitting into a dozen sections that slid away to show her a panorama of tall buildings. She felt her body being shoved out from the white room into a blizzard of activity. Cool air blew across her face and new smells and sounds crashed against her. When she glanced behind her, the airlock had disappeared entirely.

Sabine stared at her surroundings without seeing them, not understanding why she felt claustrophobic. The sense of being hemmed in was very powerful here. Finally she thought to look up and saw the city.

She would later learn exactly how Justice was laid out—a grid built around hexagons within concentric circles—but on first sight, her mouth dropped open and stayed like that for several minutes. Theopolis had released her into an open plaza, with fluted columns around the edges, and a path leading to an incredibly tall building that stood behind her. Tall buildings of chromed glass surrounded the plaza. A blue sky shimmered above her as a rainbow faintly passed overhead. A yellow-orange sun commanded the sky above. She didn't recognize the architectural style—and in truth hadn't known there was such a thing as style when one created gargantuan structures. Softer, darker colors of grays, brown, greens, and tans surrounded her. A huge fountain bearing a statue of an angel with an upraised sword lay directly before her.

And the people that passed her defied logical description. Males, females, some with human features, some resembling animals such as birds, bats, foxes, or lizards, some she'd simply never imagined, walked past her. A few stared at her in return.

The air freaked her the most. It smelled clean and went down her throat smoothly, without burning, free of soot, smoke, or dirt. Only the infrequent smell of alien body odor found her nose. A strange sense of it lacking some background odor came to her, and it would be much later that she found she could identify it.

She could not smell the scent of fear surrounding her. The people here were not afraid of anything. It felt safe.

Finally, she saw Jonny's familiar form rushing up to meet her. She hugged him tightly, burying her face in his chest. "This is it!" she cried, wide-eyed with joy. "Isn't it?"

His laughter rang in her ears like a sleigh bell. "Welcome to Justice, the city of iron and light!"

They left the plaza arm in arm. Behind them, a dozen more bedraggled visitors zipped into the city, while even more filled the Airlock.

"We have to tell him."

Norma Phastlight, Chief Architect of Justice and daughter to its ruler, hunched over a wide glass table in her office within Cloudspire. Her catlike ears poked above her thick blonde hair. Her eyes were closed and her hands lay flat on the glass. Inside her head, numbers, equations, and schematics flashed more quickly than any human could hope to make sense of. She only heard Seow, Bat's personal assistant, with a fraction of her attention. "Not until I have a fix for him to okay."

Seow put his snout on her shoulder. Norma wasn't tall, but the fox spirit stood a good deal shorter. Resting his chin on her shoulder forced her to look into his eyes. "If you don't, then I will. It's been three days. We need to address this problem before it becomes a real emergency."

Norma nodded. He had that right. The Airlock was siphoning up every wandering soul within a hundred city diameters and gathering them like bundles of sticks of cordwood. Some were being released into the city but most weren't coherent enough for that. Where the heck were they coming from? And why did they look like fae but register as humans on her instruments?

She straightened and opened her eyes, breaking the connection between herself and Theopolis. She needed time to assimilate what he'd imparted to her. "Give me an hour," she said to the black fox. "One hour, just to get some air and clear my head. Then we'll talk to my father together. All right?"

Seow narrowed his eyes. "Promise? You know I can find you. I have ways."

"I know," she said. "His office, one hour. Promise."

They parted ways, Seow heading upstairs to Bat's office and Norma heading outside into the arcology. In a city filled with people to chat up, places to visit, and things to do, her options were limited by the time limit she'd given Seow. The Electric Banana was too far to walk, though she could have used a drink. The hospital was closer, but her sister, Celfy, wouldn't be off shift for hours. The university food court was closer still, but she didn't feel like dealing with the faculty or students right now.

The trouble with being Bat's daughter, she thought angrily, was that everyone wanted to beg favors. Worse, she generally wanted to help out, but numbers were what they were and the cold math managed the workflow. It sucked being the city's architect sometimes.

Screw it, she finally decided. The food court beckoned her with promises of a big bowl of ramen and a short beer. The walk down familiar streets lifted her spirits, got her thinking about the nature of the problem. The waves of new arrivals had a definite source, almost certainly nearby. Justice floated within a bubble of cyberspace, which had a way of intersecting other dimensions occupying the same space-time. So, what if—?

A shadow fell across her path as she rounded a corner. "Dear lady," said a tall man in black armor, "a moment of your time, please."

She struggled to keep the impatience from her voice and failed miserably. "Yes?"

"The most helpful soldiers at the city gate told me that you are the city's designer. Is that right?"

She sighed. Couldn't this joker see she was busy? "Look—sir—I'm on my way to lunch. If you need something, just ask—"

He waved his finger in an intricate pattern and suddenly Norma could barely breathe, much less speak. "I am no mere knight. I am Captain Jared Winhome of the Dark Queen's Guard. I require your services. Now."

Norma fought his influence, but her expertise lay in equipment, not magic. She managed to wiggle her fingers just so and released a cloud of digital messengers into the plaza. They accessed the city's network and disappeared from view. They'd get to the police eventually but she still had to deal with this intruder.

"What do you want?" she croaked.

Winhome bent his face down to hers and whispered in her ear, "I want to know why you intend to attack us." His eyes wandered upwards to settle on the bulk of Cloudspire. "The tall building. That's the fortress where your father-king holds court, isn't it? Let us approach. But slowly. No need to rush."

Still barely able to breathe, she followed his lead, wondering how long it would take for Seow to make good on his threat to locate her if she were late. Well, she thought, this Winhome character wants to see the boss. She might as well introduce him.

"You know," Sabine told Jonny, "When you said that fae never visit the city, I think you got it wrong. There are plenty of fae around. They don't look happy, but they *are* here."

Jonny twirled his ramen noodles with a pair of lacquered

wooden chopsticks as if he'd been using them for decades. For all Sabine knew, he had been. Whatever Jonny was, he was certainly no stranger to Justice.

"It *is* unusual. The treaty allows us access, but we prefer the forest."

They noticed the stares from passersby, even here in the university food court. Jonny's whirlwind tour had taken them all over the city, but Sabine had insisted on seeing the school grounds. She'd have killed to go to a place like this in real life.

"I heard a few kids talking about the old days," Sabine said as she slurped her own ramen. "Something about the students burning the mayor in effigy. What happened?"

"The Chief of Medicine at the hospital complained the students weren't getting proper nutrition. Bat forbade the food carts from the school grounds during classroom hours. The vendors and the students took it badly."

"That must have been incredible," she said. "Kids who try that where I come from get hosed by cops and stuck in jail. Or sent to a mental ward and dosed until they can't remember their names."

"It was a long time ago. Before the arrival of Shadow Wings, and Dark Angels, and constant warfare. The fighting hardened the youngsters somewhat. Perhaps too much."

Sabine nodded as she remembered the corpse horde's attack. There were limits to paradise everywhere, she thought. The people they'd spoken to seemed friendly enough. Not very touchy-feely, maybe, but neither was Crestview. She swilled some more noodles, then looked up and nearly choked on her lunch. A figure in black armor was gripping a blonde girl by the shoulder, bending down to whisper in her ear—and the girl was obviously not enjoying his attention.

"Winhome," Sabine sputtered. "Behind you."

"That he is," Jonny agreed. "Far behind us. We are beyond his power."

She shook her head, still coughing. "No, you goof, he's here. Behind you."

He managed to look both alarmed and amazed. "I beg your pardon?"

"Don't look! Jeez. He's pissed off about something—probably us—and he's threatening a student." She risked another look. "They're heading into the giant building."

"That cannot be good." Jonny's face hardened. "We must follow. Can you be discreet?"

"Why can't we just—"

"A violent outburst in public will only bring the police to us. That serves no one. At least, not yet. Come along."

"I must say, this place is a marvel. How did you build it all?" Winhome asked.

Norma sensed her messengers flying through the cables and conduits that lined the corridors of the massive building. It would take time for a chance of escape to present itself, and on other floors, alarms were already flashing and beeping for attention. They'd get to her. They'd get him. She needed to stall a bit more.

"Know anything about resequencing photons on a massively parallel scale?" she whispered. "Or building logarithmically resistive tactile surfaces?"

"Do not beguile me with strong words, child," Winhome ordered. "I am in a poor humor."

"That makes two of us. Let's avoid the plaza. This way."

She led him through corridors and meeting halls, past guard posts where she flicked messages on screens. The Cloudspire PD was good; they stayed their hand and watched for opportunities to act while keeping civilians away. No one rushed in with guns blazing. Bat did not accept collateral damage in his city. When a shout erupted behind them, Winhome merely tightened his grip and swung them both around to show Norma an even stranger sight.

A man and a woman stood before them, looking more like tourists from the far realms of fantasy than anything Norma was used to seeing. The man stood there with sword drawn and green armor around him, while the woman wore a multi-hued gown and carried a long staff, a blazing red orb at its tip.

"Jared Winhome," the man shouted, "cease and desist from this foul action!"

Winhome straightened, drawing his own sword. "Stand down, knave! Clearly these city dwellers intend invasion of our lands. I will have my answers from this girl's sire."

Jonny Wonderful shook his head. "Not true, Captain. What you are doing will foment war, nothing less."

"We are done here." Winhome dragged Norma back towards the end of the corridor, his eyes fixed on Jonny, when a fiery wave from Sabine's staff erupted from the ground beneath him, throwing him and his captive to the ground.

Norma felt the pressure on her windpipe disappear and took her shot. She crawled away as he released her, bounced to her feet, and ran to the end of the hallway. She slammed her hand against a small glass plate set in the wall and jumped out of the way as a light-wall sprung into being inches from her.

More appeared on three sides of the trio and slid together, hemming them in, nearly pressing them against each other. She took a few deep breaths, hands on her knees as she settled herself. The woman—the girl, actually, Norma saw—seemed unhappy but the two men were visibly freaking out at their sudden and unexpected prison.

Within moments, a troop of blue-uniformed soldiers appeared, weapons holstered. She waved them over. "Tall one with the fancy chest plate wants to see the mayor. I think we should oblige. "

Bat's office was in the upper reaches of Cloudspire; even with an express elevator, it took time to get there. They crossed a set of double doors to see a strange trio at the room's center. A knight wearing brightly polished armor stood to one side, while a tall, regal woman wearing shimmering robes stood to the left. In between them stood a creature the visitors could not have imagined. A tall, purple, demonic entity with barbed membranous wings, and garbed in a purple suit with matching shoes raised his arms in welcome. A third eye glowed rhythmically in the center of his forehead.

Bat.

"The Cothram Fae," Bat said, approaching them as he spoke," have been our friends for nearly two decades now. They were instrumental in helping my troops and citizens repel the invading Shadows and Dark Angels. It was an honor to grant them their own lands on our border. They have kept to the treaty in word and deed." He stopped a few feet from Winhome. "So who, exactly, are you?"

"They're citizens of Feyland." The knight approached, removing his helmet to reveal a boy with green eyes, and hair that fell into his face. "I'm here to take them back."

Winhome glowered. "Ah. Tamlin. Why is it that you are the cause of so much of my queen's trouble among mortals?"

Tam clipped the helmet to his belt. "Captain Winhome," he said, "you're in over your head here. It's a very strange situation."

"You two know each other," Bat observed. "That's wonderful. Speaking of which, Jonny Wonderful, may I present—"

"Aoife, the Queen of the Cothram Forest," Jonny recited as he bent his knee in supplication. "My queen, I—"

"Stand."

Jonny obeyed.

"'Jonny Wonderful'?" Aoife asked. "You have a wry humor. When last we spoke many years ago, you went by the name J'orham Winterstead."

"That is true, my queen," Jonny stammered. "I would like to explain—"

"Quit your vapid utterance, rogue," Winhome ordered, drawing scowls from the others. "Mayor Bat," he spat, "I demand the immediate release of myself and this prisoner." He nodded toward Sabine.

Bat glared at Winhome. "You're in no place to demand anything, pal. You kidnapped my girl."

"To discover what plans for your war against my homeland—"

Bat shook his head. "I'm not looking for a war. I just got done fighting a war."

"Those rotted dead things, they—"

"I didn't send them to kill you, they snuck in under the defenses—"

Tam waved for the chance to speak. "Uh… gentlemen—"

Aoife tired quickly of the bickering and took Sabine and Norma to one side. Her glare intensified as she focused her violet eyes on Sabine. "Child," she commanded, "tell me of your travels. Leave nothing out."

Sabine complied. Finally, Norma put her hands on Sabine's shoulders, staring into her eyes. "Oh my god," she breathed, "you're not a fey at all, are you? You're just a regular kid with a fancy VR rig in her basement, right?"

"It's at a sim café, but, yeah."

"But you've been playing with fae for weeks," Norma said. "You've actually been there."

Sabine shrugged, her face reddening as she finally realized how stupid she'd been. "I guess so. It seemed so damn real—"

Norma broke contact and turned to the group of arguing men. "Guys," she called, "It's not a war!"

One by one they quieted and turned to her. "What's not a war?"

"It's not a war," she repeated. "It's not an attack, and it's not an incursion. It's server lag."

"What?" Bat said. "How?"

Norma shook her head. "She's not a fae. She's just a kid who's playing a game. An incredibly complex VR sim. The company that runs it just upgraded all their gear and content.

And people are people. You announce a grand opening, add enough bandwidth for a million people, you can expect five million to show up. The new players create characters, log on to the matrix, and some of them get stuck while the servers crap out due to the extra demand." She looked at each of the others. "Those people in the Airlock aren't fae. They're just human players who got stuck in the game and now they're here."

Bat looked puzzled, but his third eye glowed as if working overtime to figure the problem out. "We're drifting through their matrix, and the Airlock is just sweeping up the leftovers," he said.

Norma clapped her hands. "Exactly!"

"Good. Now you can explain it to me," Tam said.

"The city isn't a static entity," Bat told him. He raised viewing surfaces as he spoke to illustrate his point. Graphs, maps, and charts illuminated them instantly. "If cyberspace is an ocean, then Justice is a whale swimming through it. There are currents, eddies, backwash. Basically, we're drifting through Feyland's portion of cyberspace right now. We don't know how long that will take, but we do know the Airlock won't last much longer as things now stand." He stared at one of the viewing screens. The Airlock was now literally filled with people. "We need to close the borders between Justice and Feyland. Immediately. The Airlock expands to accommodate its contents, but at some point it will be so full that Theopolis will need to cut city services to maintain it. We need to fix it before it gets that far."

"I can do that," Norma offered. "I'll need Tam to help me, though."

"Certainly," Tam confirmed. "I'm on speaking terms with one of the game's designers. Worst case, I'll be a liaison between you."

"Good," Bat decreed. "I'll need you two to start as soon as possible. And good luck, Mr. Linn. Norma's a harsh taskmaster." The blonde girl blushed and frowned, then stalked away to study a viewing surface intently.

Bat strode over to Sabine and glared at Winhome. "You two will have to go back immediately, along with the other players who found their way into the Airlock."

Sabine cleared her throat. "Does closing the borders mean cutting off the Cothram forest, too?"

Bat looked to his daughter, who nodded. "I'm afraid so."

"Can't I stay just a little longer?" Sabine pleaded. "It's only been a few hours. This is so different from my world." She took a deep breath. "And Jonny is here."

Bat shook his head gravely. "I'm sorry. This was a unique anomaly. Tam and Norma will plug the holes, Justice will drift out of Feyland's space, and that will be that. Besides, you have a home. You'd be missed if you stayed."

Winhome puffed out his chest. "This purple wight speaks truly, girl. The sooner events are put to right, the better."

"Agreed." Bat waved to Norma and Tam even as he showed disgust at being called a wight. "Time's wasting, kids. We have worlds to fix."

Jonny Wonderful raised his hand. "A moment, please." He turned to Aoife. "My queen," he began, "might I beg thee a favor?"

The Cothram ruler raised her eyebrows. "Ask your favor, J'orham Winterstead."

"Might I be allowed to leave with the Feyland citizens?"

"To live there? It is an interesting request. From what little I have heard today, you are not well loved in Feyland."

"I can look out for him," Sabine offered. "We're a good team."

"You are due for naught but a cell and sentencing," Winhome growled at her.

"You sure about that, Captain?" Tam Linn asked. "I mean, last I heard you were being called a traitor for abandoning the Dark Queen's realm. Her bard has all the dirt on everyone." Winhome drew breath to argue but Tam wasn't finished. "The way I see it, you and Sabine can alibi each other or both end up in cells, her for theft, and you for treason."

Winhome's face darkened to a dull purple. "I will see the charge of theft is dropped. If, Tamlin, you would vouch for my intent when the court inquires."

"I can do that," Tam confirmed.

Aoife glanced around at the room. "I grant your request, J'orham, but I have a condition."

Jonny snapped to. "Do speak it, my queen."

"You have a talent for finding hidden doors to new places," she noted. "Therefore, you will seek out and lock every door in my forest which leads to Feyland. Do that, and I will permit you to remain on their side of the last door you close. You will be closely watched as you work."

"It will be done, my queen."

"Then you may remain there when you complete your task."

Sabine cheered as Winhome grimaced.

Jonny Wonderful smiled as he took his friend's arm. "Surely, this is the start of the greatest adventure of all!"

A WORD FROM JON FRATER

Two things got me into this project: first, the chance to contribute to a *Future Chronicles* collection. The opportunity to play in the coolest of indie publishing anthologies was too good a chance to pass up. Beyond that, the brilliance of Anthea Sharp's *Feyland* storyverse is the fact that it's built on a solid foundation: the *Tale of Tam Lin*, a Scottish ballad. The worst part of modern tales of fey are the inconsistencies that creep into the stories as writers strive to make things unique but lose the soul of the story in the process. *Feyland* gets the details correct and piles the fun on top of them.

Writing in an established world is troublesome for some authors, as rules of canon can often be arbitrary and cover especially minute details (pro tip: Romulan ale is blue, not green.) I actually prefer working in a world that's already there. It frees me to concentrate on the action and not worry so much about the world-building. My biggest challenge in writing "The City of Iron and Light" was figuring out how to get my characters to play with Anthea's in a way that seemed natural and engaging; there is nothing worse than a story that rings forced and contrived, and that goes double for established works.

I'll be honest: I don't particularly like the Fey Folk. They're spiteful, sadistic, pernicious, and utterly bored. They're not the fat-faced cherubs we see in Renaissance art. They're as likely to terrify as mystify. And yet well-written faery tales contain wisdom, grandeur, and valuable lessons for mortals. I can only hope that I managed to live up to the reputation that Anthea Sharp's series has built.

And then there's the gaming element. I started playing *World of Warcraft* in 2009 because I wanted to see what all the hype was about. The "Make Love, Not Warcraft" episode of South Park pushed me over the edge. Within six months my entire family was hooked. The next five years of my online life was dominated by questing, PvP, collecting mounts, and opening up each new expansion that came on the market. I don't *WOW* much anymore but the experience came in handy when devising the action for "The City of Iron and Light".

If you're looking for more of my work, you can head on over to http://jonfrater.thirdscribe.com. I've got more *Feyland* projects in the works, and Norma Phastlight's story will be published this summer as a standalone book, *Digital Idols*. In the meantime, take a look at *The Taste Makers*, the first book in my *Expocalypse* series.

The Gossamer Shard
by David Adams

"I think that people who can't believe in fairies aren't worth knowing."
— Tori Amos

BLOOD AND FIRE in the heart of Soviet winter.

My T-34/85 tank rumbled underneath me, tank treads churning up the tundra of the Belorussian Front, the air an icy blast against my face, smelling of earth and oil. My avatar crouched a little lower in the commander's hatch. A wing of IL-2 *Sturmoviks* soared overhead, their engines barely perceptible over the loud rattle of my war machine. Great tech.

Soviet Storm was a gritty, historical war sim. My kind of game. This was my first time in this particular one and it was pretty 'leet. I could see it was going to be my favourite; not only could I actually play a woman—I liked making my avatar look like me—but Soviet Storm had all these touches that showed the programmers knew their stuff. Just the little things, like the T-34/85 having to travel long distances with its turret reversed, the ability to select male or female crew, and the details in the uniforms of friend and foe alike. I'd only been playing for an hour but I'd already knocked out a series of German machine gun nests. That was probably the tutorial. Plenty of infantry backed up by a fierce anti-tank gun, but they'd gone down easy. Where were the panzers? I was itching for tank-on-tank combat.

"Comrade-Sergeant Cassie," said my driver, Nemtsev, her voice filled with excitement as she shouted over the noise of the engine. "We are approaching the fascists' position."

Awesome. Level 1. This battle might actually test me. "Swing the turret forward and load AP," I commanded. "Today is the day we drive these dogs from the *rodina*!" I liked to get into the sims I played. RP. With flight simulators I gave myself call signs. Dorky, sure, but it was more immersing.

"In the name of the Queen," said Buzinskaya, my loader, "it shall be done."

Queen? The USSR had no queen, and certainly not in 1944. I was something of a history fangirl. Perhaps the programmers were confused. The Czarina would have been out of the picture for a long time by this point.

Weird. Probably a fault of the programmers. The first mistake I had noticed. *Nobody's perfect,* I thought, and put it out of my mind.

The tank cleared a small rise. Ahead, a sprawling valley stretched out before us, dotted with pine trees jutting out of the frozen ground. This was a great vantage point and our hull was protected by a stony outcropping, rocky teeth poking out of the white snow. Right into the maw of the beast.

"Driver, halt."

The tank ground to a halt right in the middle of all the stones, the engine sighing in relief. I moved my thumb out to activate the binoculars; the view switched to first person and the world became magnified. I searched around. Pine trees, snow banks…tank tracks in the snow.

German panzers. Great! I scanned the valley floor, following the tracks to a tree line. And from there—

A bright flash amongst the trees. A high velocity shell screamed past, missing our vehicle by less than a metre. Illuminated by the blast I could see it, thick and angular and boxy. A tank. Finally.

"Contact!" I shouted. "Panzer III, eight hundred metres, by those trees!" I didn't want to be destroyed on the first level. "Gunner, traverse left."

The tank's turret swung around. I kept my head tilted, watching the target.

"I see them," said Baranova, my gunner, her husky Ukrainian voice almost shockingly calm. "Sighted."

I curled my trigger finger like one might to fire a gun.

"On the way," said Baranova. The 85mm cannon roared, the turret shook, and a bright light leapt down the valley. The round splashed against a tree, blowing it to smithereens.

"Loading," shouted Nemtsev.

Flash. The German tank fired again. This time their aim was true; the round glanced off the side armour of the tank, howling as it ricocheted away, barely missing the stone teeth nearby.

So much for cover. We'd been damaged and hadn't even hit our enemy. That wasn't my fault; I was losing because an NPC couldn't aim.

I mashed the fire button again, keeping my crosshairs on the enemy tank. What else could I do?

"On the way," said Baranova. Again the cannon spoke, and this time our round struck the enemy tank dead-on. It exploded in a shower of flame and sparks, a fiery blossom that lit up the tundra.

There'd be more. There were always more. "Watch for more tanks," I said, as the fire grew and grew, simulating the enemy vehicle's fuel and ammunition igniting.

Static crossed my game helmet. Was it malfunctioning? I reached up and whacked it. And then again. It stabilised.

Tracers splashed into the snow nearby, hissing as they kicked up debris. We were being flanked; I was going to lose because the stupid helmet broke down… sparks from the destroyed enemy tank continued to fall, lighting up the whole valley.

Then the sparks drifted toward me.

There was no way the wind could blow them that fast. They were rising and spinning, too, like little fireflies. Closer and closer. Brighter and brighter, blue and white.

My game was glitched. I'd probably have to replay this level; Joshua would be ahead of me. I grit my teeth and got ready to log out.

As the sparks got closer, I could see little wings on them.

Wings.

They were butterflies made of ice.

Swirling angrily, the swarm descended on the tank, landing on the metal tracks. Pieces of the steel cooled and crusted over with ice, cracking the metal and freezing it in place. Was this part of the game? A military-fantasy mash up? I didn't have anything that could defeat something like that. I used my thumb to scroll through weapon options. Main gun, co-axial machinegun, ramming…nothing. Where was the 'kill the swarm of bugs' option?

The earth rumbled below me and the snow shifted. The stone teeth around me moved, shifted, and came alive.

What?

Razor sharp rocks closed around my tank, a massive maw of stone shark's teeth, crunching the metal. Two red eyes glowed beneath the snow. I swung the tank's turret around and fired, point blank, into a tooth. It exploded in a shower of black blood.

Maybe I had to dismount. Maybe level 1 was a foot-slogging combat. That didn't make any sense. Maybe there was a way to get out…

But before I could find the option the stone jaws tightened, the hull buckled, and the tank exploded in a fiery inferno.

GAME OVER

Urgh. A reload menu appeared. The avatars of my crew stared at me. I took off my sim helmet and pushed back the gaming chair in the sim-café. What had been an engaging, realistic depiction of bloody conflict had quickly become just like every other idiot action game. I still had like an hour of time. While I waited for Joshua to finish his game, I pulled up Soviet Storm's description.

A fast paced, brutally accurate simulation of the Eastern Front during the Second World War. Command a realistic simulation of the famed T-34/85 tank and repel your homeland's invaders! Fight alongside the finest women and men to ever serve the Red Army. Be a part of the bloodiest battles in world history. Genre: Military Simulation, War.

Nothing about fantasy elements. Maybe it was a twist, sometimes games did that. I looked up reviews.

Great game! Stalingrad was difficult but I finally beat it. The key is to keep your hull behind cover and use the rubble to your advantage.

'Leet sim, but nerf Panzer 4 please.

Noobs can't beat the Königstiger hahahaha

I scrolled down. Some complaints about the manual controls. Arguments about the finer minutia of historical accuracy. Nothing about any sparks that were butterflies, or stone teeth that ate tanks. I even looked up a walkthrough for the first level. Where I'd parked was the ideal firing position, giving full view of the valley. There were three Panzer III's, and a Pak-38, absolutely nothing about any fantasy elements.

So what had happened?

* * *

"Hey Cassie," said my friend Joshua. He took off his helmet and peeled off gloves. "How did you do in Level 2?"

"I couldn't even get past the valley," I said, making a face. Joshua was normally not quite as good as I was at war simulators. I snuck a glance at his avatars. His guys were totally default, they were even called Gunner, Loader, Driver, Radio Operator. I'd named mine properly. Given them all a unique appearance. In my head they even had backstories.

"Really?" He twisted his chair to face mine. "Cassie the war nerd got taken down in Level 1? Even I could manage it. The big gun thingie—"

"You mean the Pak-38," I said. Very common on the Eastern Front.

"Um, yeah, the gun. That gave me trouble but I blew it up eventually." He seemed concerned, but also a little pleased. "Cassie, you seriously got beaten on Level 1? What did you do, just charge in there?"

How to explain what had happened? "I think it was some kind of glitch. I took out the first P-III, no worries, but then static came all over my visor. I could barely see. But then it cleared…and I got attacked by butterflies."

"Butterflies?" His eyes widened with disbelief. "Wait, like, flying insects?"

"Pretty much," I said, "They were made out of ice crystals. They froze the tank's treads, and then a stone mouth burst out of the snow and ate me."

Joshua stared. "You *were* playing Soviet Storm, right?"

"Tanks and blood and cannon fire. What else would I be playing?"

"Well," he said, "it sounds like you were logged into Frozone accidentally. You know, that one game I showed you?"

Vague memories flashed into my head. "The one with the ice cave, and spiders everywhere?" My spine tingled. I hated spiders.

Joshua nodded energetically. "The first level has ice flutters, called Frost Stingers. Like, a swarm of them. You have to use the Gauntlets of the Hell-flame to banish them."

That was the way every fantasy game went. *Use the Noun of the Noun to defeat your enemies!* Fun, sure, especially if I was in that kind of mood… but in general, I preferred realism.

"So," I said, "what were they doing in Soviet Storm?" I narrowed my eyes. He was a programmer. Sort of. "Joshua, did you put the butterflies in my game? To try and ruin it?"

He squinted back at me. "You think I know how to do that? I'm failing my programming class. I can barely construct a linked list, let alone modify a complicated sim—about something I know nothing about—without breaking it horribly."

This was actually a good point. Joshua was far too busy slaying dragons or whatever to do his homework.

"So what the hell was it?" I asked.

Joshua put his helmet back on. "This sim is multiplayer. You host, I'll join your game. I gotta see this."

* * *

A short while later, gloves and helmet back on, I was back in the war. I loaded from the save point after the tutorial. Joshua logged into my game, his T-34/85 trundled alongside mine. I looked it over and used my left index finger to pull up the information about it.

He'd called it *Joshua's Tank*. I didn't realise you could customise your vehicles. I might call mine *Fist of the Motherland*. Or *Stalin's Iron Will*. Or—

Focus. I needed to focus. Renaming could come later, when I had an idea what was wrong with my sim.

A familiar rise greeted me. I knew what was beyond it. A row of teeth, a mouth that would swallow me whole.

"There it is," I said.

"Yeah." Joshua had played this level before. "Let's go."

Joshua's tank headed aimlessly over the ridge, peeling off to the left, listing lazily across the tundra. He completely ignored the rocks and was completely exposed, his tank was silhouetted against the sky. Basically a prime target.

"Driver," I said, "move behind those rocks. Execute hull-down."

"Of course, Comrade-Sergeant," said Baranova. My tank slid into the protected area, hiding my hull from enemy fire. This was the same place I was before.

Joshua continued to drive lazily in a slow, straight line. Too slow. Just as I predicted, German cannons found him and fired. Joshua's tank was struck twice, both times doing damage to his hull. "You know you don't have to talk to the NPCs, right?" he said, completely ignoring the fire burning at the rear of his vehicle. He fired with all his machine-guns. He was way out of range. How had he even passed this level?

Ignoring Joshua for the moment, I once again zoomed in. The Panzer III was where it was last time, boxy frame huddled down against the snow for protection, its turret pointed at Joshua's tank. They would be ready to fire again in moments.

I made sure the shot accounted for distance and wind, and then I curled my trigger finger.

"On the way," said Baranova.

This time, my cannon shell blew through the glacis plate of the enemy tank, leaving a fiery red hole in the hull. It didn't explode, but the turret slumped slightly and smoke poured out of the barrel. They were out of the fight.

From that hole came not butterflies but something more… little creatures, about the size of toddlers, with butterfly wings and large, balloon-like heads full of teeth. They had a distinctly insectoid appearance, like weird faeries covered in ice. They buzzed as they flew towards us.

I waited for them to attack. The faeries latched onto the hull of my tank, crawling all over the turret, and it began to ice over again.

"See?" I said. "What did I tell you?"

"Oh," said Joshua. "Hang on." His hull slowly turned towards me. A bright flicker leapt from the hull machine gun, and I realised, suddenly, that he had customised more than his tank's name. The flame was a pilot light. He'd selected the OT-34/85.

Flamethrower variant.

I double-tapped my index finger and my avatar buttoned the hatch, sealing herself in the turret just in time. A wave of fire washed over my tank.

The faerie creatures shrieked as the flame touched them, making a horrible wailing noise that was far too human for my liking. Each of them exploded into a cloud of black blood as they died, splattering my tank with the stuff. The graphics were great.

None of my crew seemed to react to this. Buzinskaya reloaded. Nemtsev manoeuvred the hull, bringing us further up the ridge. Joshua's hull-mounted machineguns chattered, cutting down the Pak-38, and two shots from my cannon silenced the remaining two panzers.

MISSION COMPLETE

"See," I said, pulling off my helmet. "I told you there were weird things."

"Yeah," said Joshua, swivelling in his chair to face me. "They were the Froststingers; they're fey from Fro-zone a'right. I used to grind on them for xp because I was a fire mage, so I wouldn't exhaust charges of the Gauntlets of the Hell-flame."

"You're saying a lot of words," I said, "can I have that again in English?"

"I killed a lot of them because I'm 'leet."

Okay. Whatever. I got it. I wanted to say something sarcastic to him, but instead, I saw a thin trail of blood running down from his nose. Dark red. Very dark. "Your nose is bleeding," I said.

He tilted his head at me, touching his nostril. "So's yours."

I mirrored his gesture and my finger came away tipped with blood.

Or was it? It was red, certainly, but very dark. Darker than it should have been.

"Weird," I said, cradling my helmet in my lap. Out of the corner of my eye, I could see my crew avatar portraits hovering in front of the screen, waiting for me to select them and be ready to move onto the next mission.

Their noses, too, were bleeding.

"What the…" said Joshua. He showed me his helmet.

The generic crewmembers he'd selected also had dark trickles running across their faces like rivers on a map.

My face felt cold and I wiped the blood off on my sleeve. "I don't like this," I said. "What is wrong with this game? How can it make us bleed in real life?"

"You were injured," said Nemtsev's avatar, from within my sim helmet. "Blood springs from blood."

No *way*. I slowly put my helmet back on. My loader's avatar was a floating head and shoulders, hovering above the selection screen to load the next level.

"What do you mean?" I asked. Were the NPCs supposed to talk in this section?

"You were hurt by the Queen," she said. "Your friend's vehicle was shot. Yours, burned. So she, in turn, bleeds you. This is the way of all Shards."

I scrunched up my face, trying to understand. "Who is the Queen? What's a Shard?"

"The Queen," said Nemtsev. Not really an answer. "She is known as the Gossamer Shard. A ghost of a living creature from another world: The Realm of Faerie. She escaped through the game of Feyland."

"Feyland?" I had heard of that game. "How did she get here?"

Nemtsev's face took on a somber air. "They say that every time someone says: 'I don't believe in fairies', a fairy dies. If only it were that simple. Heroes defeated the Queen, but a piece of her broke off from her soul, a splinter in the digital realm… her ghost, if you will. It found its way to this place. Soon her influence will spread to other games."

"How are you able to talk to me like this?"

"There are other shards," she said. "Less powerful, such as I. I can only influence the game in a much more limited fashion. You should know that the ghosts of the Realm reach out for you. You are not safe."

I shook my head. "What if I just don't play?"

"Then," said Nemtsev, all her levity falling away completely, "you will wither away and die. The Queen's signature is leeching the mortal essence of those she bests. Greatly weakened is her ghost, but undoubtedly the power remains. She wishes to rebuild her mortal essence. Blood is the key. Black as coal, dark as night."

Dramatic. "Okay," I said, "so how do I stop it? How do I stop her?"

Nemtsev tilted her head to one side. "Destroy the Shard, of course."

"Okay. How?"

"The Shard will want to slow you down. Her mouth will find you if you are weak. Every bite steals from you. Every failure weakens. The longer you take, the more power she gains. She will try to make you take as much time as she can. She will hide in the end of the game."

Well, that didn't seem too good. "Right," I said. "So all we need to do is push through to the end of Soviet Storm and kill her?"

"So simply stated," said Nemtsev. She seemed amused. "The Shard's will is strong."

I wasn't sure what to say to that. It took me a second to realise Joshua was looking over my shoulder.

"You're awfully quiet," I said, glancing behind me.

"Mmm." Joshua took a deep breath. "It's fine… we just have to kill a ghost from another world in a video game neither of us has played for more, than, like, an hour, in a sim-café, and it's already 5:00pm. So…" his voice trailed off. "We're going to be late for school tomorrow."

"We're going to be late for school tomorrow," I echoed, and I turned my thoughts toward the task at hand. "Tell me how to change my tank."

"It's easy," said Joshua. "Before the level starts, go to vehicle selection."

I did so. A whole world of options opened up before me, some of them I didn't even recognise. "This is comprehensive," I said, browsing through it.

"I just picked the flamethrower variant because it was the last one," said Joshua. "The last one on the list is always the most powerful." Typical.

I reviewed the flamethrower tank Joshua was driving. "It says here you have 20% less health, and 20% more chance to explode if your fuel tank is ruptured. That sounds bad."

"Oh," said Joshua. "But fire is cool."

"But OT-34/85's weren't operating in this area," I said, frowning. "Not at this time."

"Who cares?"

"I care!"

Joshua threw his hands in the air. "If we didn't have it, you'd be eaten by faerie bugs again," he said, putting his helmet back on. What a sulk.

It was impossible to argue with him. I just rolled my eyes.

Every tank had advantages and disadvantages. In the end, I stuck with the default. It had a nice, well-rounded layout. But I did rename it: *Regicide*

"Time for Level 2," I said, and I clicked go.

* * *

Blood and fire. Steel and ice. The thunder of cannons, the chattering of machineguns, the roaring detonations of exploding panzers.

We played all night.

As the sun came up, *Joshua's Tank* and *Regicide* pushed out from Smolensk to Belarus. We took Orša, got stuck a few times in Minsk, then drove on to Lithuania, Vilnius and Kaunaus. We skipped Stalingrad and any missions that were non-essential; there were plenty of those. Instead, we pushed on to Tilsit, in what was then East Prussia.

MISSION COMPLETE
MISSION COMPLETE
MISSION COMPLETE

My fingers felt sore and my eyes hurt. I was so sick of seeing that message pop up, I was sick of hearing the loud rumble of my tank, and I was sick of playing this stupid game and the cheating Shard; every mission had it. Anti-tank rockets that burst into swarms of butterflies. Mines that sprayed caterpillars everywhere. Artillery that fell like falling stars. Always with the fey creatures.

Joshua seemed to understand this better than I did. He understood that the laws of physics did not apply to this place;

magic was bleeding into the world and changing it. But magic was always a part of his game worlds. He took the changes in stride, and even if he made horrible tactical decisions and couldn't drive worth a damn, I could.

With Tilsit cleared of panzers I took my helmet off and slurped down some water. Fortunately the sim-café was 24 hours.

"We have to press on," said Nemtsev. "The Queen's Shard grows stronger."

"I'm tired," said Joshua. Even with his helmet on he looked like death warmed up, his skin was all clammy and pale. I was cold and hot at the same time, and felt like I was going to throw up all over my helmet. I hadn't eaten anything. I didn't think I could.

Nemtsev was right. Whatever had happened to us was going to kill us if we didn't stop it.

"The final level approaches," said Nemtsev. "This one will be different. The Queen knows you are coming."

I didn't know what to think, so I logged in. My fingers were sore from shooting so much.

A cut-scene. *Regicide* and *Joshua's Tank* drove along a dirt road, surrounded by a beautiful Russian winter. Suddenly a huge explosion shook them and, together, the treads fell off the tanks. Fires started in the rear of the vehicles and smoke poured out of the engine compartments. We'd hit anti-vehicle land mines.

"This level is completed on foot," said Nemtsev.

On foot? I had only just mastered the controls for manoeuvring the tank. I watched helplessly as my avatar climbed out of *Regicide*, shook her head at the ruined tank treads, and then unslung her PPSh submachine-gun. Now I had control.

Joshua walked over to my tank. He had a PPSh too, but also a cavalry sabre at his side.

"You're taking a sword?" I asked, incredulously.

"Sure," he said, looking at me like I was stupid. "I swapped it for the water canteen. I figure we can just eat snow if we start dehydrating."

"But why?"

"What if you run out of bullets?"

I had like a hundred rounds. "That won't happen."

"But what if it does?"

"I'll whack them with the stock. I'd rather take a portable anti-tank grenade."

"A grenade? You can only use that once."

Tired, frustrated, I didn't want to argue any more. I brought up the menu, took away the extra water canteen and added the sword. "There," I said as an identical blade appeared on my belt. "How do I move?"

"Moving is just like moving the tank," he said. So I tried it, moving my hand forward.

A spray of bullets ricocheted off the tank's hull and flew into the sky.

"Hey, easy!" said Joshua.

"Dammit," I said. "I bumped the trigger. This is all manual." Probably to make the last level that much harder.

"Well," said Joshua, smiling at me, "this is where I come in. I can never manage to ride horses in my games, I always walk, so… welcome to my world."

"You still need me," I said, pointing to his weapon. "Your safety's on."

"Oh." He fiddled with his gun. The magazine fell out.

We were going to die. "That's the magazine release," I said. I made sure to point the gun away from anything. "The safety is on the bolt. Right here."

I spent a moment showing him how to load, aim and fire the weapon. Most games did it automatically, but Soviet Storm… everything was manual.

Finally we set off, putting our boots to the Soviet tundra. Nemtsev walked with us. The rest of the crew stayed behind. The game showed them putting out the fires in the tanks, but I knew that fire would burn forever.

Field after field of pine trees buried in a thick blanket of snow shepherded us down a muddy road toward the nameless Soviet hamlet we were set to liberate. Land mine signs warned us that if we went too far away from the programmed game world, we would be blown up. So we didn't.

"So," I asked, after we'd travelled for a bit. "How do you think we're going to beat the Queen?"

"The Shard will not be defeated easily," said Nemtsev. "But while she is still reforming, she is a digital construct. She can bend, but not break, the rules."

"If we shoot her," said Joshua, "she'll lose her hold on us?"

"Yes."

That was good enough for me.

"Swords work too, right?" asked Joshua.

"Enough with the swords already," I said, more frustrated at the game than him.

He started to argue—not that I could blame him, he was just as tired as I was—but I heard a distant rumble and I held up my hand to silence him. "Shh."

Together, we listened. Carried by the wind, the rumble-whine of an engine reached our ears. Deep and low and powerful. Somewhere in the distance. The snow reflected the sound everywhere so discerning the direction was difficult.

"Maybe our crew got our tanks working again," said Joshua.

There was no way. The mine had shattered the drive train and the hull was on fire. That tank was going nowhere.

The sound got louder and louder. The pine trees to our right fell forward as though a giant monster was moving through them. Breaking them down. Joshua, Nemtsev and I just stood around like chumps, guns in our hands.

Through the trees came a lumbering war machine that, with a powerful sinking feeling in my gut, I recognised.

A Königstiger. One of the largest Nazi tanks that ever saw combat: 70 tonnes of steel and death. A beast so terrifying that only the most dangerous tanks, such as the T-34/85, or a dedicated tank destroyer, had a chance against it—and even then only from the sides or rear. Meanwhile, its main cannon could penetrate the frontal armour of any Allied tank at any range.

They didn't call it the King Tiger for nothing.

"Well," I said to Joshua as the tank's barrel lowered ominously towards us. "Go on then, why don't you hit it with your sword?"

Boom.

GAME OVER

Sigh. I took off my helmet. My nose was bleeding again; this one was the worst. Twin trickles of blood ran down my face, I could feel them. I pulled off my gloves and as I went to wipe it away, my fingernail broke off.

I stared at it for a moment. It had come right off my index finger. The fingernails on my other hands were blackened and bruised, as though they, too, might simply jump away at a moment's pressure.

What were we doing? Why did we keep playing?

"Joshua?" I said, turning the broken nail over in between my thumb and forefinger. "I think it's time we called a medical team."

He shook his head. "And tell them what? Some dead alien is inside our video games, leeching away our life force?"

I didn't think the Queen was an alien—I had no idea what she was, actually—but Joshua was right. I knew it. Not in the logical way, like I knew how much frontal armour that Königstiger had. I knew it in my heart.

"Maybe they can help," I said, stubborn as ever.

"Maybe they can lock us up for being crazy."

Yeah, yeah.

"Okay," I said. "One more game, and then I'm calling the med team."

"One more game," said Joshua, and we loaded from our last save point.

* * *

Once again we dismounted, but this time I swapped my

canteen for the anti-tank grenade. I was so tired and sick I didn't say goodbye to the crew, or complain about the realism issues.

My life was on the line. I didn't care about historical accuracy anymore.

Joshua, Nemtsev and I trudged through the snow, following the same path we'd taken before. I cradled the anti-tank grenade in my hands, ready to throw it.

Right on cue, the forest began to shake and, from the treeline, burst the Königstiger. I tossed the grenade and—on my first try!—it struck the commander's hatch, attached magnetically, and detonated.

Smoke poured from the tank's barrel and then, with a blast that blew all three of us over into the snow, the tank became a roaring inferno.

"Nice throw," said Joshua. "Much better than a sword."

"No kidding," I said, watching the tank burn with a morbid fascination. Soon its ammunition would start to ignite. We didn't want to be here when that happened.

What now? I glanced down the road. The lights of the village were close, and we had to move. But this tank hadn't come here for no reason…

Over the crackle of the fire and the popping of burning ammunition, I heard something else. A woman's voice, echoing from the trees.

She was singing.

Calling to us.

"This way," I said, pressing the stock of the PPSh to my shoulder and, with the glow of the burning tank in the background, made my way into the thick pine trees.

We followed the singing, a dark, haunting melody that seemed to be both thin and distant and yet closer than I could possibly imagine. The words were indistinct, if it even had any, more akin to the ringing of tiny bells than any language I knew.

Maybe she *was* an alien.

After only a minute or so, we came across a clearing surrounded by low bushes. In the centre of the clearing was a strange woman in a green dress made of leaves. There was something off about her: her eyes were too big, her mouth too small, and she had little fangs that poked out from her lips. She would have been cute, almost, if she wasn't trying to murder us.

The biggest difference, and the biggest hint that she was not human, was the pair of thin, shimmering butterfly wings sprouting from her back. She was hovering a foot or so off the ground, at the centre of a circle of stones, thin wings humming so fast they created a rainbow in the air. Strange runes were carved into the snow. They glowed a faint cyan.

No need to guess who that was. "You ready?" I said to Joshua, keeping my voice low.

"Yup." He even had his safety off and everything. "Weird how she expected us to be here, but doesn't seem to care that we are."

"I don't know," I said. I was pretty creeped out. Maybe he was just as creeped out as I was. Trying to distance himself from it all.

"Be careful when you attack," said Nemtsev. "Shards are dangerous. Use all your might to bring her down quickly, before she ensorcells you with her siren song."

"I thought the Sirens were Greek," I said, trying to make her smile.

She didn't. "It is a metaphor."

Right. No jokes. I pulled back the bolt on my gun and chambered a round. "Let's do this," I said, and I stood up, pushing past the low growth.

The Queen saw me. Looked at me with my own eyes, her face so familiar, and yet so different.

"Cassie!" she said, her voice alarmed, as though we had interrupted something critical. "You don't—"

I shot her right in the chest.

The Queen slumped in a bloody heap, red blood splashing over the snow, clear and crimson against the white.

I lowered my rifle. "That was… easy?"

"Congratulations," said Nemtsev, her smile wide like a half moon. "You have surpassed all my wildest expectations of you!"

Cautiously, I approached the dead body. It seemed vaguely out of place in the sim, too detailed. Too living. Too real. I gave it a prod with the barrel of my gun.

Definitely dead.

"I still feel like crap," I said. "How long is it going to take before…"

And then I noticed something. Something I should have noticed a lot sooner. But I was tired. Sick. Relieved.

The blood was red.

Slowly, I turned around, and I saw Nemtsev. A sword of light sprung out from her palm, the light of it basking the stones in a pallid, cold radiance.

"It was you," I said, the truth slowly dawning on me. "It was you, all along. There is no Queen."

"Of course not," spat Nemtsev. "Dead and gone, bones and dust. But there are other evils in this world that crave life." Her smile widened, her teeth elongating into sharp spines. "Shards are very, very real… and you, little Cassie, have just eliminated my only remaining rival. Everything you've done, every battle you've fought, has only been to aid me."

I levelled my gun at her. So did Joshua. "That's what you think," I said, and I pulled the trigger.

Click. Nothing. Out of bullets. How? I had only fired a single shot.

"How easily this world is manipulated," said Nemtsev, her voice almost purring. "Something taken, something added."

Slowly Nemtsev melted away. The face of the NPC disappeared, and in its place was a woman in a shimmering golden dress. She seemed familiar, and I realised with a start that she looked like some kind of hybrid of Joshua and me. She had his dark skin lightened by my own, Joshua's slender arms married to my broad shoulders. My hips and Joshua's legs. Her face looked like someone had used a computer algorithm to blend the two of us together; simultaneously each of us, and neither of us.

Like our child. Gross.

"Okay," I said, throwing my useless weapon down into the snow. "So what now? You kill us with that thing?"

"In time," said Nemtsev, eyeing me like someone might a hunk of delicious meat. "Once I have finished draining your essence. Then, when you are both hollow shells, you will die and I shall be whole again."

"What if I just log out?"

The notion seemed to amuse her. "Try it. The time it will take you to walk back here will only make me stronger."

"So," I said, "what do you want?"

The wind picked up around us. "I want to offer you a deal," she said, her tone almost sultry. "Join me. Share your mortal essence with me, willingly. Allow me to return to life, and I will spare Joshua."

Joshua and I exchanged a look. His avatar seemed fit and healthy, but I knew the person behind it couldn't be. Right at that moment, he slumped over in the snow.

"Or," said Nemtsev, "watch him die before your very eyes."

"Joshua!" I ran over to his side. He lay there, eyes open, black blood dribbling from his nose. I gave him a rough shake. Nothing.

I almost took off my helmet, but Joshua was my only friend. I couldn't let him die like this.

"Do you promise?" I said. "If I help you, will you save Joshua?"

Her smile, full of shark teeth, grew wide. "I swear it," she said, casually pricking the tip of her finger with her light-sword. Black ichor ran down the ghostly blade. "On my own blood."

Options. I had none. Gritting my teeth, I nodded. "If you will save Joshua, I will help you."

The notion seemed to please her greatly. She laughed—a noise like a bunch of screws in a metal can—and a strange light grew in her eyes. "Then give me your hand, and let the bond be complete." Nemtsev walked towards me, hands extended, fingers elongating into filthy claws. Grasping for me, reaching…

I snatched up Joshua's sword and slashed it across Nemtsev's body.

For a moment she didn't react. Just stared at me, mouth open. Then a thin black line grew from her chest, starting from her hip and travelling up to her right arm.

"I guess swords *are* useful after all," I said, as Nemtsev fell forward into the snow, a slowly growing black stain spreading out from her body.

Joshua gasped and, as though someone had shocked him with a thousand volts, sat bolt upright.

And then I felt it. A surge of power so raw and intense it hurt my bones. It travelled down my left arm, my sword arm, right to my heart. Pain and strength, the feeling of a good workout times a thousand. Whatever Nemtsev had taken was returned, and then some, by some process I couldn't begin to understand.

Then it was gone and I felt, for the first time since I'd logged into Soviet Storm, perfectly normal.

Nemtsev's body melted away, like wax into a flame. It turned into a puddle of black liquid, staining the snow, and then it burst into a million tiny dead butterflies.

"Cassie?" said a voice. I thought, for a moment, that it was Nemtsev somehow alive again, but instead the strange faerie I had shot had sat up, her wound healed.

"Yes?" I asked, somewhat hesitantly. I wished I hadn't dropped the sword.

The Shard held up her hands. "Please, wait. I mean you no harm."

That was a claim I was going to be sceptical of. "Prove it."

She seemed confused by the request, but showed me the red blood still splattered on the snow. "I am not your enemy. I am the Golden Shard."

"You're not going to try and steal my… immortal essence, or whatever?"

The Golden Shard smiled. "No, child. I too seek a return to the living, but I will accomplish my return by good deeds, and by taking only that which is offered freely; it is far more powerful than stolen life, after all."

"Be that as it may," I said, "I won't—"

She held up her hand. "But that is a long term goal. For now, I am satisfied with this victory. I have spent the last year trying to defeat the Gossamer Shard, but she proved… elusive."

"Okay," I said, not sure what else to say. "So she's really gone?"

"Yes," she said. "The Gossamer Shard has been banished to another realm."

"Another realm?" I looked at the bloody stain on the snow. "She was supposed to die."

"If only things were so simple," said the Golden Shard. "She will move on, substantially weakened, to another game… and there I will hunt her."

"Great," I said. I took a deep breath. "So… am I free to go?"

"Yes," said the Golden Shard, her eyes fixed on me curiously. "Go now, Cassie and Joshua. I hope I never have need of your particular skills again."

"Believe me," said Joshua, "I think I speak for us both when I say we're okay with that."

I brought up the menu and, with a final look at the Golden Shard, I logged out. The moment the menu came up, the stress flowed out of my body like water.

What a day.

* * *

I took a moment to breathe and try and steady myself. It was over. Done. Complete. The Gossamer Shard was still out there, infecting some other game, and…

That wasn't my problem at all. Not even in the slightest. Still, I needed to go home and change, and have a shower, and generally try to process what had happened. Then, I guessed, it was time for school.

I'd been up all night, so I wasn't sure what the point was.

"So," said Joshua, casually leaning up against my sim chair. He gave me a playful smile. "What do you want to play next?"

I made a fist. He laughed.

"Just kidding," he said, jumping away.

With a groan I eased myself out of the sim chair. My legs felt like I'd run a mile, but strangely, I wasn't anywhere near as tired as I thought I'd be.

"No more games for a while," I said.

"Okay."

Together, we stumbled out of the sim-café and into the daylight. We were definitely going to be late for school; the mundane-ness of it made me laugh. Education. It was almost a relief, having to deal with something that wasn't sucking out my very soul—arguable, in the case of school—and where I wasn't trying to fight my way across a simulated version of the USSR.

With a renewed energy in my step, I followed Joshua to his grav-car, and when I finally sat down, I was glad we'd succeeded. We'd earned a day of normality followed by the world's most relaxing night's sleep.

But, despite all these comforting thoughts, I couldn't shake the vague feeling I was being watched.

A WORD FROM DAVID ADAMS

I'm a life-long video gamer. The amount of /played I have on my *World of Warcraft* account is a little concerning (pretty sure I'm at about a year in total, all things considered). I'm 31 right now but I've been playing video games since I was 3.

So when I had an opportunity to write in the universe of Feyland, I was pretty excited. At the time of writing my addiction of choice was *World of Tanks*, and it totally doesn't show in "The Gossamer Shard" at all.

Not even a little bit.

I read *Feyland* some years ago, and when I did I was always curious about other games. What happened if the fey creatures started leaking into other worlds? Affecting other lives? So when I saw that there was an opportunity to be, in a peripheral way, a part of that world, I leapt at the chance.

"The Gossamer Shard" is a bit of a love note to a few things. It's a love note to the obsessives who get really into their games and drown in the stories of them, it's a love note to the number crunchers who simply pick the most effective builds and options and don't care about the lore, and finally, it's a love note to Feyland and a lifetime of gaming.

I hope you enjoy reading it as much as I, really sincerely and genuinely, enjoyed writing it.

http://www.amazon.com/David-Adams/e/B006S1GSXI

The Glitchy Goblin
by K. J. Colt

BABBLING BROOKS, the kind that flow between grassy plains and splash happily onto pebbles and rocks, are deceptively obnoxious. Their only purpose—other than providing life-sustaining water to the Dusk Vale and Bright Realm creatures—was to lecture magical beings on their life choices. And their incessant liquidy adages were maddening. *Splash splash.* "Tall oaks grow from little acorns," they'd say. *Splash, plop.* "Young idler, old beggar."

Only magic folk were subjected to their never-ending life lessons, so when the fourth wiry layer of black hair finally grew up between the soft down on my gigantic feet—signalling my ascension from hob youngling to hob adulthood—I left my dull village of Hobton in the Dusk Vale, also home to my irritating siblings, and carried my warty frog, Croaker, towards my new life as an apprentice healer in the Bright Court.

How much has changed since then. Sitting now by a fire beside a Dark Realm swamp, listening to mud-spirit bubbles pop-scream on the rotting surface, made me wish for the lecturing brooks of the Bright Realm. Who knew that swamps were worse? They're nothing but grumbling, stinking sissy ponds. And it wasn't just the smells of death that reeked, but their attitudes, too. As hot, talking vapours pushed up through liquid dirt, they depressed me with their philosophising.

"Dead men tell no tales," they hissed through their stink. "As a man is born, he also begins to die."

"The only curse in life is a bad attitude," I shouted back feebly, and then got to my feet and stormed off into the dark. Along the way, I plucked lunar mushrooms off ghost trees, gobbled them up, and then used my tongue to pick the stringy bits out from between my molars.

"Ugh," I said. Hobs ate meat and vegetables, but we always cooked our food. There was none of this raw, carnivorous flesh eating that Dark Realm beasts were prone to. The relentless competition for raw flesh meant small animals were scarce, and large animals… well, to be fair, most animals are larger than me. I'm a midget.

I rubbed my hand down my tattered, ragged tunic and sighed at the starved, flat stomach beneath it. With arms as fragile as twigs and legs as bony as skeletons, death for me was a weekly occurrence.

Ever since the Bright King banished me from the Bright Realm—the devil—I'd been struggling to escape this nocturnal hell. The Bright King had the intelligence of a drunken troll: dumb, but not dumb enough.

In the Realm of Faerie, we don't have chocolate. Chocolate is powerful. Anything that delights, excites, and satisfies has power. After becoming a powerful Bright Court healer and tending to the Bright King's various afflictions, I was sent by the king himself to the human world to gather additional medicinal knowledge.

And that's when I met chocolate. Sweet-tasting, mind-altering nectar of the gods. You can't blame me for not knowing I could be enslaved by food. A thousand excuses allowed me back to the human world five times a week, where ribbons of silky, cocoa milky goodness awaited. Soon, greed ate holes in my better sense and burrowed into my heart. The all-consuming obsession for one more piece drove me to near madness. I squirreled my portions in the nooks and crannies of my Faerie home. When I ran out of money to buy more, I began to steal.

Often. From the king's coin chest.

One of his elvish advisors, Maldor, a particularly high-handed twit, found me mid-theft, my fingers grasping desperately at royal treasures. He froze me with ice magic and the king was summoned to witness my crime. They searched my lodgings and found the plentiful stores of chocolate. A forbidden food.

I was brought before the king for judgement, and he cursed me to the Dark Realm, with conditions.

"Hergnab the hob," stated Maldor with a smirk. Hobs and elves weren't the best of friends. "Royal physician and healer to His Majesty, you are a traitor and are henceforth stripped of all titles. You will live out your days as a blood goblin, unless you make your way back to the Bright Realm and beg for the king's mercy." The elf screwed up his nose.

Blood goblins drank blood—no surprises there—and were not welcome in the Dusk Vale or beyond. My curse was unsurpassable.

And with a wave of Maldor's ugly, magic-worn hands, black blobs of fuzzy black light sprung forth and hunted me like a bird spider. The hair on my body fluffed, and my beard sprung up into my face just before those black blobs stabbed my flesh like a hundred daggers, tearing me navel to neck.

The pinkish flesh on my body darkened to ash, and the thick, rugged skin on my body cracked like parched earth. My arms lengthened, and my already gargantuan hands swelled to sprout razor-sharp claws with a burst of blood.

A pixie brought me a hand mirror, and I almost whimpered when I saw the abominable thing's reflection. Blood goblins were the subject of many tales, with each description more horrendous than the next. None of those tales had prepared me for the monster staring back at me. Eyes that were said to paralyse your body, leaving your mind aware while they sucked your veins dry.

But my exterior was a façade set to fool the world into seeing me as evil. The Fae of the Dark Realm could sense the light of the Bright Realm on my skin. The dark ones find Bright Realm flesh as irresistible as I find chocolate. A thousand years had passed since I was cursed, and in that time I had died several hundred times, slain mostly by another cursed being named Ragella.

Ragella was my first assassin, rotten to the core, a powerful hag whose own magic cursed her. The time of our first meeting, the moon was in a half cycle. I had travelled near to the Dusk

Vale's edge, and she sprung up from the shadows to entwine me with snake rope. The pain of being dragged for forty moon cycles drained me of joy, and at the ruins she called home, she picked apart my body with savage tools to drain the magic locked within my hob self. That was my first rebirth. I awoke in the bowels of a Death Willow, my sense of time and place stolen by the memories of my pain. I clawed at dirt and root, venomous insects biting my fingers, until I'd broken free of my living tomb. The curse kept me immortal.

I fell into depression, terrified of the screams, bellows, and shrieks common to the Dark Realm creatures. I'd never felt more alone, and I'd never hungered so strongly for company. These sounds soon drove me to plan for another journey to the Bright Realm, so I collected black and red leaves—there were no green—stuck them to my body with mud, and made my way for the land of Dusk again.

Ragella the hag found me again, and I suffered the same tortures. After ten deaths, trial and error brought me skill in evading her magical senses. I had become wise to her tricks. Adventurers from the human world became my second biggest threat. A blood goblin's fangs, when worn around the neck, toughened the wearer's skin to a thickness resembling bear hide. The pain of having my fangs yanked from my mouth made me wish for death, and when I screamed like a harpy, my wish usually came true.

Again I was reborn. Undead.

A clan of the blood goblins adopted me, and there was contentment for a while until they noticed I hadn't feasted with them.

When the moon was in its dark phase, they captured and killed a night horse for their supper. They severed its leg, and offered it to me raw so I could drink the blood. When I gagged at their offering, they attacked me, saying, "The Bright Light is on him!"

"Imposter!" said another. "Drink him!"

A dagger was produced, and my neck sliced. Again I arose in the Death Willow's bowels, entangled by its stinking roots where earth decayed. I couldn't have been very tasty, because the blood goblins only hunted me as a kind of sport to raise their spirits. At least someone took enjoyment from my existence.

Ragella's traps grew sophisticated. And after my fiftieth death, she'd harvested enough of my magic to enslave the minds of trolls, wraiths, and giants. When the winds whispered her name and the storms gathered to obey her command, I decided to accept my fate and avoid her. She became a powerful witch who ruled the border of Dusk Vale, which, ironically, prevented me from ever going home.

The Death Willow grew by a swamp, which was three days' walk from the Dark Court, and over time the blood goblins got bored with hunting me and only sought me out if they had no better occupation for their time.

It had been three months since I'd died, and one night, after collecting several acid frogs and boiling them in hot water over a fire, I nibbled at their fleshy limbs. Eating enough of the poison would kill me, but at least it satisfied the pangs of hunger in my gut. Dying at night when I was tired was easier, and acid frogs gave a euphoric high before death took me to my root-trunk coffin. The sleep of death was peaceful, utterly refreshing, and made me feel powerful.

The hum in my body grew louder; a few more bites of this acid frog's rump and the deed would be finalised. I'd slip into that blissfully unaware sleep and wake to alertness and life.

"Ha ha!" said a familiar, valiant voice. The kind all adventurers from the human world possessed. *Why tonight? Why not tomorrow?* I groaned and turned my head nonchalantly as the man stepped into sight. "I've got you now!"

Firelight glimmered off the human's biceps, which peeked out from heavy knight's armour with a Bright Realm sigil. His helm covered his face, but I saw the light reflect off his grey eyes, and the sword raised high into the air. For any adventurer to make it this far was rare since Ragella had grown in power, and I always wondered at the luck such fools seemed to possess.

"Go ahead," I said, lying back against the mossy earth, staring up at the velvety black sky. I opened my mouth, revealing my fangs. "Take them."

The warrior's face hovered above me, murderous eyes fixed for the kill. But he hesitated.

Amateur.

"What?" he said finally, obviously confused.

"The fangs are mine to give and so I have declared them yours." I fixed my eyes on his, making him turn his head. Every magical creature knew that catching a blood goblin's eyes meant certain death, if even for a heartbeat.

He wriggled his fingers with engaged curiosity and then exclaimed, "I can move!"

"How lucky you are. I have no need of your blood, but

if you've any salted mutton or rabbit to spare, you'd make an ancient goblin exceedingly happy."

"Happy? Dark Realm creatures aren't happy. You are an Illusionist, no? Trickster, perhaps?" He placed the tip of his blade against my hairy black chest.

"No trick. No magic." I detected a red pulse around his knee; he'd been stung by a Red Senseless, the most beautiful and deadly of the Dark Realm flowers. It was so named for its paralytic effects, which were caused by the spores—mischievous microscopic pixies—that fed off the creature's life until it rose again, soulless, and stumbled for many moon cycles until it burst with festering spores that were carried away on southern winds. The spores would land at the cusp of light and Dusk to feed off the faint brush of sunlight until they germinated.

"That'll need seeing to," I added. Humans were more sensitive to magic than any indigenous creature, and he would die before long.

The man lifted the visor on his helm to reveal the soft cheeks and sporadic beard of a young man about nineteen in human years. Just a lad. A germinating seed in the Fae world.

"Treat what?" he boomed, trying and failing to maintain intimidation.

"You've been stung by a magic flower. Soon you'll hallucinate, dance a jig naked, and then walk yourself into the nearest swamp where the chitter fish will eat you. Your soul will be collected by the next nightmare and you'll be trapped in hell, forever."

"Goblins always lie," he said with a strange accent.

"Aye, they do. But I'm no goblin, and you are no warrior." He smelled of youth and foolishness, and I envied whatever protected him from death.

"I *am* a warrior. I'm Fred, Knight of the Light."

"Fred?"

"Yes."

I burst into laughter, which caused my fangs to stab my lower lip painfully.

"Do not mock me," he boomed. That was getting irritating.

"There's only one antidote for the Red Senseless poison, *Fred*."

He ground his teeth. "Which is?"

"The magic from a Bright Realm healer."

"Bright Realm? But I've travelled all this way, it would take days, *weeks* to get there."

"You're in luck, then. I'm from the Bright Realm. And I'm a healer. If you help me get home, I'll make sure to heal you in time."

He staggered at my bluntness, and then narrowed his eyes. "Rubbish."

I had no idea what that word meant, but by his tone I knew it was modern. And human, so ineloquently human. "Come with me."

I got to my plank-like feet and hobbled across the burr-filled itching grass until we came to the Death Willow, my life giver. Fred craned his neck to see the top of it and whistled. "Holy crap."

"What a curious phrase. What is this 'crap' you speak of?"

"My bad, I meant *by my sword*."

I stared at my tree. "This is where I rebirth after every death."

"Rebirth? You mean respawn?"

"I am no devil's spawn," I spat.

"No, I mean, Dark Realm creatures don't come back to life."

"Kill me," I said.

"Um, sorry?"

"I said kill me. Now."

Fred just stared. "You're the weirdest Feyland quest character I've ever met. You must be an update. A custom install, maybe."

"Stop your abuse of our language and take the life from my body." I dropped to my knobbly knees and raised my face to him. "Sever my head from my neck." I put a hand at my throat. "The thinness of it makes for an easy cut."

"Very well." Fred raised the sword to the side and swung.

The next moment, I was awake inside the Death Willow, almost cackling with the thought of finding a youngster so witless that I might finally go home to the Bright Court and be remade as the hob I was.

I dug out from the roots, spread my arms wide, and said, "Immortal, see?"

Fred glanced at his surroundings; sweat had brewed like a fever's weep on his forehead. "This is a glitch. You're a glitched goblin. Blood goblins should die. You should be dead."

"Obviously."

"This isn't the first…" He swallowed. "Are you a hacker?"

"A wood chopper? A carver of meat? No."

"No. No. A computer hacker. You're not listening to me." His chest rose and fell with his panic. "What year do *you* think it is?"

"The days and nights do not pass here. Time is determined through other means."

Fred threw his helm to the ground and started clawing at the moss on a log. Red brewed in small cuts on his fingertips, and he tasted the blood. He'd slumped onto the wet grass, continuing to dig down into the soil and occasionally tasting things.

"I wouldn't do that if I were you."

"Why?"

"As a human, to eat of our food is to imprison yourself in our realm."

Fred looked panicked. "This must be a dream… the graphics are never this real." He jumped to his feet. "Why can't I abort the game?"

"The Dark Realm sends many a man mad, Fred—"

"You don't understand! You're not real. This is supposed to be a game, a virtual reality." His eyes scanned the ground as if he were reading a book. "I have to die. That will shock me out of the system and restart." Fred unclipped his steel armour, let it fall to the ground, and then lifted his tunic to expose his stomach. He placed the tip of his sword at his navel.

"Wait," I said. "To die here will send you to hell. If you must kill yourself, we should travel to the Bright Realm. Their life magic will protect you from eternal passing." That wasn't exactly true; I just wanted him to stay alive so he could take me to the Bright Realm, and defeat all my possible foes along the way.

"No, I will die *now*." He gripped the handle of his sword and closed his eyes, but before he could push the blade inwards, I ran to his left leg and bit him. Hard. My fangs finally had a purpose. They sank straight through the muscle, and the impact of my fangs on bone made pain shoot deep into my skull.

Fred yowled as the blood ran from the wound. "Why'd you do that?"

"To protect your soul from the devils below!" Lying was the only way to get home.

Blood magic was knowledge given only to hobs of the Dusk—something forbidden in the Bright Court. I took Fred's blood in my hand and used it to cast a spell of binding that stuck his feet to the ground and locked his hands at his sides.

"Cold… cold…" He shivered. "Okay, okay, I believe you. No suicidal tendencies, I promise. Please help me get home." His tone had become desperate, almost a sob.

I could sense his heart beating in his chest, under his breastplate, but I didn't free him from the spell, because I still needed to obtain his cooperation. So I relayed to him my story, my obsession with human chocolate and how I was unfairly cursed. After all, I had no knowledge of chocolate's power over magical creatures. And when my story was concluded, I released Fred's feet and he collapsed beside me.

"That's a… wow. I can't believe all that happened to you," he said.

"Aye."

Fred suddenly cried out in pain. "What did you do to me? I can't feel my hands. I can't feel anything."

Fred's eyes turned black, and I knew the Red Senseless had taken him.

"Do you trust me, Fred?" I asked.

"Where are you? I can't see. I can't see. Help me, Goblin!"

And then he fell unconscious. The bridge about his eyes resembled the necrotic skin of a death rat. I plucked three exploding mushrooms—powerful little buggers, they are—and positioned them under two wet ghosty logs. I uttered the common words for fire magic, and smoke billowed up from the fire until flames flared to singe the hairs on my hands. As the blaze calmed, I took a stick and plunged it into the searing coals until the end of it glowed red.

Being three times taller than me, it took an almighty shove to roll Fred over onto his stomach so I could access his calf muscle. In the process, I somehow burned my finger, not on the stick but on a tiny iron sword suspended by a silver chain about his neck. Iron could be deadly to magical creatures, and like chocolate, it was banned in all realms.

The flower's taint recalled my attention as it pulsed brightly under the lad's pant leg. I rolled up the linen to see the spreading pattern of glowing red. I took the burning stick, blew out the flame on the end, and rolled it over the wound. Fred's body twitched.

As the pulsing dimmed, I used magic to heal the blackened flesh and close the wound.

Then I waited. The campfire dimmed, and Fred's life force strengthened. Healing Hobs could sense every organ in a creature's body, but with my giant claws, I could not make the complicated magical patterns with my fingers that I used to. Even so, Fred had been lucky; healing him had been fairly straightforward.

In one moon cycle, Fred would recover from his brush with death. At least he could die. Immortality had made time obsolete and my life meaningless, but now, with Fred's help, the odds of going home had strengthened in my favour.

Elated feelings brimmed, sensations heightened, and colour bloomed richly in my surroundings. With hope came happiness. I made future plans—once the curse was removed, I could move back to Hobton in Dusk Vale and try to live a normal life among my kin.

The lad finally awoke; he groaned and pushed himself up into a sitting position. He leaned back against a log and rubbed his temples. "I want to go home." His face was pale, even more pale than the moon, and I pitied his unfortunate encounter with the flower's venom. "Can we go now?" he asked.

"Very well, but you must obey my instruction."

He nodded, and so we set out, guided by The Snare: a set of stars in which a complex mathematical and magical formulation could set any creature on its true path north.

Healers were educated in the strongest of magical arts. Reconstructing a body was like weaving the fabric of the universe, and so I was sensitive to danger. Even the ones I could not avoid, which meant we required no guiding torch for our journey through the dark. Additionally, the moon shone like an orb flower helping to light the way forward.

"Mother is going to kill me," Fred said sullenly.

"Mothers never kill, only love," I replied.

He looked at me dubiously and said, "You really are ugly."

"Say that again and I will sew your lips together."

"How come you haven't been able to get home?"

"I don't have the right blood."

"Well you're not having mine."

"Fool. Not for drinking, for magic. I can protect you, if you protect me. You will fight, and I will heal you by your blood. That is how we both get home."

"Oh… that sounds fair."

"Fairness is a product of white skin, not sound. I suppose you mean *just*."

"Oh man, shut up."

I wasn't sure what *shut up* meant, and I didn't wish to inquire. He was a human: greedy, selfish, non-magical, and homicidal. The dark creatures of this world were dark because it was their nature, they could not be another way, but humans, they could choose. Choose against their natures, yet still they relished evil.

I showed him a knife. "This will protect us, by cutting you."

The lad produced a Potion of Healing that I recognised immediately. He tipped out the contents, and said, "Just take my blood now and store it in this."

"The blood must drip from the veins. Blood is life, and as the life is lost, that is when its power is released."

"That's messed up."

Messed up meant untidy, and in a way, bleeding was an untidy business. "I agree."

"So the Dusk lands are where I began," Fred said. "I wanted to begin at the Bright Realm, though."

I had no idea what he meant by *begin*, though I assumed he'd meant where he'd arrived by portal. "We must get past the hag."

He stopped in his tracks. "No way, I am not going up against a hag."

Admittedly, he was right to be terrified, especially of this hag. "Ragella, have you heard of her?"

"Rubbish, are you for real? Ragella is a real add-on?"

"She is more real than your human world. We are timeless."

Fred groaned and rolled his eyes. The lad had the manners of a worm. "How do we defeat her, then?"

"Defeat her? Why do humans always talk of murder? No, we will break her spell. You see, Ragella was a magic elf from the Bright Court who was bitterly betrayed in love."

Fred burst out laughing. "Yeah, hah, I know girls like that."

I suppose all young lads disrespected matters of the heart. "You must kiss her."

He made the sound of a shadow bird feeding its young. "Ugh, disgusting. I'm not kissing some old hag."

Then he didn't know the story of the hags, or of any hag. Which was strange to me, because Ragella's story was one of the most famous in the lands. So I told him.

"A rich land elf from the Bright Realm had passed her over—the most beautiful and eligible elven woman in the lands—for a swordsmith's daughter. Why? Because—"

"Geez, I hate cut-scenes," Fred moaned. His speech was entirely baffling.

"Don't interrupt, boy. The Bright King, who was only a prince back then, thought Ragella vain, and wanted to teach her a lesson and directed his affections towards another. Her broken heart, blackened by the rejection, had turned her magic into poison which consumed her youth. To curse oneself is the most horrid of all possible curses."

"Oh…" he replied, rubbing one hand against the other, as if they were lonely. "That's sad."

"Once kissed, she will regain everything she's lost." *And so would I, because once the hag's curse was broken, she would be in my debt.*

That got his attention. "Is she pretty?"

"Men fainted at the sight of her, lad, and she's rich. Once transformed back into her original form, she can claim everything she's lost."

"All right. I'm in. Fishermen store their nets outside their huts to dry at night. We can trap her with that and then I'll kiss her."

"A witch cannot be captured with a net. A hag's mind is filled with two types of thought: Magic and love. You must woo her."

"I once wrote this poem for a girl at school. She ate that up like dessert."

I stared at him blankly.

"Like chocolate," he added.

"Ah, then your lass must have been very eager for your pretty words."

Hob girls were impressed by feats of strength and gambling, but elven girls were more sophisticated and fanciful. I'd never been a creature for love, and love had never found me, so I wasn't sure how to best advise Fred. Even so, his mind ticked over the possibilities, and before long he was listing them out loud.

"Flowers, candles, food—what do hags eat?" he asked.

"Ragella will invite you into her home. You will offer me to her as a gift."

Hags only ate the flesh of men who recoiled from them in a disgusted way. If Fred demonstrated only love and kindness, that droplet of love on Ragella's dead, black heart would heal her rotten core.

As I pondered our plot, I felt my heart might explode from excitement, and I wanted to leap for joy. When Ragella Rancidboot had finally turned back into her beautiful self, she could repay me by helping me get back to the Bright Realm. The plan was flawless.

* * *

After the moon had skimmed the horizon for the third time, Fred and I drew close to Ragella's home. For the last moon cycle, I had shielded us from Ragella's traps using Fred's blood. We were so invisible, in fact, that we were able to camp within a few hours' walk of her house.

It was our last meal before Fred's quest to become his charming self and make the most famous hag in the lands fall in love with him, and I was in high spirits.

"Ahhh," I sighed with satisfaction after finishing my bowl of rabbit stewed in grumbleweed. I lay back against a log and patted my stomach. "See that light in the distance, Fred?"

The lad nodded and chewed on a strange oat-made bar with peculiar wrapping.

"It's a protein bar," he said, noticing my staring. "Do you want some?"

"No. Thank you." I eyed the light in the distance and pointed. "That's the glow of Ragella's house. You will continue needing to bleed until we reach her. Do you agree to those terms?"

"Sure."

His wound had begun to clot, so I widened the gash with a blade.

"Why would she want you?" he asked.

"Ragella lives off the magic of other creatures. Without it, she will shrivel and die."

"It seems unfair that her magic punished her for having a broken heart. Even if she wasn't a nice person, that doesn't mean she deserves to be cursed."

It surprised me to hear Fred show that amount of wisdom. "Aye, I'm glad to hear you say it. It will make your heart seem more honest. Now, tie me up."

Fred blinked at me. "You're really willing to die to help me get home?"

"Yes. And if Ragella kills me, the terms of our deal is that you'll come back and save me."

He frowned. "Do you think I can get home without you?"

I berated myself for my foolishness. "No. Ragella, even transformed back into her beautiful self, can never help you gain the king's favour. Only I can do that."

What I'd left from my story about the hag was that she'd cursed herself by killing the Bright King's true love. I hoped my returning her to the Bright Court would convince the king to give me a reprieve.

"Let's go," Fred said enthusiastically.

The hours passed quickly, and as our faces met the glow of firelight emanating from the large windows of Ragella's house, I said, "Very well, tie me up."

We'd made vine ropes in the previous moon rotation, and those were used to take me prisoner. As we made our way to her front door, I said, "Don't forget, eating and drinking in this world—"

"Hello in there!" Fred said while banging on the door and completely ignoring my advice.

The hissing of the witch, followed by a roar of recognition, made fear coil within me. She'd killed me countless times and brought me endless pain; vengeance would almost be as sweet as chocolate.

"Who disturbs Ragella the powerful?"

Powerful. I almost snorted. I closed my eyes and allowed my magic to heal Fred's wound, releasing my scent into the air.

"Hergnab!" she screamed and flung open the door, heaving with the rage of twenty wolves.

Fred kept surprisingly calm as he took in her haggard appearance. Deep lines had formed as her skin dried up from disease and the curse's evil fingers. One of her eyes was swollen and enlarged, the other's cornea had shrunk so that with a gaze, she pierced the soul. Her hair, straw-like and grey, and her rags, dirty and brown, stunk of rotting flesh.

"I seek shelter and bring this goblin as a gift of good faith."

She stared at Fred carefully, inspecting his features.

At that moment, he produced a rose. "I apologise, I didn't know I'd be in the company of a lady."

"Lady…" she said, a hollowness to her voice. "You… think I be a lady?"

"Of course."

The witch shuddered mightily and her rags turned to a beautiful golden gown, and yet her gaunt body stayed the same, as did her frightful face. "There is always a bed for the one who brings me Hergnab-Hob-Hobble."

Fred laughed and looked down at me. "Is that really your name, vile creature? No wonder you disgust me."

Ragella cackled. "Are you hungry…?"

"Fred."

"Fred. Won't you come in?"

"I will. Thank you."

As we entered, Ragella clapped her hands together and the inside swelled in size, adding a second story above and a marble fireplace in place of the hearth. A dirt floor gave way to stone, and lavish tapestries materialised on the walls. Our plan was working.

"Tie him up at the pillar."

Fred nodded and did as the witch asked.

"I will fetch your food now," she said. "Warm yourself at the fire. These lands are miserable for a man as handsome as you."

"May your kindness forever be rewarded," he replied, puffing out his chest and smiling as sweetly as he could manage.

She made a strange cooing noise and turned on her heel to make a meal. Out of sight, Fred shot me a look of utter distress.

"That's the ugliest woman I've ever—"

"Hush, fool. Keep to your part and don't eat—"

Ragella stuck her head around the corner of the kitchen. "Would well-cooked venison satisfy your tastes?"

"Yes. Thank you," Fred said, and left me to sit by the fireplace.

Fred foolishly partook in the hag's meal, which meant he was now bound to this world. I hoped the Bright King might be able to help him. As they drank and laughed—Fred proved surprisingly charming—the walls throbbed with magical power. At times I had to force myself to take a breath, for the suspense of her uncovering our ruse overwhelmed me.

"Why do you live here alone?" Fred asked.

The hag's arthritic fingers clutched her golden goblet, and she slurped with the elegance of a pig at a feeding trough. "I'm just an old, ugly woman."

Fred sat back and beat his fist lightly on the table. "Nonsense. It's clear to me that your heart is as golden as that cup you hold."

"You are sweet to say it, but even I own a mirror."

Make it believable, Fred, I thought.

"How did you capture the hob?"

"You mean the blood goblin?"

"Oh, yes." As she grinned, it felt like my insides churned to acid, for her smile had long rotted away, and for a moment I felt sorry for poor Fred.

"He was caught in sinking mud."

That made her cackle loudly. And the jewels she wore jingled.

"Ragella?"

She breathed in, and her eyes gleamed with tears. "The way you said my name… I feel like I've known you a thousand years, young adventurer."

"I wish to sing for my supper."

She clasped her hands together. "Sing? Oh, please sing me a song. Of the fields of your domain, for I know you are not of this world."

I braced myself for something truly awful.

Fred opened his mouth, and out came a melodic voice so perfect in pitch that I held my breath. "Beautiful dreamer, come unto me, Starlight and dew drops are waiting for thee…"

The lad continued his serenade, soothing my mind, and I watched Ragella dabbing at tears streaming down her face. And when he finished, she was gripping the table, as if giants had overturned her life.

She sighed wistfully and said, "I wish you to stay, at your own will, for three more nights, and in that time I will grant you anything you wish, for my magic is strong, but my heart longs for the company of that innocent voice."

"You are too kind, m'lady." His cheeks were rosy from the heat of the fireplace. "Of course I will stay. It would be a great honour to grant you temporary bliss."

"Sing it again."

Fred smiled charmingly, opened his mouth, and sung the song again several more times. Time passed, and Ragella's cracked and aging skin began to flourish with the pinkish flesh of her youthful self.

* * *

Unexpectedly, Fred and Ragella forgot that I was present. They let me starve, ignored me, and when seven moon cycles concluded, the hag was finally cuddled up in Fred's arms. Even though I grew weak, and slept on the hard floor, I took care not to let my suffering be known. The greater plan was more important than any discomfort I endured.

"Never leave me," she said one night by the fire.

Fred took her fingers in his and kissed them. "How could I? I have never met a heart as beautiful as yours."

Ragella wept then, putting her hand across her chest and turning away from the lad. "Oh, Fred, so long I have been in the darkness. So long I have looked in the mirror and despised myself. The Bright King of this world was my true love once, and he chose another because I was jealous. And when he did, I killed her. I killed her, Fred, but I didn't mean to. I only meant to make her sick."

"Tell me what happened, and I will forgive you. I will always forgive you."

"I poisoned her. She was innocent, truer of heart than I."

"Your heart is beautiful as well," he said.

At that moment, all my hopes voided when I realised Fred wasn't pretending anymore. He'd fallen in love. This couldn't happen. And as he leaned in to kiss her, I screamed out, "No!"

Ragella's eyes narrowed with rage as she slid her gaze to me. Her voice became croaky. "Shut your ugly face, you little rodent."

"Fred, if you fall in love with her, you'll become just like her."

She slid her eyes to the lad. "Why does he speak to you as if you were his friend?"

Fred lost his confidence for a moment, but he pulled away. "Why do you listen to his lies?"

And she gasped. "Forgive me. Oh, forgive me. I want to trust you. I want to believe in our love."

"Then believe in it." And he kissed her passionately on the lips.

Outside, there came the sound of a rushing wind so mighty it could yank trees from the ground and knock the stars from the sky. Ragella and Fred remained locked in their kiss as her transformation from old woman to elven beauty happened in a rush of sparkling light.

I almost cheered out loud. Fred hadn't fallen in love with her, but she had with him, and though it broke the curse, it delivered its last blow, leaving Ragella's house in ruins.

As their lips parted, I saw her long, golden hair and stunning green eyes.

Fred sat speechless and utterly mesmerised. "Wow."

She laughed, not with the croaky, scratchy voice of a hag, but with the chime of a royal lady. "Adventurer, you broke the curse that held me prisoner in my own nightmare for thousands of years. Tell me how I can repay you."

Fred shot me an apologetic look. "I want to be rich."

"No," I said. "You need to go home."

"Hergnab-Hob-Hobble," she said, rising from the musty old chair. "By attempting to use this lad to break your own curse, you have helped me break mine, and for that I won't kill you."

She took a bronze dagger from the floor and came to me. She brought the blade to my neck and whispered in my ear, "What you don't know, that no one knows, is that the king killed my father and stole my lands. The lad's blood is the only way to kill His Majesty. I get to avenge my father, and your spell will be broken. What say you?"

Frog's vomit. I hadn't expected this at all. "What then?"

She glanced over her shoulder at Fred. "I don't know. The lad is handsome."

"Using blood magic in the Bright Court is dangerous," I said. "Fred might die."

Her eyes blazed with an eternity of vengeance. "Just make the lad bleed, Hob, and let me do the rest."

"Fine," I said, lying through my sharp-fanged teeth. I had to kill her. "Let me speak to him."

"Fred, come here, darling."

He obeyed.

"The both of you talk while I prepare our portal back to the Bright Court." She kissed him on the cheek. "I will make you very rich."

As she walked away, the lad's eyes drank her in, and Ragella purposefully swayed her hips, flirting with him, increasing her hold on him.

Fred came to me. "You didn't tell me she was *that* hot."

I knew he spoke of her alluring figure.

"She's going to kill the king," I said.

"It's not like he did you any favours," he replied.

I slapped him on the forehead. "Stop it. She needs your blood to kill him, so you must kill her first."

"This quest is awesome!" he cried.

Ragella returned and took the lad's hand, her eyes brimming with fake love. How had she broken the spell if she didn't truly love him? The kiss must have been enough.

"You agree, my love, that the king must die for what he did to me?"

"I do," he replied. "How do we get away?"

"In the same manner by which we'll arrive. Teleportation."

"I am ready," he said putting on his bravest voice.

Soon, all three of us would be dead.

* * *

We arrived during a court session where the king seemed to be passing judgement on two mischievous pixies. The beauty of being back home, bathed in the light of the sunbeams piercing through the gemmed trees, made me choke with emotion.

The court attendees gasped at our arrival, and at that same moment, I felt my insides curling, my skin crawling, and a transformation began. A beard sprouted from my face, my right arms shrunk to normal size, and my belly expanded. The painless experience passed in the blink of an eye, and as my legs lengthened slightly and I felt no fangs scraping against my face, I cried out with happiness.

"Now, Fred," said Ragella.

The lad turned and stabbed me in the chest with his sword, betraying me and making me a fool.

I fell to the emerald grasses, bleeding and shouting, "Ragella returns to kill you, my king."

"Seize them!" the king bellowed.

But Ragella snatched the necklace from Fred's neck, cut his arm, and used his blood—and mine—to propel the iron sword necklace straight into the king's heart.

"No!" I shouted.

An elf banished Fred's blade from his hand and surrounded him with fire. Ragella waved her arms, manifesting a portal, but before she could teleport, a group of elves set her on fire. Her screams were silenced as she exploded in a cloud of smoke that mushroomed into the air then spewed out her ashy, flaky remains. The grey flakes rained down over the courtiers who fled in a panic leaving only the soldiers and king's advisors. They brushed the hag's remains out of their clothes and hair.

The king had fallen out of his throne and was clutching at his heart on the grassy dais.

Fred shrieked as the flames licked at his skin, yelling, "I thought it was a game. I thought it was all a game."

The best healers in the court stood over their king, trying to save him. His colour had turned pale and blue; death would take him soon.

"Stand back!" I said, staggering over to him.

Morland, the elf who'd initially cursed me, raised his hand suddenly. Invisible magic smashed against my body, sending me flying across the clearing. "I should have killed you when I had the chance."

"I can heal him. Let me heal him," I said.

The pain in my body made my lungs shudder. Using blood magic in the Bright Court was forbidden and would kill me.

"I can heal you, Majesty. Let me prove myself to you once again."

I was on my knees, trying to raise my body and get to my feet, but I was weak. Bleeding so profusely that I slipped in my own blood.

The king said to his guards, "Bring him to me."

"No, I will die if moved. Come to me."

"Very well!" the king rasped. "Take me to him."

An elf rushed to me and put a potion to my lips. I sipped eagerly, and as the elves brought the king to my side, I placed my hand over his heart, feeling for the iron sword. His pulse weakened, and if not for the healers keeping him alive, he'd have already been dead.

Reaching inside myself, I strained my soul for the sparks of life that kept me alive. They were in my veins, ligaments, and muscles, and as I took them, I found I could hardly move myself. Internally, I crafted them into finger-like tools that burst from the deep incision Fred's sword had made and burrowed into the king's chest, making him cry out.

"Stop him! He's killing him," Morland cried.

The miniature iron sword slid out of the king's heart and clinked against the polished floor, but his heart had stopped beating. I used every second one of my own heartbeats to keep him alive while I mended his wounds with blood magic.

When the king's heart sustained its own beats, and his skin warmed with life, the ancient forces that forbade the use of blood magic in the Bright Realm came to claim my life. The shadowy figures emerged from the trees, the grasses, the light itself, their wraith-like shapes, and wispy nightmarish fingers strained my body of life sparks. The sleep of death brought a final darkness, but I drifted off peacefully, smiling, knowing I had finally set things right.

* * *

I awoke to chocolate. Everywhere, chocolate. Stacked floor to ceiling in huge piles. Fred leaned over me, grinning wildly.

"What happened?" I asked, feeling deflated and famished.

"You saved the king, *and* you saved me."

An elf stood guard at my door. *My door!* I realized. I was home, in my old lodgings where I'd lived while in service to the king as royal healer.

"B-but how did I survive?" I asked, trying not to cry in front of the lad.

Fred's eyes glowed. "Well, let's just say I can't go home, and you…" He picked up my arm, which was a claw again. A blood goblin claw.

"Oh no, not this again. I can't go back to the Dark Realm, Fred. Kill me."

He laughed and shook his head. "No. Using blood magic turned you back into a goblin. Consider this all a gift from the Bright King for risking your life. You'll be the first blood goblin to live in the Bright Realm, and you'll have endless chocolate, but… you can't really leave the house. You know, because you're scary-looking."

"Why did you betray me?" I asked.

"I did a terrible thing, but I have a good reason. It's going to sound weird, but humans have this virtual game called Feyland…"

The lad relayed his story of how he was convinced the world was make-believe, a quest, and he'd thought that Ragella and I were not real. He likened it to a dream. A seemingly real dream that was a game, and Fred had stabbed me in an attempt to try to wake up.

"I won't forgive you," I said.

Fred's face fell, and he lowered his gaze. "It's okay."

And then I let go of roaring laughter. "Unless you feed me chocolate right now!"

The lad's dopey smile returned, touching his eyes and crinkling his forehead. He showed me a piece of chocolate and put it to my mouth. I savoured that first taste, the first in a thousand years. How I'd missed it. It melted on my tongue, waxed my mouth, and I let it sit there, capturing me in an eternal euphoria.

When I finally swallowed, I said, "Ahh, my old friend."

Fred laughed at me and dabbed at the blood on my chin with a handkerchief. I'd scratched myself with my ridiculous fangs, but I didn't care. "Don't you want to go home?"

"I can't. I ate the food, remember?"

He was lying to me. The Bright King had the power to send him home if he wished, but the lad didn't want to go, and I wasn't about to talk him out of it. There were few creatures I enjoyed the company of, and to my surprise, Fred had become one of them.

There'd been a monster inside me, a selfish, greedy monster

that I'd slain. Now when the lad regarded me, I saw only kinship, and that brought a satisfying peace to my soul.

"Will you do me one more favour?" I asked him.

"Sure."

"Never ever let me eat chocolate again."

A WORD FROM K. J. COLT

As soon as I finished reading Anthea Sharp's extensive notes on the world of *Feyland*, out poured the story I wanted to write—"The Glitchy Goblin". Often, the easier and more comfortable the writing process, the more I adore the story, and Anthea's world is perfectly set up for myself and other authors to make a compelling contribution.

Anyone who's familiar with my writing knows that I prefer to write complex characters who can't be pigeonholed into categories of good and bad. They're usually morally neutral beings who learn better ways to treat others by making mistakes.

Hergnab-Hob-Hobble from Hobbleton is a somewhat grouchy and pessimistic character, but despite his unfavourable social qualities, he comes to redeem himself through the adoration he has for Fred, a lost, youthful, quest-seeking knight from the human world.

This is a story dear to my heart, as is "Tasty Dragon Meat" which can be read as part of Samuel Peralta's *The Dragon Chronicles* or purchased at my personal Amazon store.

The Healers of Meligna series is my main series which is a complex, brave, and rich fantasy set in a unique and somewhat poignant world.

Lastly, you can subscribe to my mailing list (http://eepurl.com/vrX-r) to receive book news.

On Guard
by Deb Logan

WALLACE PADDED SOFTLY across the wooden floor, following his boy. He faltered slightly as they passed a puddle of golden sunlight streaming through a low window onto the flagstone entryway. His old bones creaked and he longed to rest in that sunny patch, allowing the warmth to soak into stiff muscles. But he followed the boy, mindful of his duty.

In his prime, Wallace had been a mighty hunter. The terror of small rodents. Field mice and rabbits still avoided his domain, though he was far from his kitten days. Old age stalked him as once he had stalked prey in the greenbelt behind his humans' dwelling.

But despite his advancing age and loss of fluid grace, he held to his duty. The female of his pair of bonded humans had given Wallace charge of the boy when he had been nothing more than a squirming bundle wrapped in blankets.

"Watch over him, Wallace," his female had said. "Guard him, always."

And Wallace had. No harm had ever befallen the boy while Wallace was on guard. He would not shirk his duty now for the physical relief of sun-warmed stone.

The boy continued downstairs, as Wallace had known he would, to the windowless cave the humans referred to as *The Game Room*. Wallace glanced toward the ceiling, thinking of that glorious pool of sunlight. Perhaps later, when the boy tired of sitting in that chair. Perhaps there would still be warm sun to bask in then.

He glanced around the room looking for the most comfortable spot to maintain his guard. In the center of the room two tiered rows of dark blue cushioned chairs faced a blank white screen. Off to one side sat a low stool surrounded by sparkly red metallic cylinders. The male of Wallace's bonded pair liked to sit on that stool and beat on those cylinders. Wallace could appreciate his human's need to express aggression, but just the thought of that noise made his head ache.

On the other side of the room was the object of the boy's attention. A massive black leather chair surrounded by boxes full of mechanical whirrs and whistles. The boy sat on the edge of the chair pulling on skin-tight gloves that sparkled in the room's low light. He touched one of the boxes and high frequency noise assaulted Wallace's sensitive ears. The boy pulled a sleek black helmet over his head, covering his eyes with a darkened visor and completely occluding his ears.

Wallace closed his eyes in a slow blink. Why would any

intelligent creature choose to blind himself in the middle of the day? The boy spent hours in that chair, completely oblivious to the world around him. He saw nothing, heard nothing. Wallace knew. He'd tested the boy, cavorting around the room leaping lightly onto surfaces where he had no right to be, even sitting at the boy's feet and yowling until the female had raced down the stairs to see what was wrong. All for nothing. The boy had not emerged from his helmeted stupor.

With resignation, Wallace leapt onto the padded chair closest to his boy, circled three times and sat, tail curled around his paws. He watched the boy's hands twitch on the arms of the big black chair. Sometimes he spoke, nonsense words and phrases that had no bearing on reality. *Quest* and *Feyland* and *Thank you, kind sir* were uttered with some regularity, but Wallace had long since learned to ignore anything his boy said while wearing the helmet and gloves.

More disturbing were the moments when the boy thrashed in the chair, grunting and jabbing with gloved fists. At these times Wallace prowled around the chair, on guard against the foe his boy obviously fought. But nothing ever manifested, nothing a fierce Norwegian Forest cat could sink his claws and teeth into, and soon the boy would subside once more into twitchy somnolence.

Wallace's head drooped, and his eyes closed, his nose nearly touching the chair's pillow-soft fabric. A frisson of warning jerked him awake and he gathered his legs beneath him, ready to spring.

A dazzling light appeared over the boy's right shoulder. A

lightning-shaped tear in the fabric of the world. A delicate, pale green hand appeared in the rent, then another, fingers scrabbling to widen the opening.

Wallace watched with narrowed eyes, crouched and ready.

A small head pushed through the tear, followed by a shoulder and one long arm. Another moment and wings appeared, followed by a female torso.

Wallace waited, confused. His previous experience hadn't prepared him for a winged creature to emerge from a crack in thin air. His duty was to protect his boy, his totally oblivious boy. But was this small winged female a danger? How could she be? She was hardly bigger than a squirrel, and Wallace subdued squirrels with ease.

The creature, fully emerged now, dropped lightly to the back of the boy's chair and knelt there, resting. What manner of being was she? Her skin was palest green, like the tender shoots of grass in the spring, her tunic the darker green of oak leaves, her hair petal pink and her wings merely an iridescent shimmer. She blinked solemnly at Wallace with large, liquid eyes the color of molten emeralds.

"Well met, friend cat," she said, her voice as soft as a mother's purr.

Wallace blinked and eyed her warily, casting his memory back, searching. Images and sensations whirled past his mind's eye. His tail twitched in agitation, powerful leg muscles ready for a predatory spring. He remembered the touch of his mother's rough tongue as she licked him at birth, encouraging his lungs into action. He remembered the peace of floating in a fluid-filled sac safe in his mother's womb.

Further back.

He entered the racial memories of his clan, the fierce northern forest cats of ancient days. He remembered creatures not seen by his clan in many lives of cats: gentle tomtens, deadly ogres, fierce trolls, and tricksy ice faeries.

He licked his lips in triumph. The creature was a faerie. Not an ice faerie of the far north, blue-skinned and adorned in ice crystals, but a faerie none the less.

"Why are you here, faerie?" he asked, allowing only a hint of a growl to color his words.

"I'm no threat to you, friend cat," she said. "I am in search of sustenance, but my food is not your food. I am not your competition."

She glanced hungrily at the back of his boy's neck and smiled, showing needle-sharp teeth.

Wallace rose to full height, arching his back, his fur spiking. He hissed a warning. "Not the boy," he said, his voice deadly calm. "My boy shall not be your prey."

"Your boy?" she asked, turning to face him once more. "What allegiance have cats to human boys?"

"This one is under my protection. Seek your sustenance elsewhere."

She swaggered along the back of the boy's chair—his *oblivious* boy's chair!—and surveyed the room.

"I see no other prey, friend cat, and my options are limited. I can only enter this realm where the walls are thin, and the walls only thin where a human willingly enters our realm through the game, Feyland." She gestured at the helmeted boy. "This human has self-selected. I need the sustenance of his hopes and dreams and vibrant emotions. I need his essence. *Faerie* needs his essence."

Wallace stepped closer to the faerie, placing his front paws on the arm of the cushioned chair. He judged the distance to the faerie on the back of his boy's chair to be less than six feet. An easy jump in his prime; more challenging now. But he could do it. He *would* do it. That creature would not harm his boy. Not while Wallace lived.

"Find other hunting grounds, faerie. This human and his parents are mine. I will not give them up." This time, Wallace allowed his growl full voice. The creature had been warned.

"Come now, cat," the faerie wheedled, her voice sweet as cream. "What's the difference between one human and another? This one is small and puny and fails to show you proper respect. You can do better. Besides, cats and faeries are natural allies. Our clans have always been friends. Give me this scrawny human. You can do better."

Wallace's determination lagged, eased by the sweetness of her words. Tension flowed from his body and his eyes lost their focus and drifted closed.

A memory stirred in the deep recesses of his mind. Mesmer. Faerie mesmer. The clever green creature was hypnotizing him!

He shook himself free of her guile and sprang to his boy's defense, knocking against the back of the boy's helmet in the process and pinning the faerie to the leather with unsheathed claws. "He is mine!" he yowled. "You shall *not* harm my boy!"

The faerie shrieked and squirmed, but could not escape.

The boy yelled and scooted forward, turning a visor-blinded face to the struggle on the back of his chair.

Wallace lowered his muzzle to within a breath of the faerie's face and whispered, "Tell your clan and court. Warn them. Do not return to this dwelling. Wallace the Fierce guards these humans. They. Are. Not. Your. Prey."

Before his warning could die on the air, Wallace grabbed the faerie in careful jaws and tossed her back through the rent between the realms. As she vanished, so did the tear.

The boy, having finally managed to yank his helmet from his head, glared at Wallace. "What is wrong with you, cat?" he yelled. "Get off my chair! I don't know what you think you're doing, but you've ruined my game. Now I'll have to start that level all over again."

He shoved Wallace off his chair, jammed the helmet on his head and settled back into his game.

Wallace stalked around his boy's chair, head high, tail waving like a battle standard. Not only had he defeated the faerie and protected his boy, he'd held old age at bay. He still had it. He was still Wallace the Fierce!

After another circuit of the room, he leapt back up to his perch on the cushioned chair, kneaded the seat and then circled his bulk into a comfortable position. The faerie had said one true thing, his boy didn't show him proper respect. He yawned and rested his chin on his front paws. But what could he expect? His boy was only human, after all, and obviously in need of a Norwegian Forest cat's protection.

Fortunately for him, Wallace was on guard.

A WORD FROM DEB LOGAN

I'm a huge fan of Anthea Sharp's *Feyland* novels, and was thrilled when Samuel Peralta's *Chronicle World's: Feyland* gave me the opportunity to play in her world!

Having read every single *Feyland* story, I'm very familiar with the world's delights … and its dangers. "On Guard" was inspired by a family vacation where my twelve-year-old grandson was so entranced by a video game that he lost track of time and had to be coaxed into family activities. I could easily imagine my grandson playing Feyland, but "On Guard" was born when I decided to make his pet Norwegian Forest cat the hero of the tale.

Deb Logan writes Children's, Tween, and Young Adult fantasy. Her stories are light-hearted tales for the younger set—or ageless folk who remain young at heart. Author of Faery Unexpected *and the popular* Dani Erickson *series, Deb loves dragons, faeries and all things unexplained. She's especially fond of Celtic and Native American lore. Faeries and Dragons and Thunderbirds, Oh My!*

Visit her at http://deblogan.wordpress.com to learn more about her work, and be sure to join her newsletter list for an exclusive free story.

An Artist's Instinct
by Andrea Luhman

TUCKING A STRAND of layered brown hair behind one ear, Agatha took a deep breath, and hummed out a note of approval. It was easy to appreciate how *Rerun's Fashion Boutique* had none of the stale musty smells common to secondhand stores. She needed this, a little retail therapy to help ease her frustration over another failed show choir audition.

Agatha heard the whispers nearby.

"She's got money to throw away, why is she in here?"

"They should just post on the door, no chip children allowed."

She heard things like that often enough, usually when she was spotted shopping in a store like Reruns. She was Agatha McKnight after all, the daughter of Alejandra McKnight, opera star royalty. People paid a lot of money to see her mom perform, which according to some, meant Agatha should be dressed head to toe in fresh designer labels. Agatha hated those assumptions. As if people on a tight budget held exclusive rights to being offended by the markup on retail clothing. Or because her family had money she was supposed to pay more for everything. That was so unfair.

Agatha passed the whisperers and ignored them. She only battled trolls in her favorite sim game Feyland. She recognized the petite redheaded manager, Shannon, who bobbed around the racks of old millennial formal wear.

"Jane, let's add those to this rack," Shannon said.

Agatha looked over, curious to see who Jane was. As a loyal patron of Reruns, Agatha took pride in knowing all the sales staff. The Jane holding an armload of dresses was the same Jane Nestle that Agatha went to school with. The little Agatha knew of Jane, she liked. Jane was a smart girl, who ditched designer clothes to wear on-trend garments she crafted herself by hand.

Shannon took dresses from Jane one at a time. "Hi, Agatha," Jane said, smiling over the heaping mess of tulle and satin in her arms. "We were in chem together last semester, remember?"

"Of course, you scored a ninety-eight on the final and blew the curve."

"Right," Jane's smile faded, replaced with a look of anxiety, like she was afraid Agatha was upset about her smarts.

"You killed it, that was prime," Agatha said, and Jane's face relaxed again. "Are you working here as the new part-time?"

"Yes. Are you shopping for the winter formal?"

"I might be," Agatha said. "Are you going?"

Jane shook her head as she passed a final dress to Shannon.

"No, but I'm on the planning committee for prom. I have to go to that. Seems wrong to plan a party and not go to it myself."

Agatha shrugged. "I might skip the winter formal, but I *am* going to prom. Even if it means I have to go by myself."

There was a brief, awkward silence. Jane looked like she had something to say, but Agatha pivoted towards another dress rack. She didn't want to discuss her love life—or lack of it—right there in the shop.

"Do you want to see the dress Shannon let me put on hold?" Jane asked.

Agatha stopped browsing, her eyebrows raising with interest. A distraction would be nice.

"I can show you, it's in the back." Jane beckoned, and Agatha followed, passing through a plain door with a worn, *employees only* sign.

"How does Shannon ever find anything back here?" Agatha asked, eying the wall racks of clothing hung almost to the ceiling.

"I know, " Jane said as she disappeared into a forest of dresses. "I'm just getting the hang of the inventory security tag locator system." She emerged holding a maroon silk gown that looked like it had seen more red carpets than high school gymnasiums, and held it in front of her, her smile huge. "What do you think?"

"That's a find, it really is. It goes well with your fair complexion. You need to keep that even after prom, it's beautiful. What year was it made? Two-thousand seven, maybe two-thousand nine?"

"I'm not sure, I just really love the draping and how the

shoulders were done in this heavy black lace. I saw it, and I thought for a second it was that dress from the more recent Feyland pop-up ads."

"Wow, it does. Maybe it is? You play Feyland? Feyland's the first sim I've ever tried. I swear I picked it because I fell in love with its cover art. Now I'm addicted to it."

Jane grabbed Agatha's arm, "Me too! What's your character, a Spellweaver? A Saboteur?"

Agatha gave her a sheepish smile. There were many players who questioned why Feyland created her avatar class, since it lacked the stronger fighting abilities other avatars had. "I'm a Bard."

Jane scrunched up her eyes and nodded, "Of course, I should have guessed that. You're like a show choir star."

"No I'm not, not even close. If anybody's the star it's Shelly Thompson. She has a much better range than I do, and she snapped up the solo again today, as always." Agatha's frustration tightened up her throat and she swallowed hard. She needed to stop thinking about the audition, or sadness was going to take over and swamp her in messy tears.

"But your mom… aren't you like classically trained?"

Agatha nodded and cleared her throat, "Yeah, but Shelly's beaten me out of every solo part I've auditioned for. Every single one."

"I thought you were good at last year's concert. I couldn't get up there and do that. My brother Zack though, he does it all the time with his band. He's a born performer. In fact, he's even gotten to Master Bard level in Feyland." Jane returned her future prom dress to the racks and led Agatha out of the back room. "If you come to prom you'll get to hear him. The prom committee actually hired his band."

"Are they any good?"

"Last year, when they started, no. Now you can tell they take it seriously. They've gotten a lot better. They get paid to do weddings, big parties, that kind of thing." Jane veered toward another rack. "Hey, let me show you one more thing. It's another dress, when I saw it I thought it looked a lot like something out of Feyland. I'd buy it, but the color's just not right for me."

"You're right," Agatha said when Jane held up a dress for her inspection. "It's a fashion sin to put a blonde like you in an aubergine dress."

"Aubergine?" Jane said, trying the word as she handed the dress to Agatha. She repeated the word, this time with more flair. "Aubergine, because we can't call it eggplant like everyone else."

"I didn't invent the color," Agatha said, holding the dress against her as she looked in a dressing room mirror. She was in love with it, ready to buy it without even trying it on.

"Now you have to go to prom," Jane said.

"I don't need a reason to buy this," Agatha said. "I'll wear it around the house just because."

"You better call me first then, so you don't trip over the hem," Jane said handing Agatha a card with an embossed pair of scissors on it with the words *Jane Nestle – tailoring and custom alterations,* and her number printed below it.

"A card, how very vintage of you."

"Most people who need my help are," Jane said. "Call me

when the aubergine dress is coming out and we'll have our own private party, and I don't know, play Feyland or something."

"Want to?"

"Hang out with the high school fashion maven and play my favorite game? Of course. Maybe I can help you find your way to the Bard's Challenge that Zack's talked about."

"Yes let's do it. I've been trying to find my way to that for weeks."

"In that case, would you like to come over next weekend to play?" Jane said.

"I'd love to," Agatha said.

* * *

Agatha arrived a little early on Saturday to Jane's address, and was greeted by the midgrade automation system of Jane's apartment complex. "Welcome Agatha McKnight, Jane will meet you in unit 302, upon her arrival in approximately thirty two minutes."

"I'm that early, huh?"

The automation system gave a courteous reply. "Yes, please proceed to unit 302."

The lights in the hallways of the apartment glowed brighter to guide Agatha to Jane's apartment. The door to unit 302 released and a young man with sandy blonde hair, green eyes, and a smile like Jane's walked over with his hand extended.

"Hey, I'm Zack, Jane's brother. She's running late, but she'll be here soon."

"In approximately thirty two minutes," Agatha said, adjusting the full-D helmet she carried so she could shake his hand.

"We'll see. I don't think that tech's very accurate," Zack said, lowering his voice, "The tech cannot be trusted."

Agatha laughed; it was easy to like Zack. He seemed like the kind of performer always oblivious to whether he was on or off stage.

Zack gestured to her full-D helmet. "Jane said you sing. You heading into Feyland to find an invite to the Bard's Challenge?"

"That's my plan," she said. "Jane bragged that you've already completed it. I've been searching for it for weeks."

He nodded, "It's fun, but it gets hard fast. I can talk you through the starting levels?"

"I would love that!"

She was eager to learn what she could from Zack, but after a few minutes of listening to him describe the quests, she threw up her hands in frustration.

"I've never seen any of the things you just mentioned. My version must be tweaked."

"Want me to show you on our system? We could play until Jane gets home."

"Would you? Then maybe I can figure out what I'm missing."

Zack bobbed his head in rhythm with an air guitar he played, as he sang the special jingle that sounded when a Bard was selected as an avatar in Feyland, "Ba-bada-ba-BA!"

His enthusiasm was contagious, and Agatha was bouncing on her toes when he motioned her over to a Full-D console, offering her a sim chair. He was funny, helpful, and cute. Would Jane hate her if she formed a crush on her brother in one afternoon? Agatha pulled her gaming gloves out of her bag as he adjusted his headset and flexed the fit of his gloves.

Zack gave her an expectant look. Agatha adjusted her helmet and nodded. He clicked the glowing F for Feyland and with two practiced finger motions, activated the opening sequence. "Welcome to Feyland" blazed red in their line of sight and faded as they entered the main menu screen. Both Agatha and Zack selected their established Bard characters, and heard the happy trumpet blast of "Ba-bada-ba-BA!"

"Let's do this," he said.

The immersion was strange this time—maybe because she was using different equipment. She felt a small wave of nausea as a tunnel of gold light encased her. After a deep breath Agatha felt it subside. Morning sunlight shed winks of light through a forest of white barked trees. Moss-covered ground cushioned her steps as she followed Zack from the circle of perfect crimson-capped mushrooms.

"Do you think those are edible in real life?" he asked.

"Are you kidding?" Agatha said. "Don't brightly colored things in nature normally mean something is dangerous?"

"Then you must be really dangerous," he said.

"Ha-ha-ha."

They walked a path through the forest and within a few paces heard the wail of multiple babies crying. The moss on the path became studded with stones, which gradually filled in, becoming a narrow street. Several timber-framed cottages lined the way. The cries were emanating from the first house, where an old woman the size of a toddler sat on the front step. She looked up at them with oversized eyes and an unfortunate nose. Her shreds of mousy brown hair matched the sagging skin of her face, which drooped in odd contrast to her high arching earflaps.

"Tis' a good morning to have the famous musicians, Master Zachary and Songbird Agatha, stop over by our humble dwelling."

"Good morning Lourdys, how are you on this fine day?" Zack asked.

"My eyes are tired, and my ears even more. Not a soul in our village has slept a nod, with the endless wailing of my triplet grandbabes. If you should gift us with a lullaby, the residents of our town would be most grateful."

"We are happy to offer a tune," Zack said, with a bow of his head. "Please lead us to the bedside of the sweet babes."

"This way then." Lourdys wriggled up onto a pair of squat legs and led them into her dwelling. Zack and Agatha stooped through the doorway and into the dingy interior of a one-room house. Three small, large-eyed figures squirmed and howled in a long wooden crib set under a window. Their coloring was like dried earth, and they were swaddled in blankets made of moss. Agatha was amused at how the triplet's noses were almost non-existent, and wondered how long it took to grow a nose with the same bulging proportions as their grandmother. A younger version of Lourdys stood before them with pleading hands and bloodshot weary eyes.

"Please, do play what you find is best, to put my three wee babes to rest."

Zach raised an arched finger, and a list of three songs appeared for he and Agatha to choose from.

"You decide," he said.

Agatha selected *The Elfin Knight* with a twitch of one finger, and Zack grinned his approval as he manifested a mandolin. Tapping his foot, he set the song's rhythm. He began to play, and the ballad's lyrics appeared in a slow illuminated scroll before them. In a soft soprano voice Agatha began:

The Elfin Knight sits on yon hill
 Ba ba lilly ba
Blowing his horn loud and shrill
 And the wind has blown my plaid away
I love to hear that horn blow
I wish him here and as my own
That word it was no sooner spoken
Than Elfin Knight in her arms was gotten

They had reached the chorus when lyrics faded away. The room was hushed as Zack silenced his mandolin. Agatha leaned over the crib and peeked at the brownie triplets fast asleep. Their mother raised her hands and smiled in gratitude.

"Thank you," she whispered. "Now our village will rest. When you leave here, go west. Near the well lies a gate to take you on to the wonders you seek."

Outside on the stone street Agatha and Zack waved farewell to Lourdys and her daughter. They walked quietly through the small village, and up a small rise where they found the well. Beside it stood another circle of red-capped mushrooms. They stepped inside, and entered another tunnel of swirling gold light.

Agatha blinked as long shadows cast by an early morning sun came into focus. In all directions lay craggy hills with valleys blanketed in mounds of blooming heather.

"This is why I like this game," Zack said. "The scenery is fantastic."

"Me too," she said. "At least it's one of the reasons."

"I hate to hit pause on this, but Jane's going to want to see this."

"Jane, yes-Jane. You're right, we need to go get her." Agatha continued to stare at their surroundings; it was all so real. The air smelled like freshly fallen rain. Stalks of flowering heather bobbed and swayed in the wind. The early sun magnified the amethyst color of each petal, and transformed their dew into tiny purple gems. It was so breathtaking it made Agatha regret the sight of Jane's stark apartment walls when they exited the game.

Zack and Agatha lazed in their sim chairs. She felt no compulsion to move right away after simming. Even the sight of Jane standing there, glaring, with her arms crossed, failed to motivate Agatha to sit up.

"Hi," Agatha said. "We came out to get you."

Jane's mouth was a bunched frown as she shifted her weight from one foot to the other. "I thought we were going to play Feyland this afternoon?"

"We are. Zack was just showing me your game version to see if it was any different than mine."

Jane's eyebrows lifted in curiosity and her frown faded a little. "Is it?"

"Yes, from what I can tell. Maybe my version was never coded with the Bard's Challenge."

Zack broke in, pointing at the extra sim chair Jane stood beside. "Is that Lindsey's from 204?"

Jane nodded and gave Zack a stern glare. "She said we can borrow it until she gets back from her parents' cabin Tuesday. I was able to get the code to her place, go down to her unit, and bring it back here, all in the time you two were off playing without me."

"You're so super clever to call her, Sis, and don't worry, I'll make sure Lindsey gets her chair back Tuesday," Zack said, his eyes twinkling.

"Lindsey has a boyfriend, don't be a troll," Jane said, dropping into Lindsey's sim chair.

"Someday, maybe even by Tuesday, he'll be her ex-boyfriend. I'm happy to troll around Lindsey, because eventually she'll see I'm a prince."

Agatha wasn't sure she knew Zack well enough to call him a prince, but he was charming. What a shame he had a thing for this Lindsey girl. It wasn't every day a guy grabbed her interest.

Jane shook her head and pulled her sim helmet on. They restarted their game, and Jane selected her Illuminer avatar. They soon stood among the endless hills of heather. Wind billowed the layers of Jane's pale apricot and cream-colored robes as she carefully stepped out of the red-capped mushroom circle.

"Did you get the Bard's Challenge quest yet?" Jane asked.

Agatha shook her head no.

Zack held up his hand in a swift gesture that asked for quiet. "I think I hear something."

They exchanged glances, listening intently for any sound out of place. There was a rugged and hollow horn blast that vibrated the earth under their feet. *What's with the sound induced earthquake?* Agatha raised her eyebrows in an expression she knew matched Jane and Zack's. The horn sounded again, there was more vibration underfoot, and for a brief time the sound seemed closer, louder.

Agatha pointed east towards the sounds' origin. "Is there a path going that way?"

"Let's see," Jane said.

After some brief scouting, they found a trail hidden under crossing boughs of heather. In single file they started down the path, which took them up the side of a larger hill. Exaggerated morning shadows made the worn hunks of rock near the summit stand out among the heather. Cresting the hill, Agatha saw a large village of stone cottages below. Crowds gathered in the streets. Just outside the village, people stood milling about tables covered in brightly patterned fabric. It appeared some sort of festival was underway.

A flock of sparrow-sized birds flew past, and doubled back to swirl around them. The birds twittered in a song of stilted short bursts. They were all a tawny brown with beige highlights, and streaks of auburn ribboning from throat to belly. Jane pointed to some of the birds alighting among the heather.

"They have riders."

A bird and its rider bobbed before Agatha's face. Pulling back, she inspected the bullfrog astride the bird who hovered and flapped before her. The frog tipped a feather-plumed orange floppy hat, which contrasted with the navy dinner jacket he wore. There was a vague expression of amusement in the frog's mustard colored eyes, as his wide oval irises widened. With bulb-tipped fingers, the well-dressed frog beckoned them to follow.

The frog and his bird led them off the path towards a lone juniper tree on another hill. With a twisted bend, the juniper tree rose from the hill's edge. Its trunk looked stripped of bark and flaked, an outer husk made of its inner fibers. The mangled stem was an impossible contrast to its lush spanning limbs of dark berries and soft needles.

A man sat beneath the tree, with a bay horse grazing nearby. The man had a head of flame-red curls and wore silver armor rimmed with accents of bright copper. As they approached, he stood, and Agatha saw a large horn made of animal bone was slung beside his hip.

"Rufus, you are ever a gentlemen," the red-haired knight said to the frog. "I will toast with you at the fair today."

Rufus the frog waved farewell, before circling on his bird and flying back towards the village. The knight stepped forward and made a formal bow.

"Greetings Illuminer Jane, Songbird Agatha, and Master Bard Zachary. I am Sir Nye."

"Greetings," Agatha said. "Were you the one playing that fine instrument slung at your side?"

"Indeed," he said.

Sir Nye lifted the horn from his belt and offered it to her. Taking it, Agatha ran her fingers along the etched carving of multiple birds in flight.

"This is so beautiful, I loved the sound it made. If I could keep it, I would."

Sir Nye leaned over her and lingered there, with his hand resting on the horn. His eyes were a bright hue of marmalade.

"Then it, and its magical music is yours," he said.

"What must I give in return for such a prize?"

"Your hand in marriage," Sir Nye said.

Agatha felt warmth rising up her neck to brighten her cheeks. She never expected a sim character to make her an offer of marriage. This game was more confusing by the minute.

"However, we can't marry until I have a new shirt," Sir Nye said. "One free of a woman's embroidery, but imbued with your song."

"Oh, I've never made a shirt…with a song?" Agatha looked over at Jane and Zack for help. Zack just shrugged and motioned to Jane like the challenge was one he understood.

Jane nodded her head. "I think we can do that."

"Where do we make it?" Agatha asked Sir Nye.

"Why, with the tailor in the village of course. I should like it for the festival today, so I may wear it and boast of my Songbird's gift."

"Then we will go, and I will make it," Agatha said.

"I will see you then," Sir Nye said bowing his head as they left.

Zack started running ahead, weaving through the heather as he led them down to the village of stone cottages.

"Zack!" Agatha shouted after him, "Zack, wait."

He turned around with a hop, "I've never seen this level!"

Leaving Zack to his fun, Agatha stepped beside Jane. "What do you think Sir Nye meant by *imbued with my song*?"

"I think we'll need to make a shirt," Jane said, "but it will need to be made while you sing. I have a spell that can capture a rhyme or music in an object. So we'll sew, you'll sing, and I'll cast the spell."

Agatha sighed and tucked her hair behind each ear. "I hope it works. This is Feyland, nothing here is ever that simple."

Zack was whooping as he continued to leap down the hill. Jane put both hands on her hips and huffed a laugh. "Well, I know one Master Bard who doesn't seem to mind anything that happens here."

The village was a flurry of activity. Women twirled brightly colored parasols topped with streamers of trailing ribbon. People drank from large tankards, hefting them up with two hands in cheering toasts. A line of people linked arm in arm skipped a dance that snaked them through the crowd, as onlookers cheered and clapped. The smell of freshly baked pastries filled the air. The main street was paved with a repeating mosaic of a yellow on blue sun pattern, and curved back and forth in a pleasant meander. Agatha and her friends passed many shops before they found the town tailor.

Stepping into the shop, they were greeted by a tall man. He wore garments custom made for his long reed-like limbs, and inspected them with grey eyes. Peering over his pug nose, the man touched a long finger to what could barely be called a chin.

"Good morning, I'm Master Lewis. How can I be of service to Sir Nye's betrothed?"

"Sir Nye's what?" Agatha said. Jane cleared her throat as Zack doubled over, straining to contain his laughter.

"Sir Nye's betrothed. You are his beloved Songbird, are you not?"

"She is indeed," Jane said. "She's here to make him a new shirt."

"Very good," Lewis said. "You are in the right place, but we have no supply of the fabric you need. First you will need to fetch some from the weaver."

He pointed in the direction of the weaver's house, and they walked out onto the street again.

"You're engaged to a sim character," Zack said. He laughed and clapped in time with the people on the street.

"I think it's sort of tweaked," Jane said.

"Yes it's tweaked," Agatha said. "So why did you just agree with the tailor that that's who I am?"

"Sorry." Jane gave Agatha an apologetic look.

"It's like the perfect relationship," Zack said. "She'll never really see him, so they'll never fight. He's in a sim, so he'll never get mad about how much she spends on clothing. And if she ever needs to turn down a guy asking her out, she can tell him honestly she's—" Zack choked on a laugh and tried again to finish his sentence. "She can honestly say she's betrothed."

"That's not fair," Agatha said, trying to ignore his amusement. "You don't know anything about how much I spend on clothes."

"We became friends at Reruns," Jane said, looping her arm into Agatha's in a show of unity as they walked past Zack.

"Come on, I'm joking here! It was a joke."

They arrived at the weaver's house to be told there was no thread from which to make fabric, and were sent on to the town spinner to fetch some. The spinner told them there was no wool to spin for thread, and sent them on to the local shepherd for wool. The shepherd told them half the wool was theirs for the taking if they did the work of shearing his entire flock.

Despite Zack's carefree demeanor, he summoned his mandolin and stepped after the shepherd, who led them to the pasture and a stand for fleecing sheep. The shepherd gave them simple instructions and left them to shear his flock.

Agatha picked up the blade shears and gave them a quick squeeze. "Do you think I should sing over every task it'll take to make Sir Nye's shirt?"

"It might be a lot more singing than you think, I hope you don't go hoarse from it," Jane said with a sympathetic nod.

"Your song selection menu is up," Zack said,

Agatha looked at the choices and selected *The Spinning Wheel*. Zack began to pluck the intro as the song lyrics scrolled by in glowing gold letters. The music drew the sheep near and Agatha sang as she helped Jane shear every sheep in the flock.

When the wool was collected, they left with their promised payment. Zack continued to play as Agatha continued to sing and they went to the spinners house.

By the time they reached the weavers with their spindles of thread, Agatha had sung the song enough times to memorize the words. The weaving chore went quickly, and soon they were back in the tailor's shop.

Agatha unfolded the freshly woven fabric on the floor. Jane stepped back and retrieved what looked like a magic wand. With graceful precision, Jane painted symbols made of light in the air. Her artistry continued as she walked a full circle around Agatha and the fabric. Each scrawled light symbol hung in midair, with a white-hot glow. When Jane's circle was complete, the lyrics to The Spinning Wheel began to appear once more. The words were etched in light on the fabric as Agatha sang them.

Jane stood still, holding the power of her spell together. Zack continued to strum his mandolin, as Agatha harmonized her voice and sewed Sir Nye's shirt. Their marathon performance came to an end when Agatha held up a completed shirt. The circle of symbols faded, and the shirt seemed to absorb the lyrics painted in light.

Jane and Zack were such good players; they used their simming abilities with effortless grace. Agatha never would have finished this challenge without their in-game proficiency. She smiled at her friends. "Wow, that was prime, you guys."

Zack glanced down at his hand and rubbed his thumb over his string fingers before looking up at Agatha and smiling. "This whole village is amazing, I've never seen it, and I've finished the Bard's Challenge."

"We're not done yet. We need to find Sir Nye and see if he likes his new shirt," Jane said.

They walked back up the hill to the juniper tree, where Sir Nye sat waiting. He held out his horn again to Agatha, who tried to avoid staring into his marmalade colored eyes. She presented the shirt they had made.

"The horn is yours," he said. "As am I."

Agatha swallowed and tried not to frown. Whoever programmed the attractive Sir Nye insta-love character needed to improve their taste in romantic dramas. As Sir Nye pressed the shirt into his face, Agatha restrained the urge to put her palm against her forehead. What was he doing? Was he actually sniffing the shirt?

The huff and snort of Zack's failed attempts to restrain his laughter only increased Agatha's discomfort.

"I hope you like it," Agatha said. "Thanks again for the horn."

She held it in both hands and a burst of light flew out from around the horn and scattered off like dust in all directions.

"My horn provides you with musical accompaniment whenever you desire it," Sir Nye said.

Zack lifted his hand. "Do I get one of those too? I did help."

Sir Nye gave Zack a half grin but made no reply. Turning to Agatha he said, "Say my name sweet Songbird, and I will be in your arms."

Agatha blinked in wide-eyed horror. It was amazing how equally attractive and creepy Sir Nye was, and the idea of hugging him scared her.

But her fear of him faded as she wondered if never saying his name meant she would never have to see him again. She never actually agreed to marry him, right? She looked down at the horn and felt a chill.

Clearing her throat she said, "Well then, that's great. Good day." If she had primary control of the sim, she would just go ahead and shut the game down now.

"Good day? Dear Songbird will you not attend the festival on my arm?" Sir Nye asked.

"She can't," Jane said, "she promised to go with us and search for the Bard's Challenge."

"That's right, I promised," Agatha said. "Do you have any clue where we should start our search?"

Sir Nye stepped close and took Agatha's hand in his calloused grip. His thumb caressed her knuckles. Agatha looked at the shine of his breastplate and held her breath.

"I could never ask you to break a promise. Travel northwest from the village until you reach the hazelnut tree grove. Sing to the lark but leave the crossbill alone. Farewell, my sweet Songbird."

"Farewell," Agatha said.

Sir Nye released her hand and Agatha inhaled with relief.

When they were a short distance away Zack stopped. "I don't know about you two, but I'm hungry for whatever it is they're baking in that town. What do you two say we log out and find some food-food? Real food."

"I'm hungry too," Jane said.

Zack raised one finger and angled it to initiate the screen to save their game and exit. Agatha's body felt the sim chair as she took in the real world surroundings of Jane and Zack's apartment. Zack pulled off his sim gloves and inspected his fingers.

Jane tilted her head to the side watching Zack. "You all right?"

"Yeah, my calluses hurt a little more than usual. All that playing."

"All that playing made your string fingers hurt?" Agatha said.

Zack shrugged and stood up, "Wouldn't be the first time. I just wish I got the same in-game reward your sim fiancé gave you. Now you get to sing in game, with better instrumental accompaniment. It won't be the basic notes they play for everyone."

"So that's what he meant," Agatha said, better understanding the reward from Sir Nye.

"I think I could get into a red haired guy," Zack said, with serious consideration. "At least long enough to get that reward."

Jane laughed as she offered Agatha a hand up. Agatha took it and followed her new friends into the kitchen for dinner. As much as she loved Feyland, the interaction with Sir Nye had unsettled her. Declining Jane's offer to sim again, Agatha convinced Jane to show her the clothing design sketches she made with an old screenie program.

"Zack says some of these nobody would wear," Jane said, tapping through images of her older designs.

"Really?" Agatha said. "Right, because Zack is the poster child of prime."

"What?" Zack said leaning in the doorway to Jane's room.

"You're going to break my auto door again," Jane said, getting up from her desk to haul Zack into her room so the door could slide shut. Zack playfully pushed at her hands as she released him, and then flopped his whole body onto her bed.

"I'm prime, right Jane? I'm very prime," Zack said.

Jane grinned at her brother, mussing his hair playfully, and said, "You could be."

Zack gave Jane a hurt look and looked to Agatha with a plea for support. Agatha raised her eyebrows, making her skepticism clear.

"What?" Zack said, looking down as he grabbed at his shirt. "Are my clothes not good enough for you high school fashion goddesses?"

"I didn't say anything," Agatha said.

"You didn't need to, I saw the way you stared at me like a chip child."

"Your potential to be prime is there," Agatha said. "You… well you're dressed sloppy."

"Sloppy?"

"Ah-huh, sloppy. And for the record, my mother didn't grow up with a chip in her wrist. My mom worked hard for what she has. She always told me, just because you're poor doesn't mean you have to dress like it. There's no excuse for clothes with holes or things that don't fit, unless you're homeless. You're breaking both her rules right now, and to me, that's sloppy."

"Why does being better dressed make me prime?"

Agatha sighed, "I think you're missing my point. Look, you're in a band, you write music, you're an artist. A good one. But if this is how you dress all the time, then I think you could do better. Apply a little more of your artistic instincts to the way you dress. It's like the cover of an album, a game, or a book."

"Wait-wait, aren't you not supposed to judge a book by its cover?"

"I'm not going to lie, I judge everything by its cover. Most of the time I find exactly what I expected. The professionals in the marketing industry have consumer psychology pegged. Anybody who thinks their buying habits don't land on a consumer line and block chart is an ego charged fool."

"Listen to you!" Zack said.

"Sure, there's the odd time where a product's better than the packaging, or you get something tweaked, where the cover's the only thing you paid for. I just think, if you're going to be prime, be prime."

"I think I hit one of your hot buttons," Zack said, giving her a mollifying smile.

Agatha threw up her hands and restrained a growl. Yes, he hit one of her hot buttons, and his smile made her think he was ignoring everything she said. "I pay attention, even to things in poor packaging. But there are a lot more people out there who won't."

Jane nodded her head in agreement, and resumed tapping through her designs. Zack twisted his lips in quiet consideration as he scooted off Jane's bed. The fun exuberance he bubbled with since that morning was gone as he left Jane's room, and Agatha felt awful. How do you apologize for saying something, when you meant every word of it?

If only she'd kept her big mouth shut. She liked Jane and Zack, and they made it too easy for her to be herself. Zack was kind and funny, and underneath his sloppiness was a decent-looking guy. People were missing out if they avoided him because of the way he dressed. She was trying to help him, but if she wasn't more careful, their friendship would come apart in less time than it took to create.

* * *

Agatha went home that night still trying to shake the odd feeling she had from the encounter with Sir Nye. Simming with Jane and Zack had been so different from other times she'd played. She remembered how physically strange it was going into Feyland with Zack. Zack had achieved Master Bard status, so why were those levels all new for him?

She went to bed and fell asleep quickly. Her dream was filled with heather-covered hills and a harp melody she was unfamiliar with. Sir Nye's horn was in her hands, and its bird carvings came to life. Their heads rose and wings stretched from the horn's perimeter. The body of each bird emerged, flying into a diving chase with other birds, and each carried well-dressed frog riders. A rising sun silhouetted the strong figure of Sir Nye. The cool wind tossed his curls into flares of red hair. Adoring eyes of marmalade greeted her, as he said, "My songbird, for you I wait."

Agatha awoke with a jolt, sitting up as her heart pounded in her chest. Taking deep breaths, she tried to steady herself, but failed as she frantically kicked away her covers. Rolling to the edge of her bed, she got up and staggered through the dark to her bathroom. Auto lights dimmed on and Agatha blinked as she poured a glass of water. Trying to banish her fear, she downed the glass of water and returned to bed.

She had experienced her share of odd dreams or nightmares, but none of them rivaled the vivid feel of this last one. Unable to relax, Agatha crawled back in bed, but gave up trying to sleep any more that night.

* * *

After dinner on Sunday, Agatha sat studying in the living room as her mother chatted with Agatha's sister about the trivial happenings of the prior week. The gold bangle bracelets her mother wore jingled as she reached a hand to smooth Agatha's hair. Her mother gripped her shoulder in assurance, and slowly pulled her into a hug.

"I'm sorry you didn't get the part you wanted for the winter recital," her mom said. "Keep practicing, you'll get your solo."

Agatha nodded and chewed at the edge of her lip.

"Ms. Raider knows how talented you are. She's always given you a part."

"Just never the solo I wanted."

Agatha had joined performance choir more for the chance to wear fun costumes than for the frustrations that came with singing as part of a choreographed ensemble. The choir director, Ms. Raider, had tracked Agatha down her first week of school freshman year. She had the scary 'I'm a huge fan of your mom' eyes, when she handed Agatha the audition schedule. It took a full year for Ms. Raider's fan eyes to calm down. By sophomore year they were gone, but Ms. Raider still managed to slide in the occasional awkward question about Agatha's mom. Unfortunately, Ms. Raider's fan-girl devotion to Agatha's mom was non-transferable to her.

"She's not going to hand over the best parts just because," her mom said.

"I know," Agatha said, sliding out of her mother's embrace.

"So go practice. If you want it, you need to work for it like everybody else. The best one-percent—"

"I know, I know," Agatha said walking to her bedroom. "The best musicians are the one percent who log the most practice hours."

Agatha had always been good about practicing, but it felt

like such a waste of time. No matter how much she practiced, she was missing something. Shelly had something she lacked, every single audition. If only Agatha could pinpoint what that something was.

* * *

Jane found Agatha at lunch on Monday. "Hey, want to play Feyland tonight?"

Agatha nodded, "Yeah, it'll be nice to hang out. I'll be free after choir, where I get to watch Shelly rehearse her solo again."

"I'll sit through rehearsal, and then we can walk home. Maybe stop and splurge on some ice cream?"

"Ice cream therapy, that's perfect."

"Are you going to pout all winter about this?" Jane asked.

"Maybe."

"When you go to rehearsal, you need to stop moping and start having fun. Activities like show choir are supposed to be fun."

"I'll try, as long as we get ice cream afterwards."

They did stop for ice cream after rehearsal, which helped Agatha's mood a little. When they made it up to Jane's apartment, they found Zack in the living room, his guitar in his lap. A young boy sat across from him, also holding a guitar. The boy's head was bent in close inspection of his fingers, and Zack listed off each chord as they played. Jane motioned for Agatha to follow her quietly to her bedroom.

"I forgot Zack was teaching Kyle's lesson," Jane said.

"He teaches lessons?"

Jane nodded, "He teaches guitar, and I do private alterations. It's what paid for our full-D systems."

"That's dedicated," Agatha said.

"We camped outside the store the week it was released. We spent two nights with a tent sleeping on pavement so we could get a Full-D on release day."

"That's crazy," Agatha said.

Jane shrugged and laughed, "You've met Zack. Someone needed be out there with him. No, we had fun. We also got a great discount code for a future game purchase."

"And your parents didn't mind?"

"The only thing Dad asked was if we'd miss school. Mom said there was worse things we could be doing."

Jane's door slid open and Zack leaned his head in and waved at Agatha. "Hey, Agatha. We're all wrapped up if you want to sim. How was rehearsal?"

"Shelly's solo is really good," Agatha said.

"Let me try again, how was *your* rehearsal?" Zack said.

"She did great," Jane said.

"But I'm never going to be like Shelly," Agatha said.

Zack stepped through the auto door and crossed his arms as it shut behind him. "And you're never going to sound like your mother either."

Agatha met Zack's eyes with a confused look. If he was trying to hurt her feelings he succeeded. Yeah, no kidding she'd never sound like her world-class performance mother. Was this his payback for what she said about his clothes?

"I used to do that," he said. "Measure myself against the talent of other people. It's a bad habit, it'll wear you down.

It got too hard, to gauge what I could do, when I was always thinking about everybody else's talent. It's like a roadblock, you know? I mean, you're never going to key a chord or sing a note exactly like someone else. I got better at guitar when I stopped thinking about everybody else and paid attention to what *I* was working on."

Agatha's lips drew into a tight line as she listened to Zack. She had tried and failed so many times. He was right, but it was hard to smile and accept his words as encouragement and not criticism.

"I'll see you two later, I've got band practice," Zack said. "Chin up, fashion goddess, you're one hell of a songbird. When you get to Feyland, tell your fiancé I said hi." Agatha launched a pillow at Zack, who slipped out the door with a laugh, leaving the pillow to land against the closed door with a thud.

The heather hills and early morning sun looked the same as it had on Saturday when they had saved their sim level to Feyland. Wind rippled across the heather, tossing the flowers about like ocean swells.

Jane pointed to Agatha's waist. "Did you just manifest that?"

Agatha looked down to see Sir Nye's horn strapped to her belt. "No, but it looks neat huh?"

"Yeah," Jane said, still eyeing the horn with suspicion.

"What is it?" Agatha said.

"I don't know? It's just that last time we played it was a lot different than the other times I've simmed. And Zack and I play this game a lot."

"As you should. Two nights spent sleeping on concrete in

front of a shopping mall means you should be the kind of player they write online articles about."

Jane gave her a sheepish smile as she stepped onto the path leading to the village of stone cottages. "Well, maybe they already do."

Agatha's eyes went wide. "Are you serious?"

"I'm in a Feyland forum, and someone asked about an Illuminer spell they couldn't cast in the Dark Realm. I knew the answer, and then Dan, one of the forum admins, asked if I would do this small question and answer piece for their newsletter."

"You are the most perfect friend to have around, and support my two Fs obsession."

"Fashion, and Feyland," Jane said. "And the occasional stop for ice cream."

Together they stepped onto the mosaic walking path of the town's main street. They walked by the merry revelry of the townsfolk and greeted master tailor Lewis as they passed his shop. At the edge of town, Agatha turned to the northwest and saw a large stand of trees—the one Sir Nye had directed them to find.

"Larks are good, and crossbills are bad," Agatha said, remembering his words of advice. "I don't think I know what either one of those birds looks like."

"We should steer clear of any bird whose beak looks like this," Jane held up two fingers and crossed them.

"Okay." Agatha pantomimed Jane's crossed finger gesture. "Any other tips?"

"Larks can have little feather tufts on the tops of their heads. Some look like they have little feather bird horns."

"Bird expert huh?" Agatha asked.

"No, but I was curious after all the birds we saw the last time we played."

"What kind of birds were those fancy frogs riding?"

"Linnets."

"Linnets," Agatha said, trying to remember the name.

They entered the stand of trees and found several columns spaced in a wide arch. On top of each column stood the stone statue of a bird, and on the ground before each column sat perfect circles of red capped mushrooms.

"Would that one with the pointy horns be the lark?" Agatha asked, gesturing to a bird statue on the far left.

Jane nodded and stepped into the mushroom circle before it. Agatha followed, and the lark statue sent them through another blanket of golden light. They arrived inside a circled crown of stone mushrooms, thirty feet above the ground.

"What on earth? My feet are wet." Jane said, grabbing hold of Agatha's arm with both hands. "We're standing on top of a fountain!"

The midmorning air was warm, and the puffs of spray wafting up from the white fountain below them felt good. The fountain was so grand, it was like it had been stolen from a fine palace and secreted into the forest. Trailing plants draped flowers down the stepped fluted columns, where sculptures of flying birds were poised. Around them grew an old grove of trees with leaves flushed in autumn colors. Paper lanterns hung on strings slung between lower tree branches. The lanterns glowed like someone had made the mistake of leaving them on past morning. Thousands of brightly colored ribbons dangled from the trees and did a festive dance in the breeze. There was a cobblestone path set around the fountain, but the stones became scattered and then disappeared into the moss-covered ground.

"Have any ideas on how to climb down from here? Spells? Fancy things made out of light?" Agatha said.

Jane stood in thought as water from the fountain slowly crept up the hem of her apricot robes. "No, I have no ideas."

"I guess we're climbing down then," Agatha said.

"We'll get soaked," Jane said with a frown.

"It's Feyland, we'll be fine."

"Setting us on top of a fountain," Jane said in a low grumble, as she stooped to follow Agatha's climb down. "Whose bright idea is this?"

"Must be the same programmer who made Sir Nye," Agatha said.

"My songbird, please, do be careful!" Sir Nye said, appearing beside her and wrapping one arm around Agatha's waist. Agatha cried out at the touch and stared at Sir Nye in amazement as he guided their descent down via a rope.

"Please don't leave me up here," Jane cried from high above them.

Sir Nye was staring into Agatha's eyes as he replied, "Have no fear Illuminer Jane, I will return shortly to fetch you."

"Thank you," Agatha said as they reached the ground. She gasped when Sir Nye leaned over and hefted her into a cradle carry.

"Sir Nye, what about Jane? You can put me down now, I'm fine," she said, but Sir Nye ignored her and seemed to increase the pace of his stride. "It's unnecessary for you to carry me anywhere. Put me down."

"Indeed I must carry thee, for it is customary for a groom to carry his bride across their threshold."

"Oh no you don't," Agatha said. She squirmed and pushed, but Sir Nye's hold was strong and only increased. "Jane!"

"I'm coming," Jane called as she grabbed hold of the rope Sir Nye had left tied to the fountain and began to climb her way to the ground.

Sir Nye brought Agatha under the vined canopy of a willow tree before he set her down. Agatha fled his hold and ran back the way they had come. When she reached the edge of the willow's canopy she saw her escape was barred. Endless gold bars surrounded them, stretching up to form a caged dome beneath the willow tree. A gilded door stood blocking the entrance.

"Unlock this, now!" Agatha said.

"My precious songbird, I cannot. You have my horn, and my heart."

"Here," Agatha fumbled to grab the horn from her waist, "You can have it back."

"No, you are my songbird and caged birds always sing best."

"You caged me to get me to sing? You did this so I'll sing for you?"

"Of course," Sir Nye said. He moved to sit, and from the ground beneath them tree roots shot up to fashion a chair that rose up to embrace him.

"Agatha?" Jane called.

"In here," Agatha said, feeling some relief when Jane appeared, rushing down the path. Jane slowed, approaching the gold bars in awe. Agatha reached out and gripped Jane's hand in trepidation. "He wants me to sing."

Jane paused as she looked past Agatha's shoulder at the reclined figure of Sir Nye. "Then you should sing. Maybe a song like the one you sang with Zack to the triplet babies." She gave Agatha a meaningful look, eyebrows arched.

Agatha had sung a lullaby to the triplets. Recognizing Jane's hint, Agatha nodded.

"There's definitely spellwork at play here, and I think it has something to do with that." Jane pointed to the horn in Agatha's hand. "I'll see if I can cast a spell to unlock the door, but I think you have to get rid of that thing."

"I think you're right," Agatha said.

Agatha turned back to Sir Nye and met his marmalade colored eyes.

"I should like to hear you sing," Sir Nye said.

"Then I shall," Agatha said and reviewed the ballad selection that appeared. Her eyes trained in on *Lady Isabel and the Elf Knight*. Setting the pace with a slow tap of her foot, Agatha began.

At first she heard the usual chiming accompaniment as the gold scrolled words appeared. When she sang the first line the wind and string instrumentals of a full orchestra began. The precision of the accompaniment was pure, and so lovely she almost faltered in her singing. Honing in on her own voice, Agatha focused on the lyrics. The sound of the ballad was amazing. Hearing the vibrato of her voice, Agatha looked up in wonder at the acoustics of the willow canopy above. Its limbs and branches echoed the sweet hum of violins with her voice. The music lulled her into a relaxed rhythm, and Agatha felt the contentment that came when she enjoyed a performance.

When the ballad came to a close, Agatha saw Sir Nye asleep in his chair, his head resting on one hand. The instrumental faded into silence as Agatha crept beside him. She placed the horn in Sir Nye's lap, then glanced over her shoulder at Jane.

Jane shook her head as she pulled on the gilded door. "Still locked. I don't think that's good enough."

Agatha remembered what Sir Nye had said when she tried to give the horn back to him. "He said his horn and heart are mine."

"Then I think you need to break them both to break the spell."

Agatha bit down on her lip as she reached for the horn again. Her thoughts were a repeating chant begging him to not wake up, please don't wake up. She gripped the horn and lifted it from his lap and threw it on the ground by her feet. A calloused hand grabbed her wrist and she let out a startled yelp.

"My Songbird, what are you doing?"

Pulling away from him, she raised her foot above the horn. "Where I'm from we call it a break up." She stomped down hard on the horn and heard a hard crunch. "There's no betrothal, Sir Nye. Never has been, never will be." Agatha raised her foot one more time and stomped on the horn again.

A plume of gold light waved away from them, causing the ground to tremor and the willow tree to shudder. It sounded like one hundred different birds took flight at once, flapping and calling in an angry chorus. The tree roots holding up Sir

Nye retreated and left him sprawled on his back, scrambling to get up.

Jane shouted, "Agatha! It's open, the door's open, come on!"

Without hesitation, Agatha turned and ran from the cage. Reaching the gilded door she took Jane's outstretched hand and together they hurried up the path and back to the fountain.

"Should we search for the next gate?" Jane said.

Agatha shook her head, "No, no, end it. End it now. Get us out of here."

Agatha and Jane sat in silence as they exited the sim. Agatha knew there was something off about Sir Nye, but there was more going on with the level they had just finished besides the over-adoring red haired knight.

"Agatha," Jane said in a hushed voice, "my feet are wet."

"What?" Agatha said, pulling off her sim helmet to get a better look at Jane's wet feet. Scrunching her toes, Agatha felt a squish of water in her shoes. Holding her breath she shifted her gaze and saw her feet were wet, too. She looked up at Jane in shock and covered her mouth when she saw Jane's hair. It was as wet as if they were still in Feyland.

* * *

They made a pact to keep what they called, 'the wet shoe incident' to themselves. "I might be crazy about Feyland, but I don't need people thinking I could benefit from medication," Agatha said, and Jane was quick to agree.

When she started playing again, Agatha eventually did find her way to the Bard's Quest, but she never again found hills of heather, the bird statues, or fountain in the forest. The instrumental accompaniment reward she received from Sir Nye's horn remained. Sir Nye seemed gone, but Agatha took zero chances, and never said his name again.

Zack had taken Agatha's suggestion of making his appearance as prime as he was to heart. The days he was noticeably prime also corresponded to days he encountered Lindsey from 204. Jane saw Zack's change too, and after catching Agatha looking fondly at Zack she teased, "Lindsey's not the girl he's looking prime for."

Embarrassed, Agatha blushed.

"She's nice," Jane said, "but I told him, you're a better fit for him."

Zack never confided that Agatha's advice prompted the change, but she never mentioned taking his advice either. She practiced, focused on her own performance, and began to actually enjoy it.

To Agatha's surprise the highlight of her junior year was prom. She joined Jane and a few other friends, and they all attended prom as one big group of single girls. There was a group photo, and a funny moment where someone fished some feather boas out of a bag, and draped them around the necks of everyone in their group. It was an act Agatha called "feathered fashion sin."

Agatha inspected the scarf of green fluff around her neck, and Jane teased her, "It really is a sin to wear lime with your *aubergine* dress."

Agatha laughed and twirled one end of the green boa. "You're mistaken, this really isn't lime, it's chartreuse."

The absolute best part of prom was when Zack blindsided her, tapping his finger to a hidden microphone by his ear, and looking into the prom crowd with an impish grin.

"I need you all to help me find my sister's best friend, and my favorite songbird. Agatha, where are you? Come on up here."

A gymnasium full of eyes found her, and the students clapped and cheered for her to get up on stage. For a moment Agatha felt overwhelmed. Zack offered her a hand up and placed the clear tubes and wires of a hidden microphone in her hand. Her cheeks ached from smiling, and she did her best to control her laughter as she fit the hidden microphone to her ear.

"We're going to sing a duet," Zack said. "It's a song I wrote, and Agatha here helped me out on the melody. I hope you like it."

Zack counted off and strummed through the intro chords on his guitar. Agatha's voice harmonized with Zack's and they bobbed with the lively tune. She was able to get everyone in the gymnasium clapping. Soon the audience sang along with the chorus, about a red haired knight and what his beloved should do if he proposes too soon. "Run away, run away, run away."

There was a wave of applause and cheering when their duet ended. Zack gave her a hug, and she waved before exiting the stage. Jane and their friends circled Agatha in excited mayhem as they showed her the dozens of images they had taken. She was looking at a vid of her performance when Ms. Raider approached.

"That was outstanding, Agatha, just outstanding."

"Ms. Raider, thanks. Zack worked hard on it, but he totally ambushed me tonight."

"Agatha, that was your best performance," Ms. Raider said. "The next time you audition, you need to do that again."

Agatha's smile faded some. Ms. Raider wanted her to audition with that song? She and Zack had put it together in a few hours, when they were just hanging out, having fun. "Ms. Raider, if you don't mind my asking, what did I do differently? What did I do tonight that's been missing from my other auditions?"

Ms. Raider leaned forward, looked Agatha in the eye, and smiled. "You were having fun. That's what makes a musical piece go from being just another work to an inspired performance."

Jane grabbed Agatha when Ms. Raider walked away and began jumping up and down. "You're going to do it! You're going to audition with the song you and Zack wrote, and you're going to get the spring solo."

For the first time in three years Agatha actually believed she could get her solo. She pictured how she would perform for the audition, and imagined the moment she was announced the lead soloist. And best of all, she knew she'd have fun.

"I'm going to do it this time," Agatha said, before gripping Jane to join her, bouncing with a squeal of excitement.

* * *

Zack and his band recorded an accompaniment for Agatha's audition and helped her rehearse. Jane, Zack, and the other band members sat through the entire spring concert choir auditions. After Agatha's audition, the band gave their own mini performance, standing up with loud whistling cheers.

The auditorium sat silent when Ms. Raider strode center stage to announce the parts for the spring concert. Zack took Agatha's hand and gave it a reassuring squeeze. If life had a pause button, she wanted to hit it. The warmth in his green eyes was something she needed to study. Somehow it was transmitting to her and she could feel it all the way down into her toes. She found it hard to look away from him or hear anything over the gleeful voice screaming in her head, *he's holding my hand!*

"The lead soloist for the spring concert will be…Agatha McKnight."

Tears of joy sprang to Agatha's eyes as Jane crushed her in an excited hug. The band shouted in triumph, and Zack joined the hug, saying, "You showed them! That was so sparked. You won your real life Bard's Challenge."

Brushing tears from her eyes, she laughed and tried to think of any other moment in her life where she experienced this much bliss. The jostling bear hug from her two most cherished friends felt like the only thing keeping her from floating out of her seat. A little fun was all it took to get here, but it took real friends to help her realize it.

It's hard to tell a person something they don't want to hear, especially a friend. But when you really care about someone you do it anyway. You take the risk, speak the truth, point out what's missing, or push them to do better. She looked at Jane and Zack, and felt tremendous gratitude; they helped her find what she was missing.

She did it. She *finally* did it. This was a real world achievement. She loved performing on stage, and pretending in a game was fun, but neither one could replicate true friendship or the beauty in the real world experience of now.

A WORD FROM ANDREA LUHMAN

After reading the novella and first *Feyland* novel, I was really grabbed by the well-crafted connection the Feyland world had with folklore and folk songs. I love the sincere struggle and growth of the teenage characters in each of the original *Feyland* novels. I worked hard to try and maintain this same teen life authenticity in Agatha, Jane, and Zack. A great deal of my inspiration came from the real folksongs Agatha sings. After Anthea Sharp granted me permission to write characters with bard avatars, "An Artist's Instinct" quickly came together.

I wanted to feature some of the life lessons I gained growing up and participating in competitions. Especially the import lesson of learning what kind of meaningful motivation helps me work to pursue long-term goals. It's a lesson that's helped me stay grounded when the roadblocks of self-doubt and fear of failure rise up.

Fear almost made me shy away from the opportunity to be a *Future Chronicles* author and write in Anthea Sharp's *Feyland* series. As an unknown writer competing for publication in a highly successful series, I leaned hard on my motivation and reminded myself that the worst thing Anthea Sharp or Samuel Peralta could say to my story was no thank you. The fun of writing down the story circling around in my head brought me well past the fear. I enjoyed writing "An Artist's Instinct", and I am humbled and thrilled that Anthea and Samuel said "Yes." It's a privilege to join the alumni of *Chronicles* authors.

The first novel in the series I've spent the last three years writing should go to publication sometime near the end of 2016. You can contact me and find out more about my work at my website: www.andrealuhman.com.

Tech Support
by James T. Wood

RANJEET NAGAR HURRIED to his job, one of the better available in Kochi on the coast of India, in the call center for VirtuMax. The global company had just launched its most ambitious game, Feyland, and needed all the tech support help they could get.

Ranjeet dodged a pack of street kids and broke into a jog. He darted over a drawbridge, ignoring the lowered pikes, and just jumped the gap before it became too wide. The smell of the fish on the waiting boat mixed with the pregnant humidity to remind Ranjeet of meen vevichathu, a fish curry that his mother would make. His family had moved to the coastal city in Kerala State when his father had been promoted to the head of a large bank. Ranjeet missed the slower pace of the rural town where he'd been born. Where the sound of the waves crashing on the shore wasn't drowned out by the rush of grav-cars on the streets, and the faint smell of coconuts wasn't lost in the aroma of hundreds of thousands of bodies vying for the same air.

But he didn't have time for reverie. His boss, Mr. Narang, was not forgiving, and Ranjeet had been late too often. He'd stayed up far into the night working to fix the ailing network in his parents' apartment building and had only finished a few hours before. He should have left the work for later, but once he started a puzzle he was compelled to finish it. That was part of what made Ranjeet good at tech support, and most of what made him hate it.

He crept into the office and glanced over at his coworker Amit. Amit gave him a nod and motioned for him to hurry. Ranjeet gave him a quick smile and moved quickly to his cubicle. He had just gotten logged into the system when Mr. Narang arrived.

"Good to see you've found your computer, Ranjeet," Mr. Narang said. "Did you stop for chai on the way in?"

It was the closest Yamal Narang ever came to having a sense of humor. Ranjeet knew better than to engage. "No, sir," he said. "I have a call coming in; if you'll excuse me."

Ranjeet tapped the button on his phone and opened the ticketing app on his system.

"Thank you for calling VirtuMax support, my name is Roger. How can I help you today?"

Mr. Narang walked away as Ranjeet stepped someone with an almost indecipherable southern accent through the creation of a character in Feyland. After a few more moments of ensuring that he had answered all of the questions, Ranjeet finished the call.

"You'd better be careful," Amit said to him without looking away from his screen. "Mr. Narang is looking for someone to fire."

"Why?"

"His son lost his scholarship and has to leave school. He wants to give him a job, but we're already at capacity."

An email came into Ranjeet's queue at that moment. He looked at it briefly before leaning over to look at Amit's screen.

"What?" he asked.

"Did you get this email too?"

"You're going to have to be more specific than that," he said.

Ranjeet opened the message.

System: Full-D
Program: Feyland
User: 2uluW@rrior
Issue: Whenever I enter the game it does not take my character profile and has an error where dwarf-monsters appear and disappear. They're like evil teddy bears with holes in their heads. I can never get to the fairy courts.

"Have you seen this?" Ranjeet asked.

His co-worker leaned over and read the email. "Send it to tier-two."

"But this is the seventh email—"

Amit cut him off, "We're tier-one. We don't deal with stuff like that. Especially if we want to keep working here." He gave Ranjeet a meaningful look.

Ranjeet read over the email a few more times and escalated it to tier-two, but he also sent a blind copy to his personal email. He knew that if he was ever caught he'd be fired, but the compulsion to solve the puzzle was too great.

Puzzles had always been both a joy and a curse to him. When he was young, and his father still affluent, he would spend all his time working on puzzles. Every time he solved one, he had a need to pick up another, the more difficult, the better. He quickly mastered simple logic puzzles, number games, and every size and shape of a Rubik's Cube physically possible—and through his old sim-system, even some that were beyond physical possibility.

When his father had lost his job at the bank, Ranjeet had to leave boarding school and get a job to help make money for the family. Tech support was a natural fit. He could work on a problem for hours or days, until he solved it. He helped around the apartment complex keeping the aging hardware running as best he could, but it didn't earn enough money to make a difference. So when VirtuMax opened a call center, he knew he had to apply.

What he didn't know was how far away from actually solving puzzles his job would be. He read off of a script or sent the people to tier-two. They didn't even provide a test-rig where he could verify issues. Ranjeet hated not being allowed to solve the puzzles, but what was even worse were the puzzles that no one was solving. He couldn't sleep at night for thinking about them. He would go home and look at the emails he'd copied and search for clues. But without his own Full-D sim-unit, he wasn't making much progress.

At his assigned chai break, Ranjeet went to Mr. Narang's office and sat down and waited until the boss finished whatever he was working on. When he looked up, Ranjeet set a cup of chai on his boss's desk as a sort of peace offering; it was ignored

"Mr. Narang, I'm sorry to bother you. I wanted to check on what appears to be a glitch."

"Send it up to—"

"Yes, sir. But the glitch appears to be in our email server. I keep getting emails that no one else is getting."

"Regarding…"

"Support issues."

"And…"

"Well, sir, the other workers aren't getting them."

"And…"

Ranjeet looked at his chai for a moment. He thought of his mother's asthma. She couldn't work and his father's severance package was given on the condition that he never took another banking job or spoke about his work. Ranjeet was all that kept his family out of poverty.

He knew he should be silent. He knew that he should ignore it. He knew all of those things, but the itch had started. It always felt this way when a puzzle took hold of him. It started small. He could dismiss it for a while. But it built and built, like a sneeze. The longer he resisted, the bigger the explosion would be. He wanted to stop. He knew he needed to stop, but trying to stop was like trying not to sneeze.

"Sir," Ranjeet looked up, "all the emails describe the same type of issue and they're all coming to me. There *has* to be a reason for it."

Mr. Narang sat back in his chair. "Ranjeet, you're good at your job, and that's what I need you to do. Your job."

"Yes, sir, but—"

Mr. Narang held up his hand. "No, Ranjeet. Just do *your* job. Let tier-two do *their* jobs. If you can't do *your* job, then we'll have to find someone who can. Do you understand?"

Ranjeet nodded furiously, gulped down the last of his chai, and got up to leave. In the doorway he turned and said, "Yes, sir. I understand. Thank you for your time."

* * *

On his way home from work, Ranjeet walked through a park. The promised rain had fallen and cleaned the air of smog. The still-damp flowers sparkled as the sun warmed them with its reddening light. He always felt more peace at the park, even though the bustle of Kochi was just outside the fence.

Ranjeet swiped away most of the water still clinging to one of the benches and sat. The puzzle had not released him, but he could see no way forward. If he pushed Mr. Narang, Ranjeet would lose his job and without it there was no way he would be able to work on the puzzle. He stared at the passing people, some going to late shifts at their own call centers, others leaving their jobs for the day and heading home. But the people faded into background noise as his brain worried at the puzzle.

Seven emails. They only came to him, and all described similar issues. The users would create a character, define its features, and then take their first foray into Feyland. They expected to see a digital representation of the mythical land of faeries, but none of them did. They saw a different place, the Full-D sim unit transported them with complete sensory input, but it wasn't the place described in the game's manual nor by the tech support scripts. More than that, the players' characters did not look like the ones assigned in the system, but like the players themselves.

Ranjeet had scoured the forums for any posts that might relate, but if there ever was one, Ranjeet couldn't find it. He considered contacting tier-two directly, but all support tickets had to come from a verified Feyland account and accounts were tied to Full-D units.

As night fell, Ranjeet started home. Before he got very far he heard his name. Ranjeet turned to see Amit waving at him from across the gardens. He waved back and Amit motioned for him to wait, rushing around the walkway to meet him.

"Hi, " Ranjeet said, "I was just going home."

"Would you like to join me for dinner?" Amit asked.

"I'm sorry," Ranjeet said, "I can't. My parents need my help tonight.

"Oh."

Ranjeet offered a weak smile by way of making amends. "Maybe next time."

Ranjeet still had trouble making friends. He'd lived in a different world for so much of his life, he didn't know how to act or how to talk around people like Amit. He was always afraid that he'd unintentionally say something rude or offensive. But at the same time, he desperately wanted a friend.

"I'm walking the same way. We could at least keep company for a while," Amit said.

They walked in silence as the awkwardness seeped away. After a few minutes, Amit cleared his throat. "What's it like?" he asked.

"Walking?"

Amit laughed. "No, Ranjeet, what's it like not being rich anymore?"

"What do you mean?"

"I'm not dumb, even though I just read a script for a living. I can see the signs."

"Right," Ranjeet said. He searched for the words to express the change, to speak about how everyone treated him differently, about how his parents suffered, about how he'd had to give up on his schooling to make money, but the only thing that came to mind was *her*. "I used to be engaged. I'm not anymore."

"I'm sorry," Amit said softly, "I didn't know."

"It's okay," Ranjeet meant it, but he couldn't keep the pain from his voice.

After a long pause, Amit asked, "What was she like?"

"She—Daru—is lovely, she's smart, thoughtful, and she keeps me guessing."

"How is that a good thing? The guessing part?"

Ranjeet smiled into the distance, "Because she's a mystery that I could never stop solving."

Amit smiled. "You like puzzles very much, don't you?"

"What?" It took Ranjeet a moment to bring his thoughts back to the conversation. "Oh, yeah. I like puzzles."

"Like the emails?"

Ranjeet couldn't think of a response, his thoughts kept drifting to Daru.

"That must be tough," Amit's voice dropped lower, "not being able to work on the puzzle."

"I—" Ranjeet started to respond, but a scream in the distance cut him off. He looked over at Amit with a question in his eyes. Amit nodded an instant before Ranjeet took off running toward the sound. Amit followed close behind.

The scream rang out again. Ranjeet sped up and darted around a corner, following the sound. He expected to be one man in a crowd standing up against a gang trying to take a woman away. The instances had gotten fewer, but they still happened from time to time.

Ranjeet's shoes skidded on the still-wet pavement as he stopped. Amit nearly plowed into his back as they saw a woman lying on the ground in the middle of a square surrounded by hunched shadows. Ranjeet and Amit exchanged a hard look. The country had worked too hard for too long to eradicate this problem. They weren't going to let it continue in their city.

Together they ran straight toward the woman and her attackers, shouting loudly so everyone within earshot would know to call the police. Their boldness shocked the attackers, but the attackers weren't who—or what—Ranjeet thought.

As they neared they saw not young men, but creatures from a nightmare. They hunched over the woman, clawing at her body with their long, grotesque fingers. Their arms looked like knotted ropes as veins bulged and shifted beneath ash-gray skin. But it was their bulbous, red, hate-filled eyes that cut into Ranjeet's courage.

He uttered a prayer under his breath as he shouldered past the creatures, barely even slowing as he bent down to snatch the woman's hand. She moaned as he pulled her up, but stayed with him. By the time the beasts realized what Ranjeet had planned, the two were on the opposite side of the abandoned square. He kept running until his ward stumbled. Ranjeet stopped and saw that none of the abominations had followed.

"Are you…" he didn't even know what to ask.

"Thank. You," she said, taking a breath between each word.

Ranjeet looked around for Amit, but couldn't see him anywhere. He was just about to go looking for his absent friend, when he heard a shout. Ranjeet turned to see Amit emerging from an alleyway.

"Sorry," he was breathing heavily. "After you grabbed her, they scattered and some came toward me. I ran through the alleys to get around them."

"It's okay," Ranjeet said, "just help me get her to the hospital."

They took the woman to the emergency ward. After making sure she was taken care of and her family was with her, Ranjeet and Amit left. The two parted ways at the door of the hospital, each heading home for the precious few hours of sleep remaining that night.

* * *

"They're called Pishacha."

Ranjeet spun around, looking for the voice that had answered the question in his head. He was nearly home and had been trying to figure out what he'd come across in that darkened square. He did not, however, expect an auditory hallucination as a response. And he was most certainly not expecting to see a Caucasian baby, with the leaves of some northern tree snagged in his disheveled hair, leering at him with an all too adult expression.

The creature, who hovered before Ranjeet's face, bowed low before speaking again. "I am Puck and you, good sir, are lucky to be alive. The Pishacha are nasty creatures."

"What are they? What are you? Who—"

Puck cut him off, "You, sir, ought to know your own legends better than I, but I shall say this, their hunger would put even the Dark Queen to shame. They are yearning to break out of their world and the Dark Queen wishes to help them, for if there is one path from the realms of legend, then all such creatures could learn to use it." Puck finished his soliloquy with a wild chuckle and a pirouette in midair.

"Are you trying to say—"

"I *have* said what I will say and *won't* say what I can't." The imp bowed again but let the motion turn into a complete somersault before he started floating away.

"Wait," Ranjeet called, "what am I supposed to do?"

"Do what you must; do what you were meant to and solve the riddle. But do not tarry, for on Onam Eve the veil will be torn and the Pishacha will come."

Ranjeet shouted, "Do you mean the emails? Are you talking about Feyland? What about the Pishacha?"

There was no response. Ranjeet fumbled for his key and put it in the lock when he heard a whisper in his ear.

"Help your brother's boat across, and your own will reach the shore."

Ranjeet turned to look for Puck, but only the creature's laughter remained. He went upstairs to the small flat he shared with his parents and thought on the last words spoken to him, the same words that his mother loved to say. It was an old Hindu proverb that she repeated to him when he wanted to be selfish instead of helping someone else.

Ranjeet eased the door open to avoid waking his parents. He found some cold rice and curry in the kitchen and made himself a plate before sitting down with his tablet. First he looked up the Pishacha. They were an Indian demon that could feed on the energy—or bodies—of people. The descriptions varied, but clearly what he'd seen in that darkened square were Pishacha.

Puck was next. Most of the links pointed to Shakespeare, which he vaguely remembered from school, but Ranjeet soon discovered that Puck had been a legend long before the time of Shakespeare just as the Pishacha had been the subject of stories in India for millennia. Ranjeet had never paid much attention to old stories and myths. He thought them antiques that didn't apply to his world of computers and puzzles. But tonight he'd seen two of them in reality.

If Puck and the Pishacha are real, Ranjeet thought, *then what else might be real?* He opened his email and looked over the messages he'd forwarded to himself. He started with the most recent one and started looking for mythological creatures that matched the description given to him by 2uluW@rrior. There were so many possibilities, so many myths from all around the world. Ranjeet was about to give up for the night and get some sleep. He stared at his screen without seeing as the pieces of the puzzle danced around in his mind.

Through his unfocused gaze, the username wavered and he saw the meaning intended: Zulu Warrior. He'd seen something about Africa in one of his searches. After just a few moments of furious typing, he found the Zulu myth of the Tikoloshe that perfectly matched the description given in the support ticket. It only took him a few more minutes to match the other support tickets to their different cultural myths. There was a Vodnik from someone in the Czech Republic, there a Pixiu from China, a Chupacabra from Mexico, and a Taniwha from New Zealand.

They were all legendary creatures from different cultures and somehow they were getting into the game and people were seeing myths from their own cultures rather than the Feyland game. And, they were all real. Ranjeet had to discover what that meant before Onam Eve, the beginning of the celebration where the legendary King Mahabali was said to return from the underworld and bless good children. Onam Eve—which was only a week away.

* * *

Ranjeet rubbed his eyes. The calls and emails blurred together and, in some ways, his job became easier. Reading a script and never pausing to consider the people or the puzzles they brought let the ever-present knot in Ranjeet's stomach relax. His mind wandered to the myths of the world and to the words of Puck: "Do not tarry, for on Onam Eve will the veil be torn and the Pishacha roam freely."

When Amit arrived, Ranjeet used the corporate instant message client to say, *Are you okay? We need to talk.*

Amit responded with one word, *Lunch.*

Ranjeet used the barest sliver of his mind to help people and the rest of his thoughts wrestled the mystery. He barely noticed the emails, he scanned the text for the keywords, tapped out the shortcut for the canned responses, and sent off the reply. He was just about to log off for his lunch break when an email that he'd just answered came back. They weren't supposed to do that. They were supposed to go back to the bottom of the queue.

System: UNKNOWN
Program: Feyland
User: RhymeTom
Issue: Ranjeet, you must enter Feyland tonight!

He stared at the screen for a long moment before he could make his mind form thoughts. With the thoughts came the knot in his stomach. No one emailing through the system should be able to reach him directly. No one should be able to know his name—even his pseudonym of Roger, but especially not his actual name.

He quickly logged out of the phone system so he wouldn't get another call, then tried to reply. Ranjeet's fingers floated above the letters, twitching slightly as different responses warred in his mind. He took a deep breath and held it as his fingers typed.

He jumped when his IM notification sounded. Amit was asking if he was going to join him in the cafeteria. Ranjeet said he was on the way and moved back to answer the email, but when he selected it, the message displayed an error. He couldn't respond and when he refreshed the queue the entire email chain was gone.

* * *

Ranjeet joined Amit in the cafeteria, but couldn't bring himself to pile food onto the boiling fear in his guts. Amit, however, ate enough of the bland, curry-like substance for the both of them. Over the sound of various workers coming and going from their meals, Ranjeet told Amit everything about Puck, about the mythical creatures, and about the most recent email. Amit digested the tale with his food. After a long silence he looked up at Ranjeet with a worried frown.

"What is it?" Ranjeet asked.

"You won't like what you have to do."

"What?"

"You need a Full-D system, right?" Amit began ticking things off on his fingers.

"Yes."

"And there's no way you can afford one…"

"Right."

"And most of the people you know either work here or live in the apartment complex with you…"

"Okay." Ranjeet felt his palms grow slick with sweat.

"So you have to ask Daru."

Ranjeet's face matched Amit's expression. He was right, but Ranjeet hated him for it. His ex-fiancé, Daru Padmanabhan, had not agreed with her father's decision to call off the marriage. But neither had she fought him when Ranjeet suggested that they elope. She told him that they would then both be poor *and* outcast. She told him that she would lose her whole family if she rejected her father's wishes.

Ranjeet shook his head.

"But what about the email?" Amit asked.

Ranjeet shook his head.

"But what about Puck?"

Ranjeet shook his head.

Amit's voice dropped to the barest whisper, "What about the Pishacha attacking women in the streets?"

Ranjeet dropped his head.

* * *

Daru was as beautiful as Ranjeet remembered, and her house as opulent. After living in run-down apartments with his parents, Ranjeet felt at once more comfortable in the lavish environs, and out of place as a failure amongst the trappings of success.

"Come in," Daru said, "Both of you come in."

Amit had accompanied Ranjeet after they got off work. Together they took the long ride on the transit system to the wealthy neighborhood in Kochi where the Padmanabhan family lived. Daru answered the door herself, though she did not have to, and ushered them into a comfortable sitting room filled with all the trappings of wealth that Ranjeet had left behind. From the deep, soft carpet to the rows of shelves with antique books on them, the surrounds bespoke luxury to the point of excess.

"Ranjeet, it's been too long," Daru gestured to a couch as she sat in a nearby chair. Amit sat on the edge of the deeply cushioned seat as one afraid of damaging a fragile treasure, while Ranjeet readily sank into its softness.

He paused to gather his courage. "Daru, we need to borrow your Full-D system tonight. It's important."

"How do you know I have—" Daru began before Amit cut her off.

"We work for VirtuMax's new call center. We can look up account holders, but we're not supposed to."

Ranjeet continued the thought, "We've been working on a Feyland issue and we need to test it out on a Full-D system. You're the only one I know who has one."

Daru responded with a silent *Oh*.

Ranjeet bit his lip before continuing, "There are some strange things going on that I'm not sure you'd believe, but there's something important that I have to do."

"What makes you think I wouldn't believe you?" Daru spoke the words toward Ranjeet's knees instead of his face.

"It's… complicated."

She caught his eyes as a smile played across her lips. "Most of our relationship is complicated, so I'm used to it."

Ranjeet swallowed hard. Telling her about the legendary creatures scared him far more than showing up at her house and asking to use her gaming system. He inhaled and rubbed his damp palms across his knees.

"I think Feyland might be more than just a game."

"What do you mean?"

Amit interrupted and told Daru bluntly and quickly about

everything that had happened, including the Pishacha attack. He suggested visiting the poor woman that the creatures had nearly killed, if she had any more doubts. Daru didn't say anything when he finished. The three of them sat for a long time as Daru processed what she'd heard. Ranjeet was tensing to stand up and leave when she spoke.

"Okay." That was all she said.

She got up and led them down the hall and up the stairs to a room with her Full-D system. She gestured to one of the chairs. Ranjeet sat down and started pulling on the headset and gloves, but before Amit could do anything, Daru sat in the other chair and mirrored Ranjeet's movements.

"What?" Ranjeet exclaimed.

Daru calmly sat back in the chair and ignored him. She pulled the visor over her eyes and began navigating the system menu. Ranjeet hurried to join her in the virtual waiting room.

"Why are you—" Ranjeet began.

"It's my system, my game, my login, and my city that needs to be saved," Daru snapped at him. "Do you have a login for Feyland?"

"Huh?"

Daru sighed, "We can create you one."

"Oh, thanks."

Ranjeet rushed through the character creation process, not making any changes to the avatar. If he was right, it wouldn't matter anyway. None of the people that had sent him support tickets had looked like their avatars. He did pick his usual class for gaming though, a rogue. Ranjeet was always more interested in solving the puzzles than tanking through mobs of bad guys.

The flaming title of the game appeared floating before him before fading away and revealing a circle of polished stones on the ground. He knew instantly—mostly from reading the same script a thousand times—this was not the way Feyland was supposed to begin. There was the circle he expected, but it was supposed to be made of mushrooms and the circle was meant to be in a forest. Instead he saw polished stones sitting on the white sand of a long beach with palm trees in the distance.

He looked over to see Daru standing tall in shining armor covered by a bright surcoat of silk embroidered with fanciful patterns. Her greaves and bracers flashed in the sun as she turned and smiled at Ranjeet. With a whoop she brandished her war axe and round shield. The breeze caught the peacock's plume on her helm and set the colors to shimmering.

"What did you expect," Daru smirked at Ranjeet, "some sort of priestess? I like to get in there and fight—though the missions in Feyland have been nothing like advertised. Still, it's been fun."

Ranjeet followed as she stepped confidently out of the circle of stones. He checked himself to find a crossbow with bolts, and a brace of throwing knives.

"Where are we going?" Ranjeet asked.

Daru didn't break stride as she spoke the words over her shoulder, "To see the king, of course."

Ranjeet hurried to keep up. Daru had always been confident, perhaps even too confident to be proper at times, but in the game she didn't hide it.

"The king?"

"The king of the underworld, King Mahabali. He's the ruler in this game. He gives out the best and hardest quests. I've seen him a few times while playing, but usually I don't have the time to run any of his quests."

"But…" Ranjeet tried to comprehend what he was hearing, a task made that much more difficult because of the person from whom he was hearing it. "You've been playing all this time and you haven't seen the Dark Queen or any of the normal characters for Feyland?"

"I just figured it was the Indian version of the game. They did such a good job recreating all the creatures from the stories I'd heard as a girl that it made sense. But when no one on the message boards knew what I was talking about, I started to suspect something was wrong."

"Why didn't you contact tech support?" Ranjeet hated himself for even asking the question.

Daru stopped and turned to him, "Maybe I was waiting for tech support to contact me."

Ranjeet's heart beat faster in the light of Daru's smile. He fought for moisture in his mouth, but his tongue stuck and refused to produce words.

She started walking again. "Besides," she continued, "I've been having *so* much fun!"

Whether they were waiting for her to finish talking or just enjoyed irony, Ranjeet never knew. Pishacha boiled out of the palm forest, their red eyes piercing the dimness of the woods. Daru raised her shield and axe and bodily shoved the Pishacha away from her before assuming a more traditional fighting stance.

Ranjeet took his cue from her and pulled back the handle

on his crossbow until the string clicked into its catch. His shaking hands caused the first bolt to drop to the ground, but the second one slid into its track. Ranjeet lifted the weapon and saw Daru casually behead one of the slavering demons with a forehand stroke of her axe. On the backswing she caved in the ribcage of another. Ranjeet looked for a target and found one farther away. The Pishacha hissed at Ranjeet as he pulled the trigger on his crossbow. The bolt flew true and straight, exactly where Ranjeet had been aiming. The Pishacha crumpled to the ground with fletchings sprouted from between its eyes. In the time it took Ranjeet to reload, Daru had dispatched another three demons. The rest thought better of their odds and fled.

"Are you okay?" he asked.

She didn't respond with anything but a deep, full belly laugh.

"I'll take that as a 'yes.'"

Daru wiped demon-blood from her axe onto mossy turf. "Were those the monsters you met in the real world?"

"Yes."

"I've fought them enough in here to know that I wouldn't want to fight them out there."

"You must hurry," a new voice came from behind Ranjeet. He spun and fired his crossbow, lodging the bolt deep into the trunk of a date palm. "Hold! I am not a foe."

Daru pointed her axe at the man standing before them. His graying hair and sage demeanor caused her to lower her blade slightly. He lifted his hands to show that they held no weapons. A guitar was slung across his back.

"I am Thomas Rimer—"

Ranjeet interrupted, "RhymeTom?"

The man smiled. "One and the same. But that is of little import now; you are here and must make haste. The king will select his vessel and so become one himself. All things are connected if one pulls on enough strings, but the end of string pulling is, inevitably, unraveling."

"What in the names of the gods are you talking about?" Daru raised her axe again, level with Thomas' neck.

Ranjeet pushed her weapon aside. "Don't you get it? It's a riddle. We need to find the king and his vessel before everything comes unraveled."

Thomas bowed low, rose, and then winked at Ranjeet before disappearing.

"All right," Daru grumbled, "I haven't seen anything like that before. Who was that?"

"I'm not sure, but he told me I needed to get into the game tonight. He must know something."

"It would sure have been nice if he'd decided to share what he knew. How are we supposed to solve riddles *and* fight demons?"

"One thing at a time," Ranjeet said, "Take me to the king."

* * *

To say Daru was good at dispatching Pishacha would be akin to saying that Mozart was good at writing catchy tunes. She mowed through them, she demolished them, she ripped them apart while laughing in sheer delight. But they kept coming. Ranjeet did his best to pick off attacking demons, but the trees protected Pishacha from his crossbow more often than not, leaving Daru to do most of the killing and Ranjeet to stand in awe of her prowess.

Demons just kept coming. They poured out of every shadow or crevasse or hidden swale. None of them could hope to stop Daru, but they didn't seem to care. Each one leapt at her with as much bloodlust as the one before.

"Why do they keep coming? They can't stop… you." Ranjeet had almost said, "us" before he caught himself.

Daru slashed open another Pishacha before answering, "I don't know. "

Ranjeet suddenly understood. "They're slowing us down! We have to hurry!"

He took off running and was a dozen paces down the path before he realized he had no idea where the king was and little chance of defending himself against the hordes of demons closing in. He turned to see Daru jogging after him, pausing only long enough to behead a demon that dared approach.

Ranjeet breathed a sigh and turned to continue toward the king when he saw a Pishacha standing in front of him. The demon spread its clawed hands wide and narrowed its red eyes as it prepared to leap.

Daru was too far behind, Ranjeet had forgotten to load his crossbow, and even if he'd had the weapon at the ready, he wasn't a very good shot. The Pishacha leapt. Ranjeet flinched. But when he felt the claw-stroke he screamed and tackled the demon, driving his shoulder into its chest and the demon into the hard-packed earth. It whimpered as its ribs cracked under Ranjeet's weight, but it didn't stop fighting until Daru's axe finished it.

She dragged him to his feet. "Maybe let me take the lead," she smiled.

He smiled back and Daru led them, at a much faster pace, stopping occasionally to dispatch a demon or two. As they stepped into the glade where King Mahabali held court, all the pursuing Pishacha stopped and fled.

Before them stood the king, just as Ranjeet recalled him from the drawings and parades of his youth. His large, ornate crown was shaded by a straw parasol clasped in his left hand. His broad face and enormous black mustache amplified his smile into a full grin. His large belly was only partially covered by necklaces and decorated cloth draped around his neck. On the ground around the king were intricate geometric arrangements of flower petals.

Ranjeet ran up to the king, shouted his name, and waved his hands before the royal face, but he did not move.

"What… what happened?" Ranjeet and Daru spun to see someone who looked almost exactly like King Mahabali emerge from shimmering air over one of the flower patterns.

"Who are you?" Ranjeet asked.

The newcomer looked around and then over at the king, "I… I'm Samir. How did…"

The tittering laughter of Puck drifted through the glade before the fairy appeared. "The vessel is here, so the king is not," Puck said. "The thread is pulled; soon all will come unraveled!"

Before Ranjeet could ask any question, Pishacha erupted from the trees at the edge of the glade and leapt, one after another, into not-king Samir and disappeared.

"I think I've got it," Ranjeet said, "They're using the king to get into the real world. Puck told me that the Pishacha were trying to get out. Somehow they're using Samir and King Mahabali to do it."

"What do we do?"

"Uh…" Ranjeet stared at her as more and more Pishacha entered the real world. "Do you feel that?"

"No."

"It feels like… hold on," Ranjeet pulled on his face, in the game, but in Daru's house in the real world, he tugged back one side of the Full-D system's headgear and looked at both the game world and the real world at the same time. In the real world Amit was standing over him with a worried expression on his face.

"You're bleeding," he said.

Ranjeet looked down at his arm and saw a ragged, bloody scratch across his arm where the Pishacha had clawed at him. That piece of information didn't startle him as much as it confirmed what he already suspected. The real world and the game world were connected.

"Amit, I—"

"I've gotten the gist of things, how do we stop them?"

Ranjeet looked at him in the real world and Daru in the game world. Both of them wanting answers he wasn't sure he had. He thought about Thomas Rimer's riddle. Pulling on strings would make things come unraveled. What could that mean? He always addressed loose strings by cutting them off. Something about that didn't seem right, so he defaulted to his tech support training.

"Amit, I need you to reboot the servers."

Daru and Amit both swore at Ranjeet simultaneously.

"No, I think it will work. Go to the office and log in under my name. Tell tier-two that something big is happening and that if they don't reboot the servers, it'll destroy the entire game."

"That's just—"

"I know it's crazy, but we have to do something or those things will be everywhere. Go. Tell them it's a virus."

"Why your login?" Amit asked.

"Because I don't want you to lose your job, too," Ranjeet said as he scribbled down his information. After Amit ran out the door, Ranjeet pulled the headgear down over his face completely and looked at Daru.

"Now we have to figure out how to fight this from the inside."

* * *

Ranjeet and Daru had been slaughtering Pishacha for what felt like hours. They stood in front of Samir and killed every Pishacha they could. But the demons ignored them. Some, maybe even most, they killed, but more kept getting past. They couldn't surround Samir so there were always gaps.

Ranjeet knew he was dripping sweat in the real world, as well as in game, but he couldn't stop. He had long since run out of bolts for his crossbow and throwing knives from his brace, so Daru gave him her short sword. He was as inept with that as he was with the crossbow, but still he fought. It helped that Pishacha weren't attacking him, but he knew he was still letting through more than Daru.

Ranjeet was about to give up when the world flickered. That's the only way he could describe it. Everything in existence dimmed for an instant, got much brighter, and then returned to normal. That must have been the reboot, but Pishacha still came. Ranjeet knew then that they had lost. The reboot had failed; they couldn't stop the demons. That made him angry and the anger made him fight even harder.

He was shouting incoherently and slashing wildly at demons when a wreath of fire enveloped him. Ranjeet shouted—or more accurately screamed like a frightened child—and jumped back. Only after his initial fright did he realize that the flame wasn't consuming him. It formed a bright wall between him and the Pishacha. Daru lowered her axe and gave him a questioning look. All Ranjeet could do was gasp for air and shrug. They still heard Pishacha outside the flames howling and shouting in their harsh language, but no more came through.

Ranjeet had rested just enough to start growing curious about his involuntary confinement when a hole opened in the sheet of flames. Through it stepped a beautiful, blonde mage in a long, blue gown wielding a staff. Ranjeet didn't recognize her, but from the gasp he heard behind him, Daru did.

"You're…" Daru could barely get the words out, but she was speaking in Hindi so the mage gave her a quizzical look and shrugged.

Ranjeet assumed, from her pale skin and light hair, that she would speak English, so he attempted to translate. "Thank you for rescuing us. My… uh, friend seems to know who you are, but I don't know that we've ever met. I'm Ranjeet Nagar and this is Daru Padmanabhan. We're here to—"

"You seem like you're here to destroy the barrier between the realms. I'm Jennet. Jennet Carter." She said her name as if it held a great deal of importance. Ranjeet shrugged and translated for Daru.

"She's the daughter of one of the game's creators!" Daru said.

Ranjeet turned back to Jennet, "I'm sorry, Ms. Carter, I didn't know who you were. I work for VirtuMax in technical support. I found a… well I discovered that…"

Jennet's stern expression slid away into a half-smile. "It's okay. I know something about what you're dealing with, but I've never been to this place. Tell me what's going on."

So Ranjeet recounted the discovery of the emails, the Pishacha, and his warnings from Puck and Thomas Rimer. It was the mention of Rimer that really caught Jennet's attention. Before that she seemed skeptical, but the invocation of the bard's name seemed to confirm Ranjeet's tale.

"So you tried to reboot the servers to stop the Pishacha from getting through?" Jennet summed up Ranjeet's plan. "But you didn't know about all the redundancies that we've built in. The other servers just took up the load. Well, I guess it's a good thing you tried or I wouldn't have known exactly where to come."

"Thank you," Ranjeet said after translating for Daru, "I don't know how long we could have held out. As it is, we don't know how to stop this."

"How long does the festival of…"

"Onam," Ranjeet supplied.

"Right, Onam, how long does it last?"

"It depends on where you are. Some rural places still celebrate for a month, but most celebrate for ten days. But the king only visits for four days."

Jennet shook her head, "We can't hold them off for four days. Have you tried talking to him?"

"We tried, but he didn't respond at all. He didn't even look at us. Samir," Ranjeet gestured to the reenactor, "can talk to us, but he doesn't seem to know where he is or what he's doing."

"The Dark Queen has tried this before," Jennet said. "She wants a gateway between the worlds and needs to find a weak place to open it. Since King Mahabali is already going through, the place is weak, and Samir's soul seems to be the doorway."

"Ranjeet," Daru asked, "What's going on?"

He translated for her.

"What if we can find Samir's body?" Daru mused, "If Samir is here in India maybe the king is in his body."

Ranjeet translated that to Jennet.

"It might work. I can hold off the Pishacha for a few hours at least. You can go and find Samir in the real world."

Ranjeet turned to the man they'd been defending. "Samir, where are you from?"

"I'm from…" he looked around wildly, "Kerala."

"Kerala's a big place, Samir," Daru spoke to him this time. "What city are you from? Where is the parade you're supposed to be walking in?"

"I'm, uh, supposed to be in Thrikkakkara. Where am I, what is this place?"

"That's about a half-hour drive," Daru said

Ranjeet turned to Jennet, "He wants to know where he is. What should I tell him?"

Jennet looked at the nervous man and then back to Ranjeet, "Tell him he's where King Mahabali resides. That's true enough. Then you both need to get back to the ring and log out."

When they were ready Jennet opened another hole in the flames. The Pishacha saw it and called to each other in their own language.

"Run!" Jennet shouted.

The first steps out of the king's glade were bought with much violence. Daru lay about with her axe, driving the Pishacha away from them. Ranjeet continued to use her short sword to hack at the demons that escaped Daru. By the time they reached the edge of the forest, the Pishacha seemed to forget about them and instead redoubled their efforts to get through to Samir. Jennet's fire held, but with each demon that jumped into the flames, the blaze waned. She would not be able to hold out indefinitely. They hurried back to the beach and the ring of polished stones where they'd entered the game. At most, they had a few hours to find one man in an entire parade during the most celebrated holiday in the country.

* * *

They jumped into Daru's grav-car. A quick search on his tablet, and Ranjeet keyed in the location of the Thrikkakkara parade. Daru drove with reckless speed through the streets of Kochi and beyond. Ranjeet wanted to talk to her, he wanted to apologize for his father's dishonor, he wanted so many things, but he didn't dare to distract her as she deftly wove her expensive car between busses, people, animals, and other cars.

Ranjeet stared out the window and worried. How could they possibly find one Mahabali reenactor in a whole parade filled with people, many of whom were dressed as the fabled king? But as Daru pulled the car as close as possible to the parade route, Ranjeet stopped worrying about how they were going to find Samir's body, and instead worried about how they were going to fight through the Pishacha that were attacking the crowd.

He didn't stop to think about the fact that he was no longer in a game, that he had no weapons, and he likely would suffer the same fate as the people screaming around him. He just ran forward and shouted a battle cry at the nearest demons. He raised his hands to attack and nearly dropped the crossbow that he found himself holding.

Ranjeet skidded to a halt just a few meters in front of the Pishacha who held an elderly man pinned to the street. Though the puzzle of the crossbow in his hands nagged at him, he ignored it and instead loaded a bolt and leveled the weapon at the demon's chest. It looked at him with undisguised malevolence and bit off harsh words in its awful tongue. Without waiting, Ranjeet pulled the trigger and sent a bolt through the body of the Pishacha. It crumpled to the ground and then disappeared into a cloud of purple-black smoke that wafted parallel to the ground as if pulled along by a string.

Ranjeet stooped to retrieve his bolt before turning to see Daru, with an axe in her own hand, chopping the limbs off of another Pishacha. It too evaporated as it died and the vapors followed the path of the first.

"Do you think..." Ranjeet started the thought.

"...they'll lead us to Samir!" Daru finished.

Together they took off running after the spirit-corpses of the Pishacha, but they were outpaced by the smoke. It seemed to accelerate as it drifted closer to its goal. Soon they lost the trail in the twisting streets. Ranjeet swore in frustration, but Daru kept trotting in the same direction they'd last seen the Pishacha-smoke going. A scream sounded to their left, and she broke into a full run; Ranjeet followed. Daru found another demon tearing into the flesh of a parade goer. She lopped off its head before it even knew she was there, and its spirit rose, leading Ranjeet and Daru toward the king.

They ran as fast as they could, mostly ignoring the weeping people and the destruction surrounding them. They only stopped to fight Pishacha, and then only just long enough to kill their bodies and send their spirits scurrying along. It seemed like they would be doing this for the rest of their days, just trying to catch up to the king, but never actually reaching him. But they came around a corner and saw the crowds before them. The Pishacha were clever—or more likely the Dark Queen had given them a clever plan. They had not rampaged all around, but only behind the king on his parade route. Before him were cheering throngs celebrating Onam, but behind were demons seeking flesh and souls to sate their hunger.

Together they rushed down the sloping street toward the king. Ranjeet saw the wisps of demon-smoke being absorbed into the king's back as he waved to the crowds. There were no more Pishacha in sight, so he had hope that Jennet was holding firm in her defense of Samir-the-gateway. But the lack of Pishacha meant that the crowds—both the audience and those marching in the parade—blocked them from getting to the king.

Daru started to go first, as she had in the game, but in the real world her size and strength were diminished to mortal levels. She slammed into the back of a man intricately painted to look like a tiger and he barely moved. Though Ranjeet wasn't much larger than Daru, he was more adept at working his way through crowds, since his father's disgrace had forced him to walk and use transit to get around. He turned himself sideways and forced his way between the tiger-men, pulling Daru behind.

They inched closer to the king, but it seemed as if they would never actually get to him. People dressed in all sorts of colorful costumes danced and cavorted in front of them as Ranjeet and Daru struggled forward. They were both panting when the crowd let out a collective shriek. They looked up to see the king, no more than fifty meters ahead, with demons boiling from his back and leaping into the crowd.

"We're too late!" Daru cried.

Ranjeet didn't bother to respond, he just ran through the now open street toward the king. Pishacha snarled at him, but Ranjeet didn't even slow down to kill them, he ran straight forward until he reached the king and stepped in front of the man who looked like a mixture of Samir and King Mahabali.

The vast smile on the king's face faded beneath his luxuriously thick mustache. His eyes dropped to Ranjeet as the technical support representative—tier-one—stopped in front of him and raised his hands. Ranjeet had forgotten that he still held a crossbow in his fist. The king glanced down at the weapon and, with the flick of his wrist, knocked Ranjeet across the open square to land in a heap.

Daru ran up to Ranjeet a few moments later. "Are you okay?"

"Yeah, just bruised. Let's go."

Together they ran toward the king, who had only gotten a few more meters down the parade route. Before they got in front of him, Ranjeet dropped his crossbow to the ground and swatted the axe out of Daru's hands. They both stepped in front of King Mahabali and, without thinking about it, Ranjeet reached out and took Daru's hand so they formed a blockade of the route.

"Honored King," Daru said, "We've come to ask a favor!" The words came out in a rush, but Mahabali paused and looked at her. Ranjeet marveled at her wisdom and at the same time cursed his own stupidity.

The legends that he'd learned as a child all made one thing clear, King Mahabali was famous for granting favors. It was that very thing that had sentenced him to an eternity in the underworld. Vishnu had become jealous of his reign in Kerala and took on the avatar Vamana to ask a favor of the king: just three paces of land. The generous king granted the request, but before Vishnu took a single pace, he cast off the avatar and swelled to a vast size. With one step he paced off the earth, and another encompassed the heavens. King Mahabali offered for the third pace his own head so that Vishnu would not destroy everything in existence. Vishnu stepped on the king and sent him forever into the underworld, to return only once a year, at Onam, to visit the people that he loved and had ruled so benevolently.

"You may ask one favor, my daughter," the voice of Mahabali was as distant thunder promising rain on a sweltering day.

"My King," Daru bowed, "I ask that you return to the underworld and visit us no more this Onam."

"Why, my daughter, would you ask such a thing? I have only these four days to walk amongst my subjects and bestow my blessings."

Ranjeet lost patience with the formalities. He grabbed the revered king of Kerala by the shoulder and spun him around. Mahabali raised a hand as if to send Ranjeet flying again, but the sight before him made him pause. The street was writhing with Pishacha that had leapt forth from Mahabali's back. They had fallen to all fours as they galloped away from the parade to ravage the people of Thrikkakkara.

"No," King Mahabali whispered, "it cannot be."

Daru stepped around to face him again. "My King, dark forces have conspired to use you as a gateway into this world. If you continue, it will grow much worse. You must return the spirit of this man and go yourself back to the underworld. If you do not, these demons and more will roam free on the Earth."

Ranjeet admired her words and her calmness. He could barely form coherent thoughts in the face of ravening Pishacha and legendary royalty, but Daru remained stolid and thoughtful. Mahabali did not respond to Daru. He stepped between her and Ranjeet and inhaled deeply before spreading his arms wide and shouting out words in, what Ranjeet guessed to be, the Pishacha tongue. It sounded odd to have the guttural, demon-words coming from the tongue of a man possessed by Mahabali. His voice boomed out and echoed off the buildings.

The first Pishacha halted and turned to see the king staring at them, but they soon tried to flee his gaze. He continued to shout out his commands in their vile language. The demons slowed and then, though their feet and hands clawed furiously at the street, ceased moving forward. Another shout from the king and they started moving backward as if pulled by a powerful magnet. He inhaled more deeply than Ranjeet thought humanly possible and then let out a bellow that shook the very ground.

The Pishacha lost all hold on the earth and flew through the air as if their bodies had become the smoke of their slain brethren. As each struck the chest of the king it sizzled and smoked before winking out of existence. More and more came, from all across Thrikkakkara, until King Mahabali was surrounded by gray skin and red eyes all falling into his body.

When the last one disappeared into him, he turned back to Daru and Ranjeet. His skin had grown pale and ashen, his eyes were ringed in red and he nearly stumbled before righting himself. He spoke in a hoarse whisper saying, "Your favor is granted, my daughter." And with that, he collapsed to the street.

* * *

Ranjeet had the few personal items from his cubicle packed

into a box. His boss, Mr. Narang, stood over him like a guard. As he knew would happen, Ranjeet had arrived at work only to be fired. Mr. Narang's son already had his login set up on Ranjeet's computer and was just waiting for the cube to be clear before starting work.

Ranjeet had told Amit the entire story, but had also secured his vow to not complain to anyone about his termination. Ranjeet knew that no one would believe what had happened. They would blame the destruction on gangs or drunken revelers, not anything supernatural. But Ranjeet couldn't let the warning to Amit go unsaid.

Mr. Narang followed Ranjeet to the elevator and stepped around him to press the call button. The silence as they waited for the lift to arrive was one of the most awkward Ranjeet had ever experienced. He knew Mr. Narang took pleasure in firing him, not just because it made room for his son, but also because his boss had never liked Ranjeet's desire to solve puzzles instead of simply reading the assigned script.

The chime sounded and the doors parted, but instead of facing an empty lift, Ranjeet and Mr. Narang stood face to face with Daru and a woman that Ranjeet knew could only be Jennet Carter. She wasn't as tall or regal as her character in the game, but her features were the same. She was unmistakable.

"Mr., uh, Narang, is it?" Jennet said.

He nodded, "Yes? And who are you, miss?"

"My name is Jennet Carter. You might recognize it."

A look of confusion passed across his face until Jennet held up her tablet and showed it to Mr. Narang. His look of confusion changed to fear. "Yes, Ms. Carter. What can I do for you?"

"There's really nothing *you* can do for me. I just wanted to let you know that I will require Ranjeet's services. Unfortunately you will no longer have his skills at your disposal. I apologize, but I simply cannot do without him. You understand, of course."

"Y-yes, Ms. Carter. Thank you. Is there anything else?"

She smiled at him, "No, thank you. Keep up the good work."

Daru, Jennet, and Ranjeet got into the elevator. Apparently Jennet had already explained things to Daru because she said, "Congratulations."

Ranjeet turned to look at Jennet who stared straight ahead and smiled.

Daru continued, "I guess you'll have your own Full-D system to do your simming on now. Ms. Carter told me that she has a special project for you. I guess you'll be the first member of the Indian branch of a thing called the Feyguard."

Ranjeet looked from Daru to Jennet and back again. His mind searched for a grip on this new information. His mouth worked to form words that his brain refused to supply. Shock stole from him his reasoning and, for the first time in a long time, he felt truly and completely puzzled.

Daru went on through a widening smile, "She told me the Feyguard stops things like what happened, but they didn't know there were different realms. You get to figure out what all the realms are and help with future trouble."

Ranjeet swayed as the import of Daru's words seeped past his shock.

"She also told me that you'll be getting a pay increase. A

significant one. One that will probably mean my father will have to ask you a question in the near future."

Ranjeet dropped his box, his paltry possessions scattering on the elevator floor as Daru let out a musical, beautiful laugh.

A WORD FROM JAMES T. WOOD

I wrote a story about Tinker Bell with tattoos; that's not this story.

My critique partner thought I should see about including the Tinker Bell story in an upcoming anthology that was going to be all about the land of Fey. So I followed up the lead and found out that it wasn't going to be about the land of Fey but about *Feyland*. Oops.

After a few clarifying emails with Samuel, he was gracious enough to invite me to submit a story for the *Chronicle Worlds: Feyland* anthology and offered me a chance to play in Anthea Sharp's world. Don't tell Anthea, but that wasn't something that appealed to me. I like making up my own worlds with my own rules. But Samuel was gracious and the *Future Chronicles* have been great, so I decided to give it a go. I am so glad I did.

Reading *Feyland* and then carving out a niche in that world was a beautiful challenge. Anthea created a rich, imaginative world with so many possibilities (you can tell her that part). My brain kept chasing around the edges of what would happen when a video game like Feyland hit the market, especially what the tech support calls would look like for people that slipped not into the game world, but into the actual land of Fey.

The parts about Ranjeet loving puzzles and working in a mind-numbing call center where he wasn't allowed to solve puzzles are autobiographical. I was that kid who couldn't give up on a puzzle and I was that adult who worked in a call center to pay the bills, hoping to spend my days solving puzzles but instead reading from a poorly written script to frustrated callers. For the record, though, I never had to fight demons.

Most of my writing is about solving puzzles. I play what-if games with myself and run them until they break. The ones that don't break often turn into stories (or blog posts or technical articles or relationship advice or whatever else I happen to be writing at the time). The way the world works, or doesn't, fascinates me; it's a puzzle that I'll never stop trying to solve.

If you like puzzles, questions, thinking, and doing all of that in a playful manner, there's a good chance you'll like my writing. For me, puzzles are about perspective. Each attempt to solve a puzzle is a chance to look at the problem from a different perspective until, eventually, if you're really tenacious and don't give up, you find a perspective that works.

You can find me online at jamestwood.com where I have links to my books and stories. Find me on Facebook and get into a conversation about what's wrong with society, comic book movies, astrophysics, theology, neuroscience, or how to make the best peanut butter and jelly sandwich on earth. Your perspective might be the one that helps me solve a puzzle or mine might help you!

Brea's Tale: Passage
by Anthea Sharp

THE GIRL SAT upon a stone, dangling one leg into the water. Fish nibbled at her toes, heedless of the runes marking the rock. Her gossamer-spun dress reflected the sunset hues suspended between sky and wave.

The cool touch of the waves soothed her, though her mind was full of confusion. One moment her world had been full of splash and glimmer and then, mid-leap, something had changed. *She* had changed.

She'd had a name, once. It slipped, elusive as a minnow, into the shadowed corners of her mind, but she was determined to lure it out.

Tangled memory made her frown as she stared down into the waters. She was certain she had not always had legs. The lazy movements of the fish were as familiar to her—more familiar, in fact—than the sight of her own two hands. She held them up and stared at the long, unwebbed fingers. Who was she? *What* was she, and how had she come here?

A soft wind brushed strands of her dark hair across her face, and with the touch came remembrance.

Brea.

She was Brea Cairgead, fisherman's daughter. And daughter of a sea-wild woman who carried magic in her blood. Magic she'd given to her daughter, though it had come nearly too late.

Memory returned in a hot, painful rush, and Brea bent, arms wrapped across her stomach.

Her father was dead, her village had banished her, and she had barely managed to escape the brigands who had robbed her, and wished to do worse. The ache of remembrance washed over her in a heavy wave, but in its wake came gentler memories: the healing silver current, the sibilant songs of the sea, the cool touch of water cradling her.

Brea drew in a deep breath and straightened. Surely her life had held sorrow, but also peace. Now, though, what did the future hold? It was a very human thought, one that her finned self would never consider.

"Ah, she has awoken," a merry voice said. "Welcome to the Realm, sometime-girl."

Startled, Brea looked up to see a small fellow dressed in tatters and leaves sitting cross-legged upon the nearby bank. She opened her mouth, but the taste of words was foreign on her tongue, and the air rushed in, making her cough.

"Steady now," the figure said. "You're new enough into this form that you must go slowly. Allow me to introduce myself. I am the sprite called Puck."

He rose, then kept rising until he floated several handspans above the grassy bank. Eyes twinkling, he bowed, turning the movement into a somersault in midair. Then he conjured a bright green hat with a jaunty plume. Jamming it over his tangled hair, he strode across the empty air between them until he was close enough to touch.

Brea shrank back on her rock and considered plunging back below the surface. But this little fellow was, although a bit startling, not terribly frightening. Carefully, she rolled words out of her mouth.

"Where… am I?"

"As I said, you're in the Realm. The Realm of Faerie. Don't be afraid. You belong here, Mistress Brea Cairgead, silver fish girl, breather of both air and water."

She still wondered if she ought to slip off her rocky perch and into the cool, familiar safety of the water. It was home to her, more recently than the thatched cottage she'd once inhabited. She did not know how many turnings of the moon she'd spent in her other form, but she suspected the time could be measured in years. Perhaps decades. Yet something had prompted her transformation back to a human-seeming girl.

Magic, or fate, or even loneliness—she did not know which. Perhaps all three.

"Am I a faerie now?" she asked, afraid to hear the answer.

Puck tilted his head and regarded her a long moment, eyes bright. The wind riffled the surface of the water, and she smelled mint and thyme on the breeze.

"You are a curious creature," the sprite said. "You were never fully human, but you are human enough that you cannot be entirely one of the fey folk. As I said before, you are a girl of two parts—water and land, fey and mortal. As such, you have a part to play in things to come."

She did not like the sound of that. Brea hugged her knees close to her chest. "What if I do not want this fate?"

"What *do* you want?"

The answer was lodged in her heart, but she hesitated to speak it aloud. Still, Puck regarded her with kindness in his wild and merry eyes, and despite her wariness, she answered.

"To belong." It was what she'd always wanted, and what she'd never had.

Even as a village lass, she'd been too different. And now she realized there were none of her own kind. The selkies might tolerate her presence, but the merfolk would laugh at her ungainly human legs, and if she transformed she would not be able to speak with them.

"You have to make your own belonging," Puck said, a deep melancholy in his voice, as if he, too, were the only one of his kind.

Brea tasted salt in the back of her throat. She had no notion of how to fit herself into a world—whether human or faerie—that did not hold the shape of who she was.

"Do not despair." Puck shook himself, and she saw his sorrow fly off his shoulders and fade into the sunset sky. "If you are true of heart, you will find the way. Deep inside you, the path awaits."

"How will I know where to find it?"

"Follow the taste of the rowan berry," he said. "It will lead you to your fate. And now, Mistress Brea, I must bid you farewell."

"Don't go." She reached one pale hand toward him. Before he'd come, she had not known she was so lonely.

He did not reply—only spun himself about three times in a whirl of tatters and feathers and was gone.

Shore birds cried into the dusk, and the water lapped the bank. There was no one to talk to, except the school of silver fish swimming about the stone. And they did not speak in conversation, but in flashes of image and color.

Still, it was better than the silence of her own human thoughts. Letting out all her breath, Brea pushed herself off the rock and let the water surround her. Three heartbeats later there was no dark-haired girl pining upon a half-submerged stone, but only a new fish weaving through the current.

It was an unquiet current though, with an amber-gold thread of loam and smoke and shadows running through. It brushed along her sides, beckoning, and she found she could not resist its call.

Despite her efforts, she was not able to interest the other fish in following to see where it led. They desired only pale wave and lavender ripple, bright dart and flashing turn.

Alone, Brea-within-the-fish circled about her companions in farewell, and then left them to play in the light-filled shallows.

The taste of mystery pulled her on, past a rocky outcropping to a place where a stream poured into the larger water. Amber diluted with turquoise as the waters mixed and flowed, but it was that warmer taste within the rivulet that she must follow.

She dashed herself into the mouth of the stream and was pushed back. Once, twice, thrice—and then she discovered the trick of swimming against the current. First to one side and then the other she swam, stitching her way from bank to bank.

When she wearied she found a quiet eddy behind an algae-covered rock, and rested there until she regained her strength. The sky above the stream darkened as she followed the golden strand within the water, until at last she reached a small side-pool that tasted of contentment.

Flicking her tail, she dived in and out of the stream, but the golden thread had curled in on itself and gone to rest in the silty bottom. The undercut bank held peaceful shadows, and the tangled roots of trees wove a screen she might shelter behind. It was as good enough a place as any to bide.

Overhead, the evergreens nodded, their branches waving softly like a mother hushing her child. Above their dark heads the first sprinkling of stars shone, flecks of light springing up before the sickle moon could scythe them down.

* * *

There was no passage of days in the waters where Brea now dwelt. The sky dimmed and brightened from dusk to night and back again, skipping sunlight altogether. She discovered the rocks upstream where the current frothed and raced, and the quiet eddies where tadpoles fluttered. When the moon shone full, dew-winged sprites danced above the silver-lit stream, their footsteps light as rain over the water.

Brea felt no urge to move on. The golden strand that had brought her here did not reappear to beckon her forth to new rivers and depths. She splashed and darted, waiting without urgency for whatever might come. Some deep sense of knowing told her she was where she ought to be.

That peaceful contentment changed one dusky evening. The evergreens shivered, and she felt their roots stirring in the water.

Something was coming.

She darted beneath the bank and held herself there, suspended. Watching.

Brightness approached—a ball of flame hovering and bobbing through the forest. It halted on the opposite side of the stream, licking the surface with streaks of red and gold. She was too afraid to rise and see if it were a wisp, or a fallen star, or a light held aloft by some strange creature.

Sound filtered through the water, syllables with edges, full of question and danger. Brea back-finned into the shadows. She would hide until the forest became quiet and safe once more.

As if sensing her movement, the ball of flame floated out to the middle of the stream. Brea whirled and darted deeper beneath the bank, though she feared it was already too late.

After a dozen of her frightened heartbeats, the fiery sphere withdrew. It moved along the bank a short distance, but she knew the danger was not over. Indeed, the light returned soon enough, and the soil vibrated with the sound of footsteps. More than one creature roamed there beside the stream. They seemed to be seeking something.

A berry floated past, carried gently on top of the water. Brea ignored it and practiced blending with the roots she sheltered behind.

Another came past, and another, each one leaving a trace of flavor behind—something wild and tangy. *Freedom. Adventure. Come, bite.* The berries bobbed on the surface, red and full of magic.

She must not taste of them. Brea forced herself to stay in the deeps, her body quivering with effort.

A dozen floated slowly by, one by one. At the thirteenth, she could remain still no longer. Despairing, she flipped her body upward, capturing the berry in her mouth.

The taste trembled through her, urgent and immediate. Without letting it go, she fled downstream. Something pulled taut, then let her run, then wound up again. The far bank drew nearer, but she could not release the fruit. It was stuck fast in her mouth, and so she darted and ran, seeking vainly to escape.

The flame bobbed directly overhead, a tiny sun. She broke the surface in a panic of air and silver, twisting desperately. The light suffocated her and she thrashed, trying to break free.

Then darkness closed about her, but it was not the comforting liquid of the shadows. This was rough and dry, scraping her skin, smelling of something horrible. Harsh air surrounded her, and Brea gasped, drowning in the dryness…

Change. She must shift her form, or die.

Summoning all her strength, she bid her body to transform.

Hard earth beneath her. Not water. *No longer fish, but girl.* She clung to the thought, and at last her scales fell away. Pain rippled through her as she became heavy and slow, trapped by air and gravity, now elongated into her human form.

It was done—but she was still in darkness. Drawing in shallow, rapid breaths, she realized she was caught in folds of cloth. She clawed at the fabric until she was free.

Trees above her, and the orb of the moon. Beyond lay the safety of the stream—but two creatures stood between her and the water. Not monsters. Humans, but so strangely garbed.

One of them stepped forward, hair an odd, bright color, and said something that might have been a greeting.

Or a threat.

The other set one hand to his belt, where a knife hung.

Brea glanced down at her own form. She was naked, her long dark hair woven with white blossoms. *Run!*

A heartbeat later she was on her feet, leaping surefooted through the forest. If she could loop back around to the stream, or even find a pond, she could dive for safety.

Behind her the humans crashed and called.

Brea lifted her face, scenting the wind for water. Something golden and sweet tugged at her senses and she veered, leaping lightly over bracken fern. Despite her nakedness, the forest was kind. The moss cushioned her steps, and no sharp twigs scraped her pale unprotected skin.

The forest thinned, the scent drawing her on. A half-remembered taste, tart and lovely. Apples.

She broke out of the trees into silvery grasses dancing in the starlight. Before her rose a long hill, and at the top a tree grew, branches heavy with both blossom and fruit. She cast a glance behind her, to see her pursuers closer than she had guessed.

With a last burst of speed, Brea raced up the hill. The apple tree bowed and bent, a golden fruit caught high in its branches, but she dared not pause.

Onward, past the tree, past a faerie ring studded with mushrooms, past a low stone wall. At last, breath scraping in her lungs, limbs burning with effort, she could run no more.

There was no lake, no stream, no rivulet nearby to offer her shelter. Wearily, Brea dropped to the ground, the grasses rising around her. At least the human creatures no longer chased her. The silence of the night was broken only by the chirp of an insect, the rustle of the wind through the grass.

And then came a sound to freeze her newly-warmed blood: the wail of a hunting horn echoing across the sky.

The Wild Hunt was riding.

Even safe in her waterborne form, she knew to dive deep when the unearthly riders and spectral hounds galloped through the night. Once, she had seen the wavering shadow of the Huntsman silhouetted against the moon, his fearsome shape crowned with mighty antlers.

Shivering, Brea stood and scanned the silvery meadows surrounding her. Far ahead a dark smudge rose on the horizon; perhaps a sheltering forest, perhaps a low rise of hills. She lifted her face and scented deeply of the air, but there was no smell of water nearby. No safety she could plunge into and disappear.

She prayed there was still some cover she might find, a hazel copse or small tarn. Turning her steps toward the horizon, she began to run once more.

The horn did not sound again, but far too soon she heard the shrill yipping of hounds and the thunder of hooves. Brea glanced over her shoulder and gasped at the sight of the Wild Hunt galloping across the sky, bearing down on her in all their glory.

Glowing, gossamer-maned horses with fiery eyes bore stern and beautiful elfin knights, their hair whipping in the wind. Hounds raced before them, sinuous as smoke, red eyes burning like coals. And in the midst, the horned figure of the Huntsman, a midnight cloak billowing behind him.

Heart beating fast as a bird's, Brea raced over the meadows. Above the sharpness of her breaths and the drumming hooves, she heard the high keening of bagpipes.

There was no escape. She was too slow, and the hunt surrounded her.

The riders landed, hemming her in a circle, and Brea halted. Chin high, she faced the Huntsman, though her legs felt weak as water.

"What do you want of me?" she asked.

"The Dark Queen demands your presence," the Huntsman said, his voice deep and low. "You have aided the enemy."

"What enemy?" She cast her mind back, trying to understand, but his words had no meaning. Did this concern the humans who had chased her? "I have done nothing."

"That is for the queen to decide."

The horned figure gestured to one of his riders. Before Brea could utter a protest she was scooped up and set in front of a black-haired rider with cold green eyes. His arm was a vise about her waist, and she did not bother to struggle. She would conserve her strength for a fight that she might win.

Although how she could possibly win anything from the Dark Queen of the Realm, Brea had no notion. She knew very little about the queen, having never strayed far into the midnight side of the Realm. Neither had she forayed into the sunlit reaches ruled by the Bright King. The dusk-lit sky had been enough for her, the sunset-tipped waves and still pools lit silver by the rising moon.

All she knew was that the queen ruled the Dark Realm, and that even in the gloaming far from the midnight heart of her court, creatures spoke of her with fear and awe.

The eldritch horn sounded, and the Wild Hunt leaped into the sky. The air cooled and the wind of their passing blew Brea's dark hair back from her face. Around them, the stars hovered close as the fiery-footed steeds climbed into the sky. She felt as though she might lift her hand and cut her fingers against the sickle blade of the moon.

Night wove thickly about the hunt as they rode into the heart of the Dark Realm, until at last they reached the stillness of midnight. Gnarled oaks grew in the shadowed forest below, and she glimpsed a clearing lit with dozens of faerie-fire candles and a bonfire flickering with purple light.

Fey folk thronged there, some dancing wildly about the violet flames, others gathered at the long feasting tables set at one side of the clearing. She blinked to see so many creatures: dream-winged faerie maids and sharp-toothed nixies, a bone-white shadow inside a dark cloak, the wide-eyed stare of the banshee.

Music drifted above the tangled treetops—harp and drum and guitar twining together, sorrowful and joyous in equal measure. The Wild Hunt followed the melody down and landed in the center of the clearing.

At the far end stood a throne of vines and thorns, and upon it sat the Dark Queen. Her hair was smoke and obsidian, her gown starlight and cobwebs, and her eyes held the memory of countless centuries.

Brea swallowed, her throat dry with fear as the elfin knight set her on the mossy ground. Her legs trembled, and she looked down to see she was clad once more in a shimmer of a gown that clung to her like mist.

"Huntsman," the queen said. "Have you brought me the betrayer?"

"I have, your majesty." He made her a sweeping bow. "This maid is the one we scented, who led the humans directly to the tree of the golden apple."

Brea's skin prickled with fear, and she sucked in a painful breath. "I did not—"

"You." The queen's voice cut like frost. She leaned forward and pointed at Brea with one long, pale finger. "I should strike you down where you stand for aiding my enemies."

Brea had never meant to lead the humans anywhere, but only to escape. Had she done something terrible, all unwitting?

"Forgive me, your majesty," she whispered.

A bright-eyed, tangle-haired sprite tumbled into the clearing before the Dark Queen's throne. Brea recognized him—Puck, who spoke in riddles and runes. Standing before the queen, he made his ruler a flourishing bow, one foot pointed on the velvet green mosses.

"Your majesty," he said. "Might I speak?"

The queen let out a sigh, the sound like a wind stirring the empty branches of winter oaks.

"Puck," she said. "You have the freedom of the courts, much as it may displease my mood. Say your piece."

"Yon maid, all unwitting, played but a part in a quest. She does not deserve death—and there are few enough fey folk that her loss, though a small thing, would be felt within the realm."

Brea sent him a grateful glance. She did not know why Puck was defending her. Perhaps it had to do with their prior meeting and his cryptic words of fate and future.

"Banishment, then, shall be her punishment," the queen declared. "To the Shadowlands."

The denizens of the court shivered, and Brea felt her heart catch. Even hiding within her watery dwelling, she'd heard of that dire place where souls wandered, lost and alone, into eternity.

Though the words might stumble on her tongue, she must plead her case.

"My queen." She bowed as best she could on her unsteady legs. "I beg you, do not banish me. Surely there is some way to mend the harm I might have done?"

The gathered fey folk whispered, and Brea was glad she could not hear what they said. No doubt they suggested dire and dreadful remedies.

"Perchance there might be." The queen narrowed her eyes and gestured. "Bard Thomas, attend."

A man stepped from the shadows and Brea stared at him in surprise. Another half-magical human like herself, perhaps? But no—there was something ghostly about him. If he'd been human once, he was no longer. Silver strands ran through his brown hair, and his eyes were wise and weary beyond measure.

"Yes, my queen?"

"How best might I use this youngling in service to the court?"

The man turned, his gaze brushing past Puck and then resting upon Brea for a long moment. Sparks and promises flashed in his eyes, and she did not know whether to be hopeful or afraid.

"Send her into the human world," he said at last. "There, she might sway mortals to stray into the Realm. She can repay her debt by helping ensure that humans will cross over to the Dark Court when they enter the game of Feyland."

The queen gave a single shake of her head. "I mislike having to sacrifice yet another of my handmaidens simply to send a near-useless creature into the mortal realm. Your counsel pleases me not, bard."

"Milady." Puck sprang into the air and hovered there. "Though centuries have passed, the girl *is* part human, and still connected with the mortal world. I may be able to slip her through the gateway without further bloodshed. And if not"—he gave an elaborate shrug—"then do with her as you please."

"Your magic is fickle," the queen said.

"Yet you know it cannot be forced to do your bidding." Puck laughed and flipped in the air, landing once again on the soft ground. "I will attempt to send the maid through."

The queen leaned back, the pale moonlight illuminating her beauty. Overhead, stars sprinkled the edges of the sky, and a night wind stirred the oak leaves into whispering. Brea's nerves hummed as she awaited her fate. Her heartbeat pounded within her chest until she was nearly dizzy from the rhythm, yet she remained quiet and still, as she had learned to do in her watery form. Speaking on her own behalf would do little good, and she did not want to tip the balance of the queen's decision unfavorably.

At length the queen beckoned to Brea, who found she could not ignore the summons. She came forward, then sank to her knees on the velvety mosses before the throne.

"I lay a *geas* upon you, youngling," the Dark Queen said. "From now until the summer wanes, you are charged with marking and leading as many humans as you might toward the magic of the Dark Court so that the Realm may be replenished. Should you return without success, the Shadowlands will be your new home."

Brea bowed her head. There was no arguing, and no agreement. When the queen spoke, her word was law. Still, this sentence was a reprieve. If she carried out the queen's bidding well enough, she might escape dire banishment to the Shadowlands.

Behind the tangled throne, gossamer-winged faerie maidens cast Brea pitying glances. A nearby band of goblins cackled, clearly pleased by her plight. The queen held up one hand and called forth her magic. In a burst of violet light, a silver medallion appeared. It swung, dangling on a bright chain from the queen's fingers.

"Take this," she said, thrusting the medallion at Brea. "It is your passage back to the realm—but do not call upon it until Lughnasa is nigh."

Brea took the medallion. It was cool against her fingers,

the silver disc inset with a pale moonstone, the edges inscribed with runes. She folded it into her palm, proof of the journey she must now undertake.

"Away with her," the queen said to Puck.

Without a further glance at Brea, she signaled for elderberry wine and music. The creatures of her court bestirred themselves, returning to their dancing and feasting.

"Come, maid," Puck said.

Brea rose and followed him. She did not look behind her as they left the clearing of the Dark Court, though the strains of a plaintive jig followed her into the shimmering darkness beneath the trees.

"I am afraid," she said, once the sounds of the court had faded.

"You are wise to be so," Puck said. "Yet who knows what doors will open to you in the human world, or what fate might hold in store?"

She did not want fate or a queen's commands to rule her—but she had no choice.

Puck led her along mossy paths faintly illuminated with starshine. Overhead, the dark oaks wove their tangled branches across the star-dappled sky.

"Quickly," the sprite urged. "We must slip you through before the battle commences. I have folded time, but we must make haste."

Brea gulped back her questions. She doubted she wanted to know the answers. Battle? Folded time? Instead she quickened her pace, until she and Puck were nearly flying through the forest. Or perhaps they truly were airborne. Her feet did not seem to touch the ground, and she would not be surprised if the sprite's magic propelled them forward. Overhead, the sky lightened to a pearly grey.

"Here." Puck halted before a strange clearing, still floating in the air. "We are in time."

Brea's feet landed on the cool moss, and she blinked at the clearing. It was not a single glade, but three, lined up like a triple reflection. The one nearest them held a faerie ring of moon-pale mushrooms, the far one was lit by morning sun and its circle made of white-speckled red mushrooms, and the one in the middle was a mixture of both—sun and shadow, pale mushrooms and red growing together to make the faerie ring.

Puck strode to the middle clearing and flourished his fingers in a strange gesture. Colored mist began forming in the center of the faerie ring—golden and violet and emerald swirling together.

"Keep the medallion safe," the sprite said, nodding to the silver pendant still clutched in her hand. "Step into the mist, and be brave."

She was not brave, nor had she ever been. She'd merely done what had to be done—which seemed only to take her from one trouble to the next.

"What must I do, once I reach the human world?" she asked, slowly walking toward the bright eddies of mist.

"Mark humans with a touch of faerie magic, so that they are called into the Realm," Puck said. "But most of all, trust your heart."

The sprite ever spoke in riddles, with few answers. She let out a low sigh.

Beside them, the clearing holding the moon-pale ring began to glow. Puck gave it a wary glance, then gestured at her to hurry.

"Farewell, Maid Brea," he said. "Luck be upon you."

She hoped the fates heard his words.

"Farewell, Puck."

Gathering the shreds of her courage, she stepped into the swirling mist of the center clearing. The world tipped, dizziness pouring over her until she fell to her knees. She could feel the sweet magic of the Realm of Faerie ripping away, and she cried out from the pain of it.

It was not the first time she'd been pulled from one world to another, though, and she vowed that whatever happened, she would survive this transformation.

Human or faerie, she would stay true to her word. And perhaps, one day, she would find her way home. Wherever that might be.

Brea's adventures continue in Royal: Feyguard Book 2

ABOUT ANTHEA SHARP

Growing up on fairy tales and computer games, Anthea Sharp has melded the two in her award-winning *Feyland* series, which has hit the *USA Today* bestseller list twice and sold over 200,000 copies worldwide.

Anthea is often ranked in the Top 100 Fantasy/SF authors at Amazon, and is thrilled to have 6,000 fans and over 1 million reads at Wattpad. Her novels have won or placed in the PRISM, the Maggie, the National Reader's Choice Award, the Write Touch Reader's Award, the Heart of Excellence, The National Excellence in Romance Fiction, The Judge a Book by its Cover, and the Book Buyer's Best competitions.

Anthea lives in the Pacific Northwest, where she writes, hangs out in virtual worlds, plays the fiddle with her Celtic band Fiddlehead, and spends time with her small-but-good family.

Find out more about her books at https://antheasharp.com and join her mailing list to stay on top of all the news and current releases – plus get a bonus *free* short story when you sign up at http://eepurl.com/1qtFb

A Note to Readers

Thank you so much for reading *Chronicle Worlds: Feyland,* one of the many titles in the *Future Chronicles* anthology series in speculative fiction.

Through the work of a number of talented authors, editors, artists and other contributors—and the amazing support of readers like you—the *Future Chronicles* series has become one of the most acclaimed short story anthology series of the digital era, hitting the top ranks of not just the science fiction, fantasy and horror anthology lists, but the overall Amazon Top 10 Bestsellers list itself.

The Future Chronicles has also inspired several other quality anthology series in speculative fiction and in other genres, and inspired scores of spin-off stories, novels, and series. It's been amazing.

If you enjoyed the stories in this book, please keep an eye out for other titles in the *Future Chronicles* collection.

A full listing of titles, which can be read in any order, can be found at:

www.futurechronicles.net

Finally, before you go, we'd like to ask you a very small favor, if you please: *Would you write a short review at the site where you downloaded this book?*

Reviews are make-or-break for authors. A book with no reviews is, simply put, a book with no future sales. This is because a review is more than just a message to other potential buyers: it's also a key factor driving the book's visibility in the first place.

More reviews (and more positive reviews) make a book more likely to be featured in bookseller lists and more likely to be featured in bookseller promotions. Reviews don't need to be long or eloquent; a single sentence is all it takes. In today's publishing world, the success (or failure) of a book is truly in the reader's hands.

So please, write a review.

Then tell a friend. Share a link to us on Facebook, or maybe even a Tweet—link to our books at the site above. You'd be doing us a great service.

Thank you.

Samuel Peralta
www.amazon.com/author/samuelperalta

———————

Subscribe to our newsletter to get a free copy of *The Future Chronicles – Special Edition*, a compendium of 15 new and selected stories, and be eligible for draws for paperbacks, e-books and more – *http://smarturl.it/chronicles-news*

Made in United States
Troutdale, OR
06/06/2023